North of Always
An Enchanted Rock Romance – Book One

Published in the United States by
Jules Woods Publishing
Houston, Texas

This is a work of fiction. Names, characters, places, and incidents are products of the author's imagination or are used fictitiously. Any resemblance to actual events, locales, or persons, living or dead, is entirely coincidental.

Digital Edition: ISBN 979-8-9934857-0-6

Print Edition: ISBN 979-8-9934857-1-3

Hardback Edition: ISBN 979-8-9934857-2-0

Don't miss A thing!

Are you A VIP?

www.juleswoods.com/contact

Be the first to know

Get free giveaways

Exclusive content

Opportunities only available

through my newsletter

xoxoxo

North of Always

Spotify Playlist

Happen to Me by Russel Dickerson
Springsteen by Eric Church
Better Me For You by Max McNowen
The Moon Will Sing by The Crane Wives
Ever Leave by Alexandra kay
Boot Scootin' Boogie by Brooks & Dunn
Lose it All by Brett Eldridge
I'm the Problem by Morgan Wallen
Not at This Party by Dasha & David Guetta
Take You Home by Cassadee Pope
Cowgirls by Morgan Wallen, Ernest
God Gave Me You by Blake Shelton
High Road by Koe Wetzel & Jesse Murphy
The Dance by George Strait
Didn't I by Dasha
Don't Close Your Eyes by Keith Whitley
Bye Bye Bye by Dasha
Beautiful As You by Thomas Rhett
Stargazer by Myles smith
Lost without you by Dean Lewis and Kygo
Weren't for the Wind by Ella Langley
Second Wind by Alexandra Kay

Dedication

For the girl who found her voice,
and the boy who finally stopped running.
And for everyone still learning how to stay.

xoxoxo

About North of Always

A story about love, loss, and learning how to stay.

ELIZA

Music was my first language — the only way I knew how to make sense of pain. Every song I wrote was a piece of truth I couldn't say out loud. Then came Finn Callahan. The boy who pulled me out of the wreckage when no one else would. He was my first safe place, my best friend, and the heartbeat beneath every lyric I've ever written.

FINN

I've spent my whole life running — from homes, from foster families, from anything that felt like it might last. Eliza was the one thing I never wanted to run from. But when you grow up always waiting to be left, staying starts to feel like a risk you can't afford. And I've been risking everything since the day I met her.

North of Always is Eliza & Finn's story.

Still here, still choosing
Even when it's messy, even when we're losing
Still yours, still true
Even when the world forgets what we've been through
I don't need a perfect start
Just a place inside your heart
Still here
Still loving you

And when the lights fade down
When the noise all falls away
I'll be the breath you didn't know you were holding
I'll be the home you choose to stay

from Still Here

by Eliza Monroe

Prologue

Two years ago — Fredericksburg, Texas

Eliza swatted at her leg again. This time of year the mosquitoes were relentless. Bloodthirsty and mean. The kind of mean, thirsty swarm that only came out during the ugliest part of summer in Fredericksburg. The air was hot, sticky—making you feel like you're being slow-roasted in an oven. There wasn't enough shade in town to make a difference. Not enough air conditioning either.

It was early evening, but the sun had no intention of giving up. Not yet.

Eliza hated Texas summers. Always had.

Her sky blue cotton sundress clung to her like a second skin—sweat soaked the small of her back, ran between her full breasts, highlighting her 5'9" lithe frame and drawing the wrong kind of attention. Her long white-blonde hair was plastered to her neck, the clip having given up as she pedaled the rusted old bike toward the H-E-B just off Main Street. Dinner duty. Again.

Beans and tortillas. Always beans and tortillas. It was Texas after all.

She vowed then and there that once she was on her own and making money, she'd never eat beans or tortillas again. Which was saying something since Texas used to be part of Mexico and the Latino culture here ran deep. Texas was the home of Tex-Mex after all where beans and tortillas were a staple.

Her latest foster parents hadn't bought food in days nor given her any of the state money they got for taking care of her to buy any herself. Until today. She'd only been sent out now because they weren't sober enough to care what she came back with. Fredericksburg was small, pretty on the outside—vineyards and German bakeries and tourists who took pictures of the quaint storefronts—but under the right roofs, it could be just as ugly as any big city.

She used the crumpled bills they'd shoved in her hand, barely enough to cover a few cans and a packet of tortillas. Forget fruit or vegetables. There was never money for them. The cashier didn't smile. People never did when she showed up alone with dust on her legs and bruises she couldn't explain. Bruises from Carlos grabbing at her. It wasn't the first foster home that she had been abused in but she was determined that it would be the last. What was wrong with people? Most of the homes were decent if unsupportive. It was always the luck of the draw. Well...she definitely drew the short straw with Carlos.

Outside, the heat hit her like a wall again.

And so did Carlos.

"Damn... not him," Eliza thought. Anyone but Carlos. He scared the Jesus out of her.

His burnt-orange Mustang—loud, tacky, and always parked too close— idled along the curb. He leaned against the driver's side door like he was posing for a photo. Eliza froze for a split second before lowering her gaze and moving quickly to pass.

Carlos grinned.

"Hey, Chica." His voice had that cocky lilt she hated, oozing with sly malevolence. "Take a ride with me. We could cruise out past the peach farms, maybe park at Lady Bird Park. Get to know each other better—much better."

He stepped in front of her, running his tongue over his lips reminding her of a hungry wolf. Making her skin crawl.

Eliza stopped short. The heat of his body, the sour sweat clinging to his shirt, made her stomach churn. She hated that he was barely taller than her lithe frame but built thick and solid—broad shoulders, arms like a linebacker, and a black-eyed stare that always fixated on her chest. He must have at least seventy to eighty pounds on her.

"No," she said, forcing her voice to stay even. "I'll bike back. I have to make dinner."

"You're living in *my* parents' house now," Carlos said, leaning in. "That makes you mine. Right, mi angel?" he added, glancing behind him even though no one was there.

She'd heard rumors that he was involved with a gang of human traffickers as a low level thug, and she didn't want to become a statistic.

Sadly, Texas was a hub for human trafficking due to its proximity to the border with Mexico and the US interstate system bisecting the state.

Eliza folded her arms over her chest, barely holding in the tremble. She wouldn't give him the satisfaction, but she didn't want to rile him up even more.

Her fingers tightened on the grocery bag. Carlos had been obsessed with her light blond hair, big violet eyes, and full breasts since she had come to stay with her current foster family—his family. "I need to go. I have to make dinner," she repeated.

Carlos chuckled. "Then hurry home. We've got the whole night to break you in." He smirked and winked. "Just kidding."

His eyes said that he wasn't. Her hands shook when she reached for the rusty Schwinn bike. He didn't stop her but his dark, heavy stare stayed on her the whole way as she mounted the frame and pedaled hard toward the outskirts of town.

The hills of Fredericksburg rolled in the distance, soft green slopes hiding vineyards and private ranches. But Eliza didn't see the beauty anymore. Not here. Not while living under a roof that made her feel like prey.

She didn't know how she'd ended up here.

But she knew she couldn't stay. It was only a matter of time before Carlos was done waiting—done playing with his food.

And she had no idea that somewhere, just a few miles away, a boy named Finn had just dropped his duffel bag on the bedroom floor of that same foster house.

She didn't know that night would change both their lives forever.

But it would.

Chapter One

Lost & Found

Finn

Two years ago – Age 17

Finn dropped his worn navy duffel on the dusty, splintered floor of the back bedroom in his latest foster home and looked around. Mold-stained walls. A window that wouldn't close all the way. A twin bed with no sheet. Another temporary stop on the slow crawl toward nowhere. Eight more months. Just eight. Then he was out for good. If he believed in God, he'd thank him—or her, whatever. Freedom—he was close enough to taste it.

The place was a sagging ranch house on the edge of Fredericksburg, baked soft by the Texas sun and held together by habit. His new foster parents had met him on the porch with the kind of smiles people fake for a paycheck. She had a beer in her hand before she even said hello; he reeked of whiskey and sweat, eyes dull as pond water. Empty bottles lined the porch rail like trophies. Inside, the air was stale with beer, smoke, and something fried too long ago to name. Somewhere down the hall, a can hissed open, and a game show laugh track rose over the static hum of an old TV.

No more foster shit holes. At least when he turned eighteen he would have the freedom to make his own decisions, even if it was just deciding between one shit hole or another. He sat on the edge of the lumpy mattress, elbows on his knees, staring at the walls like they might blink. Fourth placement in two years. He didn't bother unpacking anymore. Didn't bother hoping or pretending.

Survival—that was the only thing that counted now. Keep his head down. Don't get attached. Get through school and get out.
Caring was a luxury, and he couldn't afford it.

The mantra that had served him well—watch and listen. Trust no one and always be ready to run.

Raucous laughter echoed down the hallway, loud, male, and aggressive. A deeper voice barked something in Spanish. Someone else responded, and a feminine voice spoke in English—forced, thin, almost delicate—fluttered awkwardly in response. *Please leave me alone*, he thought.

Finn shut his door and tried to block it out, but something was off. He needed to stay separate—pathetic he knew but he needed to stay neutral. To not get into any trouble. He was almost out of the system. So he pulled out his book of famous football plays and ignored the voice.

Later, after dinner—cold chicken, warm beer someone left open—the house started to quiet down. He tried to sleep, but the walls here were thin, the smell stale like old cigarettes, and the only fan in his room clicked without pushing out any air.

That's when he heard it.

A muffled sound. Sharp. Strangled. Like a scream that couldn't quite get free.

He sat up. Stilled.

Hearing another thud then crying—soft and desperate he leaned against his bedroom door.

The disconcerting sounds raised the hair on the back of his neck.

He moved fast on instinct.

Barefoot and silent, Finn stepped into the hall, grateful that he had worn pajama pants to bed. Generally he preferred to sleep naked but he'd learned quickly living in the foster system to always be dressed and ready to leave at any moment. The sound came from the second room on the right—the one with the busted doorknob. It was slightly ajar. He had a really bad feeling.

He pushed it open.

The first thing he saw was movement—a large figure hunched over a smaller one on the bed.

The second was the girl—blonde hair tangled on the pillow, her violet eyes wide with horror and fear, tears streaking down her delicate heart-shaped face. Carlos' thick hand covered her mouth and almost half her face as she fought to scream.

Horror, fear, desperation, and hope filled her eyes as they met his.

Looking at Finn like he was the only one who could save her.

In that moment he probably was.

The third thing was red.

It bled into Finn's vision, hot and blinding.

Carlos turned, annoyed, as if Finn had interrupted a video game.

"There's nothing to see," Carlos said casually, his grin dark. "Just keep walking, amigo."

Finn didn't speak.

He moved.

With one powerful shove, he ripped Carlos off the weeping and petrified girl and slammed him into the wall so hard the drywall cracked. "Get the fuck off of her."

His fists clenched, rage trembling through his arms like a live wire. Carlos cursed, momentarily stunned, but came back swinging wildly at Finn. Carlos' punch didn't land but Finn's sure did. It landed hard and so did Carlos—on the floor knocked out cold.

The girl sat up, gasping, clutching her torn dress to her chest.

Finn turned to her. And in that moment, the world shifted.

Everything shifted.

Her eyes locked on his—huge and haunted—and something in his chest cracked wide open, like tectonic plates colliding. He didn't know her name. But he already knew she would never be just another girl. Not now, and not ever.

He held her gaze, speaking gently now. "Are you okay?" He wished that he knew what to say to comfort her and make her feel safe.

She nodded once, barely. Tears streaking down her face.

Carlos came to with a start. He spat blood from his lip and looked at Finn with pure menace in his eyes. "You're gonna regret that, man."

Finn knew that he wouldn't as he stared him down. "You touch her again, and you'll regret breathing."

Carlos sneered but didn't move.

Finn reached out a hand, knuckles bloody, to the girl. "Come on. Let's get you out of here."

She hesitated, then took his hand saying softly, so softly that he almost missed it, "You saved me." His heart swelled up like in that Grinch movie when the Grinch finally learns how to care for others.

Afraid to know, he asked her, "Has he done that before?"

Expressions crossed her face clearly as Eliza responded. "Yes, he has tried but I was in the kitchen when he grabbed me and held me down on the linoleum floor but his mother came in and interrupted. She didn't do anything to stop him. He keeps intimidating me every time he sees me and giving me bruises where they can't be easily seen. He broke the lock on the bedroom door. I've been scared of him ever since I got here."

A tear rolled down her face making his chest hurt.

They walked outside into the balmy night and sat together on the back cracked wooden porch step of the house where she rested her head against his shoulder and let the tears sweep her away. Finn just held her until his shirt was drenched and all of her tears were spent.

"Thank you for stopping him."

It was the first time in a long time, if ever, Finn felt needed. Suddenly, something broke through the numbness. Something real.

That was the night everything changed. That was the day they both knew what home felt like.

Eliza — Age 16

Eliza woke slowly, the morning light bleeding through the sheer, torn curtain above the bed. The air was still humid, thick as ever, but something had changed. The house was quiet. No pounding music. No Carlos. No threats whispered through gritted teeth.

Just stillness.

And Finn.

She sat up slowly in the bed in the back room—his bed, he'd told her to sleep there for the last week while he took the floor just outside the door, like some kind of gracious, big guard dog. Except there was nothing animalistic about the way Finn had looked at her when he pulled Carlos off. He hadn't just been angry. He'd looked… furious and protective. And scared for her. Like she mattered.

She hadn't felt that in a long time. If ever.

Her throat was raw, her body tense like a coiled wire. But she was here. She had made it through the last seven nights since Carlos tried to rape her. And she hadn't done it alone. It didn't stop the nightmares from coming but at least she felt safe while she slept.

Footsteps creaked outside the door. She tensed, heart hammering. Then reminding herself that it was Finn outside the door.

"Hey," a low husky voice said gently through the wood. "It's just me. You okay if I come in?"

She recognized that voice, stood and opened the door before she could second-guess herself.

Finn stood barefoot, shirtless, in worn flannel pajama pants. His dark chestnut hair was mussed, warm green eyes that reminded her of Ashe Juniper leaves were tired but soft as he gazed at her. There was a tension in his big 6'4" frame like he hadn't slept much, if at all. She wondered if he'd spent the whole night listening for Carlos.

"Hey," she whispered.

"You sleep?"

"A little."

He nodded, but his eyes didn't leave hers. "He's gone," he said after a second. "I told the case worker the morning after Carlos attacked you about what he did. Said I'd call the cops and report them if they didn't do something about Carlos' 'crazy threatening behavior'. The fosters moved Carlos to his cousin's place out near Brownsville an hour ago so that CPS wouldn't cut off the money they get from the state."

Relief hit her so hard her knees nearly gave out.

Finn saw it. He stepped closer, careful and slow, like a panther approaching a bird that might spook. "It's over," he said quietly. "You're safe now."

She pressed her full, plump lips together, trying not to cry. But tears came anyway. Tears of relief.

He opened his arms, just a little. "Can I...?"

She nodded, and he wrapped her in his strong muscular arms.

He smelled like a mix of sandalwood, spring rain, and his own distinctive musky scent. He smelled delicious. His hands were large and calloused but gentle. His chest was warm. And in that moment, she felt something in herself start to soften—a wall that had never had a reason to lower, now quietly crumbling in the presence of this boy who saw her as more than a burden or a body.

She didn't know what to call the ache in her chest when he held her like that. He felt safe. He felt like home.

But she knew she never wanted it to stop.

Being around him made her feel more alive and more inspired than ever.

That was the beginning. Sometimes, after lights-out, Eliza would scribble lyrics and stories into a half-used spiral notebook she kept hidden in her pillowcase. They weren't always finished, and they didn't always rhyme, but they felt like truth. Her truth. She didn't know if they were songs yet. But she was starting to wonder if maybe—just maybe—she had a voice that mattered. The day she wrote a line about Finn—"the boy who stood between the darkness and me"—was the day she stopped writing in pencil and started writing in ink.

Weeks later, they became inseparable. Not loudly, not dramatically—just *constant*.

He walked her to Fredericksburg High every morning, their backpacks bumping as they strolled past the peach orchards and limestone storefronts that lined Main Street. She saved him a seat at lunch under the old oak in the quad. They took turns cooking whatever scraps were left in the fridge—canned beans, toast, rice, maybe some chicken if they were lucky.

On weekends, they escaped.

Sometimes it was to the little library tucked beside the post office. Other times, they'd ride the rusted bikes out past the edge of town to Enchanted Rock, their unofficial sanctuary. There, they'd climb to the top in silence and sit side by side, staring out at the endless Texas hills. Just sky, wind, and the faint hum of crickets.

It was the only place the noise stopped.

They never talked about that first night. But Eliza remembered. Every time he walked on the outside of the sidewalk. Every time his hand hovered near hers but didn't quite touch.

He watched her—not with pity, but with quiet fire.

Like he was trying to memorize her. Like he was making sure she still felt safe. Still felt *seen*.

He noticed everything about her. The lush, generous mouth that showed small dimples when she smiled her lovely smile at him. The large warm violet eyes that seemed to see into his soul making him feel like more than he thought he was. More than he had been told he was.

The way that the sunlight glinted off her wavy light blond hair that he was dying to fist. Her round, generous breasts, silky skin, and perfect body that he knew would feel like heaven to touch. The more he was around her, the more aware he became. He didn't want to scare her away. He needed her. Needed to keep her close. Like a bird in his hand. Any unexpected movement and it would fly away. She would fly away.

He teased her like nothing had changed. Stole the last cookie. Argued about movies. She liked rom-coms and he was an action kind of guy. He didn't know how many times they had seen "Sweet Home Alabama" or "How to Lose a Guy in 10 Days" or pretty much any classic rom-com movie with Reese Witherspoon, Julia Robert, Kate Hudson, Audrey Hepburn, or Cameron Diaz. But sometimes, when he thought she wasn't looking, he stared at her with something tighter behind his grin. Like he was barely holding something back.

A flicker of *want*.
A flash of *need*.

A *lingering touch*.

Once, she caught him watching her from the hallway while she was curled up reading one of her favorite romance novels on the couch. His jaw was set, shoulders tense. He knew he looked like he was trying to figure something out—like the puzzle wasn't the book with the half-naked man on the cover in her lap, but *her*.

When she glanced up, he didn't look away.

He just smirked and tossed a pillow at her. "You suck in your bottom lip when you read."

"What? Liar."

"Swear to God. It must be the cover art."

"Maybe but only at the good parts," she said blushing.

Shifting uncomfortably, Finn felt heat run to his groin every time he saw her tucking in her lip.

They didn't talk about the night that had bound them. And they didn't talk about what was growing between them now—slowly, carefully, like something precious both of them were afraid to touch too soon.

But it was there. The energy that vibrated between them anytime they touched.

In the quiet. In the stolen looks. In the space that used to be empty, now filled with something electric.

And Finn—
Finn was falling. Quietly. Completely.

His heart beat faster just thinking about her. Embarrassingly his pants got noticeably tighter and his palms sweaty.

He just didn't think she was ready to know.

Yet.

His friends at school couldn't understand why he wasn't dating a hot cheerleader since he was a quarterback and the football team's captain. *Been there. Done that*, he thought. Being big for his age growing up as a foster kid he had been exposed to the wonders of sex at an early age. He enjoyed sex but the closer he got to Eliza the less interested he became in other girls. He found himself so drawn to Eliza now that she was maturing—filling out in all the right places—and they spent so much time together. Other girls weren't Eliza.

She was young still. Too young and innocent for him to share his feelings.

He scared away other guys that were interested in her at school. He told himself that it was because she needed protecting from desperate, horny teenage guys like most of his teammates. That they only wanted to take advantage of her sweet nature. Underneath that he knew that it was more than that. Eliza was and had always been his.

But someday… maybe under the stars on top of that pink granite rock, with the whole Hill Country spread beneath their feet…

He would tell her how he was feeling and how much he wanted her then hope that she felt the same.

In the meantime, he kept his head down and focused on football. Being intelligent and full of pent-up rage he had to release it somewhere—on the field. The football field was the only place a broken man like him fit. He hadn't told Eliza about the worst of what he'd been through in foster care and he didn't think that he ever would. She would look at him differently if he did.

Finn didn't know the details of every scholarship form or every deadline Eliza had, but he knew she was fighting for her future with every scrap of energy she had. He watched her in quiet admiration, torn between wanting to protect her and wanting to step out of her way so she could soar.

Still, there was a part of him—a big part—that wasn't ready to let her fly too far from him.

****

Eliza had always been the kind of girl who kept her head down and her grades up. No Friday night football games, no school dances, no bonfires out by the lake. While everyone else was making high school memories, she was making scholarship applications.

She had to—college wasn't going to pay for itself, and she didn't have a family safety net to fall back on. Every test score, every essay, every extracurricular with real weight mattered. Friends came and went, but her future had to stick.

It was during her senior year—when her world was all textbooks and deadlines—that she met the woman who would change everything.

Rhetta Barnes.

She wasn't like any teacher Eliza had ever known. Forty years old, hair the color of Tennessee whiskey, voice worn smooth from both teaching and living. Rhetta had been a music teacher for nearly two decades, but before that, she'd been the real deal—a touring country singer-songwriter with an acoustic guitar slung over her shoulder and a few scars of her own from chasing dreams. She'd even had one of her own songs on the radio once, back when Eliza was still in grade school. A handful of her songs had been recorded by bigger names, sung on stages she'd never set foot on.

On the first day of class, Rhetta leaned against her desk, guitar case resting beside her, and asked a simple question.

"Any of y'all write music or play an instrument?"

A few hands went up—confident ones. Eliza hesitated. Her hand twitched halfway before she let it fall back to the desk. She didn't really think she was *good*. She just knew that sometimes, words came to her like they were meant to be sung. She could feel music even if she couldn't yet play it.

Still, something in her stirred, and her hand went up.

After class the next day, Rhetta asked her to hang back. She was flipping through some papers, but her sharp, warm eyes kept flicking up.

"Figured I'd learn a little more about you," Rhetta said, tapping the folder in front of her. "I see here you're in foster care."

Eliza nodded, unsure where this was going.

"That's a road that'll make you tough," Rhetta continued. "But tough girls still need somethin' that feeds 'em on the inside. I'm hopin' music might be that for you."

Eliza blinked. No teacher had ever said something like that to her before.

"So tell me," Rhetta said, leaning forward on her elbows, "how often do you write? And what do you write about?"

"Every day now," Eliza said quietly, then with more confidence as she went on. "I like to write about life. Things I feel. Things I've been through. Sometimes the lyrics come like… like they're telling me a story that's already there. Sometimes it's just one line at a time. Sometimes all at once. But it's always from the heart."

Rhetta's smile deepened. "That's the only way it's worth a damn."

She let that hang in the air for a moment before asking, "You ever put those lyrics to music?"

"No," Eliza admitted. "But I want to. I want to learn guitar so I can tell the whole story, not just pieces of it."

Rhetta's eyes lit up like she'd just found a hidden treasure. "Well, honey… I think we can make that happen."

That was the start of it—the first time someone outside her own mind took her music seriously. Rhetta didn't just teach her chords and strumming patterns. She taught her how to turn a lyric into a living thing. She reminded her that her story mattered, and that there were people in the world who needed to hear it.

Eliza hadn't realized how hungry she'd been for that kind of encouragement until Rhetta gave it to her.

And from then on, it wasn't just about grades and scholarships anymore. It was about a guitar, a notebook, and the possibility that the girl who'd once been invisible might have something worth hearing after all.

Chapter Two

Changing Times

Two years later

The cicadas were already screaming when Finn leaned against his truck, a faded Longhorns cap pulled low over his eyes. The heat hadn't broken all day, and the air shimmered over the road like glass. Eliza sat on the tailgate beside him, swinging her red sandals from her fingers, a half-melted Sonic drink sweating between them.

"So," Finn said, grinning at nothing in particular, "Austin, huh? You ready to be a big-time college girl?"

She rolled her eyes. "You make it sound like I'm joining the circus."

He laughed, a deep, easy sound that always made her chest tighten. "Kinda is one. You, me, Rhetta—well, maybe not Rhetta—but still, college. New start. No more Fredericksburg drama. No more shitty foster

"Yeah," she said softly, staring out past the barbed-wire fence, the sky going pink behind the live oaks. "New start."

He nudged her shoulder with his. "Hey, I was thinking. Dorms are stupid expensive. And I don't exactly trust whoever they'd stick me with. What if we split an apartment off-campus? Just for freshman year. You know, save money."

Her throat went dry. "You and me?"

He shrugged. "We've known each other forever. You're clean. I'm... mostly clean. You study. I train. We won't kill each other. Plus, we'll both be broke. Makes sense."

She forced a laugh, eyes fixed on the gravel at her feet. "Yeah. Totally makes sense."

He smiled, easy and unbothered, like it was already settled. But inside, Eliza's pulse skittered. Living with Finn. Waking up to his voice, his messy hair, his bare feet padding through the kitchen. She could already feel the ache of it, the quiet, impossible pull she'd been trying to ignore.

She smiled back anyway. "Okay. Roommates, then."

"Roommates," he said, clinking his cup against hers. "Austin, here we come."

The cicadas kept humming, the sun sank low, and Eliza told herself it was just excitement she felt. Not love. Not yet.

****

The day of Eliza's high school graduation had been hot—typical Fredericksburg June sun, bright and relentless. The ceremony was held on the football field, folding chairs lined up in uneven rows, parents fanning themselves with printed programs. The graduates were seated alphabetically so Eliza was smack in the middle.

Eliza sat in her robe, legs jittering. Not from nerves, not exactly. It was the feeling of standing on a cliff's edge. Knowing she was about to jump. She had busted her ass in school realizing that the only way out was with an education. She didn't want to be at the mercy of someone else ever again. Making her own way—with plenty of sleepless nights to show for it—she was creating the future that she wanted.

Looking around at the rows of caps and gowns, Eliza realized she didn't have much to show in the way of high school friends. No tight circle, no weekend parties, no snapshots of homecoming nights. She'd had Finn and Rhetta, she'd had her books, and that had been enough. Still, she promised herself that in Austin, she'd try harder. She'd make space for people.

When her name was called, she rose on shaking legs. The sound that met her wasn't polite applause—it was Finn's whistle, loud and proud, cutting through the June air. She turned and found him in the crowd, taller than anyone else, arms raised, grin wide.

And next to him—Rhetta. Hands in the air, whistling right alongside him, her auburn hair catching the sun like a flame. She wasn't family by blood, but she'd shown up like one, cheering louder than half the parents on those bleachers.

The sight cracked something open in Eliza's chest.

She grinned, heat rising to her cheeks, and blew them both a kiss before walking the stage. The principal's handshake was firm, the diploma stiff in her grip. A lifeline. A ticket.

Just seeing Finn there brought a flush to her cheeks. Eliza noticed the way that other girls looked at him. As though he was an ice cream cone on a hot day. She understood and realized that she felt the same way which scared her. She didn't know what to do with the feelings. Anytime he hugged her or brushed her casually her body hummed and throbbed.

Rhetta pulled Eliza aside briefly after the ceremony—just a quick hug and intriguing comment,"Got something put aside for you, but I'll hold onto it until the right time."

Back home, she tucked the diploma into her drawer beside a letter. The one with the bold University of Texas logo at the top. Full academic scholarship. Living stipend. Classes. Books. Everything covered. And more than that—it was real. She was going to Austin. She was leaving Fredericksburg. She was going to be somebody.

And even better, Finn was going too.

He got the call in March—football scholarship, full ride, guaranteed first-year placement. He'd been in shock. Not because he wasn't good enough, but because someone finally saw it and said yes. Playing for the University of Texas Longhorn's Football Team was one of his big dreams. One that he had the chance to realize now that his selection to the football team and full scholarship the school offered were finalized.

They'd celebrated the only way they knew how—with ice cream melting too fast under the Texas sun and a late-night drive to Enchanted Rock. Windows down, country radio up, the Hill Country stretched wide around them. *"Happen to Me"* by Russell Dickerson played and then *"Didn't I"* by Dasha followed from their Austin Roadtrip Spotify playlist.

But it was Rhetta's voice that lingered in Eliza's head when she lay in bed that night, diploma tucked safe in the drawer. *You did this, baby girl. All on your own. And this is just the start.*

****

It wasn't a kiss.
It wasn't a confession.
It was just a look.

That's all it took for Eliza to realize she wanted more with Finn. Not just as best friends. Suddenly she noticed him in a different way. When they hugged they held on to one another a beat too long. The slightest touch gave her goosebumps and made her cheeks flush. She wasn't sure if he had noticed and was embarrassed to ask him.

He'd been coming over to the small apartment she shared with a couple of former classmates for the summer more now that she was of age and out of foster care. She was paying to rent the dining room with an air mattress until they headed to UT for the start of Fall classes. With excuses— movie night, hanging shelves, just hanging out.

But tonight, it was Eliza wanting to be in his space more than anything. They were in Finn's kitchen that he shared with two roommates, one that he was about to move from to head to Austin and the start of university. Covered in flour, trying and failing to make chocolate chip cookies with a warped baking sheet and no parchment paper. Finn had said they didn't need a recipe. Eliza had laughed in his face and told him he was an overconfident idiot. Neither of them knew how to cook but at least she knew a recipe was the best place to start.

Then she tripped over the corner of the kitchen mat and went down like a sack of flour, nearly taking the bowl with her.

"Damn that hurts," she said rubbing her hip. "I'm such a klutz sometimes."

Finn had crouched beside her, fresh green eyes crinkling, firm lips tugging up into that half-smile she'd seen a thousand times—but this time something was different. His hand went to her cheek, gently brushing a streak of flour from her skin. She felt his touch all the way to her core— warm moisture pooling between her legs. And when she looked up, he was already looking at her—really looking at her. As though he knew the effect that he was having.

Like she was a map and he'd just found his way home.

That was when she felt it:
A yielding. A disturbance.
Something slow and seismic.
Like stars reorienting themselves in the sky.

It wasn't fireworks or butterflies. It felt like a knowing. Like two perfect halves of one whole recognizing one another. Quiet, essential, but including sexual tension between them that was off the charts. Like nothing that she had ever felt towards a man before. Like a compass needle settling on true north. Something eternal and inevitable.

And just like that, she knew. With a completeness that took her breath.
Finn was her constant. Her truth.
Her North Star. Always.

Which terrified her.

Because what if she was wrong?

What if she told him that she wanted *more* with him and ruined everything? He was the most important person in her life—had been since they met. She couldn't lose him.

So she buried it. Smiled through it. Called him her best friend and pretended it didn't hurt when he touched her arm or leaned close and didn't kiss her.

She would rather ache quietly than lose him entirely. She needed him almost as much as breathing.

And that's when it hit her:
She was in love with him. So in love it made her stomach hurt.

Which was a problem.

Because Finn was her best friend. Her only real family. Her constant. He had never indicated that she was anything other than the dearest of friends, almost sister-like in his warmth. He kept a careful distance between them. She knew that he had dated and probably slept with other girls. If some of the girls in her year could be believed, he was quite popular and sexually experienced. Unlike her.

If she told him how she felt—if she *misread* him—she could lose all of that. She couldn't risk it. Not when he was the only thing in her life that had ever felt solid and he seemed to go through women like tissues according to his teammates. He hadn't had anyone serious as far as she knew. At least he hadn't introduced her to any girlfriends. Yet.

She made it into a secret she kept just for herself.

She told herself she was being smart. Safe.

But God, it ached.

Chapter Three

The Line Between

The Blind Buck pulsed with soft neon and the twang of an old George Strait song drifting out of the jukebox. The air smelled like mesquite smoke, cheap cologne, and fried pickles. Friday night regulars filled the booths, nursing drinks, throwing darts, playing pool, and telling the same stories they'd been telling for years.

Finn sat at the corner high-top, a Shiner in hand, trying not to laugh as Merrick James leaned against the bar, throwing cowboy charm at a tall brunette in tight jeans and firetruck-red heels. She laughed at something he said—one of those full-body laughs that turned heads—and twirled a strand of her hair around one finger.

Merrick flashed that cocky, crooked smile that had gotten him out of trouble more times than he deserved. His well-worn straw Stetson tipped just enough to look lazy on purpose, dark brown Lucchese boots planted like he owned the damn floor beneath him. The National Finals Rodeo Bronc Belt buckle worn like it was a part of him. He looked every inch the rodeo star he was—dangerous in denim and already too many women's regrets.

"Jesus," Finn muttered into his bottle smirking handsome face sporting 5 o'clock shadow. "Can't take this man anywhere."

Next to him, Brooks Atwood—country singer, former wide receiver, and certified pretty boy with an acoustic guitar—grinned around the lip of his Shiner. "You know that man's allergic to celibacy."

"You're both allergic to normal human relationships," Finn shot back. "Do y'all even remember what monogamy means, or has it been wiped from your vocabulary by beer and buckle bunnies?"

Brooks chuckled. "Says the guy who just realized he's in love with his soon-to-be roommate and best friend."

Finn raised an eyebrow. "Yeah, and at least I'm not flirting with half the women in Texas while I figure it out."

Merrick returned with two Patron Silver tequila shots and the brunette's number scribbled on a napkin. He set both shots in front of Finn and Brooks, then downed a third from his own hand.

"You're welcome," he said, sliding into his seat. "And don't hate the game."

"You are the game," Finn said dryly. "Seriously, how many numbers have you collected this month?"

Merrick glanced up as if actually thinking. "Including tonight?"

"Christ," Finn groaned.

Brooks knocked back his shot. "You're just mad 'cause you got it bad."

"I'm not mad," Finn said. "I'm serious. Eliza's… different. I've always been close to her. But something shifted. I've always thought that she was beautiful but now I'm starting to see her in this whole new way—like, deeper. Not just as my best friend but…" He paused. "It's love. I know it is. I'm not interested in anyone else but her."

That sobered Merrick for half a second. He looked at Finn over the rim of his glass. "That girl's not a half-measure, man. If you're gonna do this, do it right. You don't screw around with someone like her."

"I'm not screwing around," Finn said. "That's the whole damn point."

Brooks leaned back, tipping his hat lower. "Then you better stop waiting for the perfect moment and just tell her. The longer you wait, the more it'll twist up. Trust me."

Merrick's phone buzzed. He glanced down and grinned. "Looks like I got plans after all."

"Shocker," Finn deadpanned. "Try not to break her heart—or her bed frame."

Merrick just winked. "No promises."

Finn shook his head, but something about the moment stuck—like the calm before a shift. The night outside was still and thick with the scent of rain. But in his chest, something was moving.

And this time, he wasn't running from it.

He was walking straight in.

Chapter Four

Under the Stars

Eliza and Finn reached the top of Enchanted Rock just after sunset.

Fredericksburg was a dim glitter in the distance—streetlights blinking softly between the rolling hills. The last of the hikers had long gone. Now it was just the two of them, the granite warm beneath their backs, the sky unfolding above them in an endless dome of stars.

Eliza lay on the blanket, arms folded behind her head, her hair spilling out like a bright halo on the rock. Finn lay beside her, close but not touching. They'd done this before —watched the stars together—more times than she could count. But tonight felt different.

Quieter.

Charged.

The evening vibrated with possibilities.

She tilted her head toward him hair swinging forward. "Remember the first time we came up here?"

"Yeah," he said, reaching to tuck her hair behind her ear. "You made me carry that shitty cooler up the whole rock."

"You insisted on bringing three Dr Peppers, beef jerky, m&ms, bread, and a jar of peanut butter."

"Survival essentials."

She smiled, then fell quiet again. The kind of silence that didn't ask to be filled.

"You ever think about your family? Like where they are now?" she asked quietly.

Finn's fingers tightened on the steering wheel. He was quiet for a beat too long.

"Yeah," he said finally. "More than I want to admit. My mom... she wasn't really in the picture. Drugs mostly. She was always chasing her next high. I remember her sometimes, though—how she'd sing to me when I couldn't sleep. Before it got bad."

Eliza's eyes softened.

"What about your dad?"

"Gone when I was six," Finn said. "Just packed a bag one day and didn't come back. I waited for him for a while. Thought he'd change his mind. But people don't usually come back, do they?"

"Child Protective Services picked me up from a neighbor's apartment," he continued huskily, his pain evident. "I waited in my dad's apartment for two days before getting hungry and going to the neighbor's."

She was quiet for a second.

"Mine didn't either—come back that is," she said eyes glassy. "But not by choice. Not that that's any better. Gone is still gone. Car accident. I was twelve. It was raining. They had dropped me off at ballet class and were running errands before picking me up. We were supposed to be home in time for dinner."

Finn glanced at her, something tender and heavy in his gaze. "I didn't know that."

"We never really talked about it. I guess... I didn't want to make you sad. It hurt too much to talk about. I was mad at them for leaving me, the rainy road, myself for them having to pick me up from dance class, and God for letting it happen to good people."

She continues softly, "Then my Aunt Jenny, my mother's sister, declined custody of me. Then I became a ward of the state. You know how it went from there."

"You couldn't make me sad," he said. "Not like that. It wasn't your fault or anyone else it sounds like. It's just the shitty luck of the draw. But it's wild, isn't it? We've been in each other's lives for years and there's still so much we haven't said."

She nodded. "I want to know everything about you. All of it."

"Even the messy parts?"

"Especially those. That's how you know it's real."

Above them, the stars stretched wide and bright. No city haze out here. Just the raw, unfiltered night.

"There's the North Star," she said, pointing. "You can always find it if you look."

He followed her finger, then glanced at her instead. "I don't need to look up."

She turned to him, glistening eyes catching his in the dark.

"I just mean," he said carefully, "you've always been mine. My North Star."

Her breath caught.

He said it so simply. So casually. Like it had always been true.

And maybe it had.

She rolled onto her side to face him, propping her head on her hand heart in her eyes. "Finn…"

He looked at her, really looked. And it was like everything he'd ever been afraid of saying was right there between them, pulsing like a live wire.

"You don't have to say anything," he said. "I just… I don't think I can keep pretending it's not there."

"It is," she whispered. "It's always been there."

For a long second, neither of them moved.

Then she reached for him.

Just the palm of her hand, pressed gently over his chest, feeling his strong heartbeat under her palm.

And then he kissed her.

The kiss started soft. Careful. Tender. But it unraveled fast—months, years of tension spilling out all at once. Finn deepened the kiss, slowly, thoroughly and with complete command melting her as he worshiped her mouth, tongues dancing.

Her hands slid into his dark silky hair. His calloused fingers gripped her small waist like he was trying not to shake. Her body melted into his like two missing puzzle pieces coming together. Their bodies found rhythm without asking permission.

A rush. A fire. A truth.

Home.

When they finally pulled back, their foreheads rested together, breath mingling in the night air.

Eliza smiled softly. "Still scared?"

"Terrified," he said.

"But?"

Finn looked deeply into her large vulnerable violet eyes. "But I'd rather fall into this than spend one more day pretending I don't want to."

The air cracked around them as they lay back down on the rock, her head on his shoulder now, his big hand in her much smaller one making her feel both safe and delicate.

The stars didn't say anything.
They didn't have to.

They were just there.

Constant. Quiet. Eternal.

Like love that took its time. The connection between them a melody drifting in and out of her heart.

When she returned home that night heart pounding she lay down and brought out her lyric notebook. Eliza scribbled the words *North of Always* in the margin of a blank page for the first time.

It felt like a beginning.

Chapter Five

Like Air

Finn

It was just a single kiss.

But to Finn, it felt like a bomb had gone off in his chest. And now he was walking through the smoke, blind, heart pounding, every instinct screaming one word: *Eliza*.

He hadn't meant to lean in. He hadn't meant to touch her jaw, hadn't meant to memorize the shape of her mouth like he'd been starving for it for years.

But he had.

And when she looked up at him, violet eyes wide and full of knowing—of *hope*—he'd felt it all crack wide open.

The truth.
The need.
The want.

God help him, he wanted her so badly it made his bones ache.

Not just her body. Not just the way she curled into his side when she was tired or bit her lip when she was focused. It was everything. The way she saw him without flinching. The way her laugh made the world feel lighter. The way she carried the worst parts of her past and still hadn't let it kill the best parts of her.

She was the strongest person he'd ever known.

And he was in love with her.

He'd been in love with her since the first time he saw her violet eyes looking up at him from that nightmare of a night years ago. Something inside him had clicked then, a violent kind of clarity—*protect her. Always.*

But now?

Now it wasn't just about protecting her.

It was about needing her. More than air. More than anything.

And that scared the hell out of him.

That night after the kiss, Finn couldn't sleep.

He lay flat on his back, fists tight at his sides, eyes tracing the cracks in the ceiling of his apartment. Eliza's laugh echoed through him like a ghost. He could still smell her fresh, lavender shampoo on his shirt, mixed with that intoxicating scent that was uniquely her. He could still feel the way her lips had parted under his, like she'd been waiting just as long.

And he could still hear her voice—steady but trembling—when she'd whispered, *"Don't kiss me unless you mean it."*

He meant it. God, he meant it more than anything he'd ever said or done in his life.

But meaning it didn't make it simple.

Because if he gave in to this—if he let go of the restraint he'd clung to all these years—he might never let her go. And maybe… maybe that wasn't fair to her.

He wasn't whole. He was still that young guy with anger issues and broken trust and blood on his knuckles. Still the boy who'd learned too young that love meant leaving, or hurting, or both.

What if he ruined her?
What if she woke up one day and saw how messed up he really was?

His chest clenched tight at the thought. He'd die before he let himself be the one to break her.

But then he remembered the way she'd said it: *"You've never been the one who broke me."*

The words had bent something deep in him. Not snapped—bent. Tilted his whole world toward her, toward the possibility that maybe he didn't have to be afraid of wrecking her. Maybe she was strong enough to see the cracks in him and still choose him anyway.

The next morning, he found himself changing without even meaning to.

It was little things at first. Making her coffee without being asked, leaving the mug by her textbooks with the handle turned her way. Hovering in the kitchen doorway a beat longer than necessary, just to watch her scribble notes with her brow furrowed. His hand brushing hers when they reached for the same cabinet, neither of them pulling away as quickly as they might have a week ago.

He caught himself watching her more than usual. The way her hair fell across her cheek when she bent over her notes. The way she tugged at her sleeve when she was nervous. The way she chewed on her bottom lip when she thought no one was looking.

God, that lip. He'd memorized the exact curve of it against his.

Every glance, every brush of contact, felt heavier now—charged. And he didn't want to hide it anymore.

Not from her.
Not from himself.

Still, the doubts pressed in.

At football practice, when the coach barked at him to push harder, to carry the weight of the line like he was bred for it, he thought about what would happen if he failed. Not just on the field. What if he failed her? What if the demands of football, the chaos of Austin, the girls who circled like vultures around Longhorn players—what if all of it crushed whatever fragile thing was starting to bloom between them?

He couldn't stand the idea of losing her.

Sometimes he'd catch himself staring at her across her small shared living room, the guitar Rhetta had loaned her balanced in her lap. She'd hum under her breath, fingers finding chords slow but sure. And every single time, he thought the same thing: *She's everything.*

She was more than the kiss. More than the past. She was the anchor in a storm he hadn't even realized he was drowning in.

And he wanted her.

Not just wanted her. Needed her.

Like air.

One night, about a week after the kiss, Finn came by her apartment from practice. His body was wrecked, every muscle screaming, sweat still clinging to his shirt. He expected to find the apartment quiet, but instead, there she was.

Eliza sat cross-legged on the old patterned couch, Rhetta's borrowed old guitar in her lap, the lamp casting her in soft gold. Her hair fell around her face, and her lips moved in silent whispers as she tried to work out a lyric.

She didn't see him at first. And for a long moment, he just stood in the doorway, watching.

Something shifted inside him then, deeper than the kiss, deeper than the longing. A vow.

That he would never let anyone silence her again.
That he would fight—every day, in every way—to make sure she had the space to breathe, to sing, to become.

And maybe, if he was lucky, to love him back.

It wasn't easy.

Some mornings, he woke tangled in his sheets, fists clenched, panic clawing at his throat. Fear that she'd leave him. Fear that she'd see too much. Fear that the anger still simmering in him would spill over and prove he was nothing more than the broken boy he used to be.

But those fears were shrinking now.

Because when she smiled at him across a kitchen counter, or curled against him on the couch after a long day, or looked up at him with those violet eyes full of trust—something else grew louder than the fear.

Love.

Not the fragile kind. Not the fairytale. Something real. The kind built in the trenches. Forged in fire.

And he was ready—finally—to stop pretending.

If she still wanted him.

He just hoped to God it wasn't too late.

Sometimes, when the nights ran long and sleep refused to come, Finn's mind carried him backward.

Not to the kiss, not to Austin waiting around the corner—but to Fredericksburg, to the years that had burned themselves into his skin.

The foster home.
The smell of cheap cleaning products that never covered the sour stench of neglect.
The sound of muffled crying down the hall, when Eliza thought no one could hear.

He remembered lying awake on that lumpy mattress, fists balled against his chest, listening for her. Always listening.

The night Carlos cornered her in her bedroom and tried to rape her had been the first time Finn realized what "protector" really meant. The look on her face—terror edged with resignation—had seared him alive. He hadn't even thought; he'd just moved. Dragged Carlos off her like a rabid dog and thrown himself between them.

He'd bled for her that night.
He would've killed for her if it came to it.
And he didn't regret a single drop.

But it hadn't been just that night.

It was every night after. The first week after the Carlos' attack on Eliza, during nights he slept in the hallway outside his room, while she curling up in his bed. As they became closer he would share the bed with her just holding her, keeping her safe from her nightmares. She told him that she slept better knowing he was there. He'd lie awake for hours, staring at the ceiling, knowing her body was just on the other side of a thin slab of wood and later lying next to him. Wanting to open the door, to gather her up in his arms and promise her she'd never feel that way again.

But he never did.
Because what kind of boy, what kind of man, reached for someone that broken? That vulnerable. He didn't have any idea how to have a real relationship.

So instead, he would whisper through the crack of the door: *You're safe. I'm here.* And every time she'd whisper back: *I know.*

That was enough. It had to be.

Years later, those nights still haunted him. Not just the fear, but the ache. The ache of wanting to protect her, to hold her, to make her laugh so the shadows in her eyes would scatter.

There had been moments, even back then, when he'd caught himself staring too long. At the way her violet eyes seemed to cut through the dark like headlights. At the way her fingers tapped nervously against her thigh when she was trying not to cry. At the way she leaned into him instinctively, as if her body knew something her mind didn't yet.

Once, she'd fallen asleep on the couch after a long day of school. He'd been sprawled on the other end, pretending to watch TV. She'd shifted in her sleep, curling toward him, her head almost on his lap. He'd sat there frozen, barely breathing, every nerve on fire.

He could've brushed her hair from her face.
Could've bent down and pressed his lips to her temple, just to know what it felt like.

But he hadn't.
Because back then, he told himself she deserved more than a boy with bloody knuckles and a hair-trigger temper.

She deserved more than him.

And yet, through the years, she kept looking at him like *he* was the one who saved her. Like *he* was steady ground.

That look only made the walls around his heart harder to keep up.

Because every time she leaned her head on his shoulder after a long day, every time she laughed at something stupid he said, every time she trusted him enough to show him her cracks—he wanted.

And wanting her felt like breathing. Automatic. Necessary. Impossible to stop.

The kiss changed everything and nothing at the same time.

Everything—because now he knew she wanted him too, at least a little. He'd felt it in the way she kissed him back, not hesitant but certain. He'd heard it in her voice when she told him not to kiss her unless he meant it.

But nothing—because the instinct that had been his since that first night in the foster home still pulsed steady in his chest: protect her. Even from himself, if he had to.

That was the battle tearing him in two.

Part of him wanted to pin her to the wall and tell her he wasn't letting her out of his sight, not in Austin, not ever. Wanted to claim her so fully that no one could ever look at her without knowing she was his.

But another part of him—the part that remembered her whispering through his bedroom door, the part that remembered how fragile she'd been in those first years—knew he couldn't be selfish. He couldn't cage her in.

She deserved the world.
And if she wanted him to be part of it, he'd walk through fire to earn that place.

The longer he sat with it, the clearer one truth became:

He had always loved her.

Not in some teenage-crush way. Not in a fleeting, here-and-gone way. But in a way that had settled deep into his bones and refused to be shaken loose.

He loved her in every whispered *you're safe.*
He loved her in every laugh he pulled out of her on the hardest days.
He loved her in every sacrifice he made without ever naming it love.

And maybe that was why the kiss had felt like an explosion—because it wasn't the beginning. It was the culmination of everything he'd been holding back for years.

He was done holding back.

When Finn closed his eyes now, he didn't see the cracks in himself. He saw her—sitting on that couch with her guitar, hair falling in her face, singing quietly like she was still afraid the world might take her voice from her.

He saw her smile when she teased him about being grumpy in the mornings.
He saw the flush on her cheeks when she caught him watching her.
He saw every little piece of her stitched into him so deeply he didn't know where she ended and he began.

And he knew, with a clarity that felt unshakable, that he couldn't go back.

Whether it was Austin or Fredericksburg or anywhere else, it didn't matter.
She was it for him.
She always had been.

The question now was whether she'd let him prove it.

Chapter Six

Aftershocks

Eliza

It was just a kiss.

That's what she told herself, over and over, as she sat at her desk with her history notes spread out like some kind of flimsy shield. Pen in hand, textbook open. Her brain screaming *focus, focus, focus*.

But her lips still tingled.
Her chest still fluttered.
Her whole body still hummed with the aftershocks of Finn's mouth on hers.

God, what had she done?

No—what had *they* done?

It hadn't been planned. She hadn't even seen it coming. One second, she was laughing at something stupid he'd said, the next... his hand was cupping her jaw, rough thumb brushing her cheek like she was something fragile. Like she was something precious.

And then... his lips.

Soft, but firm. A question and an answer all at once.

The world had tilted on its axis, and she wasn't sure it had stopped yet.

Eliza shoved her pen across the page, scribbling nonsense, because if she stopped moving, she'd fall straight into the memory. She could still feel the weight of his gaze afterward—spellbound, almost too full—like he'd just confessed something without words.

She didn't know what scared her more.

That he had kissed her.
Or that she had kissed him back.

Because she had. She'd leaned in without hesitation. She'd wanted it. Maybe she'd always wanted it.

But Finn... Finn was her anchor. Her best friend. The one person she trusted without question. If she let this turn into something else, something bigger—what if she lost him?

She'd already lost too much in her life.

And yet...

Her fingers rose to her lips, brushing where his had been, and her chest tightened with something she wasn't ready to name. Something warm and terrifying all at once.

He'd kissed her like she was worth it.
Like she was the only thing he wanted.

And for a moment—just one breathtaking, world-stopping moment—she believed him.

Eliza pushed her books aside and leaned back in her chair, closing her eyes.

She could hear Rhetta's voice in her head, steady and sure, like it had been that first afternoon in the music room: *Baby girl, sometimes life hands you a song you don't feel ready to sing. Doesn't mean it ain't yours. Doesn't mean you shouldn't try.*

Eliza's throat tightened.

She wasn't ready. Not yet.

But maybe—just maybe—she was closer than she thought. Maybe it was destined. Immutable.

Chapter Seven

Blind Buck

Finn

With a loud verse from Laney Wilson's *Whirlwind* blasting through the old speakers, The Blind Buck smelled like cedar shavings, beer, and the faint tang of sweat. It was packed tonight—end of summer always drew half of Fredericksburg's twenty-somethings here before they scattered to college or work in Austin, Dallas, wherever.

Finn hadn't wanted to come. Crowds weren't his thing, never had been. But Eliza had tugged at his arm with that grin—the one that melted him like nothing else—and said, *"One last night before Austin. You can't hide at home."*

So here he was, posted near the wall with a longneck sweating in his hand, watching her.

Always watching her.

Eliza had dressed in a way that both killed him and made him proud. Tight black jeans cut to show off her long legs, a black silk tank with thin straps that tied at the shoulders, leaving her collarbones bare, skin glowing under the low neon lights. Her vintage snub-nosed red Lucchese boots were scuffed leather, the same pair she'd worn since senior year, but somehow they only made her look more like herself.

Her hair tumbled loose down her back, hints of purple under the lights, and she wore just enough makeup to sharpen the edges of her violet eyes.

And God help him, when she laughed—when she tipped her head back and let it out full and free—it was like the whole damn bar tilted toward her.

She was beautiful. She didn't even try, and she was devastating.

Music pumped through the speakers, *One Man Band* by Old Dominion, that had the dance floor thrumming with boots and most people singing along. Eliza was out there with a group mostly made up of classmates, her hips swaying in easy rhythm, boots kicking up sawdust as she spun. She spent most of her life focussed on school or writing music so going to the bar was a major change for her but she seemed to embrace it. She wasn't trying to be sexy, not really, but Finn could see every man in a ten-foot radius watching her like moths to flame. She glowed. Almost ethereal in the light of the bar.

And one in particular—some guy he didn't recognize, tall, broad-shouldered, with a too-slick grin—was staring too long. His eyes tracked the curve of her legs, the sway of her hips, his smile darkening with interest.

Finn felt it like a match struck inside his chest. Heat. Possessiveness. Instinct.

He set his beer down harder than necessary.

She turned then, her gaze catching Finn's across the room. For a second, it was only the two of them. Her lips curled into a smile—soft, private, like she'd been looking for him the whole time.

It calmed him. But only for a heartbeat. Because the slick-grin bastard leaned in closer, saying something to her over the music. She laughed politely, but Finn knew that laugh. It wasn't her real one. It was the one she used when she didn't want to make a scene.

Finn pushed off the wall before he even thought about it, weaving through the crowd until he was at her side. He slid an arm around her waist, not tentative but claiming, his palm resting against the bare skin just above her hip.

"Hey," he murmured, eyes on her but tone pitched just enough for the guy to hear.

Her smile bloomed real this time, wide and relieved. She leaned into him without hesitation, her hand resting lightly against his chest. "Hey yourself."

The guy's expression faltered, annoyance flashing across his face, but he lifted his hands in mock surrender and backed off.

Finn's jaw tightened. He wanted to deck him just for looking too long. But Eliza's fingers brushed against his shirt like a grounding wire, and he forced himself to breathe.

"You okay?" he asked her, voice low.

She nodded, her eyes searching his. "Yeah. Better now."

Better now. Those two words rattled through him, carving something deep and permanent.

The night rolled on, laughter and music and the steady burn of whiskey or tequila loosening everyone's edges. Eliza danced more, spinning in circles with friends to *Not At This Party* by Dasha & David Guetta, then line dancing to the classic *Boot Scootin' Boogie* by Brooks & Dunn, her boots thudding against the wooden floor, hair whipping around her face. Body undulating with the beat of the music. She looked free—lighter and happier than he'd seen her in weeks.

Taking a quick, long drink finishing off his beer, Finn headed over to Eliza and put his arm around her waist. Startled she gazed up at him through long darkened lashes a question in her violet eyes. His answer was to lean forward brushing a soft but claiming kiss on her full, shocked lips then whisper in her ear, "Let's take a spin."

Holding her close they began moving around the small dance floor, two-stepping to *God Gave Me You* by Blake Shelton. The words played in his heart. He wasn't a religious man but with Eliza he could almost believe that the words to the song were written about he and Eliza.

Eliza felt every turn, every brush of his hard, strong body against hers, every beat of the song, and the words settled deep in her soul. Where Finn lived. The way the the song spoke to her heart reminded her of why she wrote music and wanted to share her it. To touch hearts, mend them and break them. Fear and love drive everyone she thought. Either running to or from one or the other. In that moment there was no doubt what she wanted to run towards and it was tied directly to the man with his arms around her. Skin pebbling as his hands, one on the back of her neck, the other on her hip seamed to burn right through her. Finn held her so close that she couldn't help but notice that he was hard all over making her crave him something fierce. Heat pooled between her legs.

Just then, the song changed to another rousing upbeat country song and Eliza was grabbed by a couple of girls that she had met and become friendly with from her senior year in music class.

"Line dance bitches!" Called Sammie. Twirling her finger in the air, red hair blazing and stomping a cream colored Corral boot as she spoke.

June, a tiny hispanic women with doe eyes, chimed in with, "Let's show 'em how it's done."

Eliza was thrilled to be included in their small girl group. So she gave Finn a look that told him "later," and went with June and Sammie.

But Finn never stopped watching.

Not when men glanced too long. Which too many did as far as he was concerned. Not when the crowd pressed too close. His body thrummed with a kind of readiness he couldn't shake, every fast-twitch muscle wound tight like he was waiting for the next blow to fall.

Because he knew Fredericksburg. He knew it never stayed quiet for long.

It happened near midnight.

He was coming back from the bar with a new drink in hand when he saw her slip away from the dance floor toward the restroom hallway. Alone.

He knew that she wasn't used to drinking and she'd had three drinks that night. He didn't want anyone to take advantage of her with her guard down so he kept a close eye out for her. Aware of everything.

His gut tightened.

He scanned the room automatically, eyes sharp. That's when he saw him.

Carlos.

Older now, broader, a faint scar cutting along his jawline. But it was him. The boy who had almost broken her. The boy Finn had dragged off her in that bedroom years ago. The boy, now a man whose looming presence disconcerted and concerned Finn.

And Carlos was watching Eliza. Hungrily. Menacingly.

Not casually. Not accidentally. Watching her with a predator's focus.

Finn's blood iced over.

Carlos moved. Slow, steady, slipping through the crowd toward the back hallway where Eliza had just disappeared with the stealth and focus of a wolf scenting and locking onto its' prey.

Finn's bottle hit the bar with a crack. He shoved past the dancers, his body on autopilot, years of rage roaring up like it had never left.

By the time he hit the hallway, he heard it—Eliza's voice, tight with warning. "Carlos. Don't." Then a whimpered cry, "You're hurting me."

The door to the women's restroom was half-open. Carlos's hand braced against the frame, his body angled forward like he was blocking her way. His large, rough hand around her throat pinning her to the wall.

Finn saw red.

He was on him in three strides, catching him by surprise knocking Carlos' hand away from Eliza's neck and shoving him back hard enough to slam him into the opposite wall. Leaving Eliza gasping for breathe and hunched over trying to get a grip on herself.

"Get your God damned hands off her," Finn snarled, voice low and lethal.

Carlos smirked through the impact, his eyes gleaming with mean recognition. "Well, if it isn't Callahan. Still playin' guard dog?"

Finn's forearm pressed against his chest, pinning him, giving him no quarter. "You so much as breathe in her direction again, and I'll—"

Carlos cut him off with a laugh, ugly and sharp. "What? Hit me? Already tried that once. Didn't stop me, did it? You think she's safe just 'cause you're watchin'? World don't work that way, boy. I got a long memory. And I don't forget people who fuck me over."

Eliza's voice cut in, trembling but fierce. "Finn. Don't. He's not worth it."

But Finn couldn't look at her. Couldn't hear anything but Carlos's words, couldn't see anything but the memory of Eliza's wide, terrified eyes that night in the bedroom of the foster house.

His fist clenched, ready to drive into Carlos's face. The only thing stopping him was the feel of Eliza's delicate hand gripping his arm firmly, tugging, grounding.

"Please," she whispered hoarsely. "Don't give him that. Don't let him win like this. You could lose your scholarship Finn. Please."

For a second, the world teetered. Finn's vision tunneled, breath ragged.

Then he shoved Carlos harder against the wall one last time and stepped back, pulling Eliza into his side protectively.

By now the bar's bouncer had heard all of the fuss and come to throw Carlos's, who was know already as a troublemaker at the car, out. Banned from the bar for life.

Carlos straightened, smirking like he'd already won something. "See you around, mi angel," he drawled, heavy dark eyes flicking to Eliza sliding down her silvery-blonde hair. "Austin ain't far enough to keep you safe."

Finn lunged again, but Eliza's arms wrapped tight around him, stopping him. Carlos slipped down the hallway and out of the bar, laughing under his breath.

The silence after was worse than the noise.

Eliza pressed her forehead against Finn's chest, her breath uneven. He held her close, one hand cradling the back of her head, the other still trembling with the need to fight. Bruises were starting to form on Eliza's neck and wrist where Carlos had pinned her.

"Are you okay?" he finally asked, voice rough. Sick at the sight of those bruises.

She nodded against him, though her grip on his shirt said otherwise. "I am now. Thank you Finn for always being there for me," she said still trembling.

Again. Those same words.
Better now.
I am now.

Because of him.

Finn's chest ached with the weight of it. Even though he had ultimately saved her from Carlos again it wasn't without bruises. They reminded Finn that no matter how much he cared, how much he loved Eliza, *it* or rather *he* might never be *enough*. Enough to deserve her.

She leaned into him then, chest rising and falling against his. He felt her heart pounding through the thin fabric of her tank, matching the hammer of his own.

"I hate that he can still get to me," she whispered. "After all these years. One look and it's like I'm back there again."

Finn's grip tightened around her waist. "That's not weakness," he said. "That's scars. And scars mean you survived."

She blinked at him, startled, then a faint smile tugged at her mouth. "You always know what to say, don't you?"

He huffed out a laugh, though it was rough. "Hell no. Half the time I feel like I'm one wrong word from screwing it all up. But with you…" He trailed off, shaking his head. "With you, it just matters more."

He hadn't wanted to scare her with the fierceness inside him, the part of him that would burn the world down if it meant keeping her safe. But maybe—maybe she already knew. Maybe she'd always known.

And maybe she didn't need him to hold back.

Not anymore.

Maybe it was time to *be more*.

Finn didn't trust himself to stay inside. Not with Carlos's laugh still echoing through the walls, not with the raw urge clawing at him to go back and finish what he'd started.

His friends encouraged him to take Eliza home.

So he pulled Eliza with him. Out of the hallway, out of the bar, out into the sticky Fredericksburg night where the cicadas buzzed loud and the neon sign hummed above them.

She didn't resist. She just stayed close, her hand clutching the back of his shirt like she wasn't ready to let go either.

The door swung shut behind them, muting the music, the voices, the world. For a moment, it was just the two of them again—like it had been a hundred times before, in kitchens and bedrooms and porches where no one else could reach them.

Safe. That word hit different. Like it rewrote the blood in his veins. Because that was what he wanted for her more than anything—for her to never feel hunted again.

The parking lot stretched quiet around them, dust swirling under the buzz of the light poles. Somewhere down the street, a truck engine revved, but here it was still, thick with everything unsaid.

Her hand slid into his, their fingers tangling like they'd been made that way.

He looked down at her then—really looked. The smudge of mascara under her eyes, the faint sheen of sweat on her temple from dancing, the stubborn set of her mouth even after what had just happened. And beneath it all, that unshakable core of hers.

God, she was beautiful. Not the kind of beauty you admired from afar. The kind that hooked into your bones and never let you forget.

"Eliza." His voice broke on her name.

She tilted her face up, waiting.

He almost kissed her right there under the neon sign, almost gave in to the thing clawing inside him. But instead, he pressed her hand against his chest, right over his heart.

"Everything in me wants to protect you," he admitted, voice low and raw. "But sometimes... sometimes I don't know if that's enough. I want more. I want *you*. All of you. And I don't know if that's selfish."

Her breath caught.

For a moment, silence. Just their hearts, hammering in unison.

Then she whispered, "Finn... it's not selfish. It's the truest thing in the world."

The words ripped something open in him.

He bent, kissed her forehead first, gently, then lingered there, breathing her lavender and sweet pea scent in. Her hair, her skin, the faint smell of lavender lotion she always wore coupled with a scent that was unique to Eliza. He could've lived forever in that moment.

Then his lips moved to hers kissing her with reverence intermingled with deep passion. Giving and taking in equal measure. Pulling away slightly, Finn gently lifted the inside of her bruised wrist to his lips which he tenderly kissed. Moving to the bruises on her neck he did the same thing then whispered huskily in her ear, "Kisses to make it all better." He pulled away grasping her hand.

But he didn't push for more. Not tonight. Not after Carlos, not after the shadows that had been dragged up.

Instead, he pulled her against him, wrapping her up in both arms like he could shield her from the whole damn world.

And she let him.

For once, she didn't try to be strong for both of them. She just leaned into him, letting him be what he'd always sworn he would be.

Her anchor. Her shield.

They stood like that for a long time, until the music from inside faded into background noise and the night itself seemed to settle around them.

Finn knew things weren't over. Carlos was back, and that meant the past had teeth again. But as long as Eliza was in his arms, as long as she looked at him like that—like he was both her safe place and her choice— he could face it.

He could face anything.

Chapter Eight

Porch light Confessions

Eliza

Eliza couldn't sit still.

Her notes were a blur, her pen useless. Every time she blinked, she saw Finn's face—his eyes heavy with something she wasn't ready to name, his lips pressed against hers like he'd meant it, like he'd been holding it back for years.

Her heart wouldn't calm down.

So she grabbed her denim jacket, shoved her notebook in her messenger bag, and did the only thing she knew to do when her head spun like this. She walked. Past the square, past Neulinger's Sweet Shop and German bakery, the one that makes the best German chocolate cupcakes and her favorite apple crisps, shutting down for the night, until she saw it—Rhetta Barnes's porch light glowing like a welcome sign.

Rhetta opened the old bungalow's screen door before Eliza even knocked, 2008 Gibson Songwriter Deluxe guitar still slung across her chest, a mug of smokey pinewood lapsang souchong tea in her free hand. "Well, look who the wind blew in. You look like a rabbit that just dodged a coyote. Come on in, baby girl."

Eliza stepped inside, the smell of cedar and the smokey tea grounding her. She sat at the worn kitchen table, words fighting to get out but tangling in her throat.

Rhetta didn't push. She just strummed a lazy chord, eyes warm, waiting.

Finally, Eliza whispered, "I don't know what to do."

Rhetta raised a brow. "About school? Music?"

Eliza swallowed. "About Finn."

That got her mentor's attention. The older woman set the guitar aside, leaning forward. "Mmm. I thought I saw something in the way that boy looks at you. He's sweet on you, Eliza. And not the 'best friend' kind of sweet."

Heat rushed to Eliza's cheeks. "He kissed me. More than once."

Rhetta's smile softened, but her hazel eyes stayed sharp. "And you kissed him back?"

Eliza didn't answer, but she didn't need to. The blush in her cheeks doing the telling for her.

Rhetta reached across the table, taking Eliza's restless hands. "Change is comin', baby girl. That's life. You can't stop it, but you can meet it with both feet steady. Just remember—don't lose yourself in the middle of somebody else's storm. Stay true to who you are. Always."

Eliza's eyes burned. "What if we try to evolve our relationship and I lose him?"

Rhetta squeezed her fingers. "Darlin', the people meant to stay will fight to stay. And from what I've seen, that boy would fight tooth and nail for you."

Something inside Eliza steadied at that, just a little. Rhetta always had a way of cutting straight to the bone and stitching her back together in the same breath.

"Worst case sweet thang, you got more stories to tell and life explored," Rhetta added.

For the first time since the kiss, Eliza felt like maybe she could breathe again. She took her time walking back to her apartment texting Finn when she got home.

Eliza: Just saw Rhetta. She's as full of sass as always.

Finn: Still thinking of you songbird.

****

Brooks Atwood slid into the stool beside him back at the bar, smelling faintly of cedar and whiskey. Brooks had swapped cleats for a guitar after high school, but he hadn't lost the swagger of a wide receiver and bronc rider. Cowboy boots tapped to some tune in his head, his grin still crooked enough to get him in trouble.

"You look like hell, Callahan," Brooks said, signaling for a beer.

Finn gave a dry snort, eyes on his glass. "Had to head to Austin for the week to start football practice at UT and they are already hard core. That obvious?"

"Obvious enough." Brooks leaned an elbow on the bar, turning to study him. "That UT grind hittin' you already? You're moving there next week and the bullshit's already started?"

Finn exhaled through his nose, jaw tight. "It's... a lot. Playbook's twice as thick. Practices twice as long. Billings is breathing down my neck about grades and film study on top of workouts. Strength coach is chewing my ass about protein counts, and the boosters—" He shook his head, taking a long pull of beer. "Feels like the weight of the whole damn state's on me."

Brooks clinked his bottle against Finn's with an easy grin. "That's 'cause it is. Longhorn football don't mess around."

Finn tried to smirk, but it felt thin. He could still hear Billings growl in his head. *You're not just carrying a ball. You're carrying the weight of Texas.*

And beneath that, the ghost of a foster dad's voice: *Figure it out.*

Brooks watched him a beat, then tilted his head. "This about the move? You and Eliza shacking up in Austin?"

Finn's shoulders stiffened. "We're not—" He broke off, sighing. "We're just... roommates. She needs a place, I got the scholarship apartment. Made sense."

"Uh-huh." Brooks took a long drink, eyes twinkling over the rim. "And you expect me to believe you'll keep it all buttoned up when you've been in love with that girl since her second year of high school? Remember that I was at the bar the night Carlos went after Eliza. I saw the way you looked and her, danced with her, protected her. Your sun rises and sets on that woman."

Finn shot him a look. "It's not that simple."

"Sure it is." Brooks leaned back, boots hooking on the stool rung. "Football's a storm, man. The girls, the fans, the pressure—it'll eat you alive if you don't know what you're holding onto. Question is—" He tipped his bottle at Finn. "—is Eliza what you're holding onto, or what you're runnin' from?"

The words landed like a gut punch.

Because maybe it was both. He was running—from the fear of screwing it up, from a lifetime of silence where no one told him how to carry weight like this. And he was holding on—tight—to Eliza, the only person who'd ever looked at him like he wasn't just a fighter, or a foster kid, or a football player.

"She's… everything," he muttered.

Brooks' grin softened. "Then don't screw it up. You try to half-ass this thing—hide behind football, or let the noise of all those jersey-chasing girls get to you—you'll lose her. And you know damn well she ain't the kind of girl you find twice."

Finn drained his beer, the words heavy in his chest. He wanted to believe he could balance it all—the game, the pressure, the girl. But for the first time in his life, he wasn't sure if the field was the hardest fight he had in front of him.

Maybe the real fight was letting himself believe he deserved her at all.

Back at the apartment, he lingered in the doorway, watching her tape the last box shut, her hair falling in loose waves around her face. She looked like the future he didn't know how to deserve.

Brooks' words echoed. *Storms don't scare a man who knows what he's holding onto.*

But what if the storm wasn't just football? What if it was everything—his past, his fear, the ghosts of all the homes he'd never belonged in?

And what if Eliza wasn't just what he was holding onto... but the one thing that could break him if he lost her?

Moving to Austin was a new beginning for them both and he hoped like hell that they were up to it.

Chapter Nine

Edge of Changes

Eliza

The boxes sat stacked by the door, taped and labeled in her careful handwriting. To anyone else, it might have looked like preparation. To Eliza, it felt like the edge of a cliff.

Austin. College. A whole new life.

She should've been nothing but excited—she had the scholarship, the fresh start, the chance to finally be more than the girl who survived. But as she zipped the last duffel shut, her stomach twisted.

Because the past never stayed buried in Fredericksburg.

And last night had proved it.

She shoved a sweater into her duffel now, hands shaking.

Her mind dragged her backward, unwilling. To the first time.

The foster home. The smell of mildew and cigarettes. Carlos cornering her in the kitchen and a few days later in her bedroom, voice dripping cruelty and grabbing at her breast. *Bet you've never even been touched or kissed. Bet I could—*

The memory was sharp as glass. His body pinning hers, the scrape of linoleum, the press of terror choking her as his body weighed her down on the bed.

And then—Finn.

He'd torn Carlos away like an animal, fists flying. She could still see the wildness in his eyes, the blood on his knuckles. *Don't you touch her!*

Later, when she sat on the porch steps, shaking, it was Finn beside her. Silent. Solid. His shoulder brushing hers, his warmth seeping into her bones. She'd wanted so badly to lean her head against him, to press her lips to his bruised hands. To tell him he was the only thing keeping her together.

But she hadn't. She'd swallowed it down. Because what if he didn't want her that way? What if she ruined the one safe place she had?

The contrast gutted her. The now versus then of her thoughts.

Then: Carlos's weight pressing her down, her voice gone. Finn's fists bleeding because he wouldn't let her drown.

Now: Carlos back again, smirking, threatening. Finn's body slamming between them, his voice steel.

And threaded through it all were the kisses.

That sweet kisses that still burned on her lips and heralded a change in their relationship.

She replayed them endlessly—the way he'd touched her jaw, tentative but hungry, like he'd been holding back for years. The way his mouth fit hers like it had always been meant to. The way her whole body had gone weightless, and yet grounded, as if she'd just stepped into the truth she'd been circling all her life.

She wanted it again. God help her, she wanted more. Much more. From Finn. Only and ever Finn.

And that was what Austin meant. Not just escape from Fredericksburg, not just freedom from Carlos's shadow. It meant possibility. A chance to stop circling Finn like a secret she couldn't name. A chance to let herself want what she wanted.

She wanted to be his girlfriend. More than she had dared to acknowledge even to herself. Every girl she had seen him with had burned her heart. The idea of him with anyone else gave her a crushing feeling in her chest.

The thought of wanting Finn made her cheeks heat and pulse jump, but it was the truth. She wanted to claim him, to know he was hers—not just the boy who protected her, not just her best friend, but the man who kissed her like she was his whole world.

And deeper still, in the quiet place she never spoke of—she thought about making love to him.

The idea bloomed and burned all at once. She'd never given herself that way to anyone, not after what had almost happened. The thought of Carlos's hands, his sneer, had always shut her down. But with Finn... it was different. She had a few fumbling encounters during high school but could never relax enough to commit herself in body or heart to someone.

With Finn, she could imagine skin on skin, his large hands steady on her small waist, his mouth whispering her name like a vow. She could imagine giving, not because it was taken, but because she wanted—achingly, desperately—to be close to him. To share herself with him.

She pressed her palms to her eyes, heart racing. Her hands gently moved down her body noticing the sensitivity the touch left in its' wake. Her breasts, her hips, then she touched that private place. It thrummed to life with her touch. She imagined Finn's hands on her that way, breathes getting shorter as her body warmed and opened. Fingers brushed and opened her swelling lips, fingers slipping in to torment herself with thoughts of Finn doing the same thing to her. She imagined his tongue on her clit. The thought launching her into orgasm. Trembling, she wondered if Finn ever thought of touching her the same way. His strong hard body on hers.

These thoughts and feelings made it difficult to be around Finn without letting on her deep attraction to him.

Wanting him terrified her. But the fear wasn't of him. It was of herself—of how much she needed him.

****

She sat on the edge of her bed, staring at the packed duffel. The hum of cicadas outside filled the silence, and for just a moment she let herself slip into a dangerous thought.

Austin. Their apartment. Just the two of them.

She pictured that first night—the boxes half-unpacked, the mattress on the floor, city noise bleeding through the thin walls. Finn dropping beside her, worn out from carrying her bookshelves up three flights of stairs, sweat darkening his shirt. She'd laugh, tease him, throw a pillow, and he'd catch it, catch *her*, the way he always did.

And maybe this time he wouldn't let go.

She imagined the way he'd look at her when there was no one else around. Not just her protector. Not just her best friend. His gaze would soften, deepen, hold her still until she couldn't pretend anymore. He'd reach for her—slow, certain—and she'd meet him halfway, lips trembling but sure.

The kiss would start gentle, like the one they'd already shared. But then it would shift, grow, until her fingers tangled in his shirt and his hands slid to her waist, pulling her closer. No fear, no past, no Carlos—only warmth, only want, only Finn.

In her mind, she saw herself whispering his name against his mouth, felt the weight of his forehead resting on hers, heard the ragged way he'd breathe when he finally let go of all that restraint. She imagined the quiet ache of choosing, of giving, of being wanted wholly—not for survival, but for love.

Her chest ached with it, her palms pressed tight against her knees to steady the rush. God, she wanted that. Not someday, not maybe—she wanted that with Finn.

And maybe Austin wasn't just escape. Maybe it was the beginning.

Chapter Ten

The Guitar

Eliza

The next morning smelled like rain and cedar when Eliza made her way down the gravel drive to Rhetta Barnes' little yellow house on the edge of Fredericksburg. The screen door creaked the same way it always had, and Rhetta was waiting on the porch swing, mug of coffee in hand, guitar case propped beside her boots.

"Well, baby girl," Rhetta said, tipping her head in that way she did. "Big day. You finally headed off to Austin, huh?"

Eliza nodded, a lump in her throat she hadn't expected. "Yeah. I guess it just feels… bigger now that I'm actually leaving."

Rhetta's smile softened. "That's the thing about change—it don't ever wait until you feel ready. You just gotta jump, and remember who you are when your feet hit the ground."

Eliza sat beside her, sinking into the familiar sway of the porch swing. For a moment, she felt like a little girl again, just another student fumbling through chord charts and trying not to cry over a busted string. Only she wasn't that girl anymore.

Rhetta reached for the case at her side and nudged it toward Eliza. "Got something for you."

Inside was a scuffed vintage acoustic Gibson Songwriter, the rosewood darkened by years of hands and heat, the pickguard scratched bare in places. Eliza traced an elegant finger along the grain, stroking it as though touching it were a religious experience.

"She's got miles on her. Lot's of miles. Just like me," Rhetta laughs, voice thick with affection. "But she'll sing if you let her. So will you, baby girl."

Overwhelmed, Eliza swallowed hard. "Rhetta, I—I can't take this."

"The hell you can't. You'll need her more than I do now. College'll shake you up, test what you're made of. When it gets too loud, you sit down with this old girl and remember—you've already walked through fire. You'll be just fine."

The tears came then, hot and uninvited. Rhetta reached over, squeezed her hand.

"One more thing," she added, eyes twinkling with a sly kind of knowing. "That Finn boy? Don't look at you like no dear friend like I told you before. He's sweet on you. You can't miss it. A boy don't stare at a girl like she's his whole sky unless he's halfway gone already. Take your shot and give it a chance."

Eliza's cheeks flushed, her heart stuttering. She tried to protest, but Rhetta held up a finger. She didn't know if Rhetta meant songwriting or her relationship with Finn.

Clarifying, Rhetta said, "I ain't saying rush. I'm saying—don't doubt what's plain as day. And don't be afraid to let someone love you true when the time's right."

Eliza hugged the guitar case to her chest, like it could anchor her to this moment. No one had ever given her a gift like this one—so heartfelt and valuable—one that showed someone believed in her. In her talent.

Rhetta leaned back, her coffee mug, today it was black coffee to get her started, balanced on the arm of the swing. The lines in her face softened, as though she was drifting somewhere far away.

"You know, I wrote him a song once," she said quietly. "Back when I thought Jace was it. My forever. Wrote it on the back of a diner napkin, 'cause that's all I had in my pocket."

Eliza's fingers stilled against the guitar strings. Rhetta had been tight-lipped about her past and the love she'd had and lost somehow. "What was it about?"

Rhetta's smile was small, wistful. "About leavin' this town. About how we'd drive until the road ran out, windows down, singin' loud enough to drown out every bad memory." Her voice dropped, almost embarrassed. "Never showed that particular one to nobody but him."

She set her mug aside and, before Eliza could speak, she began to hum— a low, trembling tune that carried more ache than words ever could. Then, soft as a secret, Rhetta sang a fragment, just enough to hang in the air:

"Take me past the county line,
Where the stars don't all look the same.
If the world forgets my name,
Sing me back again."

The swing creaked beneath them. The cicadas outside paused as though even they were listening.

Eliza felt goosebumps rise on her arms. The melody was fragile, imperfect, but it carried a weight that settled deep in her bones.

Rhetta let the last note fade, her gaze dropping to her hands. "That's the only piece of him I kept. The song. Everything else I let go."

She looked at Eliza then, her eyes sharp, steady. "That's why I'm tellin' you—write it down. The love, the loss, the hurt, the joy. Whatever it is, make it a song. 'Cause songs last. Even when people don't. But I think that your Finn might be a man who lasts."

Eliza tightened her grip on the guitar case, throat thick. She knew she'd never forget that melody.

"You'll always have a place here," Rhetta said softly. "When you need clarity, or a hot meal, or just to remember how to wrangle a G chord without swearing. You hear me?"

Eliza nodded, smiling through the tears. "I hear you."

Eliza didn't realize she was crying until her vision blurred. The melody clung to her ribs, as though Rhetta's voice had carved open a place inside her that Eliza usually kept locked tight.

She thought of Carlos—his shadow still circling Fredericksburg, still tied to her name like a threat that wouldn't go quiet. She thought of the way fear could make you disappear from your own skin. For a long time, that's how she'd lived: shrinking, hiding, staying small so she wouldn't be noticed.

But Rhetta's song said the opposite. It said *take up space anyway*. Sing yourself back, even if the world tried to strip you down to nothing.

Eliza brushed at her cheeks, but the tears kept sliding. "What if I can't?" she whispered, ashamed of the quiver in her voice. "What if no matter how far I run, he still… takes pieces of me with him?"

Rhetta didn't flinch. "Then you sing louder, sweet girl. You take back more than he ever tried to steal. Don't let fear be the author of your story. You're the one holdin' the pen."

Eliza nodded, swallowing hard, her fingers tightening around the guitar case.

But another thought broke free, softer, more dangerous. "And what if… what if the thing I want most is right next to me? What if I ruin it? I'm not sure how to belong to someone. I'm afraid of wanting it too much."

She didn't say Finn's name, but Rhetta's smile was knowing all the same. "Wantin' ain't ruin, Eliza. It's human. And if it's meant to be, it'll grow stronger with time, not weaker. Just don't run from it 'cause you're scared. Don't erase yourself for him either. Let him see *all* of you, even the pieces you think are too messy. Especially those."

The words sank deep, anchoring her. Eliza drew in a shaky breath, as though her lungs finally remembered how to work. For the first time since she heard Carlos was back, she didn't feel small. She felt seen.

When she left Rhetta's porch, glossy guitar case bumping against her leg with the Caution: *May Burst Into Song* bumper sticker, she carried not just an instrument but a command stitched into her bones:

Sing yourself back. Don't erase who you are.

And as Finn's F150 came into view, sunlight glinting off the hood, her heart knocked against her ribs with equal parts fear and longing. Rhetta's words echoed—about not hiding, about Finn being sweet on her—and Eliza knew that leaving Fredericksburg wasn't just about escaping Carlos.

It was about stepping into the next verse of her own song. With Finn.

When Eliza finally stepped outside into the heavy heat of a Fredericksburg summer, Finn was there. Leaning against his beat-up old blue Ford F150 truck, arms crossed, eyes locked on her like she was the only thing worth waiting for.

Winking, Finn said, "let's get this show on the road."

Her feet carried her forward, heart pounding. And when she climbed into Finn's old truck, Austin on the horizon, the guitar rested across her lap—her anchor, her reminder, her piece of home.

Her chest tightened.

She remembered him at sixteen, bloodied fists for her. She remembered him last night, shoving Carlos back with that same wild fire in his eyes. And she remembered the kiss, the first one and the others after it—the way it had cracked her wide open, leaving her wanting more.

She wasn't just leaving Fredericksburg. She was stepping into the unknown—into Austin, into freedom, into possibility.

And into Finn.

Chapter Eleven

Time to Move

They left Fredericksburg for Austin, the old blue truck was stuffed with books, Rhetta's guitar, duffel bags, Eliza's favorite succulent, and tons of snacks. Finn drove. Eliza had made Spotify playlists mostly made up of country and Southern rock. They stopped at every kitschy roadside stand on the way, grabbing cherry kolaches and peach cider, laughing when a rainstorm forced them under a gas station awning for half an hour.

The drive full of heated long looks.

Finn sang off-key to one of Eliza's road trip playlists, and she recorded it with mock seriousness. "Future blackmail," she teased reaching out a slender hand to brush the wayward hair away from his eye. Finn put his hand over hers and held it to him threading their fingers together.

When the country song "Baggage" by Kelsea Ballerini came on, Eliza busted out singing along. Finn was floored. He turned the radio down so that her voice was the only one soaring. Then a Carrie Underwood song came on and he was truly blown away. Leaving a feeling like warmed honey running through him.

Like mainlining whiskey straight to his veins.

His skin rose with goosebumps when she hit the high notes. He looked at her as though seeing her for the first time. He'd heard her singing softly almost under her breath as she wrote. He knew that she wrote stories and songs but he didn't know about her voice. Its' unique tone wrapped around his heart and squeezed. That and the way its' power met with exquisite vulnerability.

"Why didn't you tell me you could sing like that and why is this the first time that I'm hearing you?"

Looking uncomfortable Eliza responded shyly, "Singing's always been just for me. My second foster mother hated when I sang and told me how bad I sounded. *"Like a strangled chicken"* were her words."

"She lied. Your voice is something special just like you are," Finn replied reaching over interlacing their fingers together again. He couldn't seem to stop touching her.

Eliza felt warmth race through her body at his supportive words flushing her cheeks.

"Maybe one day I'll have too much to sing about to stay silent. Rhetta says that it's only a matter of time before it all just floods out of me like a giant tide wave that can't be tamed."

Finn looked at her saying with conviction, "You already do —have too much to say—but just enough to sing."

Mutually deciding to change the subject, they took turns reading street signs in bad accents, pointed out every cow they saw like it was the first, and filled the space between towns with dreams. About the apartment.

About classes. About maybe, someday, performing music, getting published, and playing football in bowl games.

They took turns reading street signs in bad accents, pointed out every cow they saw like it was the first, and filled the space between towns with dreams.

Reminiscing about the time they snuck out of the foster home and went to try cow tipping without success one night.

"Damn Eliza that was a pathetic attempt. You gave up before we really tried," Finn admonished.

"She was so cute! The cow looked just like Bessie, that cow on the milk carton with sweet eyes that implored you to like her," Eliza countered. "I just couldn't do it."

For a while they just relaxed into a comfortable silence as the mile passed beneath them.

At one point, with the windows down and the Spotify playlist looping back to something acoustic and slow, Eliza turned toward him.

Finn reached across the console, lacing his fingers with hers. "Austin or bust, right?"

"Right. On a lighter note—I need a serious *sugar stop*," Eliza pleaded looking at Finn's chilled profile.

"Only if we stop by Buc-ee's for jerky and BBQ sandwiches. I mean let's face it. It's not a Texas roadtrip without a stop at Buc-ee's." Finn negotiated with conviction.

They decided to make a stop in Round Rock for the city's world famous Texas sized donut to share. Half glazed and half chocolate covered but all sugary goodness. At this rate Eliza thought with chagrin, the infamous freshman 10 might have already begun. Then on to Buc-ee's to fill the gas tank and get BBQ.

When the Austin skyline finally rose in the distance, they both went quiet.

"You ready?" he asked.

She nodded. "Absolutely! Let's make this count."

He took her hand over the center console, squeezed her hand again. "North of Always."

"North of Always," she whispered. The air between them filled with tension and possibility.

And together, they drove into the rest of their lives which began by moving into their new apartment just off the University of Texas campus together.

Still unsure. Still wanting. On the threshold.

Later, after the drive to Austin and the chaos of unpacking, Eliza found herself alone in the quiet of their new apartment, which was a small two bedroom. Finn had gone to meet with the team, Coach Billings was already a hard task-master apparently, and boxes were still stacked like walls around her.

She sat cross-legged on the floor, the beautiful, old guitar resting against her knee. Her fingers hovered uncertainly over the strings, and then— slow, halting—she began to pick out the melody Rhetta had played for her on the porch.

It was shaky at first, the notes uneven, but the sound filled the small apartment, soft and unsteady like a heartbeat finding its rhythm.

The song carried her back to the cedar-scented porch swing, to Rhetta's velvet and whiskey voice saying *sing yourself back*. And for the first time, Fredericksburg felt like it hadn't swallowed her whole. She had carried a piece of home with her, something that would remind her who she was when everything felt too big, too loud, or too terrifying.

Her throat ached, but she kept playing. Each note felt like a promise—that she wasn't running away from her past anymore, and she wasn't running from Finn either.

When the door opened and Finn stepped in, sweaty from practice and grinning at her like she was the best sight he'd seen all day, she froze. His gaze shifted to the guitar in her lap, to the fragile little tune she was coaxing out of it.

"That's pretty," he said softly, almost hesitantly. "Did you write it?"

Eliza's pulse jumped. She shook her head, swallowing hard. "No. Rhetta gave me this one."

He didn't press. Just sat down across from her, close enough that she could feel the warmth rolling off him. His eyes softened as though he understood, somehow, that the song was more than music. It was armor. It was a reminder. It was *hers*.

And though she didn't say it aloud, Eliza knew the truth: Rhetta's voice was still with her, threaded through every note, anchoring her in this new life.

Later that week, the new apartment smelled strongly of fresh paint and cardboard. Half-unpacked boxes lined the living room, and the couch still had its plastic cover on. Their first place together. Both she and Finn had gotten into the University of Texas on a combination of scholarships and grants. Finn for football and Eliza for academics.

Finn had already started football practice with his new team and coach, was pouring over playbooks, and met with his advisor while Eliza had been painting the new apartment and unpacking. She was looking forward to meeting with her scholarship advisor, Mrs. Thomas and literature advisor, Dr. Langdon, later that week right before classes started. She was nervous and excited about the whole thing.

Eliza stood by the window, twisting the ends of her blonde braid between her fingers. She watched the late summer sun stretch across the neighboring rooftops. Behind her, Finn grunted as he lifted another box into the kitchen.

"This one says 'books,' but it weighs as much as a small planet," he called. "Is Pluto still a planet?"

"Those are my anthologies," she said, smiling faintly. "And not exactly, Pluto is considered a dwarf planet."

"Next time, label it 'Warning: Literature Gym Set'. Why so many books? I thought that most of the class books are online." Finn questioned with a smirk.

He dropped the box next to a stack already labeled "desk stuff," then sat on the floor with a huff. His dark T-shirt clung to him, damp from effort. She turned to face him and couldn't help noticing how different he looked now. Still Finn—same green eyes, same dimple when he smiled—but something had shifted. They were here now. On their own. Together.

"You think we're ready for this?" she asked, quiet.

He leaned back on his elbows, looking up at her. "I don't know. Are we ever really ready for anything?"

"Comforting."

"I'm serious, though. I'm nervous too. About football. Classes. Living together." He paused. "About us."

She sat beside him. "Same."

They were silent for a minute, the weight of change settling around them.

"I keep thinking," she said, "what if college turns us into different people? What if we grow in different directions?"

He looked over at her, really looked. "Then we talk about it. Fight for it. We've already been through more than most couples our age. And we made it here."

"But here is new," she said. "Here is stress and late nights and roommates who party and professors who won't care if we're tired or in love."

Realizing that Eliza had just used the L-word, Finn nodded slowly. "Yeah. But here is also waking up next to you. Making dinner at midnight. Cheering you on when you publish something. You being in the stands at my games."

She smiled, but her eyes shimmered.

He reached for her hand. "I'm not afraid of us changing, Eliza. I'm afraid of us not trying."

That made her laugh—a small, cracked almost giddy laugh that released some of the pressure in her chest.

"Okay," she whispered. "Then we try."

Finn pulled her in, her head resting against his chest. They sat like that on the living room floor, surrounded by boxes and a thousand unknowns.

Monday would come. So would challenges.

But for now, they had this moment. Their first home. The promise to stay close, even when everything around them shifted.

Chapter Twelve

Under Pressure

Finn

The Friday night lights were long gone, but the echoes still lived in him. Sometimes Finn swore he could still hear the roar of Fredericksburg's stands whenever he shut his eyes—the crackle of the PA, the cheerleaders' chants, the way the crowd had screamed his name when he made a breakaway run.

Only now, the lights burned brighter. The stadiums were bigger. Louder. Less forgiving. At UT, there were no Friday night mistakes to learn from. One fumble could cost you a scholarship, one off week could shove you down the depth chart.

Practices had begun and the weight of it—God, the weight of it—sat on his chest even now as he hunched over his Shiner at a dive bar just off Sixth.

The place smelled like cedar smoke and grease. Neon beer signs buzzed overhead, and country music bled low from the jukebox in the corner. It was half-empty, a rare pocket of quiet in Austin's usual Friday-night chaos.

But even the quiet felt loud to him tonight. His brain wouldn't quit spinning.

Earlier that week just after he'd moved into the new apartment by the university, Coach Billings singled him out.

"Callahan, in my office. Now."

Coach Billings didn't wait for an answer. He just barked it across the practice field and stalked off, visor tugged low against the sun. Finn felt every eye on him as he jogged after, chest heaving from drills.

Inside the office, the air conditioner rattled, and the walls were plastered with game tape stills and recruiting maps. Billings shut the door with a click, then turned, arms folded, his barrel chest filling the space.

"You know what it means when you wear that jersey?" the coach asked, his voice sharp but not cruel.

Finn stood tall, helmet still in hand. "Yes, sir."

"No, you don't." Billings leaned across his desk, his finger jabbing the air. "It means pressure. You think this is about you? Your stats? Your draft dreams? Wrong. It's about this program. About every booster writing checks. Every kid out there dreaming of bein' you. Every old-timer who bleeds burnt orange. You don't just throw a ball, Callahan. You carry the weight of Texas."

The words hit like bricks.

Billings paced. "We got fans who'll forgive a busted play. What they won't forgive is weakness. You understand me? You start second-guessin', you show cracks—you won't just lose your spot. You'll let down the whole damn state."

Finn swallowed hard. His hands flexed at his sides. The instinct was to nod, to promise, to say he'd carry it. But inside? Inside his chest felt like a vise.

"Yes, sir," he managed.

Billings narrowed his eyes. "Good. Now get outta here. And Callahan?"

Finn turned back at the door.

"You've got the talent. Don't waste it by thinkin' you can coast. You're not just another player. You might be the one.

Finn jogged out, helmet clutched so tight his knuckles ached.

The one.

He should've felt proud. Instead, he felt like the floor had tilted under him.

Later that night, Finn lay awake in the scholarship apartment he shared with Eliza, Billings' words chasing themselves through his head. *The weight of Texas. The one.*

It stirred up memories he didn't want but couldn't stop.

Foster home, age twelve. A creaking bunk bed, mildew smell thick in the carpet. The foster dad—Rick, or maybe Ron, he could never keep them straight—barked at him from the living room.

"You think the world owes you somethin', boy? Get out there and mow the damn lawn before I tan your hide."

Finn had bitten his tongue bloody that day, pushing the rusted mower through shin-high grass while the Texas sun baked him. Later, when the mower sputtered and died, he'd dragged it back, hoping for help, for guidance, for anything.

Rick—or Ron—barely looked up from his recliner. "Figure it out."

That was it. No teaching. No patience. Just indifference, or anger if he asked again.

So he learned to figure it out alone.

When he flunked a math quiz at thirteen, there was no father at the kitchen table, pencil in hand, showing him how to work the problems. When he scraped his knees in Pop Warner, there was no man clapping him on the back, telling him to shake it off and get back in.

All there was—silence. Or worse, yelling.

He'd learned early that no one was coming to carry the weight for him. No one would step in.

So when Billings said, *You might be the one*, all Finn could hear was the echo of that foster dad's voice: *Figure it out.*

Only now the lawn was the size of Texas.

Chapter Thirteen

The Space Between

The air conditioner hummed against the late-August Texas heat, doing its best to cool a place that still didn't feel like home. Cardboard boxes towered like half-opened secrets, newly painted walls waited for art, and the new apartment smelled faintly of fresh paint and someone else's cleaning supplies.

Eliza padded barefoot through the kitchen, the tile cool against her toes. She had tied her hair up in a messy knot that had already surrendered to humidity. A half-empty Sonic cup sweated on the counter, a casualty from the move-in chaos.

Finn was crouched in front of the fridge, head half inside, muttering to himself. He was still damp from his post-practice shower, a bead of water sliding down the back of his neck and disappearing beneath the collar of his T-shirt.

"Don't tell me you finished the last blue Gatorade," she said, leaning on the doorway.

He looked back, that crooked grin spreading. "Might have. Needed electrolytes."

"Finn." She drew out his name in mock warning.

"I'll buy more tomorrow," he promised, pulling out a bottle of water. "You want grape?"

She wrinkled her nose. "Not even if I were dying."

He laughed, low and warm. When he handed her the bottle, their fingers brushed. It wasn't an accident, not really. Neither of them moved for half a second too long, and the spark between them felt almost visible.

Eliza looked away first. "Thanks."

"No problem." He grabbed another bottle for himself and took a long drink, throat working, and she realized she was staring.

These little moments kept happening. Glances that lingered. Fingers brushing over countertops. A quiet awareness that hummed between them like static.

They spent the afternoon unpacking side by side. She assembled a bookshelf while he waged war on the couch cushions, trying to make them fit. Music played from her phone—Rhetta's old playlist, all smoky soul and summer memories.

Every little domestic moment—arguing over where the coffee mugs should go, Finn cursing softly when an Allen wrench slipped, her laughing at how crooked their first attempt at hanging a poster turned out —felt like something more. Like rehearsal for a life she wanted but was still afraid to claim out loud.

"Do you ever sit still?" he teased when she started alphabetizing her books.

"Do you ever follow directions?" she shot back, eyeing the crooked legs of the coffee table.

He squinted at it. "Modern art."

"Functional furniture."

"Tomato, tomahto."

She rolled her eyes but smiled. It was so easy with him—this rhythm they had always fallen into without trying. He made ordinary things feel light, even when her chest ached with the weight of what she wasn't saying.

By sunset, after hours of unpacking, the boxes had thinned, the apartment softening into something almost lived-in. She lit a candle on the counter, the scent of teakwood and gardenia threading through the air.

Finn collapsed onto the couch beside her, the lamplight cutting gold through his hair.

"You tired?" he asked.

"A little."

"You did most of the work."

"Not true. You did the heavy lifting."

He grinned. "Yeah, but you did the bossing."

"That's called project management."

"Uh-huh."

She smiled, leaning her head back against the couch. Silence stretched— comfortable, weighted.

When she glanced over, his eyes were already on her.

The air thickened.

"Finn…" she whispered ache in her tone. "I'll see you in the morning."

****

Finn

The apartment smelled like paint, cardboard, and Eliza's lavender shampoo. Not like Fredericksburg, not like the locker room, but something that already felt better than either.

Finn found himself watching her more than the football games he was supposed to be learning plays from. She knelt on the floor, her braid slipping over one shoulder, lips pursed as she sorted through books like they were sacred objects. They had to be in just the right order and she couldn't relax until she had them that way.

He wanted to tell her she was beautiful like that. He wanted to tell her that watching her create order out of chaos made him want to be better, steadier.

But when she looked at him with those violet eyes, laughing about him drinking all of the Gatorade which was becoming a running joke, he thought: *I'm screwed. I've been screwed since the first day she walked into my life when our eyes made contact. She had more grit and goodness than anyone I'd ever met. She had a shine.*

By nightfall, the exhaustion had hit, but she still looked luminous in the lamp's glow, curled on the couch like it already belonged to her. He dropped beside her, too close, not close enough.

"You tired?" he asked.

She said a little. He said the same. And then the silence grew thick, humming with all the things he hadn't said.

He let his hand hover on the cushion, fingers flexing, aching to touch hers. If she just shifted closer—just an inch—he'd do it.

But she didn't. And when her phone buzzed, it was like the spell snapped. It was Rhetta checking in.

He went to bed with his heart hammering and his palms aching, body thrumming, and cursing himself for being a coward. Rhetta has the worst timing he thought, a complete cock blocker.

He realized in that moment it was time for him to man-up.

The next evening, he tried to play it cool. Music played. Cooking spaghetti with meatballs wasn't exactly candlelight and roses, but when she laughed at him—really laughed—something in his chest unraveled. He felt as though he could devour her.

She darted past to steal the wooden spoon out of his hand, and without thinking, he caught her around the waist just as the first notes from "*The Dance*" A Garth Brooks classic began.

Finn reached out and pulled Eliza into his hard chest, strong arms surrounding her and began a slow two-step in the middle of their small kitchen.

The pull between them intensified at the contact. Bodies swaying, lighting up at the contact.

As the song ended, she stilled in his arms.

And suddenly, it wasn't a game anymore. It wasn't a question.

Her long, pale blond hair brushed his jaw, her breath came fast, and when she turned her head just slightly, her full, dusty pink lips were inches from his throat. His pulse kicked hard. His whole being vibrated with need.

He didn't think—he just dipped lower, brushing his mouth against the warm skin of her neck. The tiniest taste. She gasped, and he felt her tremble against him. That sound unraveled him further, made him bold enough to trail a soft, lingering kiss along her collarbone, then back up, teeth grazing gently.

"Finn…" she whispered, half a warning, half a plea.

It was the most intoxicating thing he'd ever heard.

Winding his hands in her soft, silky hair Finn pulled her mouth to his kissing her with a fierce passion that belied his restrained behavior towards her. The dam burst and all of their joint want followed freely as Finn's mouth moved back down kissing her collarbone, intent in his eyes as his hands sliding up under her blouse, leaving a trail of goosebumps in their wake while unclasping her bra deftly.

Startled, Eliza mewed then moaned as he unbuttoned her blouse sinking his face between her full-round, throbbing breasts then licking, taking turns laving his tongue back and forth over her erect, diamond-hard nipples. Hands griping the back of his chestnut brown hair and pulling his head to her overwhelmed and overstimulated breast almost overcome with powerful sensation. The yearning for something that only Finn could provide. Eliza was at sea, drowning in him.

He was ready to lose himself there—her scent, her warmth, the way her hands had tugged at his hair and curled in the fabric of his shirt—when three sharp knocks rattled the apartment door.

They froze.

Eliza's eyes went wide, pupils blown, her mouth still parted lips glossy, cheeks burning, skin flushed. Finn stepped back, chest heaving, hands still tingling from where they'd clutched her waist.

The knocks came again, louder. "Hey—sorry to bug y'all! I'm your neighbor from across the hall—Name's Daniel—y'all got a corkscrew by chance? My roommate broke ours."

"Don't be such a dick about it," yelled another guy behind him.

Daniel replied, "Apologies in advance for him. That's Chris."

Eliza scrambled to smooth her hair and pull her blouse together, laughing nervously, while Finn swore under his breath and yanked open the drawer. He opened the door a couple of inches handing off the corkscrew without meeting the neighbor's eyes, mumbling something like *no problem*.

When the door finally shut, the silence pressed heavy. The spaghetti sauce simmered on the stove, absurdly normal, while the air between them throbbed with everything that almost happened.

Finn rubbed the back of his neck, trying to steady his breath. "Guess dinner's ready," he muttered.

But what he didn't say—what he couldn't say—was that he'd never wanted anything more in his life than to go back to her breasts and keep showing her how much he loved them and how ferociously he needed her.

He'd tried, before. Other girls. Other nights. But it had never worked. Oh he'd had sex before. Enough to know that they just weren't Eliza, accepting a substitute just wouldn't cut it now that he knew that it was only ever Eliza for him.

There'd always been a moment, some small crack where he realized he was faking it—because none of them were her. None of them made him laugh when he didn't want to, or held his gaze like she did, or knew the worst things about him and stayed anyway. She had burrowed into his heart and had taken up residence there.

That was why he'd never been able to commit. Why he always bailed, always pulled away before things got serious.

Because his heart was already taken.

By the girl in the next room, probably scribbling in her notebook, probably humming to herself without realizing.

By Eliza. Always Eliza.

Later that night, he lingered outside her door. Hand lifted, ready to knock. He wanted to tell her everything—wanted to crawl into her bed and hold her until the world made sense.

But his throat locked up.

If she didn't feel the same way…if he ruined this…He considered himself a pressure player but this was a whole new level of play.

Breathing deeply, he let his hand fall to his side, fists clenched and walked away, carrying a throbbing hard-on and the weight of unsaid words, as well as unfulfilled desire, like bricks.

Back in his room, he lay awake, staring at the glow of the streetlight through the blinds. Every cell in his body burned with wanting her. Not just her body—though God, yes—but her laugh, her stubbornness, her fire, her everything.

He was in love with her. Maybe he always had been.

And he couldn't hold it back much longer.

Tomorrow would be different.
Tomorrow the storm would come, and the dam would finally break.

But tonight, Finn Callahan, tough football player, lay awake in the dark, heart aching with the kind of love that made every other girl a ghost.

The kind of love that scared him senseless.

The kind of love he knew he couldn't run from anymore.

Taking himself in hand, releasing some pressure, he thought of the curve of her breast, the way she had moaned when he kissed her, imagined what it would be like to finally slide inside her.

Claiming her.

Taking all of her.

That thought sent him over the edge.

As his orgasm raged through him, leaving him shuddering, he knew that it was a pale imitation of what it would be like when they came together in every way.

Soon. Very soon.

****

Eliza discovered that mornings belonged to them.

Her nightmares had returned, so Finn had begun sleeping in the same bed with her so that she would feel safe, which made it almost impossible for either of them to sleep. It was both too close and too far apart.

Ugh she thought. *Something's got to give.*

She often woke first, curled on her side, watching Finn sleep. His hair always fell across his forehead in soft disarray. Sometimes he muttered play calls under his breath, twitching as though his body couldn't quite let go of the field even in dreams. Other times, he was still, stone and warm, his arm heavy where it lay slung across her waist. That weight had become her anchor.

When he stirred awake, he always smiled the same sleepy smile that undid her every time. "Morning, Songbird," he whispered, voice low and rough with sleep.

The words sank into her chest like a vow.

Their rituals appeared as if they had been waiting for them—coffee for him, tea for her, mugs lined together on the counter. They brushed their teeth shoulder to shoulder in the cramped bathroom, jostling for space, elbowing each other with laughter. Steam battles erupted over who got the shower first, Finn forever insisting that football practice made him "legally entitled" to hog the hot water. She swatted him with her towel in retaliation, and he retaliated by wrapping her against him, dripping and warm, until her giggles gave way to breathless silence.

Every moment—every gentle forehead kiss, every argument over toothpaste caps or playlists—left Eliza aching. Because beneath the sweetness was pulsing hunger. A hunger she could feel building, pulsing low in her belly every time his eyes lingered too long or his hand rested a little too firmly against her hip.

Finn

For Finn, mornings hurt in a way they never had before.

He was used to waking sharp, ready for drills, for weights, for noise and sweat. But waking with her? It made him want slow. Made him want soft. Made him want to stay wrapped in sheets and sunlight forever.

And it made him want her. Badly, almost painfully.

Not just her hand curled into his. Not just the kiss she gave him before dashing to class. He wanted the sound of her breath when his lips grazed her neck. He wanted her tremble, her taste, the way she might fall apart in his arms if he ever let himself push past restraint.

And restraint was becoming impossible.

The night in the kitchen still played in his mind—her laughter when he spun her around, the way it had broken into a sharp, needy gasp when he pressed his mouth to her throat, her breast. He could still taste her skin, still hear the catch in her voice when she whispered his name. If not for the neighbor's interruption, he would have laid her out against the counter and never looked back.

Now the wanting burned like a fuse, and he wasn't sure how much longer it could smolder before it consumed them both.

Their grocery trip turned into comedy.

Eliza arrived armed with a neatly written list, determined to be efficient. Finn, meanwhile, meandered like a child set loose, tossing cinnamon rolls, neon sports drinks, and dinosaur-shaped chips into the cart with shameless glee.

"You can't live on snack food," she said, plucking the chips out again.

"Correction: we can live our best life on snack food."

"Correction," she countered, sliding the chips back onto the shelf, "your arteries will hate you before you're twenty-one."

He leaned close, brushing his lips against her ear just enough to make her jolt. His voice dropped, rough and playful. "Pretty sure you'll keep me alive, though."

Her blush betrayed her before she could answer. And when a pair of strangers glanced their way, Finn's arm went automatically around her shoulders, his gaze sharpening until they turned away.

Eliza rolled her eyes, but inside, warmth spread through her chest like a secret glow.

Kitchen Fireworks. Cooking together was chaos.

Eliza tried teaching him how to stir-fry, only to find him sneaking peppers straight off the cutting board. "That's raw!" she yelped, smacking his hand.

"Tastes fine to me."

She swatted at him again, but he caught her wrist, grinning like the devil, and suddenly he was lifting her, spinning her around the cramped kitchen. She shrieked, braid slipping loose as her laughter spilled uncontrolled.

When he set her down, his hands lingered at her waist. The air shifted.

His grin faded into something darker. Hungrier.

Instead of claiming her mouth, he lowered his head to the curve of her neck. His lips pressed there—hot, open, searching. His teeth grazed, just enough to make her knees threaten to buckle.

"Finn," she whispered, clutching his shirt.

He groaned against her skin, the sound guttural. "God, you taste like forever."

The spell snapped. Eliza pulled away, apprehension filling her as surely as the heat from his body. Did Finn mean it? Forever?

Eliza suddenly busied herself with the pan, her hands trembling so badly she nearly dropped it. Finn muttered hoarsely about the sauce, his voice ragged with what he hadn't done.

Later, she lay awake replaying it. The way his mouth had claimed her throat, the way her body had arched helplessly closer. The ache refused to fade.

Neither did his.

Chapter Fourteen

Reclaimed

The storm rolled in just after sunset.

The rain started without warning—no slow buildup, no distant thunder—just a curtain of water slapping the pavement outside Eliza's bedroom window. Their apartment smelled like lavender and Earl Grey. Finn's soaked hoodie lay near the door, making a small pond underneath, and his socks were drying nearby.

"I told you it was going to rain," Eliza said, handing him a mug of tea. No smugness, just warmth. Tension already filling the air between them.

"I thought you meant like, later-later," he replied, lips curling into a half-smile.

She laughed, and it did something to him. Sparks began growing from embers. He felt a gravity shift. Like something in him leaned closer, even if he didn't move.

She sat cross-legged across from him backlit by lamplight, her long white-blonde hair glowing like a halo, her satin, pineapple sleep shorts brushing her silky thighs. The lamp behind her painted her violet eyes gold. He didn't want to look away. A notebook lay beside her—half-open, a few lyrics scrawled in the corner. He'd seen her writing more lately. Humming quietly under her breath when she thought he wasn't listening. She had always liked to write stories but lately he noticed that she was writing what looked more like lyrics and music.

He knew that writing was not only an intrinsic part of her but also her way of coping—with everything. Past. Present. Future.

"You okay?" she asked.

"Yeah." He glanced down at his calloused hands. "Used to think I liked being with you because it was safe. Comfortable."

She didn't say anything. Just waited. She always waited for the real thing.

"But now… it's not just that. It's you. When I'm not here, I think about being here. About you. You are home to me."

Her eyes flickered and filled with hope. "I thought I was imagining it. That maybe I was just reading too much into things because I wanted it to be more."

"Eliza," he breathed.

"I'm in love with you," she said. Lips trembling. Eyes shining. Tone husky with honest longing. "I have been for as long as I can remember."

Finn's piercing green eyes eyes darkened, but not with fear.

With *clarity*.

He reached up and cradled the side of her heart shaped face, brushing his thumb gently across her flushed cheek.

"I've been in love with you since you climbed into my life with that blue sundress, a busted bike, and more fight in your eyes than anyone I'd ever seen."

A slow relieved exhale left her lips.

"I love you. I love you. I love you." she whispered. "I can't stop saying it now. I was afraid that I felt more for you than you did for me for so long."

Something snapped loose inside him. "I love you too. I think I've been loving you forever."

The air changed. Denial dropped. History caught up. Guards down, they finally embraced the risk to their relationship. When she leaned in, he met her halfway.

"Your worth it Finn." Eliza breathed. Filling her lungs with the manly scent of him.

"You're worth everything Eliza," he responded.

The kiss was soft. Then it wasn't. Suddenly years of pent up passion burst between them demanding that they acknowledge it taking away the space between them filling it with hunger and love.

They devoured one another. All hands, mouths and fingers—honoring one another as they shared their passion. Fingers threaded into hair. Hands pulled each other closer. Breath hitched and caught. Their bodies found rhythm without asking permission.

But even in the hunger, they slowed.

"I've never... not all the way," she said curled in the blanket. "You know about Carlos. You saved me. But before that—he tried. Touched me...I stopped him, but..."

Finn's jaw tensed. "Being so close to you for so long, I was pretty sure that you hadn't had a boyfriend so I thought you might feel that way." He took her hand, soft in his callused palm. "Please let me take away the memory of his hands on you. Let me replace the touch with love and shared passion. We don't have to do anything. Not ever. You set the pace."

"I don't want to feel scared like that anymore," she whispered. "I don't want to feel dirty, or afraid. I want to feel... me. I just want to be your Eliza."

Finn reached out slowly, brushing a piece of hair behind her ear. His hand lingered on her cheek, thumb stroking gently across her skin.

"You are my Eliza, my North Star. My Songbird." he said. "You always have been. That bastard and what he did, doesn't have anything to do with that."

She nodded, breath shaky. "Then make me feel it. Not because I need to forget—but because I need to know what it's like to feel safe. To feel your touch. To feel... loved."

"I want this. With you. I just need it to be slow. And I need to know I'll still be enough after."

"You already are."

She breathed out, leaned in, and kissed him again, tongues dancing to their own melody.

He led her to the center of the bed and pulled her into his arms, warm soft lips brushing her forehead, her temple, her collarbone. He kissed her like something precious—a vow, each one softer than the last. His touch was passionate. Careful.

They undressed slowly. Purposefully. Every movement asked, and every answer was yes.

When they were skin to skin, heart to heart, it wasn't about control. It was surrender. It was presence.

It was trust.

Eliza let herself melt into him. There were no ghosts here. No fear. Just the heat of skin, the rush of breath, the soft ache of release and renewal. Her body trembled, but not from fear—from want. From trust.

He whispered her name again and again like a litany, grounding her to now, to this, to them.

When he finally entered her, it was slow. Gentle. He stayed still, just holding her close, forehead to forehead.

"You're safe," he murmured. "And you're mine. Every part of you."

She kissed him then—not to say thank you, but because she wanted him to feel it too—her passion for him, her love. She appreciated his body with soft wet kisses, moving down his strong, muscular frame starting at his neck, ending with her mouth around him. Her hand pumped slowly but firmly along his shaft, pre-cum already gleaming at the tip. She licked tenderly, fisting him as she sucked him deeper, until his head rolled back and he breathed out her name like a prayer.

Finn groaned, pulled her up, and flipped them gently. He moved down her body, giving special attention to her breasts, laving and sucking hard at her nipples until the sparks shot straight to her core.

Her thighs shook with need. "Finn, please! I need you now. All of you."

They moved together then, a rhythm found in healing passion. In rebuilding. There were tears, but they weren't sad. They were honest. Every touch a reclamation. Every kiss a reminder.

Their bodies spoke where their words had waited.

His rough, calloused hands worshipped her soft skin, spanning her waist as he shifted her, finding new angles to make her cry out with pleasure. Fingers mapped the curve of her spine, the edges of her ribs, her full warm peaked breasts, the graceful, lush curves of her hips—every inch of her like he was learning her—memorizing her strength. Her beauty more potent for that strength.

When it was over, Finn tucked her against his chest, wrapped around her like armor.

For the first time since that terrible time at her last foster home, she felt clean. She felt seen. She felt safe.

She felt home.

Afterward, in the still, quiet, dark, Eliza lay against him, hand on his chest, his arms around her.

"I love you," she said.

"You're safe," he whispered into her hair. "And I love you too. Always. You're my North Star."

She smiled, drowsy. "North of Always. Reclaimed. You helped me to reclaim myself."

And outside, the storm passed.

Inside, something extraordinary had just begun.

When Finn finally drifted to sleep, Eliza carefully pulled her notebook from the floor to overwhelmed in the aftermath of lovemaking. She slid out of bed without waking him and padded quietly to the living room. The rain had stopped. Everything felt hushed. Holy.

In the hush of the room, she began to write. Words flowing from her like a waterfall, clear, powerful and true.

Reclaim Me
lyrics by Eliza Monroe

Verse 1
I felt the dark on my skin, like a bruise I couldn't name
Silhouettes of shame, wrapped in someone else's claim
Tried to breathe, but the air was made of ghosts and glass
Tried to run, but my shadow always pulled me back

Chorus
Then you touched me like I was light, not wreckage
Spoke my name like it was a song, not a sentence
Held me steady, held me soft, made me believe
That love could rewrite the story grief left me
So reclaim me—kiss by kiss, trace by trace
Remind me I'm not broken, just misplaced

Reclaim me love. Reclaim me.

Verse 2
You didn't ask me to be brave, just honest
Didn't want perfection, just presence
With every heartbeat pressed to yours, I remembered
How it feels when hands don't take—they treasure

Chorus
Then you touched me like I was light, not wreckage
Spoke my name like it was a song, not a sentence
Held me steady, held me soft, made me believe
That love could rewrite the story grief left me
So reclaim me—kiss by kiss, trace by trace
Remind me I'm not broken, just misplaced

Reclaim me love. Reclaim me.

Bridge
You looked at me, and the past lost its power
You loved me back into every quiet hour
I'm still me, but freer, louder now somehow
Because you never saw the ruin—only how to build me back

Final Chorus
So reclaim me, with every whisper, every vow
Show me I was always whole, even when I didn't know how
Hold me where I shake, love me where I fade
And I'll meet you there, every single day
Reclaim me—

Eliza closed the notebook, her hand trembling, tears on her cheeks—but they were different this time.

She set it gently on the nightstand, then curled back into Finn's strong muscled arms.

And slept without nightmares.

****

They hadn't planned for last night to be different. But it was and the morning brought stark awareness of the change.

Eliza woke up, glanced at Finn's handsome, still sleeping face shivering at the memory of their lovemaking, shocked by how much she wanted to continue what they had begun, but decided to head for the bathroom to clean up a bit. She pulled on just a sweatshirt feeling a bit nervous after the night before. She hoped that Finn still felt the way he had last night. Her body hummed with heat just remembering.

The room was quiet but charged, the soft hum of Austin traffic filtering in from the open window. The soft, morning light played across Finn's muscular chest, hair flopping into his eyes. Eliza lay back down on the bed, body aching, wrapping a leg around his, her hands tracing the scars on his chest and arm. She bent over and delicately touched his nipple with her tongue. His eyes opened drowsily and he gave her a slow smile that full of sinful promise.

She looked at him like she was done holding back. He looked at her the same way.

"Are you still with me?" Finn asked gently. Rubbing the his hands from her cheek, across the delicate lines of her collar bone, "Regrets?"

"I could never regret being with you. Ever. I want this. With you. Again and again." she knew what he meant and purred. "I think that I'll need you close— By me. On me. In me. Now. Always."

"Are you sore?" he asked huskily as he moved over her body with knowing hands. "I need to be inside you again so that I'm sure that last night wasn't some kind of fever dream."

She sat up pulling his UT Football sweatshirt over her head and letting it drop, something in Finn snapped quietly, like a rope going slack. He crossed to her slowly, arrested, like she was something sacred that needed to be thoroughly worshiped.

Their lips met with new familiarity, but this morning there was urgency under it—a hunger wrapped in tenderness. His hands trailed her spine. Hers slipped into his hair.

When he laid her back on the bed, he did it like he was placing her somewhere safe.

His hot needy mouth moved down her body, kissing and sucking, teeth nibbling her, gentle bites of pain that became pleasure. When his hot mouth was on her breast, she felt it straight to her clit. Causing her core to throb. His fingers found her entrance, circling her clit, taunting her need, then his shoulders spread her for him. Jolted as his mouth found her private place making it his. Using his tongue to drive her into a writhing mess. As she panted from desire he put in one finger, then two as his tongue continued its torturous game.

Finn growled in her ear, "Songbird, come for me. Need to feel you explode."

And she did. Like fire works on the fourth of July.

Shifting up, his large muscular body pinned her to the bed. She wasn't scared anymore. This was Finn and the feel of his large, muscular body pressed hard against hers made her hot and weak at the same time. She couldn't wait a second more. She reached down between them and felt his rock hard arousal.

"Please Finn. I need you inside me. Now." She begged.

When he entered her, slow and steady, her breath hitched. He stilled, searching her face. She nodded again, eyes wide, full of trust.

They moved together like a language only they spoke—slow, deep, wrapped in everything they couldn't say. She clung to him, fingers in his hair, name on her lips.

And when she shattered beneath him, quiet and trembling, he followed, holding her close as if the world might try and take her away.

After, they lay tangled in the sheets, her head on his chest, his fingers tracing patterns along her shoulder.

"You're everything," he murmured.

She lifted her face. "You're home."

And they both knew: this wasn't a beginning.

It was a return.

Later that morning, the light in their apartment was soft and slow. Eliza stood at the stove in one of Finn's band T-shirts, stirring scrambled while eggs making huevoes rancheros, barefoot, glowing.

Finn watched her from the doorway, shirtless, quietly stunned by how normal everything felt. How easy. How right.

She glanced over her shoulder. "You going to stand there or get plates?"

He grinned. "You cooking for me now?"

"I'm feeding myself. You just benefit from proximity." She said smiling brightly at him. Full of happiness.

Glowing.

Shining.

"I'm definitely staying close, then." he said as he moved behind her wrapping his arms around her waist rubbing his mouth against her neck and inhaling deeply taking in her scent. Her scent mixed with his. She felt him hard against her lower back.

She rolled her eyes, but the smile on her face was real as was the heat pooling within her.

It was the first time in a long time that neither of them felt like they were bracing for impact.

And that was when everything else began to shift.

Eliza opened to a fresh page in her notebook and, in quick soft strokes, wrote the words that had been building in her chest for weeks:

I didn't know home until your name fit in my mouth like a promise.

North of always, you pull me steady.

She titled it simply: **North of Always.**

Inside, something extraordinary had just begun.

Chapter Fifteen

New Names, New Halls

The cicadas sang in the heat as Eliza crossed the wide stretch of UT's South Mall, her tote bag slung over her shoulder. The morning light gilded the limestone buildings, soft and golden against the Tower's tall silhouette. It was barely 9 a.m., but Austin already shimmered with that thick, syrupy late-August-early-September humidity that clung to skin and hair like a second layer.

She tucked a loose strand behind her ear and gripped the strap of her bag tighter. Inside: a brand-new spiral notebook, pens lined up like soldiers, and the second-hand paperback of *The Republic* she'd snagged at Half-Price Books.

Her first class. First real college class.

She had lain awake the night before, Finn's slow breathing beside her, the air conditioner rattling faintly in their new apartment. She'd been replaying the last forty-eight hours on a loop: the storm, the confession, the kiss that had changed everything, the night that had shifted the axis of her world.

She'd woken that morning to his arm heavy around her waist, his lips pressed against her shoulder as if to anchor her. *North of always,* he'd whispered drowsily before drifting back to sleep.

And now, here she was—walking across the same campus where he was grinding through two-a-days, carrying both the weight of a football program and the weight of their new beginning.

Walking into the Humanities Building, the hallways smelled faintly of chalk dust and old paper, the kind of scent that clung to spaces where words lived long lives. Posters lined the walls—flyers for poetry readings, debate club, and an indie band looking for a fiddle player.

She stepped into the lecture hall for History of Western Thought. High ceilings, fluorescent lights buzzing faintly, rows of wooden chairs with tiny fold-up desks that looked like they'd been carved in the seventies.

Eliza hesitated, scanning the room. Too many eyes already sat scattered across the rows, hunched over laptops, tapping pens against notebooks. She chose a seat midway—safe, she thought. Not invisible, not exposed.

Her heart still raced from nerves when a striking, petite, curvy, girl plopped down beside her. Copper hair pulled into a messy bun, oversized thrifted sweater even in the heat, Converse sneakers scuffed and painted with tiny constellations. Her notebook was plastered with stickers: *Read More Women, Don't Text Your Ex,* and one that just said *VOTE.* Her face looked so perfectly porcelain, mouth like a Cupid's bow, and her blue eyes so huge in her face that she looked like a doll. Even the bulky sweater couldn't hide her hourglass figure.

"I'm Sophia," she said brightly, offering a crooked grin. "You look like you're new too."

Eliza blinked, then smiled, relief unspooling in her chest. "Eliza. First day. First class. Mildly terrified. Aren't we all Freshman in this class?"

"Same. Terrified. But I hear the professor's chill, so we'll panic only halfway. As far as I know there are a couple sophomores retaking the class this semester."

Eliza let out a small laugh. "Deal."

The professor entered—a short, balding man in a corduroy blazer despite the heat, with glasses slipping down his nose. Professor Dickerson. He launched into Socrates, cave allegories, shadows mistaken for truth. Eliza's pen moved furiously across the page, but her mind snagged on the metaphor.

Shadows mistaken for truth.

That was what the last few years had been, wasn't it? Hiding from Carlos's ghost. Pretending safety meant silence. Pretending what she felt for Finn was just friendship.

But last night—the last night had been the moment she turned toward the light. Finn was the sun.

By the time class ended, she and Sophia had already swapped numbers and made lunch plans. The ease of it surprised Eliza. Friendship had always been something she had to earn with cautious effort, not something that just appeared at her side like a gift.

Maybe this place would be different. It was definitely a good start.

****

The practice field across campus pulsed with heat rising off the turf. Whistles shrieked, cleats pounded, helmets cracked together with violent thuds.

Finn crouched low in a three-point stance, sweat streaming down his back under the pads. His muscles screamed, but he pushed harder.

"Callahan!" Coach Billings barked, voice sharp as barbed wire. "You want that starting spot, you better move like the devil's chasing you!"

Finn exploded forward, slamming into the blocking sled until his shoulders ached. He drove it five yards, then ten, before the whistle shrilled again.

When drills finally ended, he collapsed onto the bench, unlacing his cleats with shaking hands.

Beside him, a linebacker flopped down, helmet tucked under his arm. Short black curls, mocha brown skin, a scar through his left eyebrow, easy grin.

"Kai," he said, fist out.

"Finn."

Kai chuckled. "Man, you hit like a truck."

Finn gave a tired grin. "You're not too bad yourself."

"Where you from?"

"Fredericksburg. Small town."

"Atlanta," Kai said. "But don't hold it against me."

They laughed, and just like that, some of the tension bled away. By the time they hit the locker room, they were trading stories about the worst cafeteria food and which coach looked like he'd lost a fight with a blender.

For the first time all week, Finn didn't feel like an imposter.

The locker room was humid with sweat and Axe body spray, the air thick with the chatter of guys riding the high of practice. Metal doors clanged shut, towels slapped against skin, laughter echoed.

Finn sat on the edge of the bench, head down, untying his cleats with careful precision. He liked details, liked focusing on the small things—the knots, the laces, the steady pull. It gave him something to hold when the noise around him started to feel too loud.

Across the aisle, two wide receivers leaned against their lockers, voices carrying.

"Did you see that girl in the lit building earlier? Violet eyes. Long light blond wavy hair. Crazy hot. Great tits."

Finn's gut tightened. He didn't have to guess. Eliza.

"Yeah," the other guy said, chuckling. "I'd like to hit that," He continued smirking. "I swear she was with one of the other football players though. Big dude. Blond. Looked like he could snap me in half."

Finn's jaw ticked. He didn't look up.

"Bet he doesn't keep her long though," the first one added. "Girls like that? They figure out real fast they don't have to settle."

A burst of laughter. Cleats clattering against the concrete floor.

Kai, sitting two lockers down from Finn, shot him a glance. He must've caught the stiffness in Finn's shoulders. Kai didn't say anything, but his eyes narrowed in warning at the guys across the way.

Finn tied his cleats tighter than necessary, muscles rigid. He wanted to say something—wanted to slam his locker door hard enough to make them shut up. But his foster-home instincts came back sharp.

In those houses, silence had been survival. You didn't call attention to yourself. You didn't speak unless you had to. Words could spark fights you couldn't finish, punishments you didn't deserve.

So Finn stayed quiet. Let the words sit like stones in his stomach.

The receivers wandered off, still laughing, and the locker room buzz filled the empty space they left behind.

Kai leaned over. "Don't listen to 'em. They don't know anything."

Finn forced a smirk. "Yeah. I know."

But he didn't know how to say what he was really thinking: that Eliza wasn't just "some girl," that she was his whole damn compass. That every careless word from strangers cut deep because she was sacred to him. He wondered though who the guy was that his douche teammates had seen her with. It didn't matter he trusted her. Trusted what they had. Hearing them talk about her made him want to ram his fists down their throats. He didn't.

Instead, breathing deeply, he pulled his Longhorn's jersey on and shoved his gear into his bag, the silence clinging to him like a second skin.

As he left the locker room, the stadium lights flickered on outside, spilling white against the darkening sky. He tilted his head up, let the brightness sting his eyes.

All he could think was: He'd have to learn how to break the silence someday. For Eliza. For himself. Because if he didn't, other people's voices might drown out the truth that had lived in him all along.

At noon, Eliza and Sophia sat under a sprawling live oak on the West Mall, lunch trays balanced on their laps. The air smelled like barbecue from a food truck parked nearby, and a busker strummed guitar on the steps of the Union.

"So what's your deal?" Sophia asked between bites of brisket taco. "Lit major? Music? You've got that vibe."

"English, maybe. Or music theory. I'm not sure yet." Eliza fiddled with the straw in her drink. "I've been writing songs. My friend Madison—she does music PR and manages indie bands in Austin—keeps telling me I should actually play them for people."

"You totally should. Austin's the place for it." Sophia grinned. "Open mic nights everywhere. Coffee shops, dive bars—you can't throw a stone without hitting one."

Eliza smiled shyly. "Maybe."

Sophia studied her, then nodded. "Yeah. You've got the look of someone who's got stories to tell. And I'm nosey enough to make sure you tell them."

Eliza laughed, warmth creeping in her chest. She hadn't realized how much she'd needed this—someone new, someone who didn't know the scars of her past, someone who saw possibility instead of pain.

"Hey who was that big, hot, blonde guy I saw you with earlier?" Sophia asked eyes sparkling.

"Who? Oh, you mean West? I just met him in Biology. He was heading the same way I was after class and offered to show me where my next class was, since it's in the same building as his." Eliza replied easily.

"I have a boyfriend. His name is Finn. We live together so I'm not interested." She was shocked at how natural that felt to say. New but natural and as effortless as breathing.

"Is he seeing anyone?" Brightening, Sophia quickly asked.

"I have no idea Sophia. We just met."

****

That night, Finn and Eliza sat cross-legged in their apartment on their couch, eating Pad Thai takeout straight from styrofoam container. The apartment still smelled faintly of cardboard and paint, boxes stacked in the corners. Eliza lit a warm vanilla candle to help cover the other scents.

Finn shoved a forkful of noodles and shrimp into his mouth and groaned, after adding a squeeze of lime. "God, this tastes like heaven after practice. I'm starving."

Eliza smirked. "I met a couple of people today in my classes. Sophia. She's hilarious and has strong opinions about Jane Austen. The other is a football player named West from my Bio class. He seems grumpy but nice. Is he on the team with you?"

Finn raised his carton in mock salute. "I don't know all of the players' names yet but I think that I know who you mean. I'll introduce myself at practice tomorrow. I met a linebacker named Kai who thinks I tackle too hard for a QB."

She leaned into him, her shoulder warm against his. "Maybe this won't be so bad. I started my part-time shift at the library and it was pretty laid back and I can study when it's not too busy."

He kissed the top of her head. "We've got this."

She turned, eyes going to his mouth thinking about all of the things that they could do to each other now. She caught his eye and licked her fork then laughed huskily at the look of promise and heat in his eyes. This was new and exciting. Seeing Finn start to come unraveled at just a look and flick of her tongue left her body hot, flushed and ready for him.

Unable to resist, Finn's hand stroked up her thigh, warming skin that came alive under his touch as his mouth came down on hers with intensity letting her feel all of his previously banked passion. Her hands did what they wanted to do since she's seen him today. They traced his tattoos, biceps and abdomen. Moving with determination towards his blatant arousal.

His breath quickened, the sound of it heightening her own passion. When her lips found his cock, she licked it while looking up, big violet holding his stare.

Pulling back from him she asked him shyly. "Finn you've probably guessed that this is my first time going down on a man. Show me what you like, what you want me to do. I want you to feel good."

It turned him on even more. Her need to please him. "Eliza, you can pretty much touch and put your mouth anywhere on my cock and I'll feel good. Put your hand around the base of my cock then move it up and down. Hard. It's not going to hurt me. While you're doing that, lick my shaft up and down then put your mouth around it and suck in. The deeper you take me, the better it feels."

Trying it, Eliza was almost undone herself at the pleasure he experienced from her mouth, her touch. It was thrilling to watch this huge, strong man give in to her so completely. She was ready to do it as often as he'd let her.

"Keep going! I'm coming." He said as he did in her mouth. She swallowed it greedily as though it were a reward for making his feel so damn good.

"God Eliza…my Songbird. There are no words for this. How you make me feel."

After lying there holding one another. Without saying a word, Finn suddenly lifted Eliza laying her diagonally on the couch as he moved his body, shoulders nudging her legs apart opening her completely to his hungry gaze. Looking into her eyes, he slipped his hands under her skirt and drug her panties down her long, perfect legs.

Settling in he looked into her eyes as he bent down to lick her folds. Flicking his tongue lightly over her clit, creating shivers and heat, to race though her body at the intimate contact. Eliza had never experienced anything like the orgasm building inside. It felt even more intense than the previous ones, as though the more they learned about one another, the better they were able to create more intense pleasure. When she didn't think that she could take anymore, he put his finger inside her, working her with both tongue and finger. She went off like a rocket, crying out his name.

Holding her tight, kissing her hair, and whispering in her ear—"I love you Songbird…always. North of Always." Finn let her explode then calm, coming down from the high.

They lay together on the couch, dazed, full of exhaustion and promises. Too tired to make it to the now-shared bedroom.

Waking up later that night in Finn's arms, Eliza's eyes drifted to the notebook on the windowsill. The song she'd scribbled after their storm-lit night still waited there. New lines had come to her during lecture, too, about shadows and light, about choosing what was real.

You are the place the compass turns to.
The quiet in my storm. My North of Always.

She hadn't told Finn about it yet. But she would.

Because now—finally—she wasn't writing into the dark. She was writing toward him.

Two days later, Eliza sat in a small seminar room on the third floor of Calhoun Hall. The room smelled faintly of pencil shavings and old coffee, a faint mustiness seeping from the cracked radiator. Twelve desks were arranged in a circle, not rows. It made everything feel closer, like there was nowhere to hide.

The course: *Introduction to Creative Writing*.
The professor: Dr. Ramirez, a wiry woman with sharp eyes and a stack of bracelets that clinked whenever she gestured.

"Stories," Dr. Ramirez said, tapping her pen against a yellow notepad, "are not about perfection. They're about honesty. About showing us something only you could see. So for our first exercise, I want each of you to write a short piece. Doesn't matter if it's a poem, a fragment, dialogue—just make it real. Five minutes. Go."

Pens scratched. Eliza froze.

Her notebook lay open in front of her, blank. Except it wasn't blank—it still held fragments from the night of the storm. *North of always, you pull me steady*. Words that already felt like a secret prayer.

She could feel her pulse in her wrist as she wrote quickly, almost without thought:

You found me where silence lived.
You didn't ask for anything, but I gave you everything.
And you called it safe.

When Dr. Ramirez called time, Eliza snapped the notebook shut, panic fluttering in her chest. She wasn't ready to say those words out loud. Not here. Not yet.

Sophia, sitting two seats over, read a cheeky prose poem about running into her ex at Target. Everyone laughed. The tension eased.

When it came to Eliza, she cleared her throat. "I—uh—didn't finish. I'll share next time."

Dr. Ramirez gave her a small, knowing smile. "Fair enough. Sometimes the real thing needs more time to breathe."

Eliza exhaled. Relief washed over her. But there was something else too: the ache of keeping something beautiful locked inside.

As she left class, Sophia looped her arm through hers. "You totally wrote something. I saw your pen moving like you were on fire."

Eliza smirked. "Maybe."

"Uh-huh. I'm calling it now—you're going to blow us away by midterm."

Eliza didn't answer. But as they walked across the shaded quad, cicadas buzzing in the heat, she knew Sophia wasn't wrong.

Eliza left her creative writing workshop with a secret in her notebook she couldn't say out loud. What she didn't know, was that Finn left the locker room with words burning in his chest he couldn't force past his teeth.

Two different rooms. Two different silences. But the same truth: both of them were learning how to exist in these new halls without losing themselves—or each other.

As the first weeks of classes passed quickly, Eliza was carrying secrets in her notebook and songs in her throat she hadn't dared to sing for anyone but Finn. And Finn was carrying bruises from practice and pressure from coaches who never let him forget the stakes.

They were both learning new names, new halls, new roles—but the more the campus pulled at them, the more they felt the tug to claim each other in the middle of it all.

That tension didn't break in a classroom or on a practice field.

It broke the moment the apartment door shut behind them.

Chapter Sixteen

Between the Notes

Weeks after that first night tangled in the safety of each other's arms, Austin began to unfurl around them like a city written just for two.

The apartment still smelled faintly of coffee and paint thinner, their thrift-store furniture leaned crooked, and cardboard boxes lingered half-unpacked in corners. Yet somehow, with him moving through the space, with her laughter echoing against the bare walls, it already felt like home.

Because he was there.
Because she was there.

They didn't pretend anymore.

They collapsed onto the couch, some half-forgotten movie flickering across the screen. His arm brushed her shoulder. She leaned in. His thumb traced her jaw, feather-light but full of intent.

"Eliza," he breathed, her name falling from his lips like a prayer.

Her eyes met his.

And then his mouth was on hers.

Not soft. Not tentative.

Hungry.

Her gasp opened her to him. His tongue slid against hers, his hands slipping beneath her shirt, palms rough and seeking as they explored her skin. Fire spread everywhere he touched, pulling a whimper from her throat.

She climbed into his lap, straddling him, pressing flush against his body. The hardness she felt beneath her only made her bolder, rocking against him until his groan vibrated into her bones.

"Eliza—" he rasped, as though the sound of her name was the only thing holding him together.

His mouth trailed lower, down her throat, across her collarbone, biting lightly, sucking marks he didn't care if the world saw. "Mine," he whispered hoarsely, half to himself, half to her.

"Don't stop," she whispered, trembling, clutching fistfuls of his shirt.

He didn't.

Clothes came off in fumbling urgency—shirts tossed aside, jeans shoved down, the world narrowing to bare skin against bare skin. The shock of it made her moan into his mouth, and he nearly lost himself right there.

"Eliza," he said again, voice breaking. His forehead pressed to hers. "Tell me this is what you want."

Her hands framed his face, eyes fierce even as they shimmered. "I've wanted you my whole life."

Something shattered inside him.

And suddenly they were stumbling to the bedroom, tripping over discarded shoes, half-laughing, half-dizzy with need. The sheets tangled around them as if the world itself conspired to hold them together.

They tumbled onto the bed in a blur of mouths and laughter and gasps, limbs tangling, hearts racing like they had already crossed some line they could never step back from.

Finn caught himself above her, bracing one arm so his weight wouldn't crush her, but his other hand roamed her body like he couldn't stop himself. Her waist. Her ribs. The soft swell of her hip. Every touch left fire in its wake.

She stared up at him, her braid loosened, cheeks flushed, lips kiss-swollen. For a moment, he froze, struck still by the sheer beauty of her.

"Eliza," he whispered, like her name alone was prayer and plea.

Her hand rose to his jaw, thumb brushing the stubble there. "Don't stop," she said, voice trembling but sure.

His restraint frayed.

He bent, kissing her again, slower now, savoring. His tongue slid against hers, his groan swallowed by her mouth. His hand cupped her breast over the thin lace of her bra, thumb brushing until her back arched off the mattress.

She gasped, clutching his shoulders. "Finn—"

"Tell me what you need Babe," he rasped, his forehead pressed to hers, breath ragged.

"You," she breathed, desperate. "All of you."

His teeth clenched as though the words barely held him back from losing control. He kissed down her throat, dragging his mouth lower, tasting her collarbone, the dip of her chest. He nosed at the edge of lace before pulling it down, baring her.

The sight of her made his chest ache. He bent, taking her nipple into his mouth, sucking gently, then harder, until she cried out, hips rising to meet him.

"God, Eliza," he groaned against her skin. "You're gonna kill me."

"Then die here," she whispered, clutching his hair, pulling him closer.

His laugh was broken, almost pained. "You have no idea what you do to me."

She arched, pressing herself against him, letting him feel the slick heat between her thighs. His hand slid down, teasing at her waistband, and she whimpered when his fingers brushed over her through the thin cotton.

"So wet for me," he murmured, voice hoarse but charged with want. "Do you know what that does to me?"

"Then don't make me wait," she begged, half wild now, writhing beneath him.

He kissed her, deep and consuming, as his hand slipped inside her panties. His fingers found her, slick and trembling, and she gasped into his mouth, clutching him tighter. He teased, circling slowly, until she was bucking against him, pleading.

"Finn, please—"

Her desperation unraveled him.

He slid two fingers inside, curling just right, and her cry filled the room. Her nails dug into his shoulders, her body clamping around him as he worked her, his lips devouring her sounds like oxygen.

"That's it, North Star," he whispered against her cheek. "Fall apart for me."

And she did—arching, gasping, shuddering around his hand, her moans spilling unrestrained into his ear.

When she collapsed against the sheets, trembling, he kissed her temple, chest heaving. "Most beautiful thing I've ever seen," he murmured.

Her hand reached, fumbling for his waistband, tugging. "I want you."

He caught her wrist, breathing hard, eyes dark. "Eliza… once I start, I'm not sure I can stop."

Her gaze was fierce through the haze. "Then don't. Never stop."

His restraint shattered.

He stripped the last of their clothes in frantic movements, his breath catching when he finally pressed bare against her. Her heat wrapped around him, and he nearly lost it before even entering.

He cupped her face, forcing his eyes to hers. "Tell me again how much you want me."

Her answer was a kiss, deep and sure. "I've wanted you my whole life. In me. Around me. I'm yours."

With a ragged groan, he eased into her. They both froze—he from the sheer overwhelming tightness, she from the stretch that still stole her breath and gave her extreme pleasure.

"Okay?" he whispered, his voice breaking, his body trembling from holding still.

"Yes," she gasped, her nails biting into his back. "God, yes. Don't stop."

He kissed her forehead, her nose, her lips, like vows. Then he began to move, slow at first, savoring every sound she made. Her gasp when he thrust deeper. Her whispered pleas for more. The way her body clung to him like it had always been made for him.

"Eliza," he groaned, her name breaking from him every time he lost rhythm. "Mine. You're mine."

"Yours," she whispered, meeting him, bolder now, hips rising to chase him. "Always yours."

The pace built—slow reverence giving way to desperate rhythm. He held her tight, one hand cradling the back of her head, the other gripping her hip as if he could fuse them together.

Her sounds filled the room, every moan, every gasp feeding the fire until he was lost. When her body clenched around him again, when she cried out his name, he followed her over the edge, shuddering, breaking apart inside her.

They clung together, gasping, laughing softly, tears streaking both their cheeks.

When the tremors eased, he kissed her damp temple, holding her against his chest. "You're mine," he whispered fiercely.

She pressed her lips to his heart, still hammering beneath his skin. "Always."

They lay like that, sweat cooling, hearts slowly steadying. But the hunger didn't fade. If anything, it grew sharper in the silence.

****

It started with a kiss.

She had gotten up for water, hair mussed, shirt hastily pulled on, and when she returned, he was sprawled on the couch, watching her with hooded eyes.

One look, and the ache was back.

She set the glass down and straddled him before she could second-guess it. His hands gripped her hips instantly, possessive, like he had been waiting for her to move.

"Eliza," he rasped, eyes burning. "You're gonna undo me."

"Then let me," she whispered, kissing him hard.

This wasn't slow. It wasn't tender. It was hungry, frantic.

He yanked her shirt over her head, his mouth devouring her throat, biting hard enough to leave marks he wanted the world to see. She moaned, grinding down against the bulge in his sweats.

"God, you're mine," he growled, gripping her tighter, guiding her hips.

"Yes," she gasped, arching, her nails raking down his chest. "Yours. Always."

He shoved his sweats down just enough, pushing her panties aside, and she sank onto him in one desperate movement. They both cried out, the rawness of it stealing their breath.

"Fuck," he groaned, clutching her waist, his head dropping to her shoulder. "You feel too good. I can't—"

"Don't hold back," she cut in, breathless. "I don't want gentle. Not now."

His control snapped.

He drove into her hard, fast, the couch creaking beneath them, their gasps echoing in the dark. She clung to him, riding every thrust, meeting him with wild abandon.

He kissed her fiercely, biting her lip, whispering between thrusts. "Mine. Always mine."

Her release hit fast, sharp, ripping through her with a cry. He followed, hips jerking as he spilled into her, groaning her name like a curse and a prayer all at once.

They collapsed together, shaking, still locked, too desperate to let go.

She laughed breathlessly against his neck. "We're never gonna leave this apartment, are we?"

"Not if I can help it," he muttered, kissing her hair, still buried deep inside her, already hardening again.

And she knew—this was only the beginning.

Chapter Seventeen

The Hunger in the Ordinary

They should have been tired. After that first night—the sweetness and reverence of the bedroom, the frantic urgency of the living room—they should have been wrung out, collapsed, content to sleep for days.

But the sweet hunger didn't fade.

If anything, it sharpened.

The morning after, Eliza woke with Finn's hand already cupping her thigh, sliding higher beneath the rumpled sheet. She gasped, twisting toward him, finding his grin half-buried in the pillow.

"Morning," he murmured, his voice gravel from sleep. "Couldn't wait."

Her answer was a kiss, sleep-soft and already burning. The tea kettle went cold that morning. Neither of them made it to class on time.

That became the rhythm of their days.

Finn's practices were brutal. Pads clashing, whistles shrill, drills endless until his legs felt like lead. But every time the weight threatened to crush him, he thought of her waiting back at the apartment.

She'd be curled with a book, hair loose, a mug of tea forgotten beside her. Sometimes he walked in and just stood there, staring, chest aching with something bigger than desire.

Other times, the sight of her sent him straight to his knees at her chair, pressing kisses up her thighs until the book slid from her hands.

Once, she swatted him with it, laughing breathlessly. "Finn, this is Virginia Woolf, not foreplay."

He only smirked, tugging her closer. "Everything's foreplay if I'm thinking about you."

She tried to glare, but her blush gave her away.

Their hunger slipped into every corner of ordinary life.

Cooking dinner: he came up behind her, lips at her neck, until she burned the garlic.

Laundry: folding sheets devolved into rolling in them on the floor.

Showering: meant quick kisses against wet tiles that turned slow, slippery, endless.

One afternoon, she tried to read her literature assignment aloud—some sonnet about yearning—and Finn interrupted halfway through with, "I can think of better ways to study desire."

She tried to push him away, giggling, but he only pulled her onto his lap, murmuring against her ear: *Say the poem again. I want to hear it while I touch you.*

She never finished the sonnet.

Their world was small, yet it pulsed with intensity that made even mundane errands feel dangerous.

At the grocery store, his hand never left the small of her back. When she bent to grab something, his palm pressed lower, possessive, like he needed the world to know she was his.

At the library, he slid into her booth, spreading out his playbook beside her novels, their knees brushing until she couldn't focus on her notes.

"You're distracting me," she whispered.

"Good," he whispered back, eyes gleaming. "I want you thinking about me when you're reading about Shakespeare's sonnets."

"Shakespeare is not foreplay either."

"You keep saying that," he teased, "and then you keep proving me right."

Nights blurred. Some were slow—him kissing her temple after long practice, murmuring how much he loved coming home to her. Some were wild—her pulling him down to the rug the second he closed the door, neither of them bothering with lights.

They made love in every room of the apartment: against the kitchen counter, sprawled on the bathroom rug, tangled on the couch with the movie menu looping forgotten.

Once, in the middle of studying, she straddled him without warning, riding him with quiet gasps until the pen slid from her hand. He held her tight, his forehead pressed to hers, whispering, "I can't stop wanting you."

"Don't," she whispered back, her lips brushing his. "I don't want you to."

But the outside world pressed in.

Finn's practices grew longer, harder. Bruises littered his ribs, his arms. He iced his shoulder at night, hissing at the sting. She sat beside him, reading aloud while pressing the pack against his skin.

"You don't have to," he said once, wincing as she adjusted the ice.

"Shut up," she said gently. "I like taking care of you."

His hand found hers, squeezing. "Songbird," he whispered, and the name sounded more like vow than nickname.

Eliza had her own battles: papers, dense lectures, professors who expected brilliance. She scribbled notes late into the night, stacks of books towering around her. Finn sometimes came home to find her slumped asleep at the desk.

He'd lift her gently, carrying her to bed, whispering against her hair: "Don't burn out. I need you."

The hunger wove through it all, but so did tenderness.

She read to him. He cooked for her. She traced his scars. He kissed her knuckles.

They were learning how to live together—not just in heat, but in rhythm.

Still, the fire never cooled.

****

The first game of the season, he didn't start. He stood on the sidelines, helmet in hand, jaw tight, waiting.

Eliza cheered anyway, her voice hoarse, her hands red from clapping. She waved like he was already the star of the field.

And when the coach Billings finally called his name in the second quarter, she screamed loud enough for him to hear it through the roar.

The next plays felt like destiny. A sack that sent the crowd wild. A fumble recovery that shifted momentum. His teammates slapped his back, shouting his name, and the announcers repeated it like it was already etched in stone.

By the end of the night, he wasn't just playing—he was shining under the lights.

Eliza's chest swelled with pride.

But it also tightened, just a little.

After the final whistle, chaos swept the field. Cameras, fans, classmates swarming. Coach Billings grinned, pounding Finn's shoulder pad so hard it echoed.

Eliza waited off to the side with Kai, clapping until her palms ached.

"Get used to it," Kai said, watching the crowd engulf Finn. "Once the hype starts, it doesn't let up."

Eliza tried to smile. "He deserves it."

"He does. But it's gonna be a lot."

Finn caught her eye across the chaos. For a heartbeat, he grinned, and the world narrowed to just that look. But then another player pulled him back, and the moment vanished.

Her hands kept clapping. Her voice kept shouting. But inside, something ached.

That night, the apartment was loud with people.

Finn had called it "just a small hangout." But small didn't look like half the team packed into their living room, girls perched on armrests, music thumping too loud.

Sophia showed, thank God. She and Eliza escaped to the kitchen, sipping white wine, watching the chaos from the doorway.

"He deserves it," Sophia said. "But damn, it's a lot."

Eliza nodded, her smile thin. "I'm happy for him. I am. I just... I feel like I'm watching him through a window now. Like I'm outside, looking in."

Sophia nudged her. "You've been his girl since before the crowd knew his name. That means something."

Eliza hoped she was right.

By midnight, the noise dwindled. Teammates drifted out, Kai herded a few stragglers, the apartment finally breathing again.

Eliza sat on the edge of the bed, scrolling through photos of the game. Finn's face filled half of them, triumphant, fierce. She wasn't in a single frame.

When he finally came in, still buzzing, smelling of sweat and cologne, he grinned wide. "Did you see the school's account? They posted the highlight reel. I'm in, like, every other frame."

"I saw."

He leaned to kiss her, but she turned slightly, and his lips brushed her cheek instead.

He froze. "What's wrong?"

"I don't know," she said, honestly. "You were incredible tonight. But I kind of felt like I wasn't even there. Like you didn't see me."

His smile dimmed, the air shifting. "Eliza…"

"I get that people want your attention now. I'm not mad about that. I just —when we got home, I thought maybe we'd have a minute. Just us. But you barely looked at me until now."

He sat, hands dangling between his knees, head bowed. For a long moment, the room was quiet.

Then he reached, taking her hands gently. "You're right. I let it go to my head. I've never had this kind of attention before. But that's not an excuse."

Her chest eased a little. She searched his eyes. "I don't need to be part of the spotlight, Finn. I just need to know I'm not getting lost in your shadow."

His grip tightened. "You're not. You're the reason I'm even standing in that light."

Her throat burned. She leaned against his shoulder. "So don't forget that when they start shouting your name again."

He pressed his lips to her hair, whispering like a vow. "I won't. You're still my North Star. My sweet Songbird."

And he meant it.

Even as the cheers grew louder in the weeks ahead, he started listening for one voice. Hers.

Because it was the only one that ever really mattered.

****

The first thing Eliza noticed, as she pried her still tired eyes open, was warmth.

Not the scratchy, unreliable kind from a too-thin blanket or the way the morning sun sneaked through blinds. This was heavier, grounding—like something had tethered her to earth itself. She opened her eyes slowly, blinking into the golden wash spilling through the curtains, and found herself staring at the large muscular arm draped over her waist.

Finn. Even though they had been sleeping together since that first night, she still woke up disoriented sometimes. Feeling his warm hard body tangled with hers made her heart shine. Love filled her as she watched Finn as he slept.

Her chest tightened. His handsome chiseled face was half-buried in the down pillow, dark lashes brushing his cheek, lips parted just enough for the soft breaths that warmed her collarbone. She almost laughed— because Finn Callahan, quarterback, the kind of guy entire offensive lines flinched at, slept like a kid. Mouth slack. Brow smoothed. Completely undone.

This was her Finn. No one else loved him like she did. No one else got to see him in this light.

Last night hadn't been a dream. Finn had led the team to victory.

Then he had woken her up during the night for a private celebration. One that left her thoroughly sated and loved. The memory sent a bolt of heat through her. The way he whispered her name like it had been locked in him for years. The dirty talk as he told her what he wanted to do to her.

The way he had moved with her—slow, yet desperate—pounding pleasure into them until she wasn't sure where she ended and he began.

She should have been exhausted. Instead, she felt alive in a way she didn't have words for.

She shifted, and his grip tightened instantly, hauling her closer even in sleep. His body knew before his mind did: hold, protect, keep.

"Morning, Songbird."

The words came low, mumbled against her skin. His eyes stayed shut, but his mouth curved in a grin.

Heat raced up her neck. "You're not even awake."

"I don't need to be to know you're here." He cracked one eye, lazy, already wrecking her with it. "God, you're really here."

Her hand smacked weakly at his shoulder, but her smile betrayed her. "Don't start."

"Too late." He kissed her hair, her forehead, the soft edge of her temple— scattershot affection he couldn't seem to stop.

It was ridiculous, how easy it felt. The years of silence, hesitation, fear— erased by the morning light stretching across their tangled sheets.

When she tried to slip away, Finn groaned and hauled her tighter.

"Nope. You're not leaving."

"I have to pee."

"Hold it."

She laughed, shoving at his chest. He didn't budge. "You're impossible."

"You're mine," he corrected, eyes finally opening, intensity cutting through the lazy haze.

The words landed like a vow. A claim.

Her throat went tight. "I know."

He kissed her then, unhurried and deep, his thumb brushing her jaw until she melted against him. The kiss built too quickly—as it always did—heat coiling in her belly, hands tangling in his hair, his chest rising fast beneath her palm.

When he finally let her go, he just sighed, soft and content, like sunlight lived in his lungs.

"Fine," he muttered. "Bathroom privileges. But I'm counting the seconds."

She laughed, finally slipping free.

By the time she returned, Finn had sprawled across the bed like a king staking claim. The light hit his bare chest, his grin smug. "You're staring."

"You're insufferable."

"Still staring."

"Get up."

"Nope. Bed's better with you in it."

She shook her head, tugging on a tee. "I was going to make coffee."

"Coffee can wait. I can't."

She threw a pillow at him. He caught it one-handed, hair sticking up like he'd wrestled the night itself.

"Fine," he relented, "coffee first. But I'm coming with you."

Which was how she ended up measuring grounds into the cheap machine with Finn wrapped around her back, chin on her shoulder, arms banded at her waist. He refused to move even when she elbowed him.

"Can't work like this," she muttered.

"Don't care. Smells good."

"You mean the coffee?"

"I mean you."

Her pulse stumbled. She set the scoop down before it clattered to the counter.

The shower was her idea. Practical. Necessary after the night they'd had. But practical became something else the moment the spray hit tile.

Finn stepped in behind her, steam already curling, crowding her against the wall with a grin that was all wolf.

"You're going to drown me," she said, half breathless, as water cascaded over them.

"Not a chance." His mouth found her shoulder, teeth grazing. "I'd never let you go under."

His hands slid over her hips, firm, deliberate, like he was staking claim inch by inch.

"Finn…" She gasped as his lips closed over her neck.

"You sound so damn pretty saying my name like that." His voice was gravel, intoxicated and wrecked at once.

She twisted, shoving his chest—but it only made him laugh against her mouth, kisses turning slippery and urgent. The water ran down the ridges of his chest, his hair plastering dark to his forehead. She thought she'd never seen anything so unfair.

He spun her gently under the spray when it got too hot, shielding her with his own body, then reached for the soap.

"Turn," he murmured.

She obeyed, shivering as his palms slid down her arms, over her shoulders, lather trailing everywhere he touched. His thumbs brushed her ribs, lower, lower—her breath caught.

"You trust me?" he asked, voice gone raw.

Her head whipped toward him, eyes wide. "Always."

Something snapped in him at that. His mouth crashed onto hers, hard enough to make her back hit tile. His hands gripped her thighs, lifting her effortlessly until she wrapped around him. Heat surged where they pressed together, bare and aching.

She moaned into his mouth, rocking against him, the slick tile at her back, the water beating down. He groaned, clutching her tighter, forehead pressing to hers.

"God, Eliza," he rasped, "I want you so bad I can't think."

"Then don't think." Her nails dug into his shoulders, dragging him closer.

His hips surged forward, grinding against her in a way that stole the breath from her lungs. She gasped, the sound echoing off tile. He cursed low, pressing kisses down her throat, nipping until her knees shook even though he was holding her off the ground.

It could have gone further—it was seconds away from going further—when the water suddenly turned ice-cold.

They yelped together, jerking apart, laughter bubbling up through the shock.

Finn nearly dropped her, but managed to set her down, both of them scrambling out dripping and breathless. She clutched a towel to her chest, grinning like an idiot.

"Saved by the plumbing," she teased, cheeks flushed.

"Sabotaged by the plumbing," he growled, dragging a towel over his head. His grin betrayed him. "We're finishing that later."

She laughed, swatting his arm. "You're incorrigible."

"You love it."

Maybe she did. No maybe. She absolutely wanted him.

By the time they collapsed on the couch, mugs steaming between them, the world outside felt like a rumor.

"This is dangerous," Eliza whispered into her tea.

Finn tilted his head. "Dangerous?"

"I could get used to it. Too fast."

He caught her free hand, threading their fingers. "Good. That's the point."

Her chest pulled tight.

After a beat, he sighed. "First real team meeting today. Coach Billings says it's where we 'set the tone.' Basically, speeches and grunting."

She smiled faintly, though a knot coiled in her stomach. "That's big."

"Eh. Just football."

She arched a brow. "You've dreamed of this since you were twelve."

He shrugged, squeezing her hand. "Yeah, but I've got more important things now." His gaze flicked, deliberate, to her.

Her cheeks burned. "You're ridiculous."

"I'm serious."

Her heart thudded as she looked away. "Well, I've got a paper due in a week. If I don't start, I'll drown."

He groaned. "Don't remind me we're students."

"Somebody has to."

He tugged her fully onto his chest, blanket and all. "Fine. After meetings, after papers—this. Always this."

And for now, she let herself believe it.

Chapter Eighteen

Late Afternoon Glow

The days after their first night blurred into something Eliza hadn't known was possible.

It wasn't just the sex. Though God, that alone was enough to make her knees weak just thinking about it. It was the way they couldn't seem to stop touching. In little ways, constant ways, like their hands had forgotten how to be apart.

She woke to his palm draped over her hip, tracing circles even in his sleep. She brushed her teeth with him pressed against her back at the sink, his chest warm through the thin cotton of her T-shirt, his lips brushing the crown of her head as he reached for the toothpaste. At first she thought he was teasing. But then she caught his reflection in the mirror—messy hair, sleepy eyes fixed on her—and realized no, this was just him. Clingy, unashamedly so.

"Move, you giant," she said around a mouthful of foam.

"No," he said simply, resting his chin on her shoulder, watching her spit. "I like the view."

"You're disgusting."

"Accurate. But also in love." He grinned, toothpaste smeared at the corner of his mouth, and she had to swat him away before he kissed her with it.

It was ridiculous. It was intimate in ways she hadn't expected. The kind of closeness you couldn't fake, couldn't plan. Domestic, almost married—but also desperate, like every second was a dare: *What if we don't get another one?*

And that desperation followed them everywhere.

By late afternoon, the apartment filled with light, golden bars stretching across the couch and spilling into the tiny kitchen. Eliza had tried to sit with her laptop, but Finn was sprawled beside her, too big for the couch, his legs spread wide until she was practically tucked between them.

"You know I actually have to work, right?" she said, glaring at the blinking cursor on her Word document.

"You *are* working." His hand slid beneath the hem of her shorts, fingers tracing her thigh lazily. "Multitasking."

"Finn." She tried for stern, but her breath already hitched.

"Yeah?" His voice was a low rumble, his grin boyish as he dipped his head to kiss her shoulder.

"Stop distracting me."

"Not possible." His lips found the slope of her neck, then her collarbone. "You're too damn pretty when you're pretending to care about school."

"I do care about school."

"Not right now you don't."

And he was right. Because within minutes, the laptop was forgotten, nudged to the side of the couch, her hands tangled in his hair while he kissed her like he owned her, like the sunlight itself bent around them. Clothes half-pulled, laughter muffled into pillows, the squeak of the couch springs betraying them to the empty apartment.

It was messy. It was clumsy. It was everything. And when it was over, Finn kissed her temple like he was sealing a promise no one else could hear.

****

By the fifth week of classes, they were reckless.

They'd snuck kisses in the stairwell before, hands clutching at each other like they were starving. But the laundry room was different. Loud with machines, half-empty in the late afternoon, smelling of detergent and faint mildew.

Eliza had been folding towels when Finn caught her wrist and tugged her back against him, spinning her into the corner. The dryer hummed beneath her, vibrating against her hips as he caged her in with both arms.

"Finn—" she gasped, half laughing, half warning.

"Shh." His mouth found hers, hungry, teeth grazing her lower lip.

Her back hit the warm metal of the machine, heat searing through cotton. His hands slid up her sides, greedy, restless. The kiss deepened until she thought she might dissolve into him entirely, her fingers knotted in the fabric of his shirt.

The sound of the door swinging open was the only thing that stopped them.

Two voices carried in, joking about detergent. Eliza froze, pushing at Finn's chest. He let out a low growl of frustration, but pulled back just enough to hide his face against her neck.

"Neighbors," she hissed.

"Don't care." His teeth grazed her skin, a quick nip that made her jump.

"Finn!"

He chuckled, low and wicked. But he stepped away finally, running a hand through his hair as two girls walked past them, one giving them a look that was half amusement, half scandalized.

Eliza covered her burning face with her hands. "We're going to get kicked out."

Finn smirked, tugging the basket from her. "Worth it."

That night, Eliza curled up on the couch with her laptop again, determined to salvage some homework. The glow of the screen lit her face, making shadows dance across her cheekbones.

Finn sprawled across the other end, flipping channels lazily. But his eyes kept flicking to her, tracing the crease of her brow, the way she chewed her lip when she typed.

"You're distracted," he said finally.

"I'm behind," she admitted, slamming her laptop shut. "I keep losing time."

"Because of me?" His grin was teasing, but there was a flicker in his eyes —uncertainty, guilt.

"Because of us," she corrected softly.

For a moment, silence stretched. He shifted upright, leaning forward, forearms on his knees. "If I'm screwing things up for you—"

"You're not." She cut him off, reaching to touch his hand. "You're…God, Finn, you're the best thing in my life right now. The best thing ever. I just need to learn how to balance both. School *and* you."

He stared at her like he wanted to argue, then blew out a slow breath. "Okay. But if you ever feel like I'm pulling you under—say the word. I'll back off."

She smiled faintly. "That's the problem. I don't *want* you to back off."

His shoulders eased, and he kissed her hand, pressing it to his cheek. "Good. Because I don't think I could."

The next morning, he insisted on walking her to her literature lecture just so they could spend a few more moments together. For some reason, that morning, he needed the extra time in her presence.

"Finn, it's broad daylight. I'm fine," she said, adjusting her bag on her shoulder.

"Humor me." He slipped his hand into hers, squeezing tight. "Crowds make me nervous."

"You're a quarterback. You literally *are* the crowd."

"Not the same," he muttered, glaring at the students brushing past them. "These guys don't wear helmets."

She laughed, but the sound softened into something warmer as he tugged her closer, tucking her against his side. He was all protective instinct, a storm of muscle and watchfulness wrapped around her.

When they reached the building, she paused at the steps. "This is me."

He didn't let go of her hand. Not immediately. His thumb brushed over her knuckles, like he was memorizing the feel.

"Go on," she urged gently. "I'll be fine."

"I know." He hesitated, then leaned down to kiss her—quick, but firm, like a seal of claim and promise both. "See you after."

She watched him walk away, tall and broad and impossible not to notice. And even with the knot of worry about homework tightening in her chest, she couldn't help the way her heart surged.

Because she knew, without question, that he'd come back for her. Every time.

Chapter Nineteen

Claiming Quiet

It started as tension. Not the kind born of distance—but of proximity. Of glances too long in crowded rooms, of touches that meant more than they should've in passing hallways.

Eliza felt it every time someone on campus looked at Finn like he was some Greek statue come to life. And Finn felt it even more when Eliza laughed a little too easily with someone else, her light catching in places he thought were only his.

By the time they got back to the apartment after first few months of classes, something simmered beneath the surface. Words unsaid. Desires pushed off by late practices and longer reading lists.

Eliza dropped her bag by the door and toed off her shoes. She barely made it three steps inside before Finn came up behind her, wrapping an arm firmly around her waist and pulling her back against his chest.

"Mine," he murmured into her ear, his voice low and gravel rough. "I don't like the way half the guys in your lit class look at you."

She turned in his arms, brow raised. "They look because I exist. That's not a crime."

Finn's grip tightened just enough to make her breath catch. "You don't get it. When you laugh like that? When you wear that lip gloss? It's like they forget you're already taken."

"And whose fault is that?" she whispered, teasing. "You haven't exactly reminded them lately."

That was all it took.

Finn kissed her like he was starving. Like the restraint he'd built for months shattered in a heartbeat. He lifted her, her legs wrapping around him instinctively as he carried her down the hall and into their bedroom.

There was nothing slow about it. It wasn't rough—not careless—but urgent. Intentional. The kind of passion that came from knowing exactly who the other person was, body and soul.

Clothes hit the floor fast, forgotten. Skin met skin, heat rising as their mouths found each other again and again. Finn's hands moved like he was mapping something he already knew but needed to relearn.

"You're mine," he whispered again, forehead pressed to hers. "Say it."

"I've always been yours," she breathed.

They moved together like instinct. Like gravity. Like coming home.

Later, when the tension had faded into something softer—when Eliza lay tangled in sheets and Finn's arms, breath slowing—he kissed her shoulder and murmured, "I'm never letting anyone take this from us."

"You don't have to," she said, turning to face him. "Just don't forget to show up."

He nodded, fingers tracing the inside of her wrist where her pulse fluttered. "I won't."

She smiled. "Then we're good."

And just like that, the quiet between them wasn't tension anymore. It was something closer to a fragile truce.

****

Saturday morning came with grey skies and no plans. Eliza sat at the kitchen table, barely touching her toast. The apartment was too quiet. Finn hadn't said much since Thursday, and she didn't know how to reach through the silence without pushing too hard.

She'd been staring at the same paragraph in her lit analysis for twenty minutes when the front door opened. Finn stepped in, hoodie pulled low, a coffee in each hand.

"I didn't know if you had eaten," he said, setting one down in front of her. His voice was low. Tired.

"Thanks," she said, wrapping her hands around the cup. "Finn... are we okay?"

He didn't answer right away. Just pulled out the chair across from her and sat down.

"I've been a jerk," he said. "You've done nothing wrong. I've just been so caught up in football and proving I belong here that I forgot—" He paused. "I forgot I already belong. Because I'm with you."

Her throat tightened.

He reached across the table, took her hand. "You know how when you're lost in the woods or out at sea or whatever, they say to find the North Star? That it's constant, even when everything else is chaos?"

She nodded.

"You're that for me," he said. "You're my North Star."

Tears sprang to her eyes, uninvited but welcome. "Finn…"

"I let everything else get louder than you. I won't let it happen again."

She got up and walked around the table, slid into his lap, wrapping her arms around his neck. He held her tight, forehead pressed to hers.

"We're in this together," she whispered. "So when you get lost, I'll remind you. And when I get lost, you do the same."

"Deal."

They stayed like that for a while—no rush, no pressure. Just breathing in the same rhythm again.

Later that day, Finn scribbled *North Star* on a sticky note and stuck it to the fridge.

Every time things got chaotic after that, one of them would just point to it, or whisper the words. It wasn't magic. It didn't solve everything. But it reminded them what mattered.

And sometimes, that was enough to bring them back home to each other.

That night, while Finn was asleep on the couch with a textbook on his chest, Eliza opened her notebook and finished the bridge to her song:

"And if I ever lose the thread, I'll follow the light where your voice has led. North of always, you bring me home."

****

Eliza woke slowly, sunlight cutting through the gauzy curtains in ribbons of gold. Finn was still asleep beside her, one arm tucked under his head, the other loosely curled around the spot where she'd been. She watched the rise and fall of his chest and felt the words humming through her fingers before she even reached for her notebook.

She sat up, wrapping a blanket around her shoulders, and padded back into the living room. The melody was still with her. A pulse. A promise. She settled onto the floor and opened her notebook again.

The page where she'd written *North of Always* looked different now. More alive. Last night hadn't just deepened their bond—it had carved something open in her. A deeper current. A new way to feel.

She added a verse:

You found me where silence lived, held me like breath in winter, like I was something sacred.

You didn't ask for anything but I gave you everything. And you called it safe.

She reread it, her throat tightening.

Music had always been her secret place. A hiding spot she didn't have to explain. Lyrics had kept her sane in houses full of strangers, in rooms that didn't feel like hers. But now, for the first time, her music didn't sound like survival. It sounded like love.

The kettle whistled softly in the kitchen. She poured tea for them both, just as Finn wandered in, sleep-ruffled and blinking.

"Hey," he said, voice low and scratchy.

She smiled, sliding him a mug. "Hey."

His eyes landed on the open notebook and the guitar propped beside the couch. "Working already?"

She nodded. "It's... starting to come together."

He leaned down, kissed her forehead, then sat beside her. "Is it about last night?"

She met his gaze. "It's about us."

His hand found hers. "Then I can't wait to hear it."

Later that day, she met Sophia at a café just off campus. They'd planned to study, but Eliza's notebook sat open between them, and her pencil never stopped moving.

"What are you working on?" Sophia asked, sipping her iced latte.

"A song. Sort of..." Eliza hesitated. "It started after something happened with Finn. Something important. Now I can't stop writing."

Sophia grinned. "That's how you know it's real. When it doesn't let you sleep until it's out."

Eliza smiled, then paused. "Do you think it's crazy if I want to play it one day? Like, at something big? Like—"

"ACL?" Sophia said.

Eliza laughed nervously. "I wasn't going to say it out loud."

"Too late. Now you have to do it."

Eliza looked down at the page. The lyrics stared back at her like a dare.

She didn't say it yet. But maybe, just maybe, she would.

Maybe *North of Always* wasn't just for her and Finn.

Maybe it was a beginning.

Chapter Twenty

Pressures Rising

Finn had known full-contact practice would hurt but after months of it he was wrecked. Everyone had warned him—upperclassmen, Coach Billings, even Kai, who told him to expect "the kind of bruises you don't remember earning."

But knowing was one thing. Living it was another.

By the time Coach Billings blew the final whistle, Finn's body felt like it had been fed through a meat grinder. His lungs burned, his arms ached from getting sacked by bodies twice his size, and his thighs throbbed where pads hadn't caught the hits. Every breath rattled with the taste of turf and sweat.

He walked off the field in a daze, helmet tucked under his arm, his shirt plastered to him. The veterans clapped his back, told him "good work," and one Coach Billings muttered, "Kid might survive the season after all." But Finn didn't feel victorious. He felt gutted.

Survival wasn't the same as belonging.

By the time he showered and dragged himself across campus, dusk had settled. He went straight home. His legs carried him to Eliza on instinct, like she was the only gravity left holding him upright.

She opened the door with a book in her hand, already mid-sentence, and froze when she saw him.

"Finn—"

He leaned against the frame, trying for a grin. It came out crooked. "Hey, Songbird."

Her eyes swept over him, taking in the slump of his shoulders, the redness around his knuckles. She set the book down immediately and tugged him inside.

"You look wrecked."

"Feel worse." He collapsed on the edge of the not big enough bed, sprawling back like he might never move again. The mattress squeaked in protest.

She shut the door, heart thudding, and crouched beside him. Up close, he was even worse—scrapes along his forearm, a bruise blooming near his collarbone, a wince every time he shifted.

"Finn." Her voice was soft, but threaded with worry. Violet eyes filled with concern. "What did they do to you?"

"Football." He tried to shrug, then winced again. "Welcome to the team. The season just gets tougher and the hits harder."

"Idiot," she muttered, already crossing to the tiny freezer for an ice pack. She pressed it gently to his shoulder, watching the tension in his jaw ease a fraction.

"God, that feels good." His eyes fluttered shut.

She smiled despite herself, brushing damp hair off his forehead. "You push yourself too hard."

"That's the point." His voice was a low rasp. "Gotta prove I belong out there."

"You already belong," she said firmly.

His lips curved faintly, but he didn't argue. Not with her.

She sat on the bed beside him, working the ice pack along his shoulder. Her free hand traced his forearm, soothing circles over scraped skin. He sighed into it, his whole body loosening under her care.

"Feels like I got hit by a truck," he murmured.

"You kind of did."

"Twenty trucks, then." He cracked one eye open, giving her that lazy grin, dimples winking, that always unraveled her. "Pretty sure you're better medicine than the ice, though."

Her cheeks warmed. "Finn—"

"I mean it." His gaze flicked over her face, heavy-lidded, hungry even in his exhaustion. "Touch me more."

She swallowed. And then she did.

The ice pack slipped aside as her hands began tracing the lines of his chest, the ridges of muscle tight with strain. She kneaded carefully, her thumbs pressing into the knots of his shoulders. He groaned, the sound low and guttural, vibrating through her fingertips.

"Jesus, Songbird—"

"Does it hurt?"

"Feels…so good," he groaned.

She kept working at him, leaning closer, her long, silver-blonde hair falling forward to brush his chest. His hand found her firm thigh, squeezing lightly, as if even being wrecked he couldn't keep from claiming some part of her.

The air thickened. His breathing deepened. When she finally bent to kiss the bruise on his collarbone, he let out a sound that was half relief, half need.

Her lips trailed upward, over the curve of his neck, until his mouth caught hers. The kiss was slow at first, tentative because of his soreness—but it didn't stay that way.

Need caught fire between them. His hands tugged her onto the bed, onto him, until she was straddling his hips, her palms pressed to his chest. Every movement drew a hiss, half pain, half pleasure.

"Careful," she whispered.

"Don't stop," he whispered back.

And she didn't.

Their kisses grew frantic, teeth and tongue, his hands threading through her hair, down her spine. The bruises didn't stop him; if anything, they made him cling harder, as if needing to prove that even battered, he wanted her more than anything.

They didn't rush it—because they couldn't. Eliza tenderly kissed all of his bruises working her way down his chest, his stomach to his hard cock. Licking the tip then taking her tongue down and up repeating the movement. His breathe ragged, his hands tugging her hair. Wrapping her mouth around him fully while fisting and pumping her hard up and down his cock. Sucking his hard length, she looked up and stared into his eyes as she loved him, taking care of him carnally. When he was close she shifted gently straddling him. His touch began flicking, rubbing her clit in circles. His eyes were hot but his body demanded slower, steadier. And yet the intensity of their union was sharper for it. Every touch deliberate, every breath stolen. It was less a frenzy than a burn, slow and consuming, until both of them were trembling.

When it ended, he held her tight against his chest, his heart hammering like he'd run another set of drills. His breath was ragged, but his smile was soft, almost boyish.

"See?" he murmured, lips against her hair. "Better than ice."

She laughed weakly, pressing her ear to his heartbeat. "You're insane."

"Insanely lucky."

He pulled her slighter body into his spooning her, then sighed contentedly. Even though football was kicking his, Eliza made him feel loved.

For the first time in his life he belonged to someone and they belonged to him.

Later, after they'd cleaned up and pulled her peach fleece blanket over themselves, Eliza sat cross-legged with her laptop balanced on her knees. The cursor blinked accusingly at the top of a blank document.

Finn lay beside her, sprawled on his stomach, head pillowed on his arms. His hair was damp from the quick rinse he'd taken, curling in messy chestnut tufts. He shifted occasionally, the mattress creaking, a soft grunt escaping when he turned wrong.

She typed a sentence. Deleted it. Typed another. Deleted that too.

"You're staring at me," Finn said without looking up.

"I'm working."

"You're not working." He rolled to his side, smirking. "You're staring."

She narrowed her eyes at him. "You're distracting."

"Not my fault I look this good broken."

"Cocky."

"Accurate." He reached out, tugged her ankle until she toppled sideways into his chest. The laptop slid to the floor with a dull thud.

"Finn!"

"Homework later," he whispered, mouth brushing her temple. "Me now. Us now."

She sighed, exasperated. But her body curled into his anyway, betraying her.

The room was dim now, lit only by the glow of her desk lamp. They lay tangled, quiet but not asleep, her head tucked beneath his chin.

"Songbird," he said suddenly, voice raw.

She tilted her head. "What?"

"I don't want to lose you."

The words landed like a weight between them. His arm tightened around her waist, his chest rising and falling against her cheek.

She swallowed hard. "It won't. You won't."

"You don't know that." His tone cracked, just slightly. "Practice, travel, games…all of it. Not to mention the struggle to keep my grades up so that I can keep playing. I've seen what it does to guys. They vanish. Relationships vanish."

She pushed up on her elbow, meeting his eyes looking like the forest depths at night in the half-light. "You're not them."

His throat worked. "But what if I can't stop it?"

"You will." Her hand cupped his cheek, thumb brushing along his jaw. "Because you care enough to worry about it. You love me. I'm your North Star. That's the difference."

For a long moment, he just looked at her, green eyes shining with something unspoken. Then he kissed her—not urgent, not rough, but soft, stirring.

When they broke apart, she whispered, "I'm scared too, Finn. But we'll figure it out. Together."

He nodded slowly, as if anchoring himself to her words. "Together."

They shifted again, finding space on their queen-size bed. Finn and she were planning to buy a new bigger bed as soon as they could afford to.

There wasn't much space now—his legs hung over the edge, his shoulders pressed into the wall—but neither of them cared.

Her laptop remained forgotten on the floor. The world outside their apartment didn't exist.

Finn wrapped around her like armor, bruised and sore but unwilling to let go. She curled into him like she'd always belonged there.

Sleep claimed them gradually, breaths syncing, limbs entwined. And in that moment the pressures of the outside world eased—if only for a night.

Chapter Twenty-One

Edges Showing

The alarm went off too early. It always did.

A white alarm clock radio glowed faint red numbers on Eliza's nightstand, its plastic frame cracked along one corner where someone before her had probably dropped it. The beeping drilled into her skull, sharp and merciless. She groaned into her pillow, dragging the patterned, peach fleece blanket over her head.

Beside her, the mattress dipped. The warmth vanished almost instantly as Finn rolled out of bed, his heavy steps padding across the room. Drawers thudded open. Zippers rasped. She peeked out from under the blanket in time to catch a flash of his bare back, muscles flexing as he tugged on a T-shirt.

"Weight room," he muttered, his voice sandpapered with sleep.

"It's barely six," she croaked.

He leaned over, pressed a distracted kiss to her cheek that was gone before she could turn her head toward it. "Coach Billings says if you want minutes, you show up early. Love you."

And then he was gone, the door clicking behind him.

Eliza lay in the dim half-light, the sheets still warm where his body had been. The air smelled faintly of fabric softener, his unique scent and last night's love making—the one scent that clung to him even after sweat.

She thought about rolling back into the warm hollow he'd left and reclaiming an hour of sleep. But her laptop, black and silent on the desk, sat like a sentinel in the corner, reminding her she'd barely started her assigned reading and was being on her Lit paper. The knot in her stomach tightened.

With a deep sigh, she pushed the blanket aside and swung her feet to the cold linoleum floor.

****

Their days got busier but they still found each other in small pockets.

Brushing teeth in the tiny bathroom, bumping hips as they spit and laughed through foamy mouths. Making scrambled eggs on her hot plate, kissing between cracked shells and sizzling pans. Sprawling on the library floor between towers of books, Finn doodling plays in the margins of her notebook until she swatted his arm.

Those moments were still bright—sparks flickering even in exhaustion. But the days grew tighter, hours more scarce, the rest of life pressing in at the seams.

That afternoon, Finn stumbled into their apartment like gravity itself had grown heavier. His shirt was soaked through, hair matted to his forehead. He didn't even take his shoes off before dropping face-first onto the bed.

Eliza glanced up from her laptop. "You okay?"

"Coach Billings still acts like he hates me." The words were muffled in the blanket.

She closed her laptop with a soft click and slid closer. "What happened?"

"Nothing. Everything." He rolled onto his back with a wince. A new bruise purpled along his ribs, blooming ugly against skin that carried a map of past collisions.

Worried but supportive, she touched him lightly, brushing her fingers along the mark. "You are sharpening," she whispered. "He'll see."

But Finn caught her hand, pressed it flat to his chest where his heart thudded hard and uneven. "What if he doesn't? I made that amazing play that saved the game and he is still keeping me under wraps. Don't know what I have to do to prove that I'm more that just a backup quarterback."

Her mouth opened, but the words caught in her throat. She couldn't promise him something she didn't control. So she leaned down instead, kissed him slow and steady, willing the tension to melt. For a moment it did. For a moment, it was just them again.

By the time she pulled back, his eyes were already sliding shut, exhaustion dragging him under.

She smoothed her palm against his cheek. *He just wants to belong,* she thought. *The same way I do.*

****

Sleep pulled at Finn, but memory stirred too. A flashback to his days as a foster kid when running was paramount.

The slam of doors in foster houses. The shouts that weren't meant for him but still landed. The careful silence he practiced, the mantra drilled into his bones:

Watch and listen. Trust no one. Always be ready to run.

He had run before—out the back door, down midnight streets, shoes too small biting into his heels. He'd run from hands that grabbed, voices that barked orders, fists that hit, places that felt temporary the second he set his bag down.

Survival had been the finish line. Keep your head down. Don't get attached. Focus on the exit.

Now he had a bed he came back to. A girl who kissed his bruises like they mattered. But the old habits clung like shadows: the silence, the instinct to pull away, the way he kept testing the floorboards for weakness, waiting for everything to collapse. Waiting for the other shoe to drop.

He knew how to run. He just wasn't sure he knew how to stay.

The next day it was Eliza dragging herself across the finish line.

She sat at her desk, towers of printouts circling her like ramparts, cursor blinking at the end of an unfinished sentence. Her Lit professor, Dr. Landon, had reminded them three times that the midterm paper was worth a third of their grade. He had also taken her aside after class to remind her that her scholarship was on the line and that she needed to step it up.

But Finn was sprawled on her bed again, earbuds in, tossing a football up and catching it lazily. Every time she looked away from the screen, her eyes landed on him—the easy stretch of his body, the sexy grin dimples flashing, tugging at his mouth whenever he caught her watching.

"Songbird," he teased, tugging one bud out. "You've been staring for five minutes."

"Because you're distracting."

"Then stop looking." He purred flexing his impressive biceps.

Unable to resist, Eliza got up, assignment forgotten, "Easier said than done."

She lay down next to him, wrapping her arms around him settling into the embrace as his arms did the same. His scent was heady and the feel of his body against hers swept thoughts of everything but him out of her mind. He smirked, victorious. She laughed, but the knot in her chest didn't ease but she couldn't Help herself.

Much later that night Eliza woke realizing that she still had to finish her Lit assignment.

The paper still wasn't writing itself. That night she didn't go back to sleep.

She got it done. Just barely in time.

Unfortunately, their laundry didn't clean itself. So Thursday night, they lugged a basket of clothes down to the basement laundry room.

The machines rumbled, hot metal scent filling the air, fluorescent lights buzzing faintly above.

As soon as the dryer kicked on, Finn pressed her against it, hot mouth urgent on hers.

She gasped, laughing against him. "Finn—someone could—"

"Don't care." His hands gripped her waist, the machine's vibration humming through her spine. His kiss deepened, feverish, as if the seconds without her touch had stacked too high to bear.

When the door squeaked open, two students shuffled in with baskets. Eliza shoved Finn back, both of them stifling laughter. Her face burned as they scrambled to look casual.

The newcomers didn't even notice. But as Finn leaned close, whispering, *"Guess we'll finish later,"* the promise clung to her skin all the way upstairs.

****

But later didn't always come.

Readings piled. Practices stretched. He fell asleep before their conversations could begin. She woke to him sliding under the blankets at two a.m., whispering "sorry" and giving her a quick kiss before drifting instantly out of reach.

She lay beside him, listening to his steady breath, missing him even when his body was right there. Feeling both the warm and cold of it.

Trailing her fingers across his cheek, she pressed a kiss to his lips. He didn't stir.

Monday afternoon, Finn insisted on walking her across campus.

The autumn air was damp, the sky the gray of unpolished stone. Students hurried past with backpacks slung low, earbuds in, caramel lattes steaming.

Finn's hand wrapped hers tight, knuckles white, like he was afraid she might slip away if he let go. Sweat still clung to his practice jersey, the acrid tang sharp in the breeze, but he didn't seem to notice. He was still starting his mornings at six in the morning. Running himself ragged.

"You'll be late," she warned as they reached her building.

"Don't care."

"Finn—"

He stopped, serious, eyes shadowed under damp chestnut hair. "I need this. Us. Even if it's just five minutes between practice and class. I need to hold your hand and know you're real. I miss being with you. Loving you. I'm running so hard to keep up and I know that you are too. I feel like every moment counts."

Her throat tightened. She squeezed back, whispering, "I'm real. I'm here. I'm not going anywhere without you." Rising on tiptoe, she brushed her soft lips to his.

Smiling faintly, he turned and jogged away, duffel heavy on his shoulder, posture sagging with invisible weight.

She turned into the building, chest tight. The world was pulling pieces from both of them, and the seams were starting to fray. She didn't know how stop, but felt the unraveling.

Inside, Sophia waved her over, and Eliza forced a smile that didn't reach her eyes.

Later that night, at their apartment, with Finn asleep again almost as soon as his head hit the pillow, Eliza cracked open her lyric notebook in the blue glow of her desk lamp.

She stared at a blank page, chewing her pen. Then the words spilled fast, almost jagged:

If you go silent, do I follow?
If you go running, do I run too?
Or am I just shouting into the dark—
Trying to hold on to something slipping through?

She looked at it, heart twisting. It wasn't polished. It wasn't even a song yet. But it felt raw, like it belonged to the same silence that sat between them lately.

She shut the notebook with the songbird drawn on the front and North of Always written in script on the front, fast, almost ashamed. Some truths were too sharp to share yet.

But the words would wait for her. They always did.

Chapter Twenty-Two

A Night for Us

The idea came from Eliza first.

Not in a grand gesture, not even in words, but in the way her fingers lingered on Finn's wrist one night while he was packing his practice bag again. The apartment around them buzzed with fluorescent light and exhaustion, papers stacked on the table, laundry in a heap, his cleats still muddy by the door. She looked at him with that soft sadness he'd been catching in her eyes more often lately, and said quietly:

"Can we just… stop for one night?"

Finn froze mid-motion, the strap of the duffel hanging loose in his hands. "Stop?"

"Not forever," she said quickly. "Just… everything. Practice, papers, alarms, all of it. Just for one night. Just you and me."

Something in her voice—a plea, but also an anchor—pulled at the part of him that had been running so long he'd forgotten how to pause. He dropped the strap and sat beside her, rubbing a thumb across her knuckles.

"Yeah," he said. "Let's do it."

Saturday night came with a little ritual neither of them had realized they missed: getting ready, separately, but for each other.

Eliza stood in front of the mirror, curling iron balanced precariously on the chipped bathroom counter, her favorite low-cut black dress swaying against her legs. It wasn't new, but she hadn't worn it since the summer, and slipping into it made her stand a little taller, made her feel like more than the girl buried under deadlines and coffee rings. Made her feel sexy. She painted a thin line of eyeliner, touched gloss to her lips, and practiced a smile in the mirror that wasn't tired.

From the bedroom, Finn's voice carried through the cracked door. "Songbird, you almost ready? I'm sweating through this shirt just waiting on you."

She laughed, the sound lighter than it had been in weeks. "Good. That's how you know it's working."

When she stepped out, his whistle filled the small room. He'd dressed in a button-down—dark blue, sleeves rolled to his forearms, collar open just enough to look like he wasn't trying too hard. His hair was still damp from the shower, and he smelled of soap instead of sweat.

"Holy hell," he muttered, eyes sweeping over her. "You're gonna ruin me tonight."

"You clean up pretty good yourself," she teased, though her pulse quickened at the way he was looking at her. Like she wasn't just Eliza-with-papers-due and coffee stains, but Eliza, the girl he chose every day.

Austin at night pulsed with life. Strings of lights crisscrossed patios, neon signs glowed above taco trucks, and music spilled from bars onto sidewalks. They slipped into the current of people, hand in hand, their laughter carried on the humid air.

Finn had picked the restaurant—nothing fancy, but nice enough that their sneakers and sweatshirts would've felt out of place. Candles flickered on the tables, and the smell of roasted garlic and fresh bread wrapped around them as they slid into a booth by the window.

For once, the conversation wasn't about assignments or practice schedules. They talked about stupid things—like which actor would play Finn in a movie ("Chris Hemsworth," he insisted, flexing until she nearly choked on her wine) and how Eliza once convinced her high school English teacher to let her skip class by claiming she had "lyrical inspiration." They swapped memories like trading cards, piecing together the parts of themselves they hadn't had time to share.

Halfway through dinner, Finn reached across the table, his hand covering hers.
"Hey," he said softly.
"Hey what?"
"Just… hey. I missed this. I missed us."

Her throat tightened, and she squeezed his hand back. "Me too."

After dinner, they didn't want to go home yet. The city felt alive in a way they hadn't let themselves feel in months. Music drifted from an open doorway down the block, a live band playing something soulful and low. Without asking, Finn tugged her toward it, his grin boyish.

"Finn," she laughed, stumbling as he pulled her onto the small dance floor crowded with strangers.
"You're not getting out of this one." He slid an arm around her waist, his other hand finding hers. "One song. Just us."

The band shifted into something slower, the singer's voice smoky over the hum of the bass. Finn swayed with her, awkward at first—he was more used to running routes than keeping rhythm—but then his chin dropped to her hair, and everything stilled.

Eliza pressed close, letting the music guide her, letting the world blur until it was only the heat of his chest against hers, the steady weight of his hand at her back.

"You know," he murmured, lips brushing her temple, "sometimes I think I don't deserve this. You. Nights like this."

She pulled back just enough to meet his eyes, her voice firm even as it softened.
"Don't you dare say that. You're my home, Finn. I don't care where we are or what's happening. It's you. Always you."

His throat worked, like her words had landed somewhere deep. He kissed her right there, in the middle of the dance floor, with strangers swaying all around them and music vibrating through the floorboards.

They walked home slower than usual, their steps unhurried, hands brushing, fingers linking and unlinking like they had all the time in the world.

Eliza kicked off her heels at the corner, carrying them in one hand while Finn laughed at her dramatics. He draped an arm around her shoulders, pulling her close as the city noise softened behind them.

On their block, the streetlights buzzed faintly, and the air smelled faintly of rain. Eliza leaned into him, her head against his arm. "Tonight was perfect," she whispered.

"Not over yet," he said, his grin crooked but his eyes serious.

Back inside their apartment, the messy stacks of books and laundry seemed smaller, less suffocating. Finn locked the door behind them, but when he turned back, he wasn't rushing. He stood there for a moment, just looking at her like he was trying to memorize her all over again.

Then he crossed the room in two strides and kissed her, slow and deliberate, his hands cupping her face.

The kiss deepened, turned hungrier, and Eliza melted into him, her heels thudding to the floor. His shirt buttons gave way beneath her fingers, each one slipping free until her palms could press against the warmth of his skin. His body was firm, still carrying the day's strength, but yielding completely to her touch.

He traced his mouth down the line of her jaw, across her throat, lingering where her pulse fluttered. She gasped softly, curling her hands in his shirt as if to anchor herself. Every brush of his lips, every breath against her skin, made the rest of the world fall away.

"Songbird," he whispered, voice raw and spellbound against her collarbone. "God, I love you."

Her answer was a kiss that stole the words from both of them. She tugged him toward the bedroom, their laughter tumbling between kisses, clumsy and breathless, but wrapped in a kind of urgency that wasn't about rushing—it was about needing to close the distance that had stretched between them these past weeks.

When they finally fell together onto the bed, it wasn't frantic. It was deliberate. Unrushed. His hands traced over her as if relearning her, mapping her curves with a patience that carried weight. She touched him back just as intently, fingertips brushing the scars, the lines, the places where the world had left marks, whispering with her touch that he was safe here, loved here.

The rhythm between them built slow, like a song beginning soft and then swelling, each movement and sigh layering into something greater. Heat pressed skin to skin, breath tangled, hearts pounding in time. Their laughter broke through between kisses, softer now, threaded with gasps and whispered words that didn't need to be explained.

Every moment was a reminder: we're still here, still us.

When it ended, they didn't fall apart but sank into each other, bodies tangled in the sheets, sweat cooling on their skin. Eliza traced lazy patterns along Finn's chest, her cheek against the steady thrum of his heartbeat. His arm anchored her close, the weight of it heavy and comforting, like he had no intention of ever letting go.

"Promise me," she murmured, eyelids heavy.
"Promise you what?" he asked, brushing her hair back from her face.
"That we won't lose this. That no matter how crazy everything gets, we'll find our way back here. Back to us."

He kissed her temple, holding her tighter. "Promise. Always."

And for the first time in weeks, sleep came easy for both of them.

But promises, they would soon learn, are harder to keep when the world pushes back.

Chapter Twenty-Three

Friction

The glow of starting at UT had begun to wear off as late November settled over Austin, the air carried a different edge. It wasn't cold, but the heat had burned off. The mornings started with mist curling along the river, and evenings cooled enough that you could almost see your breath if you tried.

The days blurred into one another: practices, classes, papers, rehearsals, workouts, commutes across campus. What had once felt like freedom—like their first breath of air after years of holding it—now felt like a grind. Their little apartment, once a sanctuary, became a halfway house between obligations: a bed to collapse into, a couch to fall asleep on, a kitchen counter cluttered with half-finished meals and stacks of books.

On campus, the floodlights along the practice fields cut sharp angles against the dusk. Finn ran until his lungs burned, until the sweat stung his eyes, until the ache in his legs blurred into something close too numb. Push harder. Don't show pain. Don't draw eyes.

That was the thing: you never gave them reason. Never lifted your head too high. Never made yourself a target. Survival was motion—quiet, efficient, relentless. Keep moving, keep running, and no one could catch you long enough to see the cracks.

Watch. Listen. Stay ready.

It had worked in foster homes—beds that weren't his, kitchens that smelled like someone else's dinner, rules that shifted with every new front door. It had worked under coaches who tested him, under teachers who assumed he was trouble before he even spoke.

It was working now. Mostly. It was the only way he knew to get through the building pressure.

****

Eliza barely saw Finn except when he stumbled in late at night, still carrying the smell of grass and sweat, his shoulders slumped with exhaustion.

She felt the shift too, though hers came in quieter ways. She had her own deadlines, her own stack of novels and draft outlines, her own calendar full of "due by midnight" reminders. Her days bled with readings, essays, highlighted margins that felt like they were swallowing hours she wanted to spend anywhere else.

Sometimes she sang—softly, late at night when Finn's even breathing meant he was already asleep. She'd scribble lines into her notebook with the lamp tilted low, words that came out darker than she expected.

That week, between lectures on Milton and long shifts in the library, she wrote:

You don't look back when you're running.
But what happens when the road ends?
If I'm the one standing still, do you see me?

She didn't show Finn. Not yet. Lately, it felt like he had enough weight pressing on him.

It wasn't that they didn't love each other. They did. Deeply and in her heart eternally. There was no one else but Finn. She knew he felt the same for her.

Responsibilities were getting in the way, creating distance between them making her heart ache. It was just that love had to fight harder now — against fatigue, against schedules, against the press of the world outside their cocoon.

****

The weight room smelled like rubber mats and chalk, like sweat steeped into the metal of the racks. Music thudded from the speakers, but Finn tuned it out, body moving through sets on autopilot.

"Billings' riding you hard," one teammate muttered between reps, wiping his forehead with his sleeve. "Said you're raw."

Raw. Like undercooked meat. Like something that could sicken you if it wasn't done right.

Finn racked the bar, jaw tight. Didn't respond. Didn't look up. Eyes forward, breath steady. Let them talk. That was safer.

Another voice chimed in, low but not low enough: "Not sure he's starter material anyway. Big frame, yeah, but footwork's sloppy."

Heat crawled up Finn's neck, but his face didn't move. No flinch. No reaction. Just silence.

He knew how to wear silence like armor. Learned it years ago when foster brothers picked fights just to see if they could break him. Learned it when new caseworkers looked at him like another file in a stack. You kept still, kept watch, and waited for the storm to pass.

Head down. Don't react. Stay ready.

But inside, the words cut.

****

Eliza was waiting when he got back, sprawled sideways on their couch with a book balanced on her stomach. She looked up, smiled, but her eyes lingered on the bruise shading purple along his forearm.

The door slammed behind him.

Finn came in, sweat-soaked and scowling, his duffel bag hitting the floor with a thud.

"How bad was it today?" she asked softly knowing by the expression on his face that it hadn't been good..

He shrugged, dropping his duffel. "Same."

"You barely touched dinner last night."

"I ate at the dining hall."

It was a lie. He hadn't. But lies were sometimes easier than explaining the truth, easier than letting her see how much he was fraying. He needed to be strong for both of them.

She glanced up from her computer. Distractedly saying, "You can talk to me, you know."

He kissed the top of her head, already moving toward the shower. "I know."

"Coach Billings changed the whole lineup," he said, his voice rough, like he hadn't spoken all day. "I've been killing myself out there and I'm not even starting this weekend. Again."

Eliza blinked up from her screen, her mind still halfway in her paper. "That sucks. I'm sorry, Finn, but I really need to finish this paper— It's due tomorrow."

"Yeah. No, I get it." His jaw flexed, sharp in the shadows. He shoved his hands into his hair, then headed straight for the shower.

The bathroom door shut behind him.

Eliza stared at the empty space he'd left, the cursor blinking on her screen like an accusation. That wasn't like him. Finn was many things—loud, protective, stubborn—but he wasn't dismissive. Not with her.

Later, he climbed into bed without a word. The mattress dipped, the sheets rustled, and that was all. He didn't pull her close like he usually did. Didn't press his face into her hair. He lay flat, stiff, staring at the ceiling.

Realizing that she'd been dismissive too, Eliza rolled toward him, the silence heavy. "I'm sorry for not talking with you earlier. But I was in the flow and the paper's due tomorrow. Finn?"

Nothing. Not even the twitch of acknowledgment. Just the sound of his steady breathing letting her know that he'd already fallen asleep.

She sighed and lay back, staring into the dark. Maybe this was what change felt like. Not some loud fight, not some dramatic break, but a series of small silences that slipped between them unnoticed, until one day they woke up and realized they were standing on opposite sides of something they hadn't seen forming.

What Finn didn't say: Talking never kept you safe. Talking gave people things to use against you. Better to stay quiet, carry the weight yourself.

Eliza sat still long after the bathroom door shut, the sound of water rushing between them. Her notebook was on the table. She pulled it closer, scrawled in sharp pencil strokes:

Even walls crack when silence is too heavy.

The next day, they found each other in passing. Finn had twenty minutes between film review and lifting; Eliza had just left her poetry seminar.

They walked together across the quad, her hand tucked in his, his grip firmer than usual, like he was anchoring himself more than her.

"You look tired," she said gently.

"I'm fine."

"Finn—"

He stopped, looked at her. Eyes shadowed, jaw tight. "Really. I'm fine."

She nodded, though she didn't believe it. And when he jogged away toward the weight room, she opened her notebook again, the words tumbling before she could stop them:

If fine is the mask you wear, who will hold your face when it cracks?

That night, he came in late. Again. Eliza was half-asleep on the couch, laptop open but forgotten. She blinked awake when the door shut, heart aching at the slump of his shoulders.

"Hey," she whispered.

"Hey," he muttered, dropping onto the couch beside her.

For a moment, she thought he might lean into her, let the walls down. But instead, he grabbed the remote, flicked on the TV, volume low.

The glow lit his face in harsh blue. His jaw worked. His eyes stayed on the screen.

Eliza shut her laptop quietly, slid closer until her thigh pressed against his. "Want to talk?"

He shook his head once. "Nothing to say."

And that was it.

She leaned back, silence stretching between them. Her pen itched for her notebook, for words to fill the gap. Later, when he finally fell asleep on the couch, she wrote:

Even anchors drift.
Even stars flicker.
Even love bends under silence.

The next morning, Finn woke with the stiffness of bad sleep and the sound of Coach Billings' voice echoing from yesterday.

Too raw. Too inconsistent.

Inconsistency got you moved. Got you traded. Got you forgotten. He knew that rhythm: homes you didn't last in, people who didn't keep you.

You stayed quiet, stayed sharp, or you ended up back on the curb with a trash bag full of your things.

So he dressed fast. Packed his duffel. Left Eliza still curled in bed.

As the door closed, he thought: *Don't linger. Don't get soft. Always ready to run.*

But for the first time in years, the thought didn't feel like armor. It felt like loss.

Eliza woke to the click of the lock, the hollow quiet after he left.

Her notebook lay open on the table where she'd forgotten to close it, last night's scrawl staring back. She traced the words with her fingertip, throat tightening.

Then, slowly, she added one more line beneath the rest:

But if you're running, and I'm standing still—
who will teach us how to stay?

Finn wasn't himself. He was still Finn, still the boy who carried her groceries in one arm and her entire heart in the other—but stress gnawed at him. Practices left him limping, bruises darkening along his ribs and shoulders. His eyes looked sunken, ringed with exhaustion. His temper snapped quicker now, little edges that hadn't been there before. The pressure to keep up was overwhelming him.

Eliza noticed.

She noticed when he stared at his textbooks and didn't turn the page for ten minutes. She noticed when his leg bounced under the table, when his pen hovered uselessly over a blank notebook. She noticed when he'd run a hand through his hair for the fifteenth time in an hour, muttering under his breath.

She noticed because she was doing it too.

Her professors didn't care about her late nights, about her ., about the fact that her boyfriend was drowning in two-a-days and film review. All they cared about were word counts, citations, and grades. She pushed herself until her vision blurred and still felt like she was falling behind.

They both were. It showed.

****

One Friday night, Finn came home so late she'd already given up waiting and crawled into bed. She woke when the mattress dipped, blinking groggily at the clock: 2:14 a.m.

Finn sat on the edge, elbows on his knees, still in his practice gear. His head hung low, shoulders heaving with exhaustion.

"Finn?" she whispered.

He didn't answer at first. Then he muttered, "I don't know if I can keep up."

The words sliced through her sleep-heavy fog. She sat up, reaching for him. "With football?"

"With everything." His voice cracked. "School. Practice. Coach Billing is breathing down my neck. And you—"

He stopped himself, shaking his head.

Her throat tightened. "And me?"

He dragged a hand down his face. "No, not like that. You're the only thing that makes this worth it. But I feel like I'm failing everywhere else. And if

I keep messing up, if I lose my spot on the team…" His voice dropped to a rasp. "What if I lose you too?"

The words rooted her in place. She wanted to tell him no, never, not possible. But she also felt the distance creeping in, the silences that scared her.

She slid closer, wrapping her arms around his waist, pressing her face to his back. "You're not going to lose me. You couldn't if you tried."

He covered her hands with his, holding tight. But the tension in him didn't fade completely.

****

The weekend passed in fragments.

They tried to find time together—coffee runs between classes, brushing teeth side by side, stolen kisses when one of them was heading out the door. But even their affection felt rushed, squeezed into the margins of their lives.

One evening, she tried to pull him toward the couch, craving the closeness they hadn't had in days. He kissed her, but there was an edge of distraction in it, his mind clearly elsewhere.

When she whispered, "Stay," he sighed and muttered something about film study.

She let him go, her eyes glossy, curling into the corner of the couch with her books.

The silence stretched again.

Monday morning, Eliza sat in the back row of her literature lecture, trying to focus on Milton while her pen hovered above her notebook. Her professor's voice droned on about epic structure, but her brain refused to hold onto it. Instead, she scribbled a phrase in the margin:

What if the epic is just survival?

She thought of Finn's bruised shoulders. The way he couldn't meet her eyes sometimes. The way she had stopped singing in the apartment because she didn't want to distract him.

Janine, the girl next to her nudged her elbow. "You okay? You look wiped."

Eliza forced a smile. "Just a long week."

As if there were any other kind.

By the end of the week, Eliza realized something: they hadn't laughed together in days.

Not really. Not the kind of laugh that left her gasping, pressed against his chest. Their conversations had turned into logistics—what time are you home, do you need groceries, did you finish that assignment. They hadn't made love all week.

Love was still there. Fierce, unquestionable. But it was buried under the mountain that comprised everything else.

And that terrified her.

That night, after Finn had passed out almost instantly on the bed, Eliza lay awake beside him. The glow of her laptop screen lit her notebook, where the new verse stared back at her.

Even stars flicker. Even anchors drift.

She closed her eyes, the words echoing in her head. She didn't want to drift. Not from him. Not now, not ever.

But for the first time since they'd started, she wasn't sure wanting was enough.

The words startled her with their ache. She wasn't sure if she'd ever sing them out loud. Maybe they were just for her, a pressure valve she needed to release.

She tapped her pencil against the desk, staring at the page until the library clock chimed the hour. Then she closed the notebook quickly, shoving it under her laptop before heading to class.

Because lately, it felt like they were both being pulled under.

The next afternoon, she pulled out her lyric notebook between classes and let her pen move without thinking. The chorus was still the same—the one she had written months ago, when everything with Finn felt endless and bright—but the new verse bled different.

In the overwhelming night, stargazing were is the light?

The words startled her with their ache. She wasn't sure if she'd ever sing them out loud. Maybe they were just for her, a pressure valve she needed to release.

She tapped her pencil against the desk, staring at the page until the library clock chimed the hour. Then she closed the notebook quickly, shoving it under her laptop before heading to class.

Because lately, it felt like they were both being pulled under.

Flipping the page her eyes lit, knowing instinctively what she needed to write. Needed to say.

You left the light on, but you didn't stay
Said you were tired, but you drifted away
Into a night I wasn't part of
Into a version I couldn't trust

You say you were lost, that you couldn't see
But I was right there—how did you forget me?
I gave you the map, the words, the flame
Now I'm here asking if you'd do it again

Chapter Twenty-Four

Boiling Over

The apartment was too small for silence, but somehow they managed to make it stretch wall to wall.

Their apartment walls felt closer, thinner. The nights dragged heavy with exhaustion, and the mornings started too soon. What had once felt like an adventure—their new life, their chance to claim something for themselves—had begun to taste like iron in the mouth.

The silence between them wasn't comfortable anymore. It pressed, sharp at the edges, a reminder of how far away they could feel even when they were sitting side by side.

The feeling and pressure of words unsaid lay between them.

Eliza sat curled on the couch, her laptop open but her essay forgotten. The cursor blinked like it was mocking her, steady and indifferent, while Finn paced between the kitchen and the bedroom, his duffel still slung over one shoulder. His body carried the sharp edges of practice—the sour tang of sweat, the stiffness in his walk, the mottled bruise rising dark along his collarbone.

"You're bleeding through your shirt," she said, trying to keep her voice calm.

Finn glanced down, grunted, and yanked the fabric away from the scrape on his shoulder. "It's nothing."

"It's not nothing. You've been coming home with new bruises every day this week. Coach Billings is pushing you too hard."

He let out a laugh—sharp, without humor. "That's football, Eliza. You think anyone else is taking it easy out there?"

"That's not what I meant," she said quickly. "I mean, I see what it's doing to you. You come home and you don't even—"

"What?" His voice cut across hers, louder than the room deserved. "I don't what? Sit around and complain? Cry on your shoulder? That's not how this works."

Her chest tightened. "That's not fair."

He dropped his bag with a thud. The sound echoed. "You want fair? Coach tells me I'm inconsistent, teammates mutter that I don't belong, and if I don't prove myself, I'm out. Out of the lineup, out of this shot, out of all of it. If I can't keep my grades up, I'll lose my scholarship. I can't afford to slow down, Eliza. Not even for a second."

The words landed heavy, harsher than he meant. But he didn't take them back.

She closed her laptop slowly, staring at the faint reflection of his silhouette in the dark screen. "And where do I fit in that picture?" she asked softly.

For a moment, his jaw flexed, muscle ticking under his skin. He didn't answer.

That hurt worse than if he had.

"Finn," she tried again, voice rising with desperation. "I know the pressure you're under. I do. But I can't be standing here invisible, waiting for scraps of you between practices. I'm not asking for hours you don't have—I'm asking for *you*, for five minutes when I'm not competing with the weight of the world on your shoulders."

His shoulders sagged, but instead of giving in, he turned away, bracing his hands on the back of the kitchen chair. "I can't—" His breath hitched, ragged. "I can't give you more right now. If I let go for even a second, it all falls apart."

The quiet stretched, thick and brittle.

Finally, Eliza whispered, "Then maybe it's not just football you're running from."

The words struck him like a slap. His eyes snapped to hers, hard, wounded, unyielding. "Don't."

"Don't what?" She sat forward, her pulse loud in her ears. "Don't notice? Don't name it? Finn, I know what it looks like when you shut down. I know where that silence comes from. But I'm not your foster brothers or your caseworkers. I'm not going to use your words against you."

His mouth opened like he might fight back, but nothing came out. Instead, he shoved a hand through his hair, grabbed his bag again, and headed for the door.

"Where are you going?"

"Out." His voice was flat, clipped.

And then he was gone, the slam of the door shaking the frame.

Eliza sat frozen on the couch, her heart pounding, the cursor still blinking on the abandoned screen. She reached for her notebook instead, the one with edges frayed from too many nights of late scribbles. Her hand shook as she wrote, the pencil digging hard enough to nearly tear the page:

Even stars flicker. Even anchors drift.
And shadows swallow what the light forgets.

She stared at the words until they blurred, her throat aching. Then she shut the notebook fast, pressing her palm flat against the cover like she could pin the ache down. Tears rolled down her cheeks in silent testament to the distance growing between them. The wall Finn seemed to be building daily.

But the apartment was still empty, still ringing with the sound of the door.

****

Finn sat on the wooden bench in the locker room, shoulders hunched forward, his jersey clinging damp against his skin. The chatter of his teammates echoed—banter, laughter, shouts across the space. He didn't join in.

He knew how to sit still, how to make himself invisible in plain sight. It was an old skill, older than football. Watch. Listen. Stay ready.

Finn stretched tape across his wrists, his reflection caught in the cracked metal of his locker door. The hum of voices carried—half-jokes, half-critiques that weren't aimed at him but weren't not about him either.

"Billings's got him running like crazy," someone muttered. "Big guy like that should own the line, but he's a step slow."

Finn pulled the tape tighter.

"Bet he's too distracted," another said. "Heard his girl's in some artsy program. Probably spending all night writing poems about feelings instead of letting him sleep."

Laughter. Quick, sharp.

He said nothing. Didn't move. Didn't blink. Let the words hit and slide.

That was survival. Don't react. Don't rise. Keep your head down and the fire burns itself out.

Except this time it didn't. The words followed him onto the field, into drills, into the weight of every sprint until his chest ached.

A couple of players walked past, talking loud enough to hear:

"Billings keeps grinding Callahan, huh?"
"Yeah, but the kid's got grit. You can't teach that."

Finn stared at the floor, jaw tight. Grit. Raw. Project. He knew the words they used about him. None of them meant safe. None of them meant permanent.

Then a shadow fell over him. He looked up.

Coach Billings stood there, arms crossed. "Callahan. Office."

The room quieted around them.

The fight came that Thursday.

Finn came home past midnight again, the smell of turf and sweat clinging to him. Eliza was waiting, lights low, a half-eaten bowl of pasta on the counter.

"You missed dinner again," she said quietly.

"Couldn't leave."

"You could've texted."

His jaw flexed. "I didn't think I had to check in every hour."

Her throat tightened. "It's not about checking in. It's about letting me know you're alive. Do you even realize how much I worry when you walk through that door looking like you've been hit by a truck?"

"I'm handling it."

"No, you're shutting me out." Her voice rose, shaky. "You think I don't notice? You come home with bruises, you barely sleep, and when I ask, you act like I'm the enemy for caring. You barely touch me."

"I miss you Finn. I miss us."

Finn's fists clenched at his sides. "I don't need another person telling me I'm not enough."

"That's not what I'm saying—"

"Yes, it is. Coach says it. Teammates say it. And now you."

Her eyes stung. "Finn, I love you. But I can't love a wall. I can't keep reaching for you when you won't reach back. Why are you shutting me out? You are my other half and I just want to be there for you and I want you to be there for me."

The words hung in the air, sharp and painful.

For a long moment, he said nothing. Just stood there, breathing hard, his silence thicker than any fight. He had retreated into himself behind some protective wall that she couldn't seem to penetrate.

Finally he muttered, "I can't do this right now," and walked straight into the bedroom, shutting the door.

****

Alone in the living room, sleep was elusive. So, Eliza grabbed her notebook like it was the only thing keeping her from shattering. Her pencil dug hard into the page:

Even walls fall if no one's holding them up.
Even love can break if silence is louder than truth.

When love is not enough. When I'm not enough

Her hand shook as she wrote. For the first time, her lyrics scared her.

She picked up her guitar and played a few cords—The a new melody she was working on. Her ache and vulnerability vibrating in each note.

On the other side of the bedroom door, Finn sat on the edge of the bed, elbows on his knees, chest heaving.

Eliza's sweet, lilting voice and the haunting melody she played broke his heart open.

He wanted to go back out there. To tell her he didn't mean it, that she wasn't the enemy, that she was the only reason he kept breathing through the pressure. How much she meant to him.

But the words stuck. It was like someone was sitting on his chest.

Talking had never saved him. Silence had. Silence was control. Silence was survival.

Only now, for the first time, he wondered if silence might cost him the one thing he couldn't bear to lose. He couldn't lose Eliza. He just didn't know how to keep her. To keep them.

He was trying his best, doing all of this for them. For their future. wasn't he? He had to prove that he was worth something. Worth her.

The next morning, Eliza's side of the bed was cold.

He found her at the kitchen table, notebook open, mug of coffee untouched. She hadn't made him his favorite morning cup of Keurig Death Wish dark roast coffee like she had every morning. She also didn't look up when he stepped in.

"Eliza," he said, voice husky, low.

She kept writing, pencil scratching furiously.

"Eliza."

Finally, she looked up. Her violet eyes were red-rimmed but steady. "If you keep locking me out, there won't be anything left to lock."

He swallowed hard, throat burning. The mantra hummed in the back of his skull—*don't speak, don't show, stay ready*—but it warred with something louder now. Something that sounded like her voice, her laugh, her love.

He sat down across from her, the silence stretching between them like a fault line.

"I don't know how to do this," he admitted. "Not with you. Not when it matters."

Her pencil stilled. For the first time in days, hope flickered across her face.

"Then learn," she whispered. "With me."

****

Billings' office smelled like leather and old coffee. The blinds were half-closed, stripes of sunlight cutting across the cluttered desk.

"Sit," the coach said.

Finn obeyed, muscles tense, bracing for another lecture about footwork, about consistency, about how close he was to losing everything he'd been clawing toward.

But Billings surprised him.

"You've been working your ass off," the coach said bluntly. "I've noticed. The staff has noticed. And with Torres out—" He leaned forward, voice steady. "You're starting this weekend."

Finn's heart stuttered.

"Coach—"

Billings held up a hand. "Don't waste time acting shocked. You've earned this. You're raw, yeah. But you've got the work ethic. You've got the hunger. And now, you've got the shot. Don't waste it."

For a moment, Finn couldn't breathe. He managed a nod, quick and sharp. "Yes, sir."

Billings' gaze softened just a fraction. "Make me proud, Callahan."

Later that day, Eliza copied the verse from her notebook into the margins of her lit binder, as if keeping the words close would remind her not to give up:

Even walls fall. Even love bends.
But if we both reach—maybe it doesn't break.

And Finn, alone in the locker room, stared at the taped mantra still scrawled on the inside of his locker—watch, listen, stay ready—and for the first time, the words felt hollow.

He touched them once, then closed the door, the sound echoing like a vow he wasn't sure he believed in anymore.

Game day. The stadium lights blazed against the night sky, brighter than anything Finn had ever stood under. The noise pressed against his chest, a thousand voices layering into a storm that made the ground shake.

"CALL-A-HAN! CALL-A-HAN!"

Every muscle in his body thrummed, sharp with adrenaline. The mantra beat in his head—watch, listen, stay ready—but for once, he wasn't invisible. He was the one the crowd was watching.

And he delivered.

A sack in the second quarter. A fumble recovery in the third. A fourth-quarter stop that made the stadium sound like it might crack open. His teammates mobbed him, helmets crashing, bodies slamming into him in celebration. Under the lights, Finn felt unstoppable.

For the first time in his life, he wasn't running from silence. He was running into sound—into a roar that wanted him, claimed him, lifted him.

****

By the time he stumbled into the locker room postgame, his body ached, his ribs throbbed, but none of it mattered. His name was already trending on the school's sports page. Students were already shouting for him outside the tunnel.

"Golden boy," Kai crowed, slapping his back. "That's you now."

Finn grinned, wild and breathless. For once, the weight in his chest felt lighter.

But when he got back to the apartment, the noise still in his veins, Eliza was waiting.

Her face lit when she saw him—then faltered when she realized the glow in his eyes wasn't for her.

He kissed her quickly, already pulling out his phone to replay the highlight reel. "Did you see that stop in the fourth? They're calling it the play of the game."

"I saw." Her voice was soft. Too soft.

But he didn't notice. Not fully. The noise was too loud in his head, drowning her out.

That night, when he finally collapsed into bed, Eliza lay awake beside him, notebook open in the dim glow of her lamp. Her newest lines stared back:

If the crowd holds you,
will you still remember the quiet?
If you're theirs,
do I still belong to you?

She shut the notebook quickly, before the ache in her chest spilled over. She was happy for him but she needed to be seen. She felt him pulling away from her. From them and she couldn't seem to reach him.

Finn's breathing evened out beside her, but even in sleep, his shoulders twitched, like he was still out there under the lights.

And she realized, after he went to sleep without even kissing her goodnight, that the silence between them wasn't just silence anymore. It was distance.

A slow tear found it's way down her face.

Chapter Twenty-Five

The Crowd and the Quiet

The fight was still in Eliza's chest, a sharp-edged thing she carried like glass in her pocket. Every step, every breath, every thought seemed to brush against it.

She hadn't seen Finn all morning. He'd left before she woke, his bag gone from the chair, the faint smell of his body wash lingering in the bathroom. He hadn't left a note.

For Finn. The noise didn't stop.

That was the thing he hadn't expected—how the roar of the crowd followed him long after the game ended. Into the locker room. Onto campus. Into their apartment. Even into his sleep.

It was easier to lose himself in it than to sit in the silence Eliza had left behind after their fight. Easier to let the cheers drown out the questions he didn't know how to answer.

Because for the first time in his life, he wasn't the kid holding back words to stay safe. He was the name on everyone's lips. The golden boy.

And the louder it got, the less he knew how to hear her.

****

For Finn the silence in the apartment still rang in his head the next morning. It followed him down the halls, into the locker room, even onto the bus that carried the team to the stadium. He could still see Eliza's face, hear the way her voice had cracked when she asked where she fit in his stopwatch.

He didn't have an answer. And he couldn't sit in that silence any longer. Suddenly, the realization that he hadn't even kissed Eliza goodnight went through his head making his heart hurt, but the feeling was quickly drowned out by the light and sound coming at him as he went through the tunnel onto the field.

So when the tunnel opened and the roar of the crowd hit him, he let it flood his chest. Let it drown out the memory of slammed doors and words he wished he hadn't thrown.

Here, under the lights, there was no silence. Only noise—glorious, deafening noise.

"CALL-A-HAN! CALL-A-HAN!"

The stadium thundered his name, and for once, he didn't have to hold still. Didn't have to bite his tongue. Taking his stress out on the field. He could hit, run, shout, and the world shouted back his worth.

For the first time in days, maybe weeks, Finn felt like he could breathe.

Finn's name continued to spill from the speakers. From the crowd. From everywhere.

"CALL-A-HAN! CALL-A-HAN!"

Eliza stood in the bleachers hours later, surrounded by students in burnt orange, the metal beneath her sneakers rattling with every stomp. The stadium thrummed—bass-heavy music pounding, voices layering into a storm.

Her throat was already raw from shouting, but she couldn't stop. Her palms were numb from clapping, but she kept slamming them together. Because he was out there. Because he'd finally gotten to start.

Not just start—dominate.

A sack in the second quarter. A fumble recovery in the third. A fourth-quarter stop that made the whole stadium sound like it might crack open. Under the lights, Finn looked like he belonged. Like he'd been waiting his whole life for this stage.

Eliza's chest was a mix of pride and ache. He was dazzling, magnetic. Everyone could see it. But as the clock wound down, and the cheers thundered, she realized she didn't know how to reach him from here.

When the final whistle blew, the field exploded. Players stormed, helmets in the air, bodies colliding in victory. Cameras swarmed. Fans leaned over the railings. The coach Billings slapped Finn's back so hard it echoed louder than the cheering.

Eliza stayed tucked off to the side with Kai and Dillon, her voice gone, her hands trembling from the cold air and adrenaline.

Kai nudged her. "Get used to it. Once the hype starts, it doesn't let up."

She tried to smile. "Guess not."

Her eyes tracked Finn across the chaos. For one second, he caught her gaze. His grin split wide, real, pure, the kind that used to be hers alone.

And then another player yanked his jersey, pulling him back into the swarm. The moment slipped.

The apartment wasn't quiet that night.

It was loud with people. Just like it had been the night he broke through and saved the game before.

Finn had invited the team back to the apartment along with a bunch of other students. But when Kai showed up with half the defensive line, plus some girls Eliza didn't know, plus Dillon the popular defensive lineman who immediately turned their couch into a throne, it stopped feeling small.

Someone had stopped on the way to get a ton of beer and chips.

The air smelled like beer, sweat and cologne, chips crushed into the rug already. Music bumped from someone's phone, and laughter spilled out louder than the Spotify playlist.

Eliza tried. She really did. She poured drinks. Smiled when people introduced themselves. Pretended not to notice when a girl in a too-tight pink tank top leaned across Finn to grab a drink, her arm brushing his chest like it was a casual accident.

Thank God Sophia came. They retreated to the kitchen, sipping Diet Coke out of ubiquitous red solo cups, watching the chaos from a safe distance.

"He deserves it," Sophia said, nodding toward the living room where Finn was mid-story, teammates hanging on his every word. "But damn, it's a lot."

Eliza traced condensation on her mug. "I'm happy for him. I am. I just…" She hesitated. "I feel like I'm watching him through a window. Like I'm outside, looking in."

It was his night but her chest still felt tight. Finn had hardly spoken to here. Everyone else vied for his attention.

Finn didn't get her a drink during the evening but Dillon did. He'd noticed Finn's preoccupation with everyone else and saw how sad Eliza looked while everyone else was celebrating. He especially noticed one of the cheerleaders, Ava, getting close to Finn and touching his arm as she spoke to him.

Dillon

While Dillon was a known *"player,"* for some reason he felt differently about Eliza and it pissed him off to see Finn ignoring her.

Dillon was attracted to her strength, talent, and stunning beauty, but it was her kind, loving heart and the hint of vulnerability. It made him feel protective and reminded him vaguely of someone else. Couldn't quite place who. He had noticed that Eliza hadn't been hanging around the team much. He knew that she was really busy, but if he were Finn that shit wouldn't stand. He'd move heaven and earth to be with Eliza. Though he could never tell her.

By midnight, the apartment had thinned. Empty beer cans and solo cups dotted the counter, the couch pillows were on the floor, and someone's hoodie was abandoned on a chair and strangely someone's show was left in the bathroom.

Eliza

Eliza sat on the edge of the bed, scrolling through photos from the game. Half of them were Finn—his arms raised, his helmet off, his grin wide. Not a single one included her.

When the door finally opened, he came in still buzzing, still glowing. His hair damp from a shower, his skin smelling of cologne layered over sweat, his eyes lit like he couldn't shut off the stadium's lights inside him.

"You see the school's sports account?" he asked, already pulling his phone from his pocket. "They posted the highlight reel. I'm in, like, every other frame. It better than the game that I hadn't started in, you know when I got a last minute touchdown."

"I saw. I'm so happy for you." Her voice was soft. Too soft for the space between them.

He leaned down, tried to kiss her. She turned slightly. His lips landed on her cheek instead of her mouth.

He pulled back, confusion shadowing his face. "What's wrong?"

She set her phone down, staring at her hands. "I don't know. You were incredible tonight. But I kind of felt like I wasn't even there. Like you didn't include me. You shined your light on everyone but me."

The words hung heavy.

His grin faltered, the glow dimming. "Eliza..."

"I get that people want your attention now. I'm not mad about that. I just —" She swallowed hard. "When we got home, I thought maybe we'd have a minute. Just us. Especially after how you left things. But you barely looked at me until now. Didn't even notice me. Dillon got me drinks during the night. Dillon for God's sake. The biggest *"player"* and by that I mean *"Manwhore"* on the team noticed me more than the love of my life did. You are crushing me with your negligence. Your thoughtlessness."

He sat beside her, the mattress dipping under his weight. His knee brushed hers. The air shifted.

"You're right," he said finally, his voice lower, steadier. "I let it go to my head. I've never had this kind of attention before. But that's not an excuse."

She forced herself to meet his eyes. Her eyes filling with tears. "I don't need to be part of the spotlight, Finn. I just need to know I'm not getting lost in your shadow. That you still see me and care if I'm there with you or not. You're making me feel less important than the people around you."

Something broke in his expression, softer than regret, heavier than guilt. He reached for her hands, holding them gently like they were fragile glass.

"You're not," he said. His thumbs brushed her knuckles. "You're the reason I'm even standing in that light."

Her throat closed, but she leaned into his shoulder anyway.

"Then don't forget that," she whispered, "when they start shouting your name again."

"I won't." His lips pressed to her hair. "You're still my North Star. My sweet Songbird."

And he meant it.

Even when the cheers got louder, when the spotlight burned brighter, Finn started listening differently. Listening for her voice in the crowd. Because it was the only one that ever really mattered. That were his thoughts until the tidal wave of success overtook them.

And he was lost to the crowd again. Lulled into a sense of complacency by the knowledge that Eliza was his. That and the assumption that she always would be. He could protect himself and still have Eliza.

Chapter Twenty-Six

The Fracture Spreads

The apartment was unusually quiet the next morning, but it wasn't peace. It was the kind of quiet that hummed, too sharp to be comfortable.

Eliza sat at the kitchen table, laptop open, books spread around her in a half-circle. She twirled her pen between her fingers, tapping it against her notebook without realizing. Her second large, hot lavender latte nearby. Words blurred on the page. A lyric had been haunting her since last night —*shadows swallow the brightest flame*—but she shoved it aside and tried to force herself back into her sociology essay.

Finn was on the couch, shoulders hunched, remote in hand as film played on the TV. Replays of the game. He'd paused it, rewound it, slowed clips frame by frame, watching his stance, the angle of his tackle.

He wasn't really there with her, and she wasn't really with him. Same space. Different planets.

"Coffee?" she asked finally, her voice too bright.

He blinked, not looking away from the screen. "Uh, yeah. Thanks."

She poured it into his mug, set it beside him. He didn't touch it.

Her chest pinched. He hadn't even looked her way. He hadn't touched her at all the morning.

She wanted to ask how he was feeling after the game, how his body was holding up, if he'd slept at all. She wanted to tell him she still heard the crowd chanting his name when she closed her eyes. But the words jammed in her throat, caught behind the memory of how small she'd felt at the party, how invisible.

Instead, she said nothing.

Instead, he watched more film.

By late afternoon, Finn was at practice again, buried in drills and playbooks, sweating through the exhaustion he never admitted out loud. Coach Billings barked. Teammates laughed. And every time someone clapped him on the back or called him "highlight reel," something inside him swelled.

It was dangerous, the way the noise fed him. Like oxygen. Like he needed it.

But even as he joked with Kai or trash-talked West, his mind flashed to Eliza. To the way her beautiful face had tightened when he walked past her in the kitchen this morning, carrying his bag without even brushing her shoulder. He realized that he hadn't even kissed her goodbye this morning.

He told himself he'd make it up to her tonight. Maybe dinner out, maybe just a quiet movie on the couch, just them. Something simple. Something grounding.

Except when practice ended a little earlier than usual, Kai slapped his helmet and said, "Bar run tonight. You in?"

Finn hesitated. The image of Eliza waiting flashed hot. But the pull of the guys was strong—stronger than he wanted to admit. He wanted to be part of them. It was easier to hang with them. Eliza was upset with him and needed to study anyway. She probably wouldn't notice if he came home a little late.

"Yeah," he said finally. "I'm in."

Eliza didn't know about the bar yet. Finn hadn't texted her all day. She only knew the apartment was too empty, too dark, and she missed him.

She strummed her guitar, soft enough to keep the neighbors from complaining, words scribbled in her notebook.

I watch you from a distance,
Your name louder than mine.
You shine like a stadium,
And I fade in the sideline.

Her throat tightened as she sang it under her breath. It felt petty, maybe, but it was true.

She glanced at the clock. 9:13. No text. No call.

She tried again.

****

It was a weightless kind of Night. The bar was alive, shoulder-to-shoulder bodies, the smell of beer and fried food hanging thick in the air. Finn leaned against a high-top, bottle of Shiner in his hand, his muscles still burning from practice but his mood looser, he felt more relaxed.

Kai threw a lime wedge at him from across the booth. "Dude, you're zoning out again. You fall asleep standing?"

"Just thinking," Finn said, smirking. "You should try it sometime."

West snorted. He had a bourbon in front of him and an expression that could only be described as *grudgingly amused*. "Thinking's for the off-season."

Kai tipped back his beer, grinning. "Says the man who watches documentaries about wolves before every away game."

"Alpha recognizes alpha," West muttered.

Laughter circled the table.

Across the bar, a group of girls hovered by the jukebox. Tight jeans, crop tops, hair that sparkled under the neon. One of them—tall, tanned, eyes like honey—made a beeline for Finn.

"Hey," she said, twirling a strand of hair. "You play for UT, right?"

Finn blinked. "Uh, yeah. Backup and sometimes starting Quarterback."

She bit her lip like it was the sexiest phrase she'd ever heard. "Figured. You look... like you hit things for fun."

Kai choked on his drink. West didn't even try to hide his laugh.

"Wanna dance?" she asked, stepping closer, fingertips trailing along the sleeve of Finn's Henley. Her nails were red. Her perfume was strong.

Finn smiled politely. "Appreciate it, but I'm good."

The girl pouted, but turned with a shrug, already moving on to Dillon, their backup quarterback, who welcomed her with open arms.

Kai leaned close. "Damn, Callahan. You're stronger than most."

Finn's smile was small. "I've got someone at home. Have you seen how hot and beautiful she is?"

"Yeah you do. Why isn't she here though? Her ass sick of your BS already," Dillon said over the honey-eyed girl. Hi hands on her hips.

Ignoring Dillon, West raised his glass. "To the unicorns who say no."

The table erupted again. The night rolled on. Fries, beer, stories, laughter.

The conversation rolled on—inside jokes from practice, trash talk about the next game, Kai's epic fail trying to ask out the girl from Econ who turned out to be the professor's niece.

Several beers in, Finn finally started to let himself relax.

But Finn's eyes kept darting to the clock. Kept wondering if Eliza was still awake. If she was still writing. If she was waiting for him.

Somewhere between the third drink and the third round of fries, Finn found himself glancing at the clock. Wondering if Eliza was still hunched over her laptop at the apartment. If she'd remembered to eat. If she was listening to music or writing lyrics in the margins of her essay. If she missed him.

His phone stayed dark. No messages.

Not because anything was wrong.

Just because… she didn't know he needed to hear from her tonight.

And somehow, that hurt more than if she'd texted angry.

He pulled out his phone. No messages.

Finn didn't think to call or text her.

But the living room wasn't dark.

The lamp on the side table glowed weakly, a little pool of yellow light in the corner. Eliza was curled on the couch, guitar across her lap, a spiral notebook open beside her. Her hair was pulled into a messy knot, a pen tucked behind her ear.

Her eyes flicked up at him as he stepped inside. Relief flickered there first—the kind that made Finn's chest tighten—then faded into something heavier. Something colder.

"You didn't tell me you'd be late. I had no idea where you were." she said. Her voice wasn't sharp, but it wasn't soft either. It landed somewhere in between, weighted with all the hours she'd been waiting. Hurt underlined the tone.

Finn shut the door gently. His chest still hummed with the bar's noise, with Kai's laughter, with the way the guys had clapped his shoulders like he was one of them now. For someone who grew up without a family and nowhere to belong, it was intoxicating. But that hum started breaking apart under the steady, still silence of Eliza's gaze.

"I know," he admitted, dragging a hand through his hair. "I'm sorry. The guys wanted to go out. I didn't—" He stopped, because the excuse sounded flimsy even in his own ears. "I should've texted you."

Her mouth twitched, a ghost of a bitter smile. "You should have."

Silence stretched between them. The clock on the wall ticked too loud. Finn shifted his weight, set his keys on the counter.

He wanted to cross the room, to kiss her temple, to tell her nothing at the bar had mattered. But he could still smell the beer on his shirt, still feel the phantom press of a girl's nails on his sleeve, even though he'd said no. He hated that those ghosts came home with him.

"Eliza," he tried again, "nothing happened. I swear. It was just beers, talking. That's it."

Her eyes stayed steady on him. Not accusing. Not disbelieving. Just tired. "I didn't think something happened. That's not the point and you haven't called me *Songbird* in weeks. We haven't made love beyond a time-induced quickie."

Finn blinked. "Then what is the point? I'm sure that I have."

She shut her notebook with a snap, setting it on the coffee table. Her hands lingered on the cover, pressing hard like she needed to ground herself.

"The point is you didn't think about me at all," she said finally. "You didn't tell me you'd be late, didn't text me once. I sat here wondering if you'd walk through that door at ten, or midnight, or never."

Her voice caught on the last word, and Finn felt his stomach drop. Fear raced through him at her words.

He crossed the room in three strides, crouching in front of her. "Eliza. You know I'd always come home to you."

She looked down at him, her eyes rimmed red. "Do I? Because lately it feels like you live two lives. One with me. One with them. And I don't know which one wins."

His chest clenched. He wanted to tell her she was wrong, that she always came first. But the truth sat heavy in his throat. Because hadn't he chosen the bar over her tonight? Hadn't he stayed when he could've walked away?

"I'm trying to balance it," he said instead. "Football—it's everything right now. But you're—" He broke off, frustration spiking. "You're everything too. I just don't know how to be in both at once."

Eliza's eyes softened for half a second, but then hardened again. "That's the problem, Finn. You don't just get to split yourself in half. You don't get to choose me when it's convenient."

Her words hit like a slap, but he didn't flinch. He deserved them.

He rocked back onto his heels, running both hands over his face. "Sometimes it's easier with them," he muttered, the words spilling before he could stop them. "Easier to just… laugh, drink, forget about how much pressure I'm under. With you—" He broke off, realizing too late what he'd almost said.

Eliza's voice was sharp now, brittle. "With me, what?"

Finn's stomach twisted. "With you, I can't pretend. You see it all. The cracks. You ask questions that I don't know how to answer. The nights I can't sleep, the times I can barely drag myself out of bed. With you, I don't get to hide. I don't get to run. Staying in that honest space with you makes me uneasy. I don't know how."

Her hands curled into fists on her knees. "So what, you'd rather hide than stay with me?"

"No!" He surged to his feet, pacing toward the kitchen, then back. His hands clenched, unclenched. "God, Eliza, that's not what I mean. I'm just

—fuck—I'm tired. I'm stretched so thin I don't know who I am anymore unless I'm on that field."

Eliza stood too, her voice trembling but steady. "Then where does that leave me? Because I can't keep being the afterthought. I can't keep sitting here, waiting for the pieces of you left over when you're done with everyone else."

Her words sliced him open, because wasn't that exactly what she'd been doing? Waiting. Holding him up. Writing songs in the quiet while he drowned in noise.

"Eliza—"

But she shook her head, stepping back. "Don't."

Her eyes glistened, but she blinked hard, refusing to let the tears fall. "I love you, Finn. But love isn't enough if you don't choose me. Not just sometimes. Not just when you remember. Every day."

His throat closed. He wanted to swear he did choose her, that she was the only reason he even survived practice, survived games. But the words felt cheap now, worn thin by every missed text, every late night, every time he let the spotlight distract him.

"I don't want to lose you," he said instead, voice rough.

Her gaze faltered then, flicking over his face, his jaw, his eyes. For a moment, he saw the softness again—the girl who had pressed ice to his bruises, who had whispered lyrics into his chest at two a.m.

But she pulled back. "Then don't make me feel like I already have."

The silence after that was deafening.

Finn stood there, breath heavy, the weight and smell of the bar still clinging to his skin. Eliza sank back onto the couch, shoulders curling inward, as if she couldn't hold herself upright anymore. Tears threatened her eyes.

He wanted to reach for her. He didn't.

Because for the first time, he wasn't sure if his hand would be welcome.

It was one of his biggest mistakes.

Chapter Twenty-Seven

Out of Sync

The apartment smelled like takeout and the faint echo of absence.

Eliza sat cross-legged on the couch, her laptop balanced precariously on a pillow as she stared down the blinking cursor. Her literature essay was due by midnight—an exploration of narrative identity in *Frankenstein*—but the words wouldn't come. Her thoughts were stuck somewhere else. Somewhere noisier. Louder. Distant.

Somewhere like the bar where Finn had gone with the team.

He'd given her a quick kiss on the way out. Said something about blowing off steam. Promised he wouldn't stay long.

She hadn't gone. Not because he told her not to—he never would. But he also hadn't made a point to invite her. She'd told herself she had work. That she needed the quiet.

And she did.

But what she didn't say was that lately, even when Finn was home, it didn't feel like he was there. Not really. His body collapsed beside hers in bed, his texts got shorter, his laugh didn't land quite the same. He was slipping into a rhythm she wasn't part of anymore.

Her phone buzzed on the armrest. A message from Sophia.

Sophia: "Want to meet for a study break? Van's bribing me with mochas."

Eliza smiled faintly but typed back:
Eliza: "Can't. Paper's eating me alive."

Then, after a second thought, she opened her camera and snapped a close-up photo of her laptop screen—her essay's header visible, along with a heart doodled absentmindedly next to his name in the corner of a page.

She attached a pink heart emoji and a *Miss you* to the pic and sent it to Finn.

Nothing elaborate. Just a reminder.

I'm still here and I'm thinking of you.

Minutes passed. No response.

She tried to focus. She really did. But instead of crafting her argument on duality and monstrosity, she found her mind replaying the way Finn had looked in his UT hoodie. The way Ava, the beautiful, slutty, bitch cheerleader, had smiled at him during the last home game. Her eyes on Finn throughout the game. Catching his eye when he looked up. How her ponytail bounced when she walked past the bench. The way that she touched him when she spoke. How her Instagram had been filled with behind-the-scenes team moments Eliza never saw firsthand that always seemed to include Finn.

She blinked back to her screen, cheeks warm with irritation. She wasn't jealous, exactly. She trusted Finn... didn't she? No...she was jealous that another woman was sharing all of those experiences with him.

Still, she couldn't shake the thought: when had they stopped *seeing* each other? When had being in love become so quiet it felt like silence?

Her fingers hovered over the keyboard, and then she did something she hadn't done in a while—she opened her notebook. Not the school one. The other one.

The one for lyrics.

She scribbled a few lines, messy and fast.

I keep showing up, keep standing still
While you chase fire I can't feel
Am I too quiet now, or just too real?

She paused, hearing the apartment door click.

Finn's voice echoed faintly down the hall. "Back!"

She didn't move.

He peeked around the corner, sweaty from practice and still in his gear. "Hey, babe. That paper kicking your ass?"

She nodded, closing her notebook halfway. "A little."

"I'll shower and then help you brainstorm if you want."

"Okay."

He disappeared into the bathroom. The door clicked shut.

Eliza looked back at her phone. Her heart emoji still hadn't been opened.

She swallowed around the lump forming in her throat, stared back at the blinking cursor, and tried to push the feeling away.

She loved him.

But tonight, she felt like a ghost in her own home.

And ghosts, she was starting to realize, could haunt even while still alive.

****

Finn had always known pressure.

It came with the pads. The weight room. The expectations.

But college ball was different. Especially at UT, where the lights were always bright and someone was always watching. Coach Billings. Agents. Reporters. Scouts with clipboards and practiced poker faces.

He'd been on fire this season—starting, now leading in yards and getting whispers about third or even *second* round draft placement.

He should've been riding the high.

Instead, he felt like he was barely holding on.

Practice ran late. Film study bled into class time. And when he finally dragged himself home, he had to get the classwork done. Eliza was usually at her desk with headphones in, typing away. She'd been different since Austin City Limits. Restless in the best way. Buzzing with energy. Inspired.

He loved that for her. He just hated how far away it made her feel.

They sat on the couch one night, half-watching a documentary about classic albums. Finn stretched out, one arm draped behind her, but she wasn't leaning into him like she usually did.

"Madison wants me to submit a sample packet," Eliza said suddenly. "Lyrics, voice notes, even just snippets. She thinks one of her artists might bite."

Finn turned to her, his chest tightening with something he didn't want to name. "That's amazing, El. Really."

She nodded, but didn't smile. "I'm scared."

"Of what?"

"That if I go for this... if something actually *happens* with it... I won't have time for us. We are already stretched thin."

Finn looked down. That quiet voice in his head—the one that always said don't get comfortable, don't trust permanence—whispered: *She's already halfway gone.*

He reached for her hand. Held it tight. "We make time. We fight for it."

She looked at him then, and for a second, he saw the girl from the top of Enchanted Rock. The one who always ran toward the light, even if her past told her not to trust it.

"We just have to keep coming back," she said. "No matter what."

He nodded. "You're my north. Always."

But the fear didn't leave.

Chapter Twenty-Eight

Cracks

It started again with a missed moment.

Eliza had been thinking about him all day. Thinking about the way he kissed her neck, how he pulled her in close like he couldn't stand the space between them. She needed that tonight—needed him. Not just the kiss. The closeness. The reminder that they were still them. The passion.

So when he finally walked through the door from practice and already peeling off his shirt, she didn't wait. She walked up behind him and wrapped her arms around his waist, kissed the space between his shoulder blades.

He flinched slightly—not away, but with surprise.

"Hey," he said, voice worn thin. "Can I shower real quick? Practice was brutal."

Eliza didn't let go. "I missed you."

"I missed you too, baby." He kissed her forehead. "Just give me ten minutes, okay?"

She nodded, stepping back. But when he came out of the shower, towel-drying his hair, his eyes were already half-lidded. He dropped onto the bed and didn't pull her in like he usually did. Didn't reach for her.

By the time she came out of the bathroom, wearing one of his T-shirts and nothing else, he was already dozing.

She climbed into bed slowly, trying not to feel small. She noticed the shirt that he peeled off. It wasn't a practice shirt it was a going out shirt and the jeans looked like his nicer ones.

"What the hell?" she thought.

"Finn?"

He stirred. "Mm?"

"Never mind," she whispered. It was too late. She would ask him when he wasn't so wiped.

The next morning, her phone buzzed just after nine. Sophia.

Sophia: "Hey... have you checked Instagram yet?"

Eliza blinked at the message, her stomach already tightening. She clicked open the app.

There it was. A photo posted to the UT football team's story late last night. A group pic—guys from the team and a few cheerleaders crammed around a table at a bar. Finn was front and center, his arm slung around Kai's shoulder. Ava—the always-there cheerleader—was next to him, laughing into her drink.

The timestamp? Twenty minutes before he'd told Eliza he was too exhausted to do anything but sleep.

She didn't even know what she was feeling—betrayal? Embarrassment? Jealousy?

Probably all three.

And it got worse.

The next day, Ava posted a close-up. Her in Finn's hoodie—his hoodie, the one that she'd given him—with a playful caption: *"When you steal from the best 😘 #HookEm"*

Eliza stared at the screen, cold sinking into her stomach like a rock.

She tossed her phone onto the couch and pressed her hands to her face. It wasn't just about a hoodie. Or a party. It was the fact that he hadn't told her. That he hadn't seen what it might mean to her. Why would she be wearing his hoodie? What wasn't he telling her?

Ava was always there.

At every game—on the sidelines in uniform, her smile practiced and camera-ready. On the travel roster for away games, flashing Finn bright eyes and inside jokes. At practice, draped over water coolers or hanging around the locker room exit, waiting for "the boys." Waiting for him.

She laughed a little too loud at his dumb jokes. Asked for "help" tying her cleats even though she'd been on the squad for years. Always touched his arm when she talked. Always "accidentally" brushing up against him during group photos.

Finn thought she was just friendly. "Ava's cool," he told Kai once. "Kind of intense, but harmless."

Kai, for what it was worth, only grunted. "You might want to pay more attention to that one. She seems a little hyper focussed on you. Does Eliza know about Ava's attention? If not, you might want to warn her or it could blow up in your face."

"Eliza knows that I love her and that I'm not interested in anyone else." Finn's replied.

The hoodie situation—The day before, Ava had spilled Gatorade on her cheerleading uniform leaving the field and asked to borrow his hoodie because she was cold. She hadn't given it back to him yet and he was worried that Eliza would notice because she knew it was his favorite. He could explain it once he saw her.

Back home, Eliza was learning to ignore the sharp pinch in her chest every time she saw Ava's tagged photos online. Or when Finn texted *long day, crashing early* and she saw a picture posted an hour later—Ava leaning against a locker with Finn laughing in the background.

She tried not to jump to conclusions. She trusted Finn. She did.

But it was hard not to feel like someone had moved into the space she used to occupy.

Dillon, Kai, West and more importantly, Ava noticed.

Finn didn't seem to.

At least Sophia and Van still saw Eliza. Saw her shrinking into herself.

"You okay?" Sophia asked one afternoon as they walked out of the writing center. "You've been kinda... ghostly."

Eliza shrugged. "Just tired...the truth is that I feel really chewed up and spit out."

"You mean, tired of Finn hanging out with Sideline Barbie?" Van said.

Eliza blinked.

"Sorry," Van added. "That was brutal. But not inaccurate."

Sophia looked at her gently. "You know you can talk to us, right?"

Eliza nodded. But what could she say? *I feel like I'm being replaced. I feel like I'm watching someone else slip into the space I built with him, and I don't know if he even notices. I don't know how to fight for him or if he wants me to.*

Dr. James Landon's praise became more common as he simultaneously offered Eliza more personalized guidance in the weeks that followed. Eliza's short story had been accepted to a prestigious literary journal, and now the professor pulled her aside after nearly every seminar.

"You have something rare," he said one afternoon. His warm brown eyes focussed on her. "Real narrative instinct. We should talk about MFA programs soon. Mentorship. Maybe more."

She was thrilled, but worried. .

How can I balance school, music, and Finn? Stressed out. Eliza recalled Rhetta telling her, *"Grades'll open one door, baby girl. Music might open the one you didn't even know you wanted. Relationships will provide the juice for your stories."*

Feeling as though she was loosing herself, that night, unable to sleep, Eliza sat in the dim light of the living room, notebook open, fingers ink-smudged and shaking slightly. She started writing—not an essay or an assignment, but a song. Her voice was quiet, almost a whisper, as she worked through the chorus aloud.

"Half a Step Behind"

You said it was practice, said you'd be late
But I saw your smile in someone else's frame
Her hand on your shoulder, my hoodie on her skin—
I used to be the one you'd bring those moments in.

Now I'm half a step behind,
Falling through the space between
What we were and what we are—
You don't even see the lean.
She's got your laugh, your arm, your time…
And I'm just writing songs to remind you I'm alive.

The song poured out of her like something she'd been holding back for too long—raw, unfiltered, and so heartbreakingly honest she had to pause and breathe before continuing.

If she's the storm you chose to chase,
Then I'll be the quiet you erased.
But I won't beg, I won't plead—
I'll bleed it out in melody.

She sat back, tears blurring the lines on the page. The lyrics weren't for the world. Not yet. Maybe not ever. They were for her. And maybe, one day, for him. By November, Eliza and Finn barely saw each other unless one of them made a conscious effort to close the distance. And it wasn't Finn.

And he wasn't seeing it—wasn't seeing Ava, or how Eliza had started walking through her days like someone trying not to break. In pain from feeling the loss of him—of them.

All of Finn's energy and attention was given to football, homework, and letting off steam with friends. He didn't seem to want her anymore. He "*forgot*" to invite her out with him saying that it hadn't crossed him mind that she might want to come and hang out after a game or practice since he knew that she was "*overwhelmed with projects and papers.*"

That was true to a point. She missed him. She missed them and wanted to be with him but she was learning that he didn't. Apparently his teammates and the cheerleaders, one in particular, were his chosen. Not her. No longer her.

She felt lost and turned around as the the North Star that she had counted on had moved and she could no longer see it.

Just like the North Star note on the fridge. Faded. Adhesive no longer holding. Unseen.

She wondered if Finn ever looked at it anymore. Ever thought of her.

By December, Eliza and Finn barely saw each other unless one of them made a conscious effort to close the distance. And he still wasn't seeing it —wasn't seeing Ava, or Eliza. She felt like a ghost of herself.

A shell. He was killing her slowly.

They were just roommates. Eliza knew that their relationship, the one only a short time ago was her everything and her forever, was on life support and she couldn't figure out how to save it. Finn needed to want it too. It's hard to row a boat with only one oar and make it to your destination.

Tears blinded her as she started editing a paper for Lit.

Chapter Twenty-Nine

Blind Spots

Finn hadn't meant to drift. He really hadn't.

But everything had changed since the season started.

Practice wasn't just practice—it was a gauntlet. Every play, every hit, every second on the field was a test of whether he belonged. Coach Billings watched like hawks. Teammates circled like competitors. The pressure to perform—to *be the guy*—wasn't just unspoken. It was carved into every muscle of his body.

"You're the one to watch this season," Coach Taylor Billings had said after a particularly brutal two-a-day. "Don't lose focus now."

Focus.

He was trying. But the truth was, he'd never had this kind of attention before. Not from men like Coach Billings, who actually looked him in the eye like he mattered. Not from the press. Not from half the campus.

And certainly not from women like Ava.

Ava, who laughed at his jokes and tossed him Gatorade like it was flirtation. Ava, who called him "Number Twenty-Two" like it was an inside nickname. Ava, who was suddenly always *there*—in the background, at team dinners, even outside the locker room, like she had a sixth sense for when he'd walk out.

But she didn't mean anything by it. She was just... around. He was a football player and she was a cheerleader. They both were on the field at the same time for practice and games and hung out all together afterward. He didn't see the problem. He didn't have any interest in her but was flattered by her attention.

What he did see was the exhaustion in his own face every night. Dark circles under his eyes. The assignments he barely finished. The lectures he half-heard while texting Kai about routes and defensive shifts.

He told himself he was doing it for the future. For them. For Eliza.

But the more the season heated up, the more he convinced himself that Eliza was *fine*. That she understood. She was buried under her academic work. That they were solid enough to go for awhile without talking much, or missing a night or two together.

She was the constant, after all. His North Star.

So, he enacted a form of willful blindness on the relationship. If he didn't notice how lonely Eliza looked or how sad that he was too tired to talk or do anything else, then he could convince himself that everything was fine. Then he could justify putting all of his efforts on winning games, passing his classes, and keeping up with the demands and expectations of everyone else.

He didn't notice the way she shrank slightly when he brushed off a kiss with a tired smile. Didn't register how quiet she'd become during dinners, or how often she stared at her notebook without writing anything down.

When Ava posted a pic of the group at the bar after practice, Finn didn't even flinch. It had been nothing—a celebration after a hard week. He figured Eliza was probably asleep anyway. He didn't even think to mention it.

That's what hurt her most.

He was tired. Stretched thin. Trying to juggle everything.

But what he didn't realize—not yet—was that in all the noise of the spotlight, he'd stopped tuning into the one voice that had always mattered most.

And Eliza? She wasn't just his peace. She was more—needed more.

She was starting to wonder what it meant when peace stopped showing up.

That night, Eliza sat alone in the living room with her guitar balanced on her knee and her notebook open. The light was soft, the apartment too quiet. She'd been trying to write something else—but the melody that came out wasn't soft or romantic. It was aching. Honest.

She wrote the words in one go, like they'd already been waiting inside her:

"You Weren't There"
You said it was practice, said you'd be late
But I saw your smile in someone else's frame
Her hand on your shoulder, my hoodie on her skin—
I used to be the one you'd bring those moments in.

Now I'm half a step behind,
Falling through the space between
What we were and what we are—
You don't even see the lean.
She's got your laugh, your arm, your time…
And I'm just writing songs to remind you I'm alive.

If she's the storm you chose to chase,
Then I'll be the quiet you erased.
But I won't beg, I won't plead—
I'll bleed it out in melody.

You weren't there—but I still stood strong,
Built melodies from everything gone.
Now I'm not waiting, not asking why,
I've got my own rhythm, my own sky.
You said I was your always, but baby, fair—
I needed someone
Who'd be there.

She didn't cry. She didn't even flinch. Her heart just felt like was shriveling up more and more without his attention and love. She just played it again, softer this time. Like maybe if she played it enough, he'd hear it. Even if he never actually heard it at all. Her heart was breaking and his absence and distance made her protective walls, the ones their love had torn down, began to rebuild—stronger and higher than ever.

****

Finn hadn't planned to check his messages that night.

He was lying in bed, thumb scrolling aimlessly through TikTok reels while the faint buzz of the team group chat lit up the corner of his screen. Kai had just posted a picture of their table from the bar—another "we survived the week" celebration. He laughed quietly at the chaos in the photo. Everyone looked buzzed, loud, dumb.

Ava had tagged him in a story too. Something about "number twenty-two and tequila." He rolled his eyes. She was always doing that. It didn't mean anything.

But then he clicked back into his texts.

That's when he saw it.

A heart emoji and *Miss you*.

And a photo. A close-up of Eliza's laptop screen. Header bold at the top, "Lit 201 Essay," and just beneath it, a doodled heart next to his name. Her handwriting. Her way of saying, *I'm still here. I'm thinking of you. I want you to think of me.*

His own heart sank.

He hadn't seen the message. Hadn't even noticed the ping when it came through. The bar had been too loud. The game highlights had been playing on repeat on the TVs. And Ava—always Ava—had been beside him, pressing too close.

Finn sat up in bed, suddenly wide awake.

His stomach twisted.

He hadn't even *asked* Eliza if she wanted to come. He'd just assumed she'd be busy. Assumed she'd understand.

And now… the way she'd looked at him the other night—soft, hopeful, reaching for him—and the way he'd told her *ten minutes* and then fell asleep?

What the hell was he doing? Had he been pushing her away?

He opened her message. It had been sent a week ago.

Finn: *Hey. I just saw this. I'm sorry, baby. I should've been with you tonight. I miss you. Can we talk tomorrow at breakfast?*

He stared at the blinking cursor after sending it. It felt like spitting into a hurricane.

Across the room, the light from the kitchen spilled across the sticky note still stuck to their fridge.

North Star.

His words. From the first week they moved in. He'd written it to remind her they'd always find their way back.

When was the last time he'd even looked at it?

He stood, crossed the room, and touched the edge of the paper. It was faded now, curling at the corner.

Like everything else.

Suddenly, it hit him—not all at once, but in a slow, sinking ache in his gut.

He'd left her behind.

Not with anger—with neglect—every moment he *hadn't* reached for her. Every night he said, *I'm tired.* Every time he thought *she's fine* instead of asking, *are you okay? All of the times he spent his free time with the team instead of her. Not even inviting her to come with him.*

She had stayed soft. Steady. Present.

And he'd gone blind.

He hadn't seen the songs. The quiet heartbreak in her eyes. The way she was always trying to meet him halfway—reaching for him while he drifted further.

He sat at the table, elbows on his knees, head in his hands.

"I fucked up," he whispered to the dark. "I really fucking missed it."

And maybe—maybe—it wasn't too late to fix it.

But it wouldn't be easy.

Not now that he'd finally seen what he hadn't seen before.

Not now that he realized: she had been calling out for him in every way that mattered.

And he hadn't answered.

Chapter Thirty

After the Whistle

The bar was loud—too loud for Finn's exhausted head, but he was here anyway, half-listening to Kai argue with Dillon over who missed a block, nursing a beer someone else had put in his hand.

It had been a good game. He'd played hard, made two big tackles and nearly picked off a pass. Coach Billings clapped him on the back like a father might, and the guys had dragged him straight from the locker room to the bar down the street. The celebration was already well underway.

Finn laughed at something Dillon said, though he hadn't really heard the joke. The truth was, he felt good. Buzzed. Seen. Like someone who mattered. He was still pumped from the game. In all of the excitement he'd already forgotten his thoughts the night before. Later he would tell himself that it was a hit to the head during that game that caused his idiocy.

He hadn't even thought to text Eliza. Even after his epiphany the night before.

Not because he didn't care. Of course he cared. But she'd mentioned something earlier about a writing center shift or a paper. Or maybe that was last week. Either way, she was probably too swamped to come out. That's what he told himself—again. Bad habits died hard.

"Hey," Kai said, nudging him. "Where's Eliza tonight? Thought she'd for sure be here after that rough game. You know offering a little TLC."

Finn blinked. "Uh… she had work or class or something. Long day."

Kai raised an eyebrow. "Did you even ask her?"

Finn opened his mouth, then shut it. Had he? He'd sent her a thumbs-up emoji earlier when she said good luck and that she loved him. But that wasn't really a question. It wasn't even a conversation.

Dillon chimed in, "Man, she's always been cool with this kind of stuff, right? If I had a girlfriend, which I don't. Not that I'm a relationship kind of guy, but even I'm sure that she'd feel left out and probably jealous of all the attention you're getting from other women."

"Yeah," Finn said, quieter. "She gets it. She knows that she's the only one."

With a skeptical look, Kai took a sip of his beer. "Are you sure Ava knows that?"

Before Finn could say anything else, Ava appeared beside him. She placed a fresh drink in front of him with a grin. "Looked like you needed a refill, Twenty-Two."

He smiled, trying to be polite. "Thanks."

She slid onto the barstool next to him, a little too close, her arm brushing his. "Big game. You were incredible out there."

"Thanks," he repeated, though the word felt hollow now.

His eyes drifted toward the door. Toward the empty seat he hadn't saved. The space he hadn't noticed was missing until someone else pointed it out.

Eliza should've been here. He should've asked. Should've wanted her here. Should've shared the night with her.

And now, he wasn't sure if he'd forgotten… or just assumed she'd always be waiting. He felt her absence strongly at that moment.

He wondered where she was but wasn't worried. Downing the drink that Ava had given him, he would see her back at the apartment.

Finn's buzz started to dull the second Ava laughed too loud beside him.

At first, he didn't notice it—just a flicker in the back of his mind. A dissonant note under all the noise. But then Kai said something else, low and pointed:

"Bet Eliza would've wanted to be here if you'd told her it mattered."

The words didn't sound accusatory. They just hung there.

Finn chuckled, rubbing a hand over the back of his neck. "Yeah. I guess I just figured—"

Kai didn't let him finish. "That she's not part of this world? Or that she's part of it enough to be ignored?"

Finn didn't respond.

Ava leaned in again. "You okay Sugar?" She had started cheekily calling him that recently.

He forced a smile. "Yeah. Just tired."

But his gaze kept drifting—to the bar door, to the corner booth, to the stool on his right that remained empty. The one she could've filled.

Should've filled.

He remembered, just barely, the photo she sent earlier. Something about her essay. Another heart emoji *Love you*. He hadn't responded. Too busy enjoying being that man of the moment. It had been during warm-ups. He'd meant to text back. He hadn't. He'd forgotten. Again.

He shifted in his seat. Realizing on some level that he had been running away from Eliza. From them. Running scared.

He could hear her voice now—not angry, not demanding. Just soft. Disappointed. The way she said *I missed you* the other night. The way her body curved into his like she was trying to remind him who they were.

He remembered the way he said *ten minutes* on more than one occasion and then never came back.

That invisible weight pressed deeper against his chest.

Ava was saying something about tailgates and team dinners, but it was a blur now.

Finn stood abruptly. "I need to head out."

Kai gave him a slow nod. "Good call."

"Tell the guys I'll catch them later," he said, already moving toward the door.

He didn't say goodbye to Ava.

He stepped outside into the cool Austin night and breathed deep.

The street was buzzing, music from the next bar over leaking out in waves. But all he could think about was their apartment. Their kitchen. That sticky note still stuck to the fridge.

North Star.

He pulled out his phone and opened her text for the first time. It came after the game.

Are you ok Finn. I saw the hit on the field. I'm so worried about you. Please come home So I can take care of you. A scribbled heart in the corner.

And suddenly, it hit him full-force.

The only thing she'd asked of him tonight was to notice. to let her be there for him. For them.

And he hadn't.

He hadn't noticed the messages. The missed chances. The slow fading of something that had once meant everything.

He started walking faster. Home wasn't far.

But tonight, it felt like miles.

When he got in, Eliza was asleep. Her songwriting notebook open and her favorite pen.

Chapter Thirty-One

The Fall

The bar that Saturday night pulsed with noise and neon. Music throbbed underfoot. Voices overlapped—shouts, laughter, the clink of glass against glass.

Finn leaned on the edge of the booth, beer in hand, sweat at his temples. Again, he hadn't invited Eliza to come with him. She was buried under a project with Sophia and Van that she needed to get done tonight. His jaw was loose with smiles, the beer bitter and cold. His third? Fourth? He'd lost count after Kai ordered a round of celebratory shots. Someone— Dillon, maybe—had toasted to the win. To Finn. To "the future face of Texas football."

Ava had given him his last drink, which he drank quickly, anxious that Eliza might be upset that he'd come out without her again.

After that, the room spun a little, but it was a good spin. Familiar. Like floating. At first. He didn't have to think. Just be.

Eliza wasn't there. she had barely spoken to him all week and he wasn't sure how to handle it. Not knowing, he lost himself in his friends and football like he had all semester.

He should've gone home.

But Ava had pulled him into another toast. Had laughed at something he barely heard. Someone had taken a picture—he didn't even register it happening.

"Finn," she purred, sliding into the booth beside him. She was too close. Her knee brushed his thigh. Her hand landed on his chest like she belonged there. "You crushed it tonight."

He smiled, dimly. "Thanks…"

His voice dragged slightly, slow. Thick.

Ava leaned in. Her perfume was sharp. Something floral and expensive. His head was heavy.

Then her lips were on his.

And for a moment, he didn't move.

He didn't kiss her back. But he didn't pull away either—not fast enough. Not publicly enough.

When he did jerk back, blinking, the lights were too bright. His mouth tasted wrong.

"Ava…" he tried to say, but it slurred. "Don't—what are you doing? You know I'm with Eliza." In the back of his brain an alarm was blaring but he couldn't seem to figure out why exactly.

She laughed. "If you're with Eliza why isn't she here. I'm always here for you. Relax. It's just a picture. It's just fun."

Around them, a few cheers rose. The guys half-laughed, half-cheered, half-stared in confused and disgusted silence.

Dillon froze halfway to the booth, beer in hand. His eyes landed on Finn, then on Ava still clinging to his arm. His whole body tensed.

"The hell is this?" he muttered, not quite to anyone.

Kai's brows knit as he leaned across the booth. "Hey, Ava—back off."

She just grinned. "It's nothing. He's had a few. Don't act like you guys haven't seen worse."

But it didn't feel like nothing.

Not to Kai. Not to Dillon. Not to the guys who knew Eliza.

Especially not to Dillon, who stood there with his jaw tight and eyes hard, looking like he wanted to punch something—or someone.

Dillon didn't like Finn. Not really. Not the way Eliza had loved him. And maybe—maybe that was the worst part. Because now, with Finn slumped and blinking, his collar stained with lipstick, Ava's mouth on Finn's. Dillon saw it clear as day.

Finn didn't deserve her.

Not like this.

And Finn—he couldn't stand, not properly. he couldn't feel his legs. Couldn't seem to move his body. Fear flooded him. The booth tilted when he tried to get up. His heart pounded off-beat, something clenching in his chest. He kept feeling someone pressing against his mouth.

Something's wrong.

The words were clear in his mind, but they wouldn't leave his mouth.

Some guy he didn't know helped him to stumble outside without a goodbye. Ava following closely behind.

The next thing he knew. He was at his apartment. He wasn't sure how he had actually gotten home. He could swear he heard Ava's voice in his ear, as well as, her laughter. All he knew was that he needed Eliza. He felt scared.

****

It started as a scroll.

She wasn't looking for anything. Just killing time between paragraphs of her essay, trying to stay awake with her third cup of coffee. The apartment was quiet—too quiet—but she was used to that now. Finn had said he'd be out late with the guys but she had made his favorite dinner because she knew he would be hungry when he got home and she wanted to celebrate his win. She expected him home some time ago, had hoped for some alone-time with him, and the candles she had lit in the apartment were earlier were burning out.

But then her thumb froze.

A video. Posted to a cheerleader's story. Tagged: #PostWinVibes #HookEm

The camera panned over a crowded bar—shouting voices, music blaring in the background. Then it landed on Finn.

Her Finn.

Smiling. Drunk. Slumped into the booth like he barely knew where he was. And Ava—Ava "always-there" Ava—on his lap.

Kissing him.

Not a peck. Not a joke.

It was messy. It was real.

And it was public.

Eliza sat completely still.

The sound around her dropped away. The hum of the heater. The buzz of her laptop. Even her heartbeat felt muted under the roar in her ears.

The only sound she heard was the cracking of her heart ringing through her.

The camera shook with laughter—someone offscreen hooted. "Damn, Finn!" A cheerleader cackled. "She's gonna be mad about that one."

The video ended.

Eliza blinked once. Twice.

Then she clicked the next story. And the next.

Ava, posing with Finn's hoodie slung over her shoulders, pouting into the camera. "Just stealing hearts and hoodies 😙"

Eliza closed the app.

Her hands were shaking.

She set the phone on the teak coffee table that Finn loved and stood, too fast. Her knees almost buckled and she swayed. Her breath caught in her throat. She thought *Oh god, I'm going to be sick*.

This wasn't confusion. It wasn't a misunderstanding. There was no defense. No benefit of the doubt. It was right there—in pixels and sound.

Finn hadn't invited her with him to the bar because Ava was there for him. Now she understood why he didn't include her in his team hang outs. He'd been with her. That's why he had barely touched her lately.

She'd been replaced and her heart shattered in her chest, leaving her gasping as breath the left her. She didn't recognize the Finn that she loved with her whole heart. That Finn would never do something like this. He had changed. She didn't recognize this man, the one she had seen in that post. That man had replaced her—with that hateful bitch. She could never love a man like that.

Finn. With Ava. Laughing. Kissing. Letting her wear the hoodie Eliza had bought him last Christmas. The one he said smelled like her. In front of his friends, everyone.

She walked to the bathroom, looked in the mirror. Her face was deathly pale. Violet eyes, full of devastation were too wide and bright with tears. She pressed her hands to the bathroom counter, bracing herself. If she didn't, her body would drop to the floor. It was the only thing holding her up.

Was this who she was now? The girl who waited at home while the guy she loved let someone else climb into the space she used to hold?

She turned off the light.

Went to their bedroom.

His side of the bed was still messy. She hadn't touched it. She sat down for one breath. Two.

Then she stood again and walked to the front door.

When she heard him fumbling with the key twenty minutes later, she didn't open it.

She didn't speak.

She just sat on the other side of the door, staring straight ahead, as his voice cracked through the wood like it had a right to be let in.

"Eliza, please—open the door."

She opened it part way. Looking at him with narrow eyes she took in the lipstick on his face, what looked horrifyingly like a hickey on his shoulder and his button-down shirt was missing.

Had she heard a woman's laughter before Finn had knocked on the door? Had Ava come to their apartment with him? How could he?

Her chest burned and her eyes started streaming.

It was enough. She'd had enough.

Finn could *Go Fuck Himself*. She was done. It was over.

And even if there was more to the story, she didn't have the strength to ask for it right now. She wasn't sure that she even cared after seeing Ava all over Finn.

She needed space. She couldn't even look at him. Her gut twisted. Her brain hurt and her heart felt as though it had sustained irreparable damage. She ran to the bathroom and puked her guts out.

Clearly—she needed to find the version of herself that didn't need to be chosen second. Not even second. She was dead last. And she needed to grow some lady balls and do that right fucking now.

Chapter Thirty-Two

Fracture

he door slammed in Finn's face before the cold even hit him. In his haze, his heart and mind knew something was terribly wrong.

It echoed down the hallway, sharp and final. The kind of sound that didn't just end a moment—it ended something bigger. Something real.

Finn blinked, slowly.

The hallway tilted. He threw up.

He pressed his hand to the door, but it felt too far away, like he was moving through molasses. Everything was fuzzy—no, not fuzzy. *Wrong.* His vision blurred at the edges. His balance was shot. His stomach turned.

"Eliza," he said, knocking hard, panic swelling in his chest. "Eliza, please —open the door. I don't—" He swallowed, tried again. "I didn't mean— Eliza, just let me talk to you."

No answer.

He banged the door even harder. "Please!"

Then he dropped to the floor, his back sliding down the wood, his legs folding beneath him like someone had pulled the strings. He tried to sit upright but couldn't hold his head steady.

That's when it hit him with greater clarity.

Something was wrong.

This wasn't drunk. He *knew* drunk. He'd had a few beers, maybe more than a few. Enough for a light buzz and a good laugh. Not blackout. Not... *this*. He couldn't remember what happened. He barely remembered the ride home. One minute he was at the bar with Kai and a few of the cheerleaders. He'd seen Ava sitting too close hanging around like always, sure, but he'd ignored it. He'd laughed with the guys, texted Eliza that he was headed out soon—hadn't he?

Had he?

What was the last thing he remembered?

Ava had offered him a drink. Just one. It had tasted sweet and a little bitter. Too sweet and he'd been thirsty and drank it quickly.

He rubbed at his face, his vision swimming again. Lipstick on his collar. Smudges on his skin. His stomach twisted.

He gagged. Caught himself just in time.

What the hell happened?

He would never kiss Ava. *Never*. He loved Eliza. He only ever *wanted* Eliza. She was the other half of his soul even if he didn't deserve her.

And now she was on the other side of the door, probably thinking he'd thrown her away like it meant nothing. Like *she* meant nothing.

He banged on the door again, but softer now, weakly.

"Eliza, I swear to God I don't remember kissing her. I don't remember getting here. Something's not right."

Still nothing. at that moment he realized that his shirt was missing.

The horror and terror of that knowledge came together in his messed up mind. Desperate, he pressed his forehead to the door, heart breaking slow and steady.

Had he just lost the only person who had ever made him feel like more than a number? More than a jersey or a body or a good story?

The person that made him feel seen and loved. He'd never felt those things before her.

Had he just lost his North Star? Thrown away the only woman he loved? Lost her? Lost himself? Because deep down he was a coward.

He closed his eyes. His heart pounded more desperately than after any football game or practice that he'd ever played.

And for the first time in years, Finn felt truly, deeply afraid—not of failure, not of pain.

But of the possibility that he'd just ruined the best thing he'd ever had.

His chest clenched tight at the thought. He'd told himself once that he'd die before he let himself be the one to break her.

But then he remembered the way she'd said it: *"You've never been the one who broke me."*

But he was the one and he did.

Finn hung his head as despair flooded him.

The bedroom door was locked and spare room smelled like dust and old books. Finn lay on the futon, fully clothed, staring at the ceiling with red, burning eyes after their neighbor Daniel heard all of his banging and unlocked it with the spare key they'd given him in case of emergency and this certainly classified as one.

His phone was still in his hand. He'd called Kai three times. No answer. Sent a message to Sophia. To Van. To anyone who might've been at the bar. Even Dillon. All he got back was silence, except for Dillon.

"Dick. Fucking dick. Always knew Eliza was too good for you." Dillon texted back.

He'd knocked on their bedroom door around midnight. Whispered her name through the wood.

Nothing.

Then passed out.

Now it was morning, pale light leaking through the slats of the blinds. His head pounded—not from a hangover, but from whatever had been in his system. He felt clearer now. And emptier. Still sick to his stomach.

After heaving what was left of his guts out, he walked to the bedroom door again, barefoot and tired in the bones.

He knocked.

"Eliza?"

No answer.

He pressed his hand against the wood. "Please. Just talk to me."

Nothing.

Then—movement. A muffled rustle. And finally, her voice, rough and cracked.

"Go away."

"Eliza, I didn't do what you think I did. Something was wrong with me last night—I didn't mean to come home like that, I didn't mean to—"

"You're a disgusting piece of shit." she said, voice rising, brittle and furious. "You don't even get to *speak* to me."

"How could you?" she continued.

His heart cracked in two. "I didn't kiss her. I don't remember it. I would *never* choose her over you. Something happened—Eliza, please."

The lock clicked.

Then the door flung open.

She stood there, eyes puffy, cheeks streaked with tears. Her hair was pulled into a messy knot, and she wore one of his old sweatshirts—like her heart didn't know yet it wasn't supposed to miss him.

"I heard you last night.. at the front door. Heard you and Ava laughing." Eliza said painfully.

"The lipstick all over your face, that hickey, and missing shirt would show otherwise," she whispered quietly. Then lost all ability to reign in her devastation.

"How could you? You broke me," she choked, voice shaking. "You *broke us.*"

He opened his mouth but nothing came out. He was looking at the wreckage of the person who used to hold him with steady hands, who had his whole heart, and he knew this pain—*this*—was his fault.

"I stayed up and made you dinner," she said, her voice rising, spiraling. "I made your *favorite meal to celebrate your win*. You never told me that you weren't coming home after the game. I lit candles. I was fighting for us. I was trying. I *still loved you*, and you came home with her all over you."

He stepped backward instinctively.

"I think that I'm going to be sick. You even smell like her."

"I swear to God I didn't know what I was doing. Eliza, I think I was drugged."

"Don't." She held up a hand. "Don't you *dare* say that to soften this. No excuses."

"I'm not—" he said quickly. "I'm not trying to excuse anything. I *want* to figure out what happened. I need to. I need you to believe that something wasn't right. I love you Eliza and I wouldn't do this."

"Do you think I *care* what you need right now?"

She was breaking in front of him, piece by piece. And he had no way to catch her.

"I know you hate me right now but…," he whispered.

"No," she said, voice quiet now, nearly a whisper. "I hate *what you did.* And I hate that I still love you while it's killing me."

She turned and shut the door again. This time, she didn't slam it.

That somehow hurt worse.

****

Eliza couldn't breathe.

Not in this room. Not in this apartment. Not surrounded by the framed photos of them together on the wall or the blanket they used to cozy up together under for movie nights, or the jacket still draped over the back of the chair that smelled like him. Looking at that picture of them on the beach in Destin, Florida, arms around one another, holding tight. Enchanted Rock where they shared their first kiss.

The love in both their expressions undoing Eliza, sinking her thoughts and love for Finn into a vortex deep inside her, holding the feelings hostage lest they be released and destroy her utterly. Leaving Eliza a shadow of herself. Until she could deal with this earthquake inside herself, she'd keep her love for Finn locked away in the deepest recesses of herself until one day she might be able to address the loss.

Most people never find their true love. She thought that she had when she met Finn in foster care. Her soul knew his. Two halves of something greater. She'd been wrong. How could your other half cause you so much pain?

She'd tried to sleep. Tried to eat. Tried to stop crying.

None of it worked.

Her heart felt like it had shattered and reassembled itself with jagged edges. And every breath scraped against them.

She sat on the floor in the corner of the bedroom, arms around her knees, hoodie sleeves pulled down over her hands. Looking down at herself, she realized that she was wearing his hoodie. Yanking it off she grabbed the scissors and started hacking at it, remembering that Finn had loaned that very hoodie to Ava.

Disgusted with herself for putting up with Finn's shitty behavior, for letting that bitch Ava take her place, she threw the tissue box down.

Her suitcase was half-packed on the bed—because even though she didn't know where she was going, she knew she couldn't stay here.

Not with the scent of him on the sheets.

Not with the silence in the hallway where he used to meet her with open arms.

Her phone buzzed for the fourth time that hour. Finn. Again.

She didn't look.

Instead, she pulled up a name she hadn't called in a while but had always known she could.

Rhetta.

Chapter Thirty-Three

Coffee and Calluses

Eliza showed up at Rhetta's porch without calling first. Her face was pale, eyes rimmed red. Looking like a haunted shadow of herself. She carried no books, small bag left in the car. Just herself, raw, frayed, and her Gibson guitar.

Rhetta didn't ask questions. She just pushed the screen door open wider and drawled, "Kitchen. Go on."

The coffee was already half-brewed—Rhetta ran on the stuff like other people ran on sleep. She poured Eliza a chipped mug, slid it across the worn table, then went to her bar and pulled out the bourbon sat down opposite her two glasses in hand.

Pouring the bourbon, Rhett said firmly, "drink." Then she let the silence stretch. Rhetta let it. Let it breathe.

Finally, Eliza whispered, "She said he's been with her. That I was just… a distraction."

Rhetta leaned back in her chair, folding her arms. "And you believe that?"

"I don't know what to believe." Eliza's voice cracked. "Everything feels like it's breaking at once. My head knows he wouldn't that something else was going on, but my heart—God, my heart's a mess. And everyone saw it. On campus. Like my private life's some kind of show, like a bad soap opera, existing solely for their amusement."

Rhetta reached across the table, laying her callused and comforting hand over Eliza's. Firm. Warm. "Sweetheart, lies only work if you let 'em settle in your chest. Don't hand that girl the keys to your own house."

Eliza blinked at her. "But what if I'm not strong enough?"

Rhetta's mouth quirked into something between a smile and a smirk. "Strength ain't about not breaking. It's about what you do with the pieces. You can sit in the dirt, let 'em cut you up, or you can melt 'em down and forge a blade. I'd say you're a blade kind of girl."

That drew the faintest laugh out of Eliza, thin but real.

"Write about it," Rhetta said, reaching for her guitar and propping it against the table edge. "Not for him. Not for her. For you. Truth has a way of finding its way into a song. And songs—well, they cut deeper than gossip ever could. The words can help you process and heal—get you the truth of things."

Eliza wrapped her hands around the warm mug, feeling the steam against her face. For the first time since Ava's words, she breathed without that crushing weight in her chest.

"You gotta release those feelings out into the world freeing yourself when you're ready—through song sweet girl. It's therapy for the soul. Write is out. Sing it out. Nobody can take your song away but you."

"You're not alone, Eliza. Not here, not ever," Rhetta added, her tone soft but iron-strong. "Remember that next time the world tries to knock you sideways. That bein' said, I believe that there may well be more to this story with Finn than we know. That boy loves you. Always has. Find out the truth or your heart'll never forgive you. "

The porch creaked as the evening wind kicked up, carrying with it the smell of cedar and dust. And Eliza thought—maybe, just maybe—she still had a voice left to fight with.

And the words flowed like the tears that wouldn't stop falling.

Chorus

If it wasn't real, why does it still ache?
If I was enough, why did I break?
You swear you didn't choose her, say the kiss was a lie
But I felt it all crumble without a goodbye
So if I believe you, if I let this heal
Tell me—will you fight like hell to prove it was real?

Bridge

I'm not made of glass, but I shattered for you
Built us a home, then watched you walk through
A door I never closed, a heart still bare
Waiting for proof you were ever really there

Final Chorus

If it wasn't real, why do I still care?
If I was the one, then why was she there?
You say it was stolen, a night you never meant
But the silence, the damage—it all still left a dent
So if I let you back in, if I start to feel
Don't just love me—prove that it's real

****

Madison Kennedy

She didn't even wait for the voicemail prompt.

"Hey, it's Eliza," Eliza said when it picked up. Her voice cracked. "Can I… crash with you for a bit?"

Twenty minutes later, Madison texted her the code to her downtown condo and said, simply: *Come. No questions until you're ready.*

Eliza had returned from Rhetta's place, the apartment empty since Finn was at practice. Exhausted but sure sharing the apartment with Finn right now was untenable. Packing her suitcase with a writing notebook, school books, computer, toiletries, and some clothes. Zipping her suitcase with shaking hands, she pulled on her favorite vintage cream cowboy boots. They always made her feel strong, like she could kick ass if need be. She couldn't bring herself to take any pictures. They followed her anyway on her phone. She didn't leave a note. She just put her hair up in a messy bun and couldn't be bothered to look in the mirror.

She just walked out. She needed to go somewhere Finn wouldn't know to look for her. The idea of looking into his lying green eyes was unbearable.

The hallway felt like a tunnel, every step echoing too loud in the stillness. In her mind she still could see Finn in the hallway after he had been with Ava. She pressed the elevator button with a trembling finger and stared straight ahead, willing herself not to throw up and not to look back.

As the elevator doors closed, she finally let the tears fall.

Madison's place was a high-rise tucked above the music district. By the time Eliza reached it, she was raw. Hollowed out.

Eliza met Madison and their friend Amber Walker working on a committee planning Austin City Limits.

But Madison didn't ask anything. Just handed her a glass of water, guest towels, and a blanket, pointed her toward the slick-looking modern guest room, and said, "We'll talk tomorrow. Tonight, you sleep. I've got you."

Eliza nodded, clutching the blanket to her chest like armor. Grateful beyond measure.

She sat on the edge of the unfamiliar bed in the unfamiliar apartment and looked out the window at the Austin skyline glowing in the distance.

And for the first time in hours, she breathed.

Not because the pain had passed.

But because she wasn't in the place where it had bloomed.

She opened her notebook before bed. Not to write a song. Not yet. But just to see if the words would come.

They didn't.

All she could manage was a single line, written crooked and soft at the top of a fresh page:

"What if the thing that made you feel safest is the one that wrecks you the most?"

She closed the notebook. Crawled under the covers.

And this time, she let herself fall apart.

Eliza hadn't spoken much in the first twenty-four hours after she arrived at Madison's place.

Madison didn't push. Being the headstrong music maven she was. It said a lot that she didn't.

She handed Eliza hot chamomile tea in the mornings and played soft records in the background—*Wasting All These Tears on You* by Cassadee Pope, *Everleave* by Alexandra Kay, *Star-crossed* by Kacey Musgrave, old Joni Mitchell, a bit of Brandi Carlile on repeat. Music that felt like balm instead of noise.

Now, sitting across from her on Madison's couch, Eliza stared at the untouched mug that bore the saying *Without music, life would B flat* between her palms. Her face red and splotchy from the tears that wouldn't stop coming. Outside, the city moved in its usual rhythm—horns, voices, the low thump of bass from a street below.

Inside, she felt like her heart had slowed to a crawl.

"I keep replaying it," she said finally. Her voice was hoarse, like she hadn't used it in days. "That image. The lipstick. The HICKEY. The way he looked—like I didn't even exist. That he barely knew me. The social media video with that bitch on his lap, him kissing her…with tongue."

Madison didn't flinch. She set her own mug down and leaned forward. She didn't know Eliza very well yet, but she knew how much she and Finn loved each other so the situation didn't feel right. She thought that there was more to the story than they knew. She was also aware that what Eliza was describing sounded more like Finn had taken drugs or was drugged. She worked in the music industry so she'd seen it all.

"Eliza," she said carefully, "what you saw hurt. No one is questioning that. But has Finn actually told you what happened?"

"He tried. I shut him down. I couldn't… I couldn't even look at him."

"Okay. So now what? You're here, and you're safe. But the ache doesn't go away just because you slammed the door."

"I know." Her grip tightened around the mug. "But it wasn't just a kiss, Maddie. It was everything. The not showing up. The silence. The way he let someone else take up my space. Feels like he erased me and she took my place. Whether he meant to or not, he let her."

Madison nodded slowly. "That is probably true, but if the other night hadn't happened. If he hadn't acted that way with Ava of his own volition, would that free up room to work things out between you. Heartbreak doesn't always explode. Sometimes it fades you out. Like someone turning down the volume on you, little by little. That doesn't mean that it's not still there—more like a banked fire that just need attention to rekindle the flame."

That made Eliza's throat tighten. Madison was right.

She pulled out her phone, thumb hovering over the screen.

Then she texted Sophia:

Hey. I'm okay. Sort of. I'm at my ACL friend Madison's.

And Van:

Still breathing. That's all I've got right now.

Seconds later:

Sophia: *Where is he? Because I'm bringing a baseball bat. you can stay with me. My roommate is usually staying at her boyfriends place.*

Eliza: *Thanks for the offer but I'm going to lay low here. Your apartment is the first place that he'll look for me and I can't face him yet.*

Van: *Say the word. We're yours, Eliza. Always.*

Eliza: *xoxo ;)*

She smiled through the sting behind her eyes. They still had her. Even if he didn't.

An hour later, her phone buzzed again. This time, the name surprised her.

Dillon.

She hesitated. Then opened the message.

Dillon: *I don't want to cross a line, but I just… wanted to say I'm sorry for what you're going through. If you need anything—talk, distraction, someone to rage at—I'm here. No expectations. Just a friend. Promise.*

Tears welled up again. Not from the message. From the *kindness* in it.

Madison glanced over. "That from the football and girlie whisperer?"

Eliza blinked. "Dillon."

Madison's brows lifted, but she didn't say anything more. Just reached out and gave Eliza's hand a gentle squeeze.

Eliza responded:

Thanks, Dillon. That means more than you know. I might take you up on that.

After she hit send, she finally looked at Madison.

"I don't know if I can forgive him. But I don't know how to stop loving him either."

Madison leaned back, her voice even. "You don't have to decide yet. Just keep breathing. Keep creating. Keep reaching for the people who remind you who you are. When you're ready maybe he can explain what he was thinking and why he behaved that way. But only when you're ready to hear it."

Eliza let herself lean into the couch cushion, the ache still present, but less suffocating.

She wasn't fixed.

But she wasn't alone either. Thank God. One thing she was grateful for were the friendships she had built since moving to Austin. They were more than she had ever had during her life and she needed them with the giant whole Finn was leaving in her heart and life. She wished that she could hate him and right now...she did.

And maybe, for now, those friendships were enough.

Hearing another ping, she looked down at her phone, opened up messages and saw that Finn had sent her another text to add to the more than a hundred texts he'd sent already, ones that she wouldn't let herself read. Finn tried to call her even more times, leaving long voicemail messages that she couldn't bring herself to listen to yet.

Maybe she'd never be able to.

Chapter Thirty-Four

Damage Done

Eliza hadn't planned to be on campus that afternoon. She'd meant to stay at Madison's a little longer—hide out in record stores and corner cafés, anywhere her name wasn't stitched to his like a wound that still bled.

But an advisor meeting with Dr. Landon had pulled her in, and now she was cutting across the quad, keeping her head down, earbuds in, trying not to exist too loudly.

She didn't see Ava until it was too late.

Grabbing Eliza's arm, she said, "Wow. You look like hell."

Eliza stopped cold, pilling her arm away from the fake, pointed red talons that fronted as Ava's nails.

Ava stood in the center of the brick walkway, sunglasses perched in her glossy hair, arms crossed over her UT cheer jacket with Finn's hoodie wrapped around her waist like she owned Finn and the whole damn university.

Sickened by the sight of it, Eliza pulled out one earbud. "Excuse me?"

Ava smiled. "I just meant… it's a bold look. The whole broken-heroine vibe. Very indie."

Barely restraining herself, Eliza's hands curled into fists. "What do you want, Ava?"

She could't believe that Finn would be so attracted to this awful woman that he was willing to lose her. Maybe she was just a seriously good actress or that good in bed. After all, Finn had been Eliza's first. Maybe he wanted someone with more experience. It would be hard to cover up all that bitch for any length of time Eliza thought.

"I thought you should know the truth," Ava said, voice faux-sweet. "Since Finn's obviously too cowardly to tell you what's been going on between us for months."

Eliza's stomach sank.

"I don't know what Finn may have told you about what happened that night but there was no drink," Ava continued. "No setup. No 'I was drugged' drama. He kissed me because he wanted to. Because he *has* been. We've been… seeing each other. You weren't around much, and—well." Her grin widened. "You know how guys are. Stepping into your place wasn't that difficult to do. You were never there for Finn and he needs a woman that puts him first."

The world shifted beneath Eliza's feet.

No. No, it wasn't true. Finn wouldn't do that. Not for months. Not in secret. Not with *her*.

"I don't believe you," she said softly, her heart refusing to believe what Ava was telling her.

Ava leaned in, just enough so her breath brushed Eliza's ear. "He used to call me by your name when we were hooking up. You really think one hoodie and a sob story means you were the only one?"

Eliza's knees buckled. Not literally—but something inside her gave out. She felt *unmoored*, like her entire identity had been tossed into the wind and shredded on impact.

She didn't know what to say. Couldn't breathe. Couldn't move. She started to hyperventilate. Just she felt her legs give out, sending her sliding to the concrete.

And that's when she felt arms around her.

Strong. Solid. Familiar. The distinct scent of linen, bergamot, and something musky.

Dillon.

"Hey," he said quietly, pulling her trembling body gently into his chest. "Come here. I got you."

She didn't even realize she'd started crying until his sweatshirt soaked up the first wave of tears. Her fingers gripped the fabric like it was a lifeline.

Ava took a half-step back, clearly surprised by the scene. Her smirk wavered—just slightly.

Dillon glanced up at her, jaw tight. "You should go. Now."

"Oh, how noble," Ava said, biting the inside of her cheek. "Rescuing the damsel. It's a new look for you. Doesn't matter. My job here is done—so is she."

Dillon didn't blink. "Seriously. Walk away, Ava. Before you say something that gets you thrown off campus."

Ava scoffed and turned, flipping her ponytail like the scene hadn't mattered.

Eliza stayed there, head pressed to Dillon's chest, her body trembling with the kind of grief that didn't feel like crying—it felt like disintegration.

"I can't... I can't do this," she whispered. "I thought I was getting stronger. But I can't take this version of him."

Seeing how fragile and delicate she was, Dillon's voice was low. Gentle. "I don't know what the hell she said, but I do know Finn. And I know he's an idiot, but he's not *that* kind of idiot. He has never given another woman his attention until that night. He tolerates the women that hang out around the team. That includes that bitch Ava."

Eliza shook her head. "You didn't see the look in her eyes."

Dillon pulled back just enough to cup her face in his hands. His thumbs brushed under her eyes. "Then let me say this: *you* are not whatever that girl tried to reduce you to. You're not weak. You're not broken. You are Eliza Monroe. You write songs that stop time and stories that punch people in the chest. You make the people around you *better*. A gentle but strong light."

She closed her eyes. Let the words soak in. Let herself be held.

Across the quad, Kai had seen everything.

He stood near the steps of the science building, arms crossed, a silent witness to the embrace. His jaw ticked. Not in judgment—but in worry.

A few hours later, he knocked on Finn's apartment door.

Finn opened it, tired, bleary-eyed and pale. "Hey. You got anything?"

Kai stepped inside. "Yeah. Something you're not gonna like."

Finn raised an eyebrow. Dark circled smudged under his eyes. He couldn't eat. Couldn't sleep. He lay on her side of the bed just so that he could smell her sweet lavender and vanilla scent still.

Kai didn't sugarcoat it. "I saw Eliza today. With Dillon."

Finn's chest tightened. "Is she okay?"

"She was crying. Shaking. Looked like hell. Ava said something to her—*hurt* her."

Finn's voice was a rasp. "Dillon?"

"Holding her. Comforting her. Like she was about to fall apart."

Finn pressed both hands against the counter, his knuckles white.

"I'm telling you this," Kai said, voice level, "because if you want her back, if you still love her—you're gonna have to fight harder than you ever did on that field."

Finn didn't answer right away.

But inside, something cracked open—pain and guilt and rage all boiling over into one sharp, gutting truth:

He had broken her. Broken them.

Now he had to become someone worth putting the pieces back together for.

First he had to prove the truth. He would never have touched Ava if he hadn't been drugged. He knew that deep in his heart and soul. He just needed proof.

Chapter Thirty-Five

Fallouts and Fire lines

Finn hadn't slept. Couldn't.

Every time he closed his eyes, he saw her face—red-rimmed, devastated. Not angry. Worse. Broken.

And it was his fault. Hands shaking, he made coffee and gave up on getting his assignments done. Surrounded by her scent and memories, nothing else mattered now but Eliza. He would give anything right now to be there for her. To share everything, all of himself with her. With the very real possibility of losing Eliza forever, the truth hit him in the gut. So busy running, he forgot to make the commitment to stay.

He didn't know how far she'd fallen until Kai told him she was in someone else's arms. Until he saw Dillon—his teammate—holding her like she already belonged to him.

That lit something in Finn's chest. Something wild. Something *primal*.

Because no matter how badly he'd fucked up, Eliza wasn't just a girl he dated. She wasn't just part of his life.

She was his life. He was the asshole that ruined them. How had he gotten so lost, so off track from what really mattered. He could live without football or friends but one thing that he was sure of…he couldn't live without Eliza. He had taken her for granted. Taken them for granted and not realized what Ava was trying to do—break them up. He was finally seeing through the heady haze of success and peer admiration.

Eliza is home. His North Star.

And there was no way in hell he was letting her go without a fight.

By noon, he was standing in the weight room doorway, fists clenched, jaw locked, watching Dillon rack a barbell like the world hadn't just shifted under all of them.

Dillon glanced up and pulled out his earbuds. "Don't," he said. "If you're here to punch me for comforting *your* girlfriend—"

"She's *my* girl," Finn growled, stepping forward, voice low and lethal. "Let's get that part straight first."

Dillon wiped sweat from his face, eyes hard. "She's not acting like yours lately. You certainly haven't acted like you're hers."

"Because I messed up. Because I let things slide when I should've been pulling her closer. Not because she stopped loving me."

Dillon scoffed. "She's wrecked, man. I saw it. You think she wants to hear your excuses right now?"

"No. But she needs the *truth*. And so do you."

Finn stepped closer, fire radiating off him. "You think I don't see it? The way you look at her. Like you're just waiting for me to drop the ball."

"You *did* drop it."

"Yeah. I did." His chest rose sharply. "But she's still mine. I'm not backing down. I'm not walking away just because another guy showed up when I was at my lowest."

Dillon's eyes narrowed. "You don't get to call dibs on her like she's a prize. You lost that right the second you had your tongue down Ava's throat, and in front of everyone just to humiliate her more. Eliza deserves better than that bullshit. "

"Fucker. I'm not calling dibs," Finn shot back. "I'm calling *love*. She's it for me. And I'm not gonna stop until she knows that again. Until she *feels* that again."

A pause hung between them — heavy and electric.

Finn's voice dropped, rough with guilt and resolve. "You can be there for her. You can hold her when she breaks. But don't forget who put her back together the first time. Don't forget who's been by her side for years. Through every panic attack. Every song. Every goddamn storm. That's me. I don't exist without her."

Dillon looked away for a second. "She deserves better than what you gave her."

"I know," Finn said, voice cracked. "And I'm gonna become the man she deserves — no matter how long it takes. I'm gonna prove it to her."

Silence.

Then Dillon nodded once, stiffly. "I'll tell her you said that."

Finn turned, but paused at the door. "One more thing."

Dillon raised an eyebrow.

"If she ever chooses you after she knows the truth about that night… I'll back off. I'll respect it. But until *she* says those words to my face? She's still mine. And I'm gonna fight like hell to win her back. So back the fuck off."

Then he walked out—burning with purpose, wrecked by love, and more certain than ever of one brutal, beautiful truth:

Eliza Monroe wasn't just someone he loved.

She was his *everything*.

He had one shot.

And this time, he wasn't going to drop the ball.
And he wasn't giving her up without a war.

But the war was already costing him.

On the field, the ball kept slipping from his hands like it wanted to punish him. Passes sailed high. Routes he could read blindfolded blurred like static.

He threw two interceptions in the first half of their conference opener—both straight into the arms of defenders he should've seen. When he jogged off the field, the student section didn't chant his name. They booed.

On the sideline, Coach Billings' jaw was locked. "You're rattled, Finn. Pull your head out."

But Finn couldn't. He looked up at the stands and saw Eliza's empty seat.

He saw Dillon watching from the bench, helmet under his arm, jaw set. He saw Ava in the cheer section, smiling like she'd already won.

His stomach turned.

By the fourth quarter, they were down by twenty-one. His offensive line gave him space. He still couldn't see straight. He forced a throw into double coverage and it got picked again.

The stadium erupted—not in cheers. In jeers.

His phone lit up in the locker room afterward. Notifications stacking like blows:

@CampusBuzz: "From golden boy to fallen star. Finn Callahan blows another game. #NotSoGolden #AvaWins #JusticeForEliza"

@LonghornNation: "Maybe if Finn kept his focus on the playbook instead of the cheer squad... #FumbledLove #QBDown"

@HotTakeSports: "Finn Callahan tanks 3 games in a row. Losing Eliza AND the season. #GoldenNoMore"

Memes followed. One of him dropping a ball photoshopped into Ava's arms. One of Eliza walking away with the caption *You played yourself.*

He stared at his screen until the words blurred.

The Golden Boy wasn't golden anymore and it didn't even matter anymore. Losing Eliza did.

Finn hadn't slept. Not really. A few seconds here and there on the guest room futon, waking every time he heard the bedroom door creak, hoping it might be Eliza. It never was. He couldn't bare to sleep in their bed without her.

By 6 a.m., he was dressed, eyes bloodshot, determination running hotter than his grief. If he'd been in his right mind that night, he would've called an Uber, gone to a hospital, gotten blood work done.

But he hadn't.

Because he wasn't.

And if there was *any* way back to Eliza—to *them*—it would be through proof.

He took a deep breath and walked into Coach Billings' office without knocking.

The head coach looked up, eyebrows raised. "Finn. Everything okay?"

"No, sir," Finn said, voice flat. "And I need your help."

By mid-afternoon, Coach Billings had gotten in touch with the manager of the off-campus bar where the team had been drinking the night Finn was allegedly drugged. Security footage existed. But it wasn't something they could just walk out with.

Meanwhile, Finn met Kai, West and Jayden, another teammate, outside the locker room.

"You're sure you only had three beers?" Jayden asked, scanning through photos on his phone.

"Three beers, plus two shots early in the evening then I was hydrating. Nothing else until Ava handed me that drink. I think she said it was a rum and Coke. I was thirsty, not paying attention and drank it quickly."

Kai crossed his arms. "You barely said goodbye when we left, man. You were zoned out. Looked like someone unplugged your brain and your body."

Jayden held up his phone. "Okay, this one—look. Timestamp's 9:58. You're sitting on the couch. Ava's pouring something into your cup in addition to the liquer."

Finn leaned in. His jaw clenched. "Zoom in."

Kai whistled low. "She's not at the bar. That's something *she* brought in."

Jayden nodded slowly. "Man... you sure you don't want to go to the cops?"

Finn shook his head. "Not yet. Not until I've got proof. If I can show Eliza I didn't *choose* this, maybe she won't walk away for good."

Chapter Thirty-Six

The Retelling

The sun was barely up when Dillon knocked on Madison's door.

Eliza had barely slept. She'd been curled on the pull-out couch, Madison's dog snoring softly at her feet, the glow of her laptop screen the only light in the dark.

She hadn't touched her guitar in days.

Hadn't written a lyric that wasn't soaked in ache.

Madison opened the door first, hair in a high messy bun, oversized UT hoodie nearly swallowing her whole.

She looked at Dillon like she already knew who he was.

"You're not who I was expecting," she said flatly.

Not here to cause trouble," Dillon replied. "Just need five minutes. With Eliza."

Madison looked back toward the couch, where Eliza was already sitting up, blanket tangled in her lap. Her eyes were puffy. Her voice came out hoarse.

"It's okay. Let him in."

Dillon stepped inside, towering but awkward, like he didn't know where to put his hands. He stood near the counter.

Eliza didn't rise.

"When I saw you yesterday," he said softly. "I mean—I heard what Ava said. Saw what it did to you."

Her jaw clenched. "She's disgusting."

"Yeah. But she's also a liar."

Eliza looked up. Something sharp flickered in her eyes. "What?"

"I talked to Finn," Dillon continued. "And before you say anything—I'm not here to take sides. I'm here because I think you deserve to hear the whole thing."

Eliza crossed her arms, spine straightening. Bracing. "Go on."

Dillon hesitated, then told her everything. The confrontation in the weight room. The desperation in Finn's eyes. His fury. His insistence that what happened wasn't what it looked like. That he was drugged. That he *didn't choose* Ava. That the kiss, if it even happened, wasn't real. It had been assault.

"He said he wasn't drunk just buzzed until Ava gave him that last drink," Dillon said. "He's trying to find footage. Talked to Coach Billings. The guys. Even Kai backed it up."

Eliza's hands trembled in her lap.

"He said you're his North Star," Dillon added, quieter now. "And he's not letting go without a fight."

The words cracked something in her.

Because that was their thing. Their vow.

She didn't want to cry. Didn't want to hope.

But she could feel the war rising inside her—grief and longing and the tiniest flicker of belief that maybe, just maybe, she didn't have the full picture.

Dillon shifted, uncertain. "He also told me something else."

She looked up.

"He said that if you ever choose me—he'll walk away. No questions asked. But until you do… he's not quitting."

The room went quiet.

Eliza swallowed hard. "He said that?"

Dillon nodded once. "Yeah. And he meant it."

A silence stretched between them—heavy and full of everything she didn't know how to say.

"Thank you," she said finally. "For telling me."

He stood there for a beat longer, like he wanted to say something else—but didn't.

Then he just gave a small, sad smile, and said, "Just don't let him come back if you're not sure. It'll wreck him. And you."

When he left, Madison came over with two mugs of coffee and sat cross-legged on the other side of the couch.

"Well," she said, "that was dramatic as hell."

Eliza let out a strangled laugh, then covered her face with her hands.

"I don't know what to believe. I know what I saw. What everyone saw, but it's not like Finn. The Finn I've know for years. It's not who he is…at least I thought it wasn't."

Madison set down her mug. "You believe your gut. And your heart. And then you let the truth do the rest."

Eliza's phone pinged. Looked down at her cell she saw that it was a text from Rhetta: "Saw that video. Don't let other people write your song for you. You're the only one who knows the real words."

Suddenly her next step became clear. She needed to see Rhetta.

"I think that I need a road-trip to get my head on straight. Visit Rhetta again. Mads I feel so wrung out, gutted and lost. Being around her grounds me. Puts me to rights. I'll head out tomorrow. Maybe a road trip is just what I need right now." Eliza said. The idea of running into Finn, Ava or Dillon was too much to take.

****

The drive back to Fredericksburg was quiet. Eliza didn't bother turning on the radio—her head was already loud enough.

When she pulled into the gravel drive, Rhetta Barnes was exactly where she expected her to be: out on the porch swing, guitar in her lap, boots propped on the railing, a Shiner sweating in the Texas heat.

"Well, if it ain't my songbird," Rhetta called, voice warm and lazy, like honey over ice. "Missed me already?"

Eliza forced a smile, but her chest was tight. She hadn't cried in days—her eyes burned like they were holding everything back by force.

Rhetta didn't push. Just patted the seat beside her. "Sit. Porch don't judge."

Eliza dropped down next to her, the boards creaking under her weight. The night smelled like mesquite and dust. Crickets hummed low in the grass.

They sat in silence for a long stretch, Rhetta idly plucking a slow, mournful chord progression. Finally, she glanced at Eliza.

"You look like someone dropped your heart in the dirt and drove over it twice."

That cracked something in Eliza's chest. A laugh—sharp, bitter—slipped out. "Pretty much."

Rhetta's fingers stilled on the strings. "Boy trouble? Still? Have to say I'm surprised. Never thought he'd mess up bad enough for you to drive all the way out here to talk."

Eliza nodded. Words caught in her throat. She didn't want to say Finn's name. Didn't want to picture the lipstick on his face, the the knowledge that she had her mouth all over him, and the way the internet replayed her humiliation like it was a game. The image of his tongue down her throat burned in her mind.

Rhetta leaned back, studying her. "Men'll tangle you up, sure as a barbed-wire fence. But the right one? He won't leave you bleeding. He'll climb through it with you."

Eliza swallowed hard. "What if I can't tell the difference anymore? What if he doesn't want to? What if we're too broken to fix?"

"That's why you write, baby girl." Rhetta nudged the guitar into Eliza's hands. "Get it outta your chest. All that hurt, all that heat—turn it into something only you can say. Don't let silence eat you alive."

Eliza's fingers hovered awkwardly on the frets. She still wasn't as good of a player as Rhetta, but stroking the wood felt solid, grounding.

Rhetta smiled at her softly, that rare, maternal sort of smile Eliza never got from anyone else. "Scholarships, school, the world—they'll try to take pieces out of you. But you already got a weapon. You got your words. Don't forget who gave 'em to you."

The porch light buzzed above them, casting the yard in a soft gold. And for the first time since everything fell apart, Eliza let herself believe she wasn't completely lost.

Later after Rhetta went to bed; Eliza dropped her hands, looked at her notebook sitting nearby.

For the first time in days, she picked it up.

And started to write. The words flowing out of her in one giant stream of conscious thought.

"If It Wasn't Real"
Lyrics by Eliza Monroe

Verse 1

You left the light on, but you didn't stay
Said you were tired, but you drifted away
Into a night I wasn't part of
Into a version I couldn't trust

You say you were lost, that you couldn't see
But I was right there—how did you forget me?
I gave you the map, the words, the flame
Now I'm here asking if you'd do it again

Chorus

If it wasn't real, why does it still ache?
If I was enough, why did I break?
You swear you didn't choose her, say the kiss was a lie
But I felt it all crumble without a goodbye
So if I believe you, if I let this heal
Tell me—will you fight like hell to prove it was real?

Verse 2

I wore your name like a second skin
Wrote our story in the margins, let you in
Now all I have are questions and ash
And a hundred yesterdays I can't get back

I don't need perfect—I never did
I just needed truth, not half-truths and ifs
So don't promise me stars while standing in shade
Come back with fire—or don't come at all again

Chorus

If it wasn't real, why does it still ache?
If I was enough, why did I break?
You swear you didn't choose her, say the kiss was a lie

But I felt it all crumble without a goodbye
So if I believe you, if I let this heal
Tell me—will you fight like hell to prove it was real?

Bridge

I'm not made of glass, but I shattered for you
Built us a home, then watched you walk through
A door I never closed, a heart still bare
Waiting for proof you were ever really there

Final Chorus

If it wasn't real, why do I still care?
If I was the one, then why was she there?
You say it was stolen, a night you never meant
But the silence, the damage—it all still left a dent
So if I let you back in, if I start to feel
Don't just love me—prove that it's real

Chapter Thirty-Seven

The Song That Knew

The bar wasn't packed, but it buzzed with low-key energy—the kind of warm, candlelit space where music wasn't just background noise. It mattered. Guitars lined the back wall. A neon "Live Tonight" sign flickered above the small wooden stage.

Madison adjusted the mic stand while Eliza tuned her guitar, looking ethereal beneath the lights making her appear otherworldly beautiful. There was a goodness and truth shining from her while her hands trembled, but her expression stayed calm. Focused. She looked like she belonged there—even if she wasn't sure she felt it yet.

"You're on in two," Madison said gently. "And for the record? This is the most honest thing I've heard all year. Play it your way."

figured. She hadn't spoken to Finn and she stayed off social media. She couldn't bare the thought of seeing him with Ava. Because she went underground and didn't follow the so called Golden Boy, she didn't know that he was never with Ava, didn't hang out after the games anymore and was staying off social media as much as he could.

After talking with Madison about her feelings, she decided to be brave and sing one of her songs publicly. She had so much in her that needed to get out. To be heard. To be healed.

Eliza nodded, her throat tight with gratitude. Madison had been the one to set this up—a last-minute acoustic showcase just off campus. "New Voices," the flyer had said. Eliza still wasn't sure if she qualified.

Across the bar, Finn stepped inside behind Kai, his hands shoved deep in his leather jacket pockets. He hadn't shaved. His eyes were bloodshot. He'd lost weight. He looked like hell.

Dillon and West followed close behind, eyes scanning the room until they found her.

"She's up next," Madison said, glancing their way with measured acknowledgment before returning to her place near the soundboard.

When Eliza walked onstage, the crowd quieted.

She sat on a stool, crossing her long legs under soft golden light, her violet eyes scanning the room until they landed on him—on Finn. Blinking quickly and shaking her head slightly. He was near the back wall, frozen.

She didn't flinch.

"I wrote this after losing something I thought I'd never have to question," she said. "And maybe it's not perfect. But it's mine."

She began to play.

Her voice was low, hushed at first. But each verse built like a slow confession. She didn't perform it—she *released* it. Line by line, like every note had been waiting inside her chest for the right moment to be freed.

If it wasn't real, why does it still ache…
If I was enough, why did I break…

Her eyes never left Finn's.

Dillon's jaw tensed. His heart ached watching her sing to someone who didn't deserve the way she still ached for him. And yet…he couldn't look away. Because Eliza, up there with a guitar and a raw voice like smoke and stars, was the most extraordinary thing he'd ever seen.

Kai whispered, "Damn," under his breath, watching Finn pale.

Don't just love me—prove that it's real.

The final line landed like thunder wrapped in velvet.

Looking at Eliza, Finn saw her. Saw the woman that he loved deeply, passionately. Fighting for her, for them was a need that couldn't be denied.

The room held its breath for one long beat… then erupted in applause.

Eliza looked down at her guitar, breath uneven. She wasn't sure what she'd expected—tears, maybe. Silence. But the clapping was real. Earnest. For her.

Madison reached her as she stepped offstage. "That's the one," she said. "That's your Austin City Limits submission. You just sang your way into something bigger."

Eliza blinked. "You really think so?"

"I *know* so," Madison said. "Now ask yourself: Are you ready to be seen like that again?"

Eliza didn't answer. Not yet.

Because her eyes had already drifted across the bar—where Finn stood still, shattered, watching the girl he loved sing the truth he'd failed to hear.

She was already being seen.

And this time, she wasn't hiding.

****

The night air was heavy with the scent of spring rain—just damp enough to promise thunder, just warm enough to feel like hope.

They walked side by side across the quad. Not holding hands. Not quite touching. As always there was a connection between them, an energy. But something had changed in the space between them. A weight lifted. A line redrawn. Finn hadn't expected her to follow him outside after she listened to the recording. But when he turned to leave... she'd slipped on her sneakers and quietly said, "Let's walk."

Now, under the amber glow of campus lamplight, the silence between them was louder than any crowd. But it wasn't angry. It wasn't even sad.

It was full.

Full of everything they hadn't said. Everything they still wanted to.

"I didn't think I'd get to hear you sing again," Finn said finally, voice low. "Not with me in the room."

Eliza looked over at him, eyes soft but guarded. "You shouldn't have been there."

"I know," he said. "But Madison told me. I couldn't stay away."

He stopped walking. She did too.

"I needed to hear it," he added, his voice raw. "Songbird, I needed to see what I'd almost lost."

Eliza didn't speak, but her gaze didn't waver.

"I know I messed up," Finn continued. "Not just that night. Before it. Every time I missed the signs. Every time I made you feel like you had to fight for my attention instead of already having it. Every time I ran and didn't stay. You were never a backup. You were never less. I was."

He stepped closer.

"You were always the one. Even when I was too blind or stupid or overwhelmed to act like it. I was there but running scared."

Eliza's lip trembled. "And Ava?"

"I don't remember anything after that drink. Not the kiss. Not the photos. Not getting home. Nothing. I swear on everything, Liza. She drugged me. It wasn't just manipulation—it was assault. I've reported it. Coach Billings is backing me. The police are reviewing the footage. We're going to make sure she can't hurt anyone else. You have to let me prove it to you."

Her arms folded over her chest like she didn't know what to do with them. Like if she let them fall, they might reach for him and not let go. After the initial trauma of that night she had pulled back in her mind, distancing herself from the emotion of the situation, deciding that something was definitely off about what happened and that Finn's behavior was inconsistent with who he had always been. Who he was.

Her heart was filled with complete knowing—that Finn had indeed been drugged. Her mind wanted proof. Even if there were proof, they would still need to work through the distance between them that allowed this situation to happen. Allowed them to grow apart.

"I'm sorry doesn't fix this," he added. "But I'll say it a thousand more times anyway. Because I love you. I've loved you since my eyes met yours in that foster house in Fredericksburg. Since before I knew what it meant."

"You didn't say it before," she whispered. "Not like this."

"I was scared," he said. "Of needing you too much. Of being that guy who loses himself in love. I was afraid of what staying meant. Running I knew how to do, it's the staying that needs work."

"And now?"

"Now I'd rather lose everything else than lose you again, but I don't expect you to just believe me after everything that's happened."

The tears she'd been holding back slipped free.

Finn's voice broke as he took a final step, not touching her, but close enough that she could feel his breath. "I'm still yours, Eliza. I always have been and I swear that I'll prove it to you. Even if you don't want me back. Even if you write me out of every song from here on out. I'll still be yours."

She looked up at him then, shattered and whole all at once.

"I never stopped writing about you," she said daring to hope.

Then she leaned forward and pressed her forehead to his chest.

He didn't move.

Not until she whispered, "I'm not ready to say I forgive you. But I want to see who we are on the other side of this."

That was enough.

Finn wrapped his arms around her and she let him—carefully, poignantly —like she was the most fragile and most powerful thing in the world.

And maybe she was. Because that night, in the middle of campus, under storm-heavy clouds and the echo of an acoustic song still lingering in both their chests, Finn Callahan held Eliza Monroe like he was already rebuilding everything he'd broken—

One breath, one promise, one heartbeat at a time.

Finn walked across the quad later that afternoon, heading back from the athletics office, when Ava caught up to him, still in her cheer uniform.

"Hey, stranger," she said, brushing her fingers across his arm like they were in on some shared secret. "The other night was… wow. Everyone is still talking about it. Did you see the response to my posts about us? We're trending campus-wide. The newest golden couple."

He stopped walking. Hiding his disgust at her touch. Not so golden he thought. Fool's gold at best and he had been a fool for not seeing Ava for who she really was and being willfully blind as to the true stalker-level interest she had in him. She's actually assaulted him. WTF. His skin crawled. He couldn't let her know he knew what she did or how he really felt about her. He had to keep his head on straight and in the game. Everything was riding on this to work.

So he said, "Yeah the new golden couple."

She leaned in closer. "I wasn't sure if you were gonna go for it. But you didn't disappoint. You *really* know what you're doing with your hands and that tongue. I knew that it was me you really wanted."

He clenched his jaw, swallowed the bile in his throat. "Glad you had a good time," he said flatly.

She smirked. "Oh, I did. And I'm thinking maybe next time we don't have to rush it in the hallway. Take it to the bedroom instead."

He looked at her, eyes sharp. "We should talk. Wednesday night?"

Ava blinked, happily caught off guard. "Really?"

"Yeah," he said. "You and me. Just us. Maybe grab a drink and… talk about everything. I want to remember more of it."

Her smile widened. "You're finally coming around. I'm so much better for you than Eliza. I can't wait to show you again how good we could be together."

He smiled too, but it didn't reach his eyes. Because if she was as careless and over confident as he thought she was, she'd slip.

And when she did, he'd be ready.

Because love wasn't always soft. Sometimes, love meant *fighting like hell* for the truth—even if it broke you first.

Chapter Thirty-Eight

Smoke, Mirrors, and Mini Skirts

Madison's heels hit the sidewalk like punctuation. Sharp. Intentional. Dangerous.

Behind her, Sophia and Amber flanked Eliza like bodyguards in leather and lipstick, dragging her into a night she hadn't asked for—but maybe needed more than she realized.

"I still don't know about this," Eliza muttered, tugging at the hem of the black satin mini dress Madison had all but forced her into. "This is not me."

Madison arched one perfectly sculpted brow. "Eliza Monroe, your ex tried to apologize with a criminal investigation. You've earned a night in heels and hell-yeah energy."

Amber grinned and handed her a soft red Sephora lip gloss. "You write songs that could break hearts in half. You deserve to feel hot while doing it."

Sophia, in her signature combat boots and mesh sleeves, copper hair down and swishing as she bumped her shoulder. "And honestly? You've got legs for days. Let the world suffer."

That earned the first real laugh Eliza had managed in a while. She did feel like a smoke show that night.

The bar—*The Amethyst Room*—was already packed when they walked in bypassing the line thanks to Madison's VIP status. A blend of neon, old wood floors, and local bands playing moody covers gave it that too-cool-to-care Austin vibe. Bodies swayed to the music, and the scent of whiskey, sweat, and strong perfume clung to the air like fog.

Their sophisticated and famous violet colored Amethyst Negroni, and violet gin cocktails were the lounges' signature.

Madison led them to a table near the back, perfectly angled for people-watching but close enough to the dance floor to bolt if a good song hit.

They ordered the amethyst gin cocktails—which were potent.

Eliza took a sip of the strong sweet pea infused concoction and felt the tension begin to unravel from her spine. Maybe this wasn't so bad.

Until she saw them.

Kai and Dillon were across the bar, flanked by a few teammates. Dillon caught sight of her first. His mouth parted slightly, eyes dragging over her like he didn't know where to look first. The dress. The hair. The fire in her eyes that hadn't burned quite this brightly in weeks.

Eliza looked away quickly, pulse skipping. If Finn weren't her North Star, Dillon would have made her pause. But he was, so she didn't. Dillon had an unusual vulnerability and quiet strength that she'd noticed which contrasted with his man-whore reputation. He deserved to find real love and she hoped that he would. Just not with her.

Kai elbowed him. "You okay?"

Dillon didn't answer. Not right away.

But Eliza didn't have time to dwell on that—because that's when *she* saw *her*.

Ava. The Bitch.

Perched on a velvet barstool like a smug little queen bee, surrounded by two of the other cheerleaders who'd always trailed after her like mean-girl footnotes. She wore a clingy red dress and too much highlighter, her glossy mouth twisted in that practiced perfect smile. The queen bee presiding.

The girls around her turned as Eliza walked by. One of them actually *winced*. Another whispered behind a hand, eyes darting between Eliza and Ava.

Ava looking like a cat who ate the cream, of course, just sipped her cocktail with the air of someone who believed she was untouchable. She locked eyes with Eliza and tilted her glass in a silent toast then smirked.

Like she'd won.

Eliza's stomach churned.

"Finn's chosen me over you. We have a romantic date night planned for Wednesday. Our love is out of the shadows now. He's forgotten about you and is completely mine now. Traded up." Ava almost purred with malicious glee.

 Heartsick, Eliza turned to walk toward the dance floor before Ave could see that her barbs hit their mark, but Madison caught her wrist gently.

"You okay?" she murmured, reading everything on her face.

Eliza nodded once. "I knew she'd be out here playing the victim. Trying to rewrite the story. I'm so mad, I just want to slap her self satisfied face. She told me that she has a date with Finn. I feel sick."

Sophia slid up beside them. "The nerve of her showing up in that dress like she's not ten minutes from jail time."

Amber stepped closer looking gorgeous in an asymmetric black dress with fine leather detailing. "Want us to dump our drinks on her? That never gets old. This situation calls for me to let my inner klutz out."

Eliza smiled, but it didn't quite reach her eyes.

"No," she said. "Let her gloat. Let her act like she's still in control. Finn said it himself—she doesn't know what's coming. Let her think she won."

Sophia raised a brow. "You're playing the long game."

"I'm not playing anything anymore," Eliza said, straightening. "I'm done playing. I'm just watching now—watching her trap herself in the lie she built."

Her voice was calm. Too calm. The kind of calm that comes just before the storm.

Behind her, Dillon was still watching. And he wasn't the only one.

Kai's gaze bounced between Eliza and Ava, catching the tension like a rope stretched tight. He nudged Dillon again.

"Don't interfere," he said quietly. "She's got a plan."

Dillon didn't speak. Just downed the rest of his beer, jaw tight.

Back at the table, Madison looped her arm through Eliza's.

"Ready to dance it out?"

Looking at the packed dance floor, Eliza smile a genuine smile, finally. "Let's make some noise and show everyone what they're missing."

And they did.

All while the girl in red watched—unsure why the room no longer bent around her.

Because power, Eliza realized, wasn't about volume. It was about knowing the truth—and letting it burn quietly until the whole world saw the fire.

****

Finn didn't mean to see it.
He hadn't gone looking.

He'd been watching game film in the common room of the athletic dorms with some other teammates when Kai walked in, phone in hand, face unreadable.
"Violet Room," Kai said, dropping onto the couch beside him.

"What?"

Kai turned his screen. "Scroll through the tagged photos."

Finn did. Slowly. Like ripping off bandages.

There she was.

Eliza. His Eliza. Long hair curled, flowing down to the middle of her back, legs bare, that tiny black dress he hadn't seen before hugging her body like sin and poetry. Her stunning violet eyes fierce. Her full mouth in a soft smile that didn't quite reach her eyes making his heart beat faster reminding his body of how long they'd been apart.

Surrounded by Sophia, Amber, and Madison—powerhouse women who weren't about to let her fall apart on their watch.

And behind them, barely in frame, was Ava. At the bar. Smirking like she still had cards to play.

Finn felt his stomach twist. He's seen the video of him kissing Ava and he wanted to puke. He had been drugged but still his lips and tongue had touched someone other than Eliza and he almost couldn't forgive himself for it.

"I thought you said she wasn't talking to anyone," he said flatly.

"She's not. But people talk. And apparently, that dress made the rounds."

Kai gave him a sideways glance. "Dillon was there, too. Some say he didn't stop looking at Eliza all night."

Finn's jaw clenched. "Of course he didn't."

Kai leaned back. "You gonna get pissed or you gonna get smart?"

"I'm gonna win her back," Finn said, low. "No matter who else thinks they have a shot."

Kai smirked. "Good. 'Cause she looked like a woman halfway done rising from the ashes."

Finn stood. "Then I'm making damn sure I'm the one waiting for her on the other side."

****

Eliza sat on the floor of Sophia's spare bedroom later that night, her notebook open, guitar across her lap. The buzz of the night was still on her skin—the lights, the bass, the burn of Ava's hate-filled stare.

But louder than all of it was Finn's face, playing in her memory like a film reel she didn't know how to stop.

She didn't trust him yet. She didn't know what the next step was, she just knew that she couldn't let him go.

But she didn't want to hate him anymore either.

She strummed a soft chord. Then another. Let the words come without questioning them.

"Smoke Signals"
Lyrics by Eliza Monroe

Verse 1
You didn't see the war in me
Until I walked away, head high, not clean
Lipstick armor, heels like fire
I danced past the wreckage, but I never lost desire

Pre-Chorus
You thought I'd burn and fade
But I lit the match and walked away

Chorus
I sent up smoke signals, baby, did you see the flare?
That dress, that laugh, my hands up in the air
I wasn't lost—I was learning how to leave
But you showed up in the echoes, in the space I still believe
Smoke signals in the night

Telling you I'm not alright
But I'm still here
Still burning bright

Verse 2
She watched me like a warning sign
You sat in silence while she crossed that line
I kept your name in every song
But I'm tired of bleeding for what you got wrong

Pre-Chorus
You say you didn't choose her
But I felt the silence louder

Chorus
I sent up smoke signals, baby, did you see the flare?
That dress, that laugh, my hands up in the air
I wasn't lost—I was learning how to leave
But you showed up in the echoes, in the space I still believe
Smoke signals in the night
Telling you I'm not alright
But I'm still here
Still burning bright

Bridge
I don't want a maybe, I don't want a ghost
I want the truth, even if it hurts the most
So follow the trail, find your way back
If you're still mine—prove it's not just talk

Final Chorus
I sent up smoke signals, hoping you'd find your way
Through fire and doubt, through every price we pay
I'm not the same, but I still believe
In the love we swore would never leave

So light a match, meet me in the flame
If you want me—say my name

Outro
Still burning
Still brave
Still waiting
To be saved

She set the guitar down and exhaled.

Madison would want to hear this one.

But part of her wondered… if Finn would, too.

And whether he'd know that the smoke wasn't just a warning.

It was an invitation. To remember. To try.

Chapter Thirty-Nine

Caught in the Light

The plan was simple.

Finn would meet Ava at *The Pavilion*, the busiest on-campus restaurant, at her request. She wanted to be seen. That much was obvious. Prove that they were the new *golden couple*. But Finn didn't care about the eyes around them—he only cared about the ears that mattered.

Coach Billings and Kai were both looped in, listening through the live call he had running from his phone, tucked safely in the chest pocket of his hoodie. The mic was open, the line recording. The police had already taken his statement, and the request for security footage from *The Blind Buck* had been processed. l

Now, all he needed was Ava to confess and confirm what he already suspected.

Ava was already there when he arrived—seated at a small corner booth by the window, legs crossed, phone in hand, practically glowing. She wore lipstick—The same shade that she had left on his face and neck that night.

She stood as he approached, pressing a kiss to his mouth like it was routine.

Finn didn't flinch. He just gave a tight smile and slid into the booth across from her.

"I was wondering if you'd come around," she said, sipping something pink with a straw. "You've been all tension and guilt since that night. I thought you might be scared off."

"Maybe I was," he said, steady. "But I've been thinking about it. About you. About that night."

Ava leaned in, lowering her voice like she was telling a secret. "It was fun, wasn't it?"

"Yeah. But the end of the night… it's a blur. I can't really remember how we ended up back at my place. I just remember that Eliza was mad."

She smirked. "Well… you weren't exactly in your right mind."

"Exactly," he said. "That's what I can't stop thinking about. I don't remember anything after that drink you gave me."

Ava's gaze flickered, just briefly. But she recovered quickly. "You were drunk, Finn. Happens."

"I had three beers and a couple shots over several hours. I've had more than that and walked home straight."

She sipped her drink, eyes narrowing. "Are you accusing me of something?"

"No," he said, leaning in. "I'm asking you. Did you put something in that drink? It sure made me feel good." He lied trying to draw her in.

Her mouth curled at the corner, but the smile didn't reach her eyes. "You liked it, though. You kissed me back. All that tongue. And your hands were everywhere."

"I didn't know what I was doing." Finn replied feeling sick to his soul but trying not to show it.

"Oh please," she said, laughing quietly. "You weren't *that* out of it. I just helped things along. Gave you a little push. You didn't want to hurt that simpering ex-girlfriend of yours."

And there it was.

Finn's heart pounded.

"I was by your side all season. Not her. She was too busy for you and you didn't want her there anyway or she would have been there for you like I was." Ava's seductive voice finished.

He kept his expression neutral. "So… you did something to the drink."

Ava blinked. A beat too long. Then she smiled again, cocky this time. "Relax. It was harmless. Just something to take the edge off. Make it easier for you to make the right choice. You were so stressed and I knew that I was the one you really wanted. I thought you *needed* it. I needed you."

His fists curled under the table, but he stayed calm. "That wasn't your choice to make. What was it anyway? I've never felt that way before." Finn prodded.

Ava shrugged. "Eliza's not here but you're here now, aren't you? With me. It was the only way to make you see what's right in front of you. It was just a little generic Rohypnol."

He had her. Ava was going to be expelled and prosecuted for Assault.

Finn sat there alone, shoulders heavy. Then he ran a hand through his hair and buried his face in both palms.

Having just moved her stuff from Sophia's place back to their apartment, determined to work out things with Finn and she couldn't do that with distance between them, Eliza walked into the restaurant with Sophia, scanning for a table. Her eyes moved past faces automatically—until they landed on *him*.

Her whole body went still. Then felt a deep cold stealing her body. Her heart.

Finn. Sitting across from *Ava*. In a booth. Leaning in. Talking like it meant something.

Sophia followed her gaze. "Shit."

But Eliza didn't move. She couldn't. Because as she stared, she noticed something off. Finn's expression wasn't easy. It was tight. Focused. Controlled. Like he was *trying* to stay calm.

And then she noticed his hand—pressed to his chest. No, not *his hand*—his *phone*.

Recording. This was the so called "date" that Ava had mentioned. In reality Finn was trying to get a confession.

Her breath caught at the realization.

She stepped behind a pillar, dragging Sophia with her. "Wait," she whispered. "Something's happening."

Back at the table, Ava was rambling.

"Oh please," Ava said, laughing quietly. "You weren't *that* out of it. I just helped things along. Gave you a little push. You didn't want to hurt that simpering ex-girlfriend of yours."

Finn slowly pulled out his phone, set it on the table between them.

Eliza and Sophia saw them speaking but couldn't hear anymore. The noise in the restaurant had increased exponentially as the band had started playing.

"You just did."

Ava blinked, confused. "What?"

Finn pressed the screen. The video call ended.

And the line went quiet on the other end—now already captured and sent. Sent to Coach Billings, West, the UT campus police and the Austin Police.

Ava paled.

"You recorded me?" she hissed.

"I loved Eliza," he said quietly. "I *still* do. And now I have proof that I didn't walk away from her. You *took* that from me."

Shaking, Ava stood so fast her drink spilled across the Formica table.

Blanching she said, "You're gonna regret this."

"No," he said. "You will. You assaulted me by taking my free will. According to the police, that's assault."

Behind the pillar was empty, Eliza had left before Finn and Ava had finished.

Her legs were jelly, her chest tight. But in her gut, in the place beyond pride and heartbreak, she finally *knew*:

He hadn't betrayed her.

He'd been set up.

She needed to let him come to her with the evidence…the proof that he wasn't unfaithful. Her heart ached for what had been done to him. His free will taken away.

And now, everything hurt in a different way. This didn't fix everything but at least he hadn't betrayed her. It was time to head back to the apartment. Now they might have a place to begin.

Chapter Forty

The Reckoning

Finn sat in the booth long after Ava was gone.

The restaurant was busy around him. A couple of college kids who'd been hunched over their laptops packed up and left as a band had begun while he was talking with Ava. The waitress had stopped checking on him, probably deciding he was one of those people who wanted to be left alone.

He was.

But also, he wasn't.

The air smelled of food and beer, overpowered by the cloying perfume Ava had left behind, still clinging to the vinyl, to his hoodie, to the inside of his lungs. He hated that it lingered. It made him feel coated, contaminated.

The table was sticky with the residue from Ava's drink. His palms left faint imprints when he lifted them. He flexed his fingers, watching the shine glisten under the now dim light, like glue, like something meant to hold him in place.

He wanted to claw his skin off.

Instead, he stared down at the phone lying in front of him.

Black screen. Lifeless. But it wasn't. It held a pulse, a weight, a threat. It carried the last thing he had to give — the truth.

The recording was safe. Backed up. Though the only person who mattered hadn't heard it yet.

Eliza.

Her name hit him like a heartbeat. A syllable that wasn't just sound but gravity, keeping him tethered when everything else inside him wanted to drift into oblivion.

He whispered it under his breath, once. Twice. Like a prayer.

Eliza.

He didn't know if she would ever want him again. He didn't know if hearing the recording would change anything. He didn't know if she had already decided he was poison but after seeing her perform her song and having a talk afterwards he was hopeful that she would still want him still. Give him another chance.

He was going to find out. He had to try.

He picked up the phone. The case felt slick in his hand, his palm damp with sweat. He pressed his thumb hard against the glass, not to unlock it, but just to feel the resistance. Like it might bite him. Like it might shatter under the pressure.

He shoved it into his hoodie pocket, grabbed his wallet, and pushed himself out of the booth. His legs felt shaky, too long and too weak at the same time.

He tossed down bills on the table—twice what the meal cost. He didn't care, this moment had been worth it. He needed to leave.

Outside, the air slapped him with cold clarity. The wind tore at his hoodie, shoved through his jeans, made his skin ache. Leaves scraped across the sidewalk in frantic little swirls, as if even the ground itself was restless.

He walked.

Every step heavier than the last.

Every step replaying the words she'd thrown at him.

You broke me.

You broke us.

He dragged his hands through his hair until it stood on end. His scalp burned. His ears rang. His chest felt like it was collapsing inward.

Still, he walked.

The city blurred around him. Streetlights flicked off one by one as the sun clawed its way up through a bruised horizon. Cars hissed by on wet pavement, splashing cold arcs against the curb. His shoes soaked through, but he didn't stop.

By the time he reached their apartment building, his hands were trembling.

You broke me.

You broke us.

He stood outside the glass doors, staring at his reflection. Pale. Haggard. Eyes bloodshot, jaw tight, hoodie clinging damp to his shoulders. He looked like someone she wouldn't recognize. Someone she shouldn't let back in.

But he had to try. He was never giving up on them. On her. His North Star. His Songbird. His everything.

The lobby smelled faintly of disinfectant and burnt coffee from the pot that always seemed to be brewing at the front desk. He ignored the elevator and took the stairs. His legs burned with the climb, but the pain felt better than the panic. At least pain was solid. Real.

By the time he reached their floor, his chest was heaving. His heart pounded so hard it shook his vision.

He stopped outside their door. Paused.

He pressed his hand flat against the wood. His breath fogged against the cool surface. For a second, he let his forehead rest there, eyes closed, imagining what it would feel like to open it and find her arms waiting.

But he hadn't earned that. Yet.

He wrapped his fingers around the knob.

He didn't knock.

He unlocked it quietly and stepped inside. The place was dim again, the curtains drawn. Her favorite vintage Lucchese cream boots were by the door. Her gold tote bag was on the counter.

She was home.

His stomach twisted. His heart raced.

He walked down the hall to their bedroom—the door was closed.

His stomach twisted until he thought he might throw up.

He moved through the living room like an intruder. Every step slow. Every breath shallow.

The hallway stretched long, shadows heavy. At the end—their bedroom door. Closed.

He stopped there.

His hand hovered inches from the wood. His chest rose and fell in uneven bursts. His forehead pressed against it.

It was like standing on the edge of a cliff.

If he knocked, everything could fall.

If he didn't, he'd already lost her.

He lifted his fist. Hesitated. It was now or never.

Knocked once. Soft.

Silence.

Then footsteps.

Then nothing.

Then the door opened.

Eliza stood there. Pale skin. Dark circles beneath her eyes. Her hair loose around her shoulders, tangled like she hadn't slept.

She didn't look surprised. Didn't look angry. She looked… steady.

Like part of her had been waiting.

Her violet eyes speared through him, questioning, strangely hopeful.

She didn't speak. Neither did he. Not yet.

Her eyes locked onto him, sharp and unreadable.

He felt the weight of them like a blade.

Neither of them spoke.

Finn's hand shook as he reached into his hoodie pocket. He pulled out the iPhone. His thumb slid across the screen. His pulse thundered in his ears.

He held it up between them like an offering.

"I need you to hear this," he said, voice raw. "And then you can slam the door again. Yell. Tell me it's over. Whatever you need. But you deserve to know what really happened."

Her gaze flicked to the phone, then back to his face.

He pressed play.

Ava's voice filled the quiet hallway.

Eliza's jaw tensed as Ava's words landed in her heart.

"You weren't exactly in your right mind."
"I just helped things along."
"You were so stressed. I thought you *needed* it."
"You weren't going to walk away from her on your own."
"She needed a reason to leave you. So I created one…Rohypnol"

"Now you can be with me like I know you've always wanted to be."

"I was by your side all season. Not her. She was too busy for you and you didn't want her there anyway or she would have been there for you like I was." Ava's seductive voice finished.

By the time the recording ended, Eliza's hand was over her mouth and she was shaking.

Tears slid down her face.

He didn't speak. Just let the silence settle.

"I didn't remember anything," he said finally, voice shaking. "Not the kiss. Not the ride home. Nothing after she gave me that drink. But I swear on everything, Eliza—if I'd known what she'd done—if I'd been *me*—I would have come home to you and I certainly wouldn't have touched that bitch."

Eliza looked like she wanted to believe him. Needed to. Did believe.

"But I didn't protect us," he said. "I let distance grow between us. I let someone like her get close because I was blind to how bad things had gotten. That's still on me."

She stepped forward. Barely.

And then she said, voice quiet, "You didn't choose her?"

He shook his head. "I never stopped choosing you. I love you more than life. You will always be my North Star. I'll be better at showing you everyday if you let me."

The air hung thick between them. Grief. Relief. Fear. Everything unspoken.

Finally, she reached for the phone.

Not to throw it. Not to replay it. Just to hold it.

Her fingers curled tight around it, knuckles white.

She stared at him. Lips trembling.

She just held it. And stared at him.

She whispered. "I believe you Finn. I think that in my heart I already knew the truth but I couldn't see beyond the image of you with your mouth on her. My heart felt too shattered."

Finn's chest caved inward. Relief tore through him so hard he almost dropped to his knees.

It wasn't forgiveness. It was vindication for Finn. He knew that they had things to sort out and work on but now he felt like they at least had a chance.

And for now, that was enough.

It wasn't forgiveness.

It wasn't healing.

It was a chance.

It was a beginning.

And for now, that was enough.

Chapter Forty-One

North Again

Eliza didn't sleep that night. Neither did Finn.

Not because of anger. Not even from pain. Neither knew where to begin.

The apartment felt like a museum of everything they'd been, and everything that had been broken. Shadows shifted across the ceiling, the clock ticked, and she lay in bed with her eyes wide open, pulse thrumming in her throat.

Not from rage. Not anymore.
Not even from pain.

From weight. From everything pressing against her chest.

She lay in bed alone, eyes open, listening to the silence that used to be shared—used to be filled with whispered goodnights and Finn's steady breath.

The recording had played again in her mind long after she'd handed the phone back to him. Ava's voice, smug and cruel. Finn's voice, steady and broken. The way he hadn't begged, hadn't pushed—just offered her the truth like it was all he had left.

You weren't going to walk away on your own. So I created a reason.

Eliza gripped the sheets in her fists, hot tears tracing down the sides of her face. Rage, sorrow, and love—God, *still* love—battled inside her like fire and wind.

But underneath it all, through every stormy thought, one thing stood unmoving:

Finn hadn't betrayed her.

Not really. He had been *taken* from her in the worst way. And still, he came back.

Still, he fought…for them.

As her tears continued sliding sideways into her hair, beneath them, through the cyclone of fury and grief, something steadier thrummed.

Finn hadn't betrayed her.

He came home. To her.

She pressed the heel of her hand to her eyes, but it didn't stop the tears.

Across the hall, she knew he was awake too. On the futon in the guest room, curled tight like someone braced for impact.

She wanted to go to him.
She wanted to throw open the door and curl into his chest and let herself sob until she couldn't breathe.

But not yet.
Not until she knew what she wanted to do with the shards of her heart.

The hours dragged. Her mind an unrelenting spiral of self recrimination for losing faith in Finn. Examining the reasons why she hadn't believed him when he had claimed innocence before he'd shown her the proof.

Finally, she realized that it had been the distance that had grown between them before that night. Finn seeming to chose everything else in his life but her. Everything else had come first to him—Teammates, football, school, public adulation. Unaware or unwilling to keep Ava at a proper distance. Moving forward with their relationship, if they both chose to, couldn't begin that same way. They would need a whole new start. He had to put her, put them first.

She rose at sunrise, wrapped herself in her violet silk floral kimono that Madison had convinced her she needed to buy, and stepped into the quiet apartment. Finn was still asleep.

She watched him for a moment. Wanting to hold him close. Missing his scent and the feel of his warm skin.

Instead she turned and made jasmine tea, the scent filling the air like memory—sweet and sharp. She set the mug on the counter and leaned against it, palms flat, eyes closed.

Later that morning, she found him sitting on the balcony. Hoodie pulled over his head. The same one from the night he had fallen apart behind their front door.

He looked up as she stepped out, his expression cautious, quiet.

She sat beside him. Pulled her knees to her chest. The breeze smelled like wet leaves and something new.

"I hated you," she said softly.

He nodded. "I know."

"I hated myself, too. For still loving you through it."

He didn't look away. "I never stopped loving you. But I understand if that's not enough."

She shook her head. "It's not. Not by itself."

A pause. The wind moved her long, pale hair across her cheek.

"But I realized something last night. You didn't just fight to prove you didn't cheat. You fought to come *home*. To *me*." She turned to him. "Even when I slammed the door. Even when I screamed in your face."

His throat bobbed. His lips pressed tight. His eyes shone like he might break—but he blinked it back.

"I don't want to start over," she continued. "I want to move forward. With everything. The damage, the truth, the love. I want to build from *here*."

Finn swallowed hard. "Even after everything?"

"You're my North Star, Finn." She exhaled slowly. "But stars don't always shine clearly. Sometimes the sky gets crowded. Or dark. But that doesn't mean they're gone. You just have to remember where to look."

She let him take it. Their fingers threaded together, trembling.

"Finn," she whispered, her voice breaking, "we both made mistakes. We both let the distance grow. I'm sorry for my part. You are my only and always Finn."

His rough thumb brushed her knuckles. His grip was soft. Too soft. Suddenly, swinging into her space, he clutched her to his chest, whispering hoarsely in her hair.

"You'll always come first to me Eliza. Songbird I almost lost you. Lost us. Never again." Finn said with conviction and possession. A tear sliding down his face.

Eyes burning with love and all of the passion they'd been denied, they looked at one another.

And suddenly, it wasn't enough.

The dam inside her cracked.

Her hands fisted in the front of his hoodie and she pulled him toward her. Their mouths collided—desperate, hungry, trembling with everything they had almost lost.

He made a low sound, half-growl, half-sob, and crushed her against him. His arms banded around her waist, fierce, possessive. Like he was afraid if he loosened for a second, she would vanish.

Their kiss was salt and fire, wet with tears, hot with survival. Her lips parted under his and he devoured her, breath harsh, unsteady. His hand slid into her hair, cupped the back of her skull, angling her exactly where he wanted. She clutched his shoulders, short red nails biting through fabric, dragging him closer.

Her chest pressed against his. His heart thundered against her ribs. They kissed like they were drowning, like breath didn't matter, like their mouths were the only place they still lived.

When she pulled back for air, her forehead slammed against his, breaths ragged in the inches between.

"Don't let go," she whispered, voice shaking.

"Never," he rasped. His fingers dug into her waist, anchoring her. "Not again. Not ever."

She kissed him again, harder, a sob trapped between their mouths. He swallowed it, turned it into heat. His hands slid down her back, gripping her hips, pulling her practically into his lap. She straddled him without thought, silk kimono falling open at her thigh, his hoodie rough against her skin.

He kissed her like she was oxygen. She kissed him like he was blood in her veins.

Every touch was frantic and heart-stopping. Every press of their mouths was apology and promise.

"I thought I lost you," she gasped against his jaw, teeth grazing.

"You're mine," he said, fierce and raw. "I'll never let anyone take me from you again. No one."

Her nails dug into his nape, holding him to her. He groaned into her mouth, like even pain was proof he was still alive, still hers.

The wind whipped around them, but they were heat. Fierce, consuming heat.

They kissed until they shook. Until her lips were swollen, until his hoodie was damp with tears, until her lungs screamed for air.

Finally, they broke, chests heaving, foreheads pressed together. His hands framed her face, trembling but unyielding.

"You're everything," he whispered, voice raw. "Everything."

Her tears slipped free, but they weren't bitter anymore. They were release.

They stayed wrapped around each other, wounded and raw, holding like lifelines—without illusions but filled with their shared love.

This wasn't an ending.
It wasn't forgiveness.
It was survival.
It was a beginning.

They sat like that—wounded, real, and holding each other like they'd never let go, It wasn't a perfect ending.

It wasn't an ending at all.

It was the start of their second beginning.

They didn't let go for a long time.

The balcony around them blurred—the wet leaves on the railing, the faint clink of her tea mug against the metal, the street sounds below. None of it mattered. What mattered was the thrum of his pulse against her temple, the weight of her in his lap, the steady burn of something alive between them.

When Eliza finally leaned back, her eyes were red but unflinching. Body still throbbing with banked passion.

"If we're going to do this again," she said, her voice quiet but steady, "we do it differently."

Finn's hands tightened on her hips. His eyes, still wet, locked to hers. "Whatever you need."

"Not just me," she said. "Us. Both of us. That's the only way we protect it."

She slid her hands down his arms, gripped his wrists. Counted off on her fingers.

She turned to face him. "Not just me. You too. This has to work for both of us. That's the only way we protect it. The distance that grew between us was created by both of us not putting the other first or communicating what we needed."

He leaned in, listening hard. Like every word she said was something sacred.

She counted on her fingers. "First: we check in. Not just how was your day, but real check-ins. If you're drifting, if I am… we say it."

"Deal."

"Second: boundaries. Ava should've never been close enough to drug you, Finn."

His jaw tightened. "She'll never be near me again."

"I believe you. But this isn't about punishment—it's about patterns. No more blurred lines. Not with friends. Not with people who want you."

"You have mine. Fully," he said. "And I'll take the same from you."

She nodded, thankful. "Third: we don't let each other disappear. Not into practice, not into classes, not into fear. If you feel distance, you speak. If I feel distance, I speak."

He swallowed. "No more ghost version of us."

"No more."

Then she added quietly, "And if either of us ever feels unsafe, unheard, or unseen... we talk before it's too late."

"We make time for date nights and time for it to be together just the two of us." Finn reached for her hand again. This time, it wasn't shaky.

It was steady. Strong.

"Okay," he said. "Let's write our new rules on the sky."

For a long moment, they just sat like that, holding on. Holding each other. Then Eliza whispered, "I need to tell you something. Something I've been scared to say out loud."

He shifted toward her. "Anything."

"I was afraid I wasn't enough for you," she said. "Not smart enough, not wild enough, not... glittering enough. You live in this world now where everyone adores you. And I kept thinking—what if one day you wake up and realize I'm too small, too quiet, too ordinary?"

Her voice broke on the last word.

Finn's brow furrowed, his thumb brushing over her knuckles. "Eliza there is nothing ordinary about you. In my eyes I see your grace, beauty, gentleness, talent, and resilience. I was afraid *I* wasn't enough for you."

She blinked incredulously. "What?"

He exhaled, voice low. "Everyone sees me under lights, under helmets, in highlight reels. They cheer, they scream, they put me on their walls. And I started believing that was all I had—that version of me. The one who throws touchdowns. The one who smiles in the pictures. The one who wins. But with you... I was terrified you'd see past that. That you'd see me tired, or broken, or lost. And that one day, it wouldn't be enough. That you'd see that I'm one bad pass, one failed class, from falling apart. That you would leave me. No one has ever stayed. So subconsciously I ran from us before you could leave."

Her breath caught.

"I got drunk on the adulation," he admitted, eyes wet but unflinching. "I let it distract me. I thought if I kept being the guy everyone wanted, I'd never lose you. But the truth is… it pulled me away from the only person I *wanted* to be enough for. You."

The words hung between them, sharp and tender.

Her heart ached. She tightened her grip on his wrists. "Maybe that's what we both forgot. You don't have to be bigger than life. And I don't have to be more than myself. What makes us enough… is each other."

Finn's chest rose and fell, uneven. Then he leaned in and pressed his forehead to hers. "You've always been enough. More than enough. You're the only thing that's ever made me want to be more—not for the crowd, but for us."

Her eyes closed. Tears slipped down her cheeks, but they weren't bitter.

This time, when they kissed, it wasn't desperate or broken.
It was quiet.
It was new.
It was the first kiss of their second beginning.

They skipped classes later that day.

It wasn't about playing hooky. It was about *presence*. Eliza closed her laptop. Finn left his phone in the kitchen drawer.

They walked for hours through campus, holding hands, stealing passionate kisses, down side streets lined with orange leaves, through the bookstore where Eliza pointed out the poetry section and Finn pretended to critique the covers. She picked out a secondhand copy of *The Little Prince*. He bought it for her without a word.

They shared fries in the quad. Watched a squirrel steal a granola bar from someone's backpack and debated whether it was "calculated theft or dumb luck."

They ignored everyone else but each other, completely absorbed renewing their connection.

They laughed.

They touched.

They breathed again.

They burned for one another.

That evening, the warm vanilla-lavender scented candles were lit again. Same ones she'd used the night she waited for him, only now they flickered in forgiveness, the promise of passion, instead of sadness.

The balcony doors were open to the fresh night air, stars glimmered in the sky, bearing witness to their union.

Eliza stood in the doorway of their bedroom. She had changed into something simple. A pretty red sundress and her favorite vintage cream Lucchese cowboy boots, a touch of makeup—her favorite Sephora lip gloss, double black mascara, and deep violet eyeliner, hair down wavy to the middle of her back just the way Finn liked. But the way Finn looked at her when he saw her made her feel like she'd stepped into light.

They didn't rush.

He touched her like she was sacred, not fragile. Like he was being given another chance to memorize her all over again. Her hands trembled as they ran down his hard, muscular chest, his broad shoulders, but not from fear. From the weight of the moment.

They undressed slowly, kisses traded like passionate vows, skin warming under hands that no longer held doubt.

As Finn unzipped her red dress, unveiling new red lace lingerie underneath his breath hissed out and hands began to shake. He pulled her flush against his front, sliding his big hands inside the back of her dress. Cupping the curve of her bottom holding her closer against his hard length. She ground against him whimpering with need. Desperately trying to get closer. It had been too long since they had felt each other. Known each other.

When they moved together to the bed, they both knew that it was deeper than just need. It was coming home.

"Finn," Eliza whispered his name like a husky prayer.

He held her like she was the last good thing in the world. Hands firm, caressing, kissing, and nibbling her collarbone moving down slowly to her full aching breasts.

"Finn, please," she cried with growing abandon. Thinking that she'd die if he didn't satisfy her need for him soon.

"You want my mouth on you? Here?" He asked as he cupped then licked the sides of each breasts and moving to her diamond hard nipples. Sucking hard and tweaking each one sending sharp tingles down her body, leaving her wet, awakening her core.

As he made his way down her body with his mouth, kissing and touching her with reverence and passion she undulated and caught fire. His mouth moved lower to the place that pulsed with need of him—Loving her folds, fingers scissoring inside her, as his tongue laved her sensitive bud. It wasn't long before she was shattering, thrown into overwhelming pleasure, her body exploding like stars under his tongue. A pleasure only Finn could sate. As she started to come down from her high, Finn lifted his fingers to his mouth, sucking them. Licking them clean with a husky growl of satisfaction.

As she began to come down from her orgasm, Finn began to build the heat back up.

Wanting to pleasure him too, she placed her small hand on his shaft moving it up and down with a building intensity, her other hand cupping his balls gently, as her mouth loved his with deepening exploration then moving it down slowly to lick the top of his shaft lovingly. When she looked up into Finn's eyes as her tongue caressed him so thoroughly, he was ready to blow. The passion overtaking him completely.

Almost frantically, he grasped her by the waist and and moved his huge, muscular body over her. He wanted to look into her violet eyes full of love and lust, as he thrust into her, wanted to see the passion and connection— the lust. Knowing that he was the only man who would see her this way. Feel her this way. Winding her shiny, blonde hair in his fist, making her delicate neck free for his attentions, he put his other arm under lower back making her arch under him.

The flame blazed into an inferno as he pressed the head of his cock against her swollen, aroused opening, then thrusting to the hilt inside her. All she could do was hold onto him, wrapping her legs around him encouraging him to go deeper, get closer. Become one soul.

"Come on songbird give me everything. No holding back. You are mine. This body is mine." Finn said roughly in her ear.

"Always." she responded as she began to orgasm. Nails digging into his shoulders. The sound of her scream tearing from her followed. "Finn! Mine!" She cried in ecstasy.

The orgasm ripped through Eliza so that only stars shown in her eyes and her body convulsed gripping him with abandon. Bliss finding her. Once he felt her erupt, it was his turn to see the stars. Experiencing the most mind-blowing orgasm of his life, and a sense of utter completion, he started to come down holding Eliza tightly against his hard, muscular body, warm with sweat. Unwilling to release her. Wanting to never let her go. To never be apart again.

They didn't speak. They didn't need to. So in the moment and overwhelmed. Sated and full of gratitude.

Afterward, tangled in sheets and each other, Eliza placed her hand over Finn's heart, feeling the beat quicken at her touch.

His spring green eyes were filled with deep love and contentment as he looked at her, "You still feel like home," she said softly. "North of Always, my love."

Finn turned toward her, eyes wet. "You *are* my home."

Breathe slowing, Eliza noticed a tattoo above his heart. One that wasn't there before. Having Finn inside her again, loving her had blotted out everything else.

She traced the image delicately with her finger. It was an image of a songbird inside it was a compass pointing north. Lyrics from a song she wrote for him around the bird in flight.

Moved beyond words, she looked into his eyes, kissed him passionately and asked, "When? Why?"

"The day after. As I came off that drug Ava gave me, saw the video, I knew immediately what I had lost. How precious you are to me. No matter what happened, even if you never forgave me, I needed you with me in my heart and branded on my skin. You're it for me Eliza."

Wrapping her arms around him, she replied huskily, "Finn my heart is yours, all of me is yours. Since ours eyes met all those years ago you've been my North Star, my *North of Always*."

She kissed him consuming them both with all of the love and passion they'd almost been denied.

Outside, the clear night was silent. Only the constellations told stories.

Inside, two people who had been broken found a new way to fit together —not perfect, but passionate and real.

And under the soft glow of flickering starlight, they began anew.

Chapter Forty-Two

Stronger Days, Louder Voices

The weeks that followed weren't easy, they both had bad habits to change but both Finn and Eliza were committed to rebuilding their relationship by putting each other first—always. Filtering out the noise around them.

But they were honest and genuine. Hopeful. Eliza found herself writing more music than doing homework. Stressing herself less and allowing herself to embrace each moment. Inspired by her challenges with Finn she wrote a song called "Second Chances" influenced by their renewed commitment to one another.

"Second Chances"
Lyrics by Eliza Monroe

Verse 1
We broke in the quiet, not in the storm,
In the missed hellos, in the love not worn.
But I still hear your voice in the smallest things—
In old songs, in tea cups, in worn-out strings.

Pre-Chorus

We forgot how to listen, forgot how to see,
But I still remember the way you breathe.

Chorus

So let's be the kind who start again,
Pick up the pieces, not pretend.
I don't need perfect—I need real,
I need to know you still feel this feel.
We don't have to be who we were before,
Just two hearts choosing more.
I believe in second chances—
And I believe in us.

Verse 2

We kissed like gravity, then drifted apart,
Got caught in the orbit of too many starts.
But you're still the one I'd call in the dark,
The map in my chest, my north, my spark.

Pre-Chorus

It's not about falling—it's choosing to stay,
To say, "I still want you," at the end of the day.

Chorus

So let's be the kind who try again,
Write our names in ink, not sand.
I don't need flawless—I need true,
Even if that means relearning you.
We don't have to be unscarred or new—
Just two people still choosing "me and you."
I believe in second chances—
And I believe in us.

Bridge

There's beauty in broken things,
In stitched seams and fragile wings.
If you'll meet me in the in-between,
We can build something strong and seen.

Final Chorus

So let's be the kind who fight to mend,
Who show up not just now, but again.
I don't need easy—I need us,
The kind of love I can trust.
We don't have to be a perfect story,
Just the truth, raw and holy.
I believe in second chances—
Because I still believe in us.

Always Yours

The apartment was quiet—too quiet for how fast Eliza's heart was beating. They had just renewed their connection and she couldn't get enough of Finn. She craved him. His touch. His very presence in the room made her want to climb him. They were insatiable.

In her tight jeans and tank, she stood just inside the door, back against it, keys still clutched in her hand. Finn was already in the kitchen, shirtless, sweatpants low on his hips, abs carved, a light trail of hair leading downward, every muscle taut like he was waiting for a signal.

He turned when he heard the click of the lock.

"Eliza," he said, voice rough, husky and full of need. Like her name was a prayer he hadn't dared to say out loud.

She dropped her bag, stepped out of her battered cream vintage boots, and closed the distance between them in a few long strides of her long sleek legs that he loved so much. He visualized them wrapped around him with her on the kitchen island.

"I don't want to talk," she said.

His throat worked as he swallowed a slow smile crossing his face making his dimples pop. "That's my girl. I don't either. Come here," he said growling.

She reached for his face. Her fingers brushed along the edge of his jaw, down the stubble on his throat. "I just want you. No doubts. No distance. Not tonight. Not ever again."

That was all he needed.

He crushed her mouth with his, not gently—desperate and aching. She gasped into the kiss and fisted her hands in his dark silky hair, pulling him deeper. Coasting her tongue against his as his hands slid down her spine and under her thighs as he lifted her easily in his muscular arms, carrying her toward the bedroom without breaking the kiss.

They barely made it there.

He pressed her against the wall just inside the door, mouth trailing down her neck, biting and kissing until her head tilted back, breath caught between a moan and a plea. He licked and kissed the pulse point beating rapidly in her neck. She dragged her tank over her head and tossed it aside, bare beneath it.

His breath hitched. "Jesus, Eliza…"

"You said I was yours," she whispered, voice unsteady but sure. "Show me."

She felt the answer in the way he grabbed her hips and ground against her, hard and wanting. His hands roamed everywhere—her back, her thighs, the curve of her waist—as if trying to memorize every inch all over again.

When he laid her on the bed, he didn't go slow. Not this time.

They were past gentle.

His mouth traced fire along her collarbone, down the valley between her breasts, until her back arched and her fingers clutched at his hair. He kissed like he meant it. Like he needed it. Like the last few weeks had carved a hollow in him that only she could fill.

When he finally sank into her, it was with a groan that sounded more like surrender. She wrapped her legs around his waist, eyes locked on his.

"I love you," she said, fierce.

"I love you more than I know how to say," he choked out.

They moved together in a rhythm that was frantic, then aching, then perfect. Every thrust, every gasp, every whispered name was a reclaiming. Of her body. Of his love. Of them.

She cried out when she came, stars exploding behind her eyes, nails digging into his shoulders.

He followed seconds later, body shuddering, breath catching as he buried his face in her neck. Neither moved. Not for a long time.

When they finally did, it was just enough for him to pull her close again, tangled in sheets and sweat and something too deep to name.

"I don't ever want to lose this again," he whispered against her skin.

"You won't," she said, voice soft and sure. "We just found our way back. We just keep getting better and better."

And in the quiet after, as their hearts slowed and the world narrowed to the warmth of their bodies wrapped around each other, they knew—

This wasn't just sex.

It was a vow.

They were each other's again. Fully. Fiercely. Forever.

It was utter bliss.

****

Eliza and Finn continued to rebuild in small, consistent ways—morning check-ins over tea and protein shakes, post-class walks, handwritten notes tucked into backpacks. They took turns cooking. Made time to just *be* together without distractions. Eliza attended every home game and cheered loudly for Finn. He told her that he needed the support and that having her there grounded him and he felt as thought he played better when she was watching.

They celebrated with their friends together after the games. If one was there, the other was sure to be also. Everyone noticed the change and were happy for them both.

No forced smiles. No pretending the past hadn't happened.

They made space for hard talks. The kind where neither raised their voice, but both held ground.

They laughed more too.

Their sex was off the charts hot. Finn's desire was insatiable and so was Eliza's. Only and ever for one another.

The hurt hadn't disappeared—but they were walking through it *together*. And each step forward was theirs alone.

The passion was back full force. They couldn't keep their hands off one another.

They also celebrated, Eliza's short story being selected for the semester's closing reading—an event open to students, faculty, and local press. It was small, but to her, it was everything.

She nearly backed out the day of.

Finn found her in the green room of the campus theater, sitting on a folding chair, chewing a fingernail and staring at her printed pages like they might explode.

"You okay?" he asked.

"I feel like I'm going to throw up."

"You won't," he said. "But if you do, I'll hold your hair back, then drag you on stage anyway. You've performed your songs in public before. Think of that moment."

She gave him a watery laugh and smiled.

"You've got this," he said, kneeling in front of her. "You're not just reading. You're *showing* them who you are. And she's incredible."

She nodded, heart steadying.

"And afterward," he added, "we get fries and a chocolate milkshake and pretend you're not a literary goddess for the night."

Eliza rolled her eyes. "Shut up."

"You love it."

"I do."

In the front row sat Sophia, Van, Kai, and Rhetta grinned with pride. Finn watched from the side of the stage after leaving her in the green room.

Sophia, dressed in all black with her signature combat boots, had brought someone new: a massive guy from the football team, Finn's teammate, who no one had ever seen her with before. He was in her Bio class.

He sat like he barely fit in the chair—blonde hair buzzed short, pale blue eyes under thick brows, arms covered in tattoo sleeves that peeked from beneath his rolled-up sweatshirt. Strong, almost blunt features. He looked like he'd rather be anywhere else—until Sophia leaned in and whispered something.

Then he smirked. Just a little.

"Eliza, remember West," Sophia had told her earlier. "He's my… current social experiment."

"More like your hostage," West had muttered. But he hadn't left her side since.

Eliza stepped onto the stage and read her piece: a fictional retelling of a girl who found her way back from betrayal, not through revenge, but by choosing to stay soft. To heal. To forgive.

Supposedly it wasn't about her and Finn. But everyone knew it *was*.

And when she finished, the applause wasn't just loud.

It was *real*.

Finn stood first. Clapped loudest. His eyes held all of the love and pride her felt for her. He couldn't take his eyes from hers.

In that moment, she felt whole again—not because of the crowd or the praise, but because she knew she'd gotten here on her own two feet. And because the man in the audience stage-side had never stopped looking at her like she mattered.

Afterward, as they all gathered outside under string lights and paper lanterns, Finn giving his teammate West a pat on the back in greeting. Eliza gave him a grateful hug.

"Thanks for coming. Your support means the world to me." Eliza told her friends.

Sophia nudged Eliza with her elbow.

"Your words hit, babe. Like, genuinely. I almost cried. Then West muttered something sarcastic and ruined it."

West, standing beside her, grunted. "I said it was 'decent,' and for me, that's like a standing ovation."

Sophia smirked and laced her fingers through his massive hand.

Finn slid his arm around Eliza's waist. "Proud of you doesn't even cover it."

She leaned into him. "Thanks for standing by me."

"Always."

Their scars hadn't disappeared. But together, they'd stopped bleeding.

And as winter settled in, they walked ahead—hand in hand—under a sky that finally felt clear again.

Chapter Forty-Three

The Fourth Quarter

The championship game was a home game that started tense and stayed that way.

It was the Aggie's versus Texas and promised to be intense and was either schools' game.

Stadium lights burned against the early winter dusk, the crowd on their side of the stadium in burnt orange, yelled loud enough to shake the metal bleachers. Eliza sat between Sophia and Van wearing Finn's team jersey, hands clenched, eyes locked on the field.

West and Dillon started in the game but it was Finn who dominated—diving tackles, quarterback pressure, shouting signals, chasing every inch like it was personal. And it *was*. This game was the result of a season rebuilt from broken moments.

The other team had size. Speed. But what Finn's team had was grit. Unity.

And when the clock hit the final 60 seconds, they were down by five.

Then came the fumble.

Finn recovered it. The golden boy striking again.

The stadium roared.

"Sweet baby Jesus… it was a nail biter for UT." Eliza exclaimed to Sophia and Van.

"Your man is rocking it, " Screamed Sophia with enthusiasm.

And with thirty seconds left on the clock, they scored. A touchdown born from chaos and exhaustion and belief.

Finn looked up in the stands for Eliza. Their eyes met and Eliza was screaming before she realized it and started running to the field—To Finn. Sophia was jumping up and down trying not to look only at West. Van was on his feet, fist in the air oblivious to Sophia's focus on West.

And down on the field, Finn ripped off his helmet and found her in the crowd moving towards him. His grin was pure light. He ran to her giving her a sweaty and enthusiastically passionate kiss, that made his teammates taunt him and give him hell. Especially, West and Dillon.

They had done it and the UT crowd went insane for their Longhorn Football Team.

On the field looking at Eliza and Finn now, Dillon was happy for them. Seeing them together now made him realize that Eliza could never have been with him. He'd never stood a chance. Her heart was already taken and it had been since she met Finn. Finn seemed to realize what he had with her and treated her like the queen she was. Their love was truly made in the stars and he was happy they figured things out and busted that bitch Ava.

He couldn't quite grasp who Eliza's vulnerable and delicate sensibilities reminded him of. Strangely his heart tried to remember. It was there just out of reach.

The celebration, later that night, took over *McAllister's*, the dimly lit campus bar that felt half-sports pub, half-dance club. The whole football team and what looked like half the school were there. Tables overflowed with plates of wings, fries, pitchers of beer. Music thumped low through the walls. A back corner had been claimed by the football team.

Eliza sat on Finn's lap, her arms around his shoulders, cuddling into his chest, his hands on her hips and thigh. He was sweaty, hoarse, and still riding the high.

"I can't believe it," she whispered into his ear. " Take that back. I can believe it. You and the guys worked hard all season. You earned the win. You were spectacular," she added kissing him possessively, passionately.

He kissed her jaw, enjoying having her in his arms, celebrating with their friends. "Yes we earned it. Every second. Every bit. I'm still grateful that the plays and calls went our way."

Across from them, Sophia sipped a whiskey sour in a black velvet top that left little to the imagination. High-waisted leather skirt. High heeled, thigh high boots that said try me. West leaned beside her at the bar, stone-faced and quiet, as usual. Looking like a Russian mob or Bratva boss from a movie. Eyes glittering as they seemed to watch Sophia's every move.

"Are you ever gonna smile like a real human?" she sidled up to him and teased, bumping him with her hip.

"I'm smiling on the inside," he deadpanned but then smirked.

She winked, "I'll take what I can get."

Later, Sophia made her way to the dance floor. Alone.

The music shifted to something deep and rhythmic, pulsing through the crowd. Her hips moved easily, arms raised, eyes closed.

Two guys slid in around her—uninvited—one in front and one behind.

Too close. One tried to grab her hand. Putting his hand on her hip, the other leaned in, his breath too hot, too familiar. Moving his hand to her stomach and pulling her into his chest, grinding himself into her. Aroused.

"Back off," she said, trying to pivot. Pushing them away. She wasn't shy and didn't mind male attention but it had to be on her terms.

But they didn't. Back off from touching and crowding her.

And then a huge shadow moved between them.

West.

He didn't shove anyone. Just *stood there*.

Massive. Cold-eyed. Tattooed arms flexing under his fitted long-sleeve tee.

"Step back," he said, voice like a steel door closing.

The guys looked at each other, laughed—then saw his face.

They backed off without a word.

Sophia's heart was hammering. Her skin felt a warmth that had nothing to do with the crowded dance floor.

"You okay?" West asked, his tone low but direct.

"Yeah," she breathed. "I just..."

She trailed off. The music shifted again. Something slower. A little darker.

"Dance with me," she said.

West blinked. "I don't dance."

"You just rescued me. That earns you a spin."

He hesitated, then nodded once.

They moved together—awkward at first. But then his hands found her hips. Her arms slid around his neck. And something in the air changed. She smiled up at him.

"See?" she said. "You *are* human."

He smirked. "Don't tell anyone."

Back at the table, Van sipped his drink and watched them.

His jaw was tight.

Eliza noticed.

"You okay?"

"Yeah," Van said too quickly.

He took another drink and looked away from the dance floor—but not before one last glance at Sophia and West.

Still dancing. Still close.

Eliza leaned into Finn's chest and whispered, "Something just got complicated."

Finn grinned, drunk on adrenaline and love. "Everything worth it usually is."

"Ready to go home and start the real celebration?" Eliza said and her hand stroked his thigh moving closer and closer to his hard length.

"Always!" Finn winked and smirked.

They left as some of Finn's teammates patted him on the back as they passed.

The door clicked shut behind them, muffling the laughter and music still echoing in Finn's ears. Eliza was slipping off her jacket, shaking out her hair, when he crossed the room in three long strides and caught her wrist.

She looked up, startled.

His green eyes were dark with adrenaline, lips parted, breath shallow.

"Finn—"

"You looked so damn good tonight—hot and mine." His voice was low, ragged. "All night, I could barely focus. You were there, smiling like that, wearing my jacket, my number, touching my arm... I almost lost it."

Her breath caught. "You won. You were incredible."

He pulled her closer, his hand flat on her lower back, his body still humming with the rush of the game. "I didn't want to celebrate with anyone but you."

"I can't wait." He kissed her—hard, claiming. It wasn't soft or slow. It was desperate and consuming. She responded instantly, pressing into him, her hands fisting in the front of his T-shirt. He picked her up, one arm strong under her thighs, and carried her into the kitchen putting her on the island, not bothering with lights, not stopping until her butt landed on the granite counter.

"I need you," he breathed against her mouth. "You're mine, Eliza. My reward. My everything."

"I've always been yours."

He groaned and kissed her again, rough with reverence. He'd fantasized about taking her in every room of their apartment and on every available surface—tonight it needed to be in the kitchen. He moved with purpose, shedding clothes in a trail behind them. Spreading her long silky legs, he stepped in between pushing his hard length against her already swollen, drenched pussy.

Grinding, he kissed his way down to her aroused nipples, her full breasts begging for his attention. He gave it gladly, cupping then laving them with his tongue and finally when she thought she couldn't stand any longer he began sucking them earnestly, passionately.

Eliza felt it from her breasts straight to her clit. So completely enthralled, shaking with arousal, she was one second from impaling herself on Finn's shaft.

Finn then tangled one hand into her hair pulling until she felt a bite of pain along with pleasure, the other gripping her hip tightly like he needed her grounded, here, now, only his. Like she might fly away if he didn't hold her tightly to him.

"I need to be inside you Songbird." He growled.

Licking and kissing every one of his cut abs. He was steel covered in heated silk. Her fingers mapped his body like she already knew every muscle, every scar, the tattoo—and she did. But tonight, it was more. Fierce. Tender. Real. Hard. Her body arched to meet him, pulling him closer, whispering his name like a prayer as he thrust into her with all of the possessive passion and love he felt. Taking her hard, overwhelming her in his passion and desperation. Claiming.

Finn didn't just want her.

He needed her. She belonged to him. With Him. Always.

Not just the touch, not just the sex. He needed the way she looked at him like he was all of the stars in the sky, as though he wasn't just a number on a jersey. Like he was still the boy who needed love as badly as he needed air. She gave him that. She always had.

When they came together, it wasn't just passion—it was memory and fire and the kind of hunger that didn't fade with time, only burned hotter.

Afterward, he carried her to their bedroom, there they lay tangled in sheets still sweaty and out of breath, he pulled her into his chest and kissed the top of her head.

Then nibbled on her ear whispering, "I love you Eliza. North of Always."

"You know you're it for me, right?" he continued.

She nodded, voice soft. "I know."

"I'm never letting you go."

She smiled against his skin. "Good. I wasn't planning on going anywhere."

Adding for good measure, "Don't think for one minute that I'm letting you go Finn. You are only ever mine."

Outside, the world kept turning. The team would watch film tomorrow. Classes would resume. But in their bedroom, in the space between heartbeats and soft kisses and whispered promises, Eliza and Finn had never felt more sure.

Together was where they belonged.

Always.

Chapter Forty-Four

Shifts and Shadows

Sophia didn't do repeats.

Not dates. Not texts the next morning. Not sitting around waiting to be seen. No expectations.

But West was different. She didn't want him to be, but he most certainly was.

They had had one hot, sweaty, passionate night after the big game. West had offered to drive her home from McAllister's Bar. She had felt the chemistry and heat between them even before she had gotten in the car. It only got more intense from there. He pulled the car over to the side of the road asking her if she was "feeling it." Then pulled her to him and kissed her soundly and thoroughly with his hot tongue leading the way. he got her so turned on and ready that when he suggested that she come to his place, she shamelessly acquiesced.

She was pretty buzzed but she remembered every dirty thing he did with her body. She loved it, every second.

Until she didn't. In the morning she woke up with her back up against his chest and with his leg over hers. Panic held her in place. What had she done?

She reminded herself that it was a one-time thing. One and done. She didn't do it very often but when she did, it was a strictly no strings experience.

For some reason fear filled her as she turned her head to look at the hard, harsh cut planes of West's handsome face.

She needed to get away. Now. before he woke up.

She didn't want any awkwardness or give him the chance to brush her off. Leave them before they had the chance to leave you. That was how she rolled. Sophia knew that any good therapist would diagnose her issues as residual abandonment and daddy issues but she didn't care.

This was her and this was now so she extricated herself from West's embrace, grabbing her clothes from the floor where they had been hastily discarded and headed to the bathroom. While freshening up as best she could, she ordered her Uber. It would be at West's apartment building in 5. She couldn't get away fast enough, so she slipped out the door without saying goodbye.

West's sharp eyes tracked her departure.

West was different and now Sophia knew that on an elemental level after their night together.

Not because he was sweet—he wasn't.

Not because he was easy—he was *absolutely not*.

But because he *showed up*. Full of brooding masculinity.

He almost overwhelmed her with his gravity. His intensity. A boiling kettle. She felt as though she were pulled into his orbit every time she was around him. It made her uncomfortable. she feared if they got to close he could crush her when they ended things. She responded so powerfully, almost elementally, to West's brand of brooding sexuality and brusk demeanor. So thoughts of pushing him away before she got to deep flooded her. It's what smart girls do. Get out before they could break you. Disappointment sucked. She preferred to set the perameters.

Unfortunately for her, they started running into each other more after their steamy night following the championship game. At first by accident—on campus, outside the gym, during post-practice hangs with Finn and Eliza. Then not by accident at all.

He didn't text much. When he did, it was blunt:

Library roof at 10? Bring a hoodie.

I'm walking you home. Don't argue.

I'm not good at this, but I want to try. You scare the hell out of me, btw.

She liked that.

It wasn't poetic. But it was *real*.

And when he kissed her again—really kissed her—it wasn't in the dark or behind closed doors.

It was in the middle of the quad at night, after she made fun of his playlist.

She'd laughed. Then he'd pulled her close, kissed her once, hard.

When she opened her eyes, he looked terrified.

So she kissed him back. Just as terrified.

Van

Van noticed it all.

He noticed Sophia texting less in their group chat. Showing up late to lit meetups. Coming to hangouts with West instead of alone.

He told himself it didn't matter.

He told himself they were just friends.

But it *did* matter.

Because he'd started seeing her in ways he hadn't let himself before. Because she *got* him. And because West? Guys like that always messed it up eventually.

They burned bright, then faded. Or imploded.

And he'd be there when it happened.

He started teasing her more. Pushing buttons. "Don't forget who actually reads your writing," he said once, casually. "Not just grunts at it."

She rolled her eyes, but something shifted. Just a flicker.

Van held onto it like a foothold.

West

He wasn't good at words.

West had always been told to be tough. His dad made sure of that—former NFL linebacker, the kind of man who loved with a fist and taught lessons with silence. When West cried at his mom's funeral, his father told him, *"That's enough. Don't be a pussy."* And that was the last time he let anyone see him break.

He'd learned early that people didn't want the soft parts of him. Girls liked the build, the edge, the reputation. His name. His jaw. His tats.

Not one had stayed for the quiet parts. He didn't blame them. There hadn't been much else to give.

Until Sophia.

Beautiful copper-haired, Sophia, who was as beautiful and delicate looking as a doll but strong enough not to flinch when he was blunt. Who laughed when he said he didn't dance—and then made him do it anyway. Who noticed when he needed space and didn't punish him for it. Beautiful, independent, and hard to get. He'd had her but still didn't know her. In some ways she was a lot like him just friendlier.

But now she was getting closer. And it scared the hell out of him.

Because what if she found out he didn't know *how* to be in something real?

What if he wasn't real? What if he didn't have anything to give?

They were sitting in his truck one night, just parked outside her apartment. Neither ready to say goodbye.

She looked at him, half-turned in the seat.

"You ever been in love?"

"No," he said.

"Why?"

He thought about it. "Didn't think I was built for it."

Sophia's mouth curled slightly. "Well, I've done the whole love thing. Two years. He cheated. Twice, actually. So don't worry. I'm not all in on fairytales either."

West exhaled. "So what are we doing?"

She was quiet for a second. Then said, "Honestly, I don't know. I think we're trying. I enjoy being with you despite my best efforts."

And then she did something simple that undid him: she reached for his hand. Rubbing the knuckles gently with her fingers. Then circling her finger on the inside of his wrist and lifted it to her lips, giving it a soft kiss and licking it lightly. A strange heat and tingling sensation went through his whole body. from that one point of contact touching him deeply.

He didn't know what to do with that much gentleness.

But he held on anyway, encircling her in his hard arms. The realization of how precious she was to him becoming clear. Terrified, he he wanted to end whatever this was between them and simultaneously hold her close forever. He was fucked.

Van

The next day, Van found Sophia in the student lounge after the creative writing group wrapped. West wasn't around. They were alone for the first time in weeks.

She was venting about a new story draft. He listened. Laughed. Said something that made her roll her eyes and swat his arm.

And when she leaned in to grab her coffee, he reached up and brushed a strand of copper hair from her face.

It was small. Quick.

But it wasn't *nothing*.

Sophia went still.

Van smiled, unsure. "Sorry, I—"

She leaned back. The space between them sharpened.

"I sort of have a boyfriend, Van," she said softly, but clearly.

His smile faded. "Right. Sorry. I wasn't—"

"I know," she said. "But just... don't."

He nodded quickly. "Totally. I didn't mean anything."

But something cracked anyway.

She didn't mention it to West right away.

But she pulled back from Van after that. She took a closer look at him. 6 ft. lean and fit, Van didn't have a fraction of West's muscle mass. He was handsome she supposed objectively, with slightly tilted dark eyes and shiny black hair from his Chinese mother and height and face shape from his caucasian father. Despite how attractive he was, both handsome and a good friend, she had never had any chemistry with him. So friend zone it was.

And he felt it.

Eliza and Finn

Back at their apartment, Eliza curled up on the couch with her favorite flowered fleece blanket, her laptop open and ignored. Finn sat next to her, scrolling through articles on his phone.

Hearing his cell ring, he answered. It was Officer Jennings from the Austin Police Department calling to notify him that they were pressing criminal charges against Ava for aggravated sexual assault.

"Given the video from the bar showing her actually giving you the drugged drink coupled with the video confession, we have a strong case. We also had a UT student come forward admitting that he had aided Ava in getting you into the car at the bar and then almost carrying you to your apartment. He is willing to testify for immunity. Given all that, since it's her first offense, she might get probation and community service or jail time." He informed Finn. "Rest easy. We got her."

Hanging up relieved, Finn looked at Eliza saying with finality, "It's over."

Elize had found out that day that Ava was expelled from the university as well, which she had already shared with Finn.

After that, for the rest of the night, they let the world wait.

Sophia

Thursday afternoons always stretched long. By the time their study session started, Sophia already had three iced coffees and a headache to match.

The university's library's corner study lounge was buzzing—paper and online deadlines, midterms, and caffeine highs. Sophia, Eliza, and Van had staked their usual table: half-covered in textbooks, notebooks, open laptops, and the smuggled-in trail mix Eliza always carried in her tote bag which included her beloved M&Ms both nut and regular, peanuts, raisins, almonds and cashews.

Van had claimed the cushioned window seat, his long legs sprawled, tapping his pen against his knee in a syncopated rhythm. Eliza sat cross-legged with her laptop perched on top of her thighs, her brows drawn in focus, long strands of light blonde hair falling into her face.

Sophia had been trying to revise a short story for workshop, but every time her phone buzzed with West's name, she lost the thread.

West: *practice ran late. where are you?*
Sophia: *library. study group.*
West: *coming. don't leave.*

Sophia's heart had done that inconvenient flip thing that made no sense for a girl who "didn't do repeats." She stuffed the phone under her notebook and pretended not to notice Van glance at her.

"You're smiling," Van said flatly.

Sophia wearing one of her cheeky t-shirts. This one featuring "Frankie says RELAX." A wink and nod to the 80's, arched a fine brow. "I'm frowning."

"Nope," Van said, twirling his pen. "That was definitely a smile. Secret-boyfriend text, I'm guessing?"

Eliza looked up at that, her eyes flickering between them with quiet interest.

Sophia forced a shrug. "Maybe. What's it to you?"

"Just gathering data," Van said lightly, but something under his tone pinched.

Before she could reply, the door to the lounge pushed open.

And there he was.

West Vaughn. All six-foot-whatever of him, broad-shouldered in a faded UT jersey, hair damp from the shower, black backpack slung lazily over one shoulder. Tattoos visible. He scanned the room, found her instantly, and for a second the hum of the library dimmed.

He walked straight to their table, ignoring the stares he always drew—size and football notoriety had its price. Sophia braced for the casual nod, maybe a muttered "hey," the version of him that never gave too much away in public.

Instead, West leaned down, pressed a kiss to the side of her temple, and dropped his hand on her shoulder like it belonged there.

"Sorry I'm late," he murmured, low enough only she could hear.

Sophia froze. Not because she didn't like it—God, she did—but because it was blatant. Not a shadow, not a secret.

Across the table, Van had gone still, his pen stopped mid-tap.

Eliza blinked once, then smiled faintly at her screen, like she knew exactly what had just happened and wanted to give Sophia an escape hatch.

Sophia swallowed, heat rising to her cheeks. "You're… not late. We're just studying."

West dropped into the seat beside her, close enough that their knees brushed. He didn't move them apart. "Studying, huh?" He glanced at her open notebook, squinting at her messy scrawl. "That's a lot of words. You write like you're being chased."

Sophia shoved her notebook toward him. "And you read like you're allergic to metaphors."

His mouth twitched, the half-smile she'd started recognizing as his version of softness. He leaned back, arm hooking casually over the back of her chair, claiming space like it was the most natural thing in the world.

The air around the table shifted.

Van

Van couldn't believe what he was watching.

West Vaughn—stoic, brick-wall, Russian mob boss vibe, never-let-anyone-in Vaughn—sitting there with his arm slung around Sophia's chair like it was a throne he intended to guard.

And Sophia… Sophia wasn't brushing it off. She wasn't rolling her eyes, wasn't laughing it away like she usually did when guys tried to be territorial. She was *letting him*.

Hell, more than letting—she was leaning slightly toward him, almost unconsciously, like she'd found a center of gravity she didn't know she needed.

Van's jaw clenched before he could stop it. He forced himself to look back at his notebook, scribbling nonsense equations in the margin of his notes.

"Thought this was a study group," he muttered.

Sophia's head whipped toward him, eyes narrowing. "It is."

West, maddeningly calm, just raised a brow at him. "Don't let me stop you, man. Carry on."

The dismissal in his tone lit something sharp in Van's chest. He wanted to say more. Wanted to push. But Eliza shot him a look across the table—a warning, gentle but clear.

So he shut up.

For now.

Eliza

Eliza watched the scene unfold with careful eyes.

Sophia's guarded edges were weakening. West Vaughn—of all people—was softening into something that looked dangerously close to tender. And Van… Van was hurting, though he'd never admit it.

She felt the tension under her skin, the way invisible lines were being drawn right here at their shared table. And she thought about how quickly things could tilt.

But she also thought about Finn Callahan. Her love. About how far they'd come. How close they'd come to breaking and how hard they were fighting not too.

She reached across the table, nudged Van's portion of the trail mix she'd brought toward him. A peace offering, maybe. Or a reminder that he wasn't alone.

Then she bent her head back to her screen, letting Sophia and West find their own rhythm, even as the air thickened around them.

Sophia

They lasted another forty minutes, though "studying" was generous.

West didn't pretend to work. He sat there, listening half-distractedly as Sophia and Eliza debated a passage in their lit readings, occasionally throwing in a dry comment that made Eliza roll her eyes and Sophia smother a laugh.

Every so often, his hand would brush her knee under the table. A subtle, grounding touch. Each time, her heart thudded harder.

Van barely spoke. When he did, it was sharp, almost clipped. Sophia pretended not to notice, but she felt the divide stretching across the table.

Finally, Eliza shut her laptop with a sigh. "I need to get home before I turn into a pumpkin. Finn's home from practice by now. Thanks for the company, guys."

Van stood too quickly, shoving his notebook into his bag. "Yeah. Same."

Sophia caught the flash of something raw in his eyes before he looked away. She opened her mouth, but the words died in her throat.

Then it was just her and West.

He leaned in close, voice low. "You wanna get out of here?"

Her pulse jumped.

"Yeah," she said. "Let's go."

Chapter Forty-Five

Connecting

Sophia

The night started like all the best ones did—without a plan.

Garlic bread in the oven. Pasta simmering in a saucepan that West had been stirring with unnecessary intensity. And her—barefoot in his apartment, hair tied up messily, emerald blouse sliding off one shoulder as she rooted around his spice rack like she had any clue what she was doing.

"You're gonna burn it," she teased, catching his wrist before he over-stirred the pasta into glue.

West shot her one of those deadpan looks that always made her grin. "I'm not burning it. You just like telling people what to do."

"Correct," she said, stealing the spoon.

"You're insufferable," he muttered, reaching for it.

"And you like it. And that's a three dollar word." She dodged backward, hip bumping the counter, daring him.

He caught her easily, his fingers circling her wrist. Heat traveled up her arm like a fuse being lit. She laughed, but the sound snagged in her throat because his huge, muscular body was suddenly right there—broad, warm, smelling faintly of cedar and soap.

"You're still here," he said quietly, like he couldn't quite believe it.

She swallowed, trying not to melt under the weight of his gaze. "Guess I am."

And God, she didn't want to be anywhere else.

West

He told himself not to look at her like that. Like she belonged there. Like she was his.

But she was standing barefoot in his kitchen, humming and dancing along to some chaotic playlist while she salted his sauce into oblivion, and he couldn't stop watching. Couldn't stop needing.

Sophia felt like danger disguised as comfort. He wasn't built for soft, for domestic, for someone who brushed against him like it wasn't a big deal. Like he wasn't dangerous.

He wanted her so bad it terrified him. Most people were.

"I Was Made For Lovin' You" by Yungblud blasted out from her Spotify playlist. "Shit, he was screwed he thought.

When she laughed—when she tilted her head back, blouse slipping down further to reveal a line of collarbone and the slight rise of her generous breasts—he thought, *this is the kind of shit that ruins men.*

And he was already halfway ruined and she was fully dressed and just making food.

Again he was fucked.

Dinner was chaos. Half-burnt bread, pasta that stuck a little too much. Distracted by the music, distracted by West, she didn't care.

They ended up on the couch, plates abandoned, legs tangled. She read aloud from her draft, words stumbling because he was watching her like she mattered. His complete focus trained on her.

"You're staring," she said, shutting the iPad.

"You're better than you think. Not that I'm an expert on literature," he replied simply.

No one said that to her—not without an agenda. The honesty of it made her heart ache.

Silence stretched. His hand found hers, thumb rubbing slow circles. Warmth pooled low in her belly.

She leaned toward him, almost without meaning to.

West

When she kissed him, he forgot how to breathe.

Slow at first, hesitant. Then hungrier. Her fingers slid into his blonde hair, tugging, and he was gone. Completely gone.

He lifted her petite frame onto his lap without breaking the kiss, her knees bracketing his hips, her mouth opening against his like she'd been waiting for this as much as he had.

Every instinct screamed at him to take, to push fast, to lose himself. But he forced himself to slow down, to savor. Because she wasn't another faceless girl at a party.

She was Sophia. And he already knew he'd never get enough.

Sophia

By the time they stumbled into his bedroom, her pulse was wild. She pulled his shirt off in one tug—and froze.

Her breath caught. My god he was built like a Viking God.

His chest, arms, shoulders—ink everywhere. Black and gray, intricate and bold, curling down his bicep and around his forearm, snaking up toward his collarbone. A full sleeve—on both arms.

"Jesus," she whispered, tracing the edges with trembling fingers.

He stiffened. Like no one had ever really looked.

"What do they mean?" she asked softly.

He hesitated.

Then, voice rough, he said, "Every one's a scar. Just prettier. Each one is a feeling, story or reminder."

Her heart twisted. She ran her hand lower, across his ribs, where another design curved—a wolf mid-snarl. "And this one?"

"Strength." His jaw flexed. "Reminding myself to always exercise it."

She swallowed, kissed his chest over the ink. "And the phoenix?"

He stilled completely.

Her fingers brushed the broad sweep of the bird inked across his back, wings outstretched, flames curling down his spine.

"That's... the one I've never told anyone about."

Her lips grazed his shoulder. "Tell me."

He paused then exhaled like it hurt. "It's... starting over. After everything burns down. After my mom died, after my dad—" He cut off, shaking his head.

Sophia pressed her cheek to his back, arms wrapping around him from behind. "That's not ugly. That's... survival and it's beautiful."

He turned, eyes raw. "You don't know how fucking much I want you."

"Then have me," she whispered.

West

He kissed her like it was a vow, stripping away the hoodie, the shorts, the thin fabric beneath until there was nothing left between them but heat.

Every inch of her was soft, curving, trembling under his touch. He memorized the sound she made when his mouth found her throat, the way her back arched when he palmed her breast, the whispered curse when his fingers slid lower, teasing, coaxing.

She was slick and ready and begging in broken whispers, and he thought —*this is what it means to be alive*.

When he finally pushed inside her, slow, steady, her nails dug into his shoulders, dragging him closer, deeper.

"West," she gasped, and the sound of his name undone on her lips nearly broke him.

He moved with restraint he didn't know he had, savoring the way she clung to him, the way she met him thrust for thrust, the way her huge doll-like blue eyes stayed open—locked on his, like she wanted all of him —only him.

And that terrified him most of all.

That she could take all of him if he let her. He just didn't know how he could survive it.

Sophia

It was nothing like she'd had before.

It wasn't just sex—it was worship. He touched her like he couldn't believe she was real, kissed her like she might vanish.

And when she came, crying his name, shaking around him, she swore the world cracked open.

He followed, big body shuddering, face buried in her neck, his whole body trembling with the force of it.

After, he didn't roll away. He held her close, strong arms tight like a shield, like letting go would mean losing her.

Her heart softened painfully. "West?"

"Yeah?" His voice was hoarse.

"You're safe with me."

He didn't answer. Just pressed a kiss to her hair and inhaled taking in the jasmine scent of her hair.

But his silence said everything.

Eliza

Across town, Eliza curled against Finn on their couch. An action movie classic, Die Hard, flickered on the screen, forgotten.

She traced lazy circles on his hand. He kissed her temple looking away from the TV into her eyes.

No urgency. No fear. Just passion, steady warmth, like gravity.

She thought of Sophia, out with West tonight, and hoped her friend was finding something like this.

Passionate, forever love that didn't roar…it stayed.

West

Sophia slept, small, curvy body curled against him, full lips parted, trust heavy in her breath.

He should've felt peace. Instead he felt panic.

Because this—her, here, wrapped around him like he was worth something—was the most dangerous thing in the world.

He couldn't lose her. And that meant, sooner or later, he'd have to let her go.

His hand tightened on her tiny waist, even as his chest locked with fear.

Don't ruin her, he told himself. *Don't ruin this.*

But deep down, he already knew—
he was going to.

Chapter Forty-Six

The Retreat

Sophia

The first morning after felt unreal.

She woke in West's bed with the dark sheets tangled around her, skin sore in places that made her smile, breath catching when she rolled over and saw him asleep beside her.

He didn't look like the West Vaughn the world saw—cocky, untouchable, carved out of stone. He looked younger. Softer. His hair was a mess. His mouth relaxed. One tatted arm wrapped around her waist like he couldn't let go even in sleep.

And she remembered every sensuous detail.

The way his mouth had dragged over her skin. The way his tattoos had moved under her hands, living maps she'd traced in awe. The phoenix spreading fire across his back. The way he'd pulsed inside her when he'd whispered her name.

She thought about how his forehead had pressed against hers in the dark, his thrusts slow and enthralling, as if every second was a prayer. How she'd felt cracked open, seen, like they hadn't just had sex—they'd stitched themselves together. Their torn pieces matching perfectly.

And she wasn't going to forget that for the rest of her life.

West Vaughn had let her in.

She smiled into his chest. For once, she didn't feel the urge to bolt.

But when she finally looked up, his eyes were already open. Awake. Watching the ceiling like it had betrayed him.

"Hey," she whispered.

His gaze flicked to her, then away. "Morning."

Something in the clipped tone made her stomach dip.

Still, she kissed his chest, right over the inked wolf snarling across his ribs. "You're impossible in the mornings, huh?"

He didn't answer. Just tightened his arm around her like he didn't want her to move.

And even as her heart swelled, a tiny whisper of fear threaded through her: *Don't shut me out*.

She got up and did the walk of shame headed back to her own place to get ready for class. West kissed her firmly but briefly, said that there was coffee made, and then said he had to get to practice. They left his place at the same time. She put her arms around his waist and leaned into him for a kiss goodbye but he pulled away quickly locking his apartment door behind them.

By noon, though, it became clear that the first thread had unraveled.

She texted him a picture of her coffee cup and a stupid owl meme.
He didn't respond.

Then she texted him: Last night…yum.

He still didn't respond.

At first, she brushed it off. He was probably busy. Practice, workouts, whatever. She gave him space.

But one day bled into two, then three.

Still nothing.

The silence grew claws, digging into her ribs. Into her heart.

Oh God, please don't tell me I let down my guard just to have my heart stomped. She thought.

West

He knew he was fucking it up.

Every second he didn't answer her texts was another shovel of dirt on the special thing they'd made. But what else could he do?

He couldn't be that man she'd seen in him—the one she thought she'd uncovered. The tenderness, the gentleness, the part of him that had made love to her like she mattered.

That wasn't him.

Not really.

It had been one night, and already he felt stripped bare. Already he hated how badly he wanted her. He wasn't weak. He wouldn't let himself be. Already he was terrified of the way she looked at him like he was worth more than fists and anger and the game.

So he shut her out. Completely.

Practice. Weight room. Home. Repeat. He buried himself until his body ached too much to feel anything else.

But it didn't work. He knew that he was being a dick.

All night, every night when he closed his eyes, he saw her. The tilt of her head when she'd straddled him on the couch. The way her nails had dug crescents into his shoulders when he'd finally slid into her. The sound she'd made when she came—breathless, desperate, his name torn from her throat like a prayer.

No one had ever looked at him the way she had that last night. Wide open. Trusting. Like he was more than the sum of his scars and fuckups.

Because every night when he closed his eyes, he saw her mouth open on a gasp, felt her nails clawing down his back, heard her whisper his name like it was salvation.

And the wanting grew until it hurt.

****

By the fifth day, Sophia snapped.

She waited outside the weight room where the football team worked out, arms crossed, wearing her tight, black *"That's bananas"* t-shirt. When West finally emerged, shirt drenched in sweat, jaw clenched, she stepped in his path.

"Really?" she said, voice sharp. "This is how you disappear?"

He didn't meet her eyes. Just brushed past her like she wasn't there.

Her chest burned. She moved to block him again. "West—"

"I'm not who you think I am," he muttered. "It was a one-and-done. Don't try to make it into more. Don't make me into more."

The words landed like a punch. Crushing her in one blow.

"I know who you are," she shot back, voice cracking but strong. "You're the guy who held my hand when I didn't trust anyone. Who told me I scared you—and still kissed me. You're the guy who made love to me like it meant something. So don't stand there and pretend it didn't."

His eyes flickered. He hesitated. For a second she swore she saw the man she'd woken up beside.

"I never said it didn't."

"Then why are you running?"

Finally, he looked at her. The weight of his stare nearly buckled her knees.

"Because if I stay, I screw it up."

The words sliced her open. She wasn't even worth him trying.

"You already screwed it up." She stepped away holding back the tears in her eyes like physical distance might hold her together. Resolve keeping her back straight and her chin up.

And then she turned and walked away.

No tears. Not then.

But later.

God, later.

Sophia

That night, the tears came.

She climbed out onto the fire escape, knees pulled tight to her chest, UT hoodie up to hide the mess of her face. The city hummed low and steady beneath her, but she felt like she'd been hollowed out.

The door creaked behind her. Sophia's text message had Eliza coming over holding her while she cried and cursed West for the selfish prick he was.

Eliza slid out, quiet as a shadow, carrying a fleece snoopy blanket, the one Eliza only used if she or a friend were sick or in this case sad, and a mug of steaming mint tea. She didn't say anything at first—just draped the blanket around Sophia's shoulders and pressed the warm ceramic mug that said "Songbirds can't be silenced" into her hands.

Sophia's throat closed. "He shut down. Pushed me away."

Eliza leaned against the railing, pulling her knees up. "Yeah."

"I thought he was different." Her voice broke. "I can't believe that I bought into him. I mean he looks like a walking felony with those tattoos, size, and mob enforcer vibe. Damn. He may as well have a Hazard sign on his big forehead. He plays football besides and they are all mostly non-relationship players. Finn excluded. I know better than to believe in a man and relationships."

Eliza wrapped an arm around her. "He is. But that doesn't mean he's ready."

Sophia shook her head hard, tears streaking down her cheeks. "I don't understand how you can go from—" Her breath hitched. She couldn't even say it out loud, how tender, how intimate, how earth-shattering that night had been. "—to nothing. Just… gone."

Eliza squeezed her shoulder. "Because wanting something that much? It terrifies people like him. He doesn't know what to do with it."

Sophia sniffed, swiping at her eyes. "It terrifies me too. But I didn't run."

"I know. You were brave my friend. That's nothing to be ashamed of." Eliza's voice was quiet. But her arm stayed steady around her friend, anchoring her.

For a long time they sat like that, Sophia crying, Eliza letting her.

Eliza clung back, whispering, "Finn came around. Don't give up on West just yet. In the meantime…I think that this is a problem that only Ben & Jerry can solve," she added.

Sophia agreed. "Cherry Garcia here we come."

Chapter Forty-Seven

Ghost Messages

West

West didn't even remember walking into the warehouse.

One second, he was pacing his apartment with Sophia's voice in his head, the ghost of her touch in his skin. Her smell still on his sheets. The next, he was standing under too-bright lights, the air thick with sweat and testosterone, the dull roar of voices egging him on.

He hadn't come to fight.

But his fists were already taped. His body was already buzzing, restless, searching for an outlet.

And his thoughts—they were all her.

him. The softness in her voice when she'd said, *You're safe with me*. Her copper hair spread across his pillow, lush curves under his hands.

It was unbearable.

So when the defensive lineman squared up across from him—a big guy from another university, Texas A&M, taller, bulkier, grinning like he wanted to make West bleed—West welcomed it.

Make it hurt, he thought. *Drown her out.*

The bell rang.

He swung first.

The first round was chaos.

A blur of fists, sweat, grunts. West landed a clean shot to the guy's ribs, took a jab to the jaw in return. The crowd whooped. His blood sang.

But even as adrenaline surged, Sophia's face was there. Her laugh in his kitchen. Her breath hot in his ear. Her body under his, arching, begging.

He snarled and threw another punch, harder.

The guy staggered back, then retaliated with a brutal uppercut that snapped West's head back. Pain exploded white-hot.

He welcomed it.

Second round.

His lip split. Blood dripped down his chin. His knuckles throbbed.

He thought of Sophia's small hands on his chest, tracing the ink softly, engrossingly, like it meant something. *Every scar, prettier,* she'd said.

Another hit landed to his ribs. He grunted, doubled over for a second—then came back swinging.

He fought like he was drowning. Like every punch was a breath, every bruise a confession.

He drove his opponent back against the edge of the mat, fury in every strike. But then—*Sophia's eyes, wide and trusting. Sophia whispering, Then have me. I want all of you. Her once distant eyes brimming with passion, connection* .

He faltered. Just for a split second.

The guy caught him clean across the cheek. Splitting skin. Creating bruises. His vision blurred. His knees buckled.

Third round.

His chest heaved. Sweat soaked his shirt. His body begged him to stop.

But stopping meant thinking. And thinking meant remembering the way Sophia had clung to him, her body pulsing around him as she shattered apart.

Her smile. The one she only gave to him.

He couldn't survive that memory.

So he pushed forward.

The lineman slammed a huge fist into his stomach, knocking the wind from him. The violence thirsty crowd roared approval.

West tasted blood. Spat it onto the mat. And charged.

It wasn't a fight anymore. It was exorcism.

Every blow he threw was her name. Every time he got hit, it was her voice breaking in his chest.

When the lineman clipped his temple and stars burst across his vision, he remembered her nails digging into his back, her thighs squeezing tighter, her cry of *West* like a plea ringing in his head.

When West slammed a fist into the guy's ribs, he remembered Sophia licking and kissing the phoenix ink on his spine, whispering *That's not ugly. That's survival.*

When his opponent grappled him to the ground and they rolled, muscles straining, West remembered the way she'd wrapped her arms around him after, holding him close like he was worth holding.

And it broke him.

Because the harder he fought, the louder she got in his head.

By the end of the third round, he was staggering. His vision tunneled, his breath ragged, his knuckles raw.

The bell rang. He was done.

The crowd erupted.

But West didn't feel victorious. He didn't feel anything except empty.

Completely drained, he stood there, chest heaving, blood dripping from his split lip, sweat stinging his eyes.

The lineman clapped him hard on the shoulder. "Good fight, man."

West didn't answer. Couldn't.

Because as the adrenaline ebbed, the ache roared back louder than ever.

Sophia's smile. Sophia's laugh. Sophia's jasmine and hibiscus-scented copper hair. Sophia's petite, voluptuous body trembling against his.

She was everywhere. And no amount of pain could burn her out of him.

He leaned against the brick wall outside of the warehouse, tasting copper. His fists shook, wrapped and ruined.

And still, all he wanted was her.

The one thing he couldn't have.

He ripped the tape from his fists and walked out into the night.

Still broken.

Still hers.

And terrified that he always would be.

Sophia

On the fire escape, Sophia leaned into Eliza's shoulder, staring out at the city lights through tear-blurred eyes. She had ugly cried enough. Now she just felt empty.

Her body still remembered West's. Every inch of her still ached for him, every nerve haunted by the memory of his touch.

But he wasn't here. He didn't want to be.

And she didn't know if he ever would be again. If she even wanted him.

Eliza's warm honey voice was steady beside her, but the cracks underneath were clear. Both of them were holding on by threads, both of them scared in different ways.

Sophia curled tighter under the Snoopy blanket, whispering, "We'll be okay. Somehow."

Eliza nodded, though her eyes shone. "Yeah."

The night hummed around them—two girls on a fire escape, both bruised, both alone in their own ways, trying to believe they weren't.

And across town, West Vaughn sat bleeding in the dark, hands raw, ribs screaming—feeling the same emptiness. A half bottle of agave Tequila in hand.

Separate.

Parallel.

Wanting each other like oxygen.

And not knowing how to breathe without it.

Sophia's voice cracked. "He shut down. Just like that. Like what we had —what we did—didn't matter."

Eliza wrapped an arm around her shoulders, pulling her in. "It mattered. To you. To him too, I think. That's what scared him."

Tears slid hot down Sophia's cheeks. "I thought he was different."

Eliza pressed her cheek to Sophia's hair. "He *is* different. But sometimes different doesn't mean ready."

Sophia buried her face in her hands. She hated how much it hurt.

Behind them, the window slid open again. Van stuck his head out, holding an open bottle of wine and a pizza. "You two planning on freezing to death out here, or should I be the hero with alcohol?"

Eliza gave him a look. "Not helping."

"Not hurting, either." He squeezed himself out onto the fire escape, handed the bottle to Sophia, and sat down cross-legged.

For a while, they just sat there—the three of them against the cold, Austin city lights flickering below.

Eliza's cell pinged. "Gotta go. I need to head home. Finn waiting," she said blushing.

Sophia continued sipping the wine, wiping her eyes with her sleeve, and let the silence hold her up.

"Are you going to be ok if I head home?" Eliza asked concerned. She'd never seen Sophia like this. So despondent.

Sophia for her part still felt cracked down the middle. But at least she wasn't alone in the breaking she hoped.

And so the night ended with them both undone—
West bleeding against a warehouse wall, fists raw from fighting ghosts.
Sophia crying into her best friend's shoulder, drinking her heart ache away where trust had been.

Both reaching for each other in silence.
Both too far gone to find the way back

Sophia and Van

The next afternoon, Sophia rode her bike beside Van on the river trail path, wind in her hair, the sound of wheels on gravel breaking the silence.

Lunch had been easy. Comfortable. They had gone to the café by Lake Travis. Van was clever. Funny. Safe. One of her favorites.

But underneath, she sensed something else—like he was trying too hard to be effortless.

When he offered to walk her bike back to her place, she smiled, said she'd be fine.

But when he hesitated at the door and said, "You know, I'm glad West blew it. He didn't deserve you."

Sophia stiffened. "That's not really your call to make."

"I'm just saying," Van added, "you deserve someone who actually knows how to stay and wants, you know, to be in a relationship."

She didn't answer.

Because maybe that was true. Maybe Van was right.

But maybe West was finally learning.

She could only hope—because her heart still ached without him.

West

That same night, West sat on the apartment balcony, staring at the skyline with a bottle of water and his phone glowing in his hand.

The wallpaper still showed Sophia. Laughing. Eyes half-closed, no makeup, hair a mess.

He'd thought leaving was protection.

But it had been fear.

And now, after what happened to Eliza—after feeling her shaking in his arms, after watching Finn refuse to waver—West finally knew exactly what he wanted.

Not just someone to save.

Someone to stand with.

And that someone was Sophia.

He hadn't been ready before.

But now, at last, he felt ready to try. To show up. To stay.

He only hoped it wasn't too late.

The next morning, Sophia walked across the quad with a coffee in hand, earbuds in, trying to lose herself in a podcast she wasn't really listening to.

She spotted Van near the library steps, but turned quickly down the opposite walkway. She didn't want to talk. Not today.

The late-summer sun was already hot on the back of her neck, and she tugged her notebook tighter under her arm, weaving between clusters of students.

She almost didn't see him.

West, emerging from the English building, head bent over his phone, earbuds dangling loose. He looked thinner. Tired. His hair longer than she remembered.

Her chest squeezed.

They were only twenty feet apart. A straight line.

But just as she slowed, ready to risk it—to say his name, to break the silence—he turned left, disappearing into the crowd.

Her throat burned.

Sophia stopped in the middle of the sidewalk, breath catching. She could still feel the ghost of him, like static in the air. But the moment was gone.

She dug her phone out of her pocket.

West sat at the top of her messages. Her thumb hovered over the keyboard.
Can we talk? she typed.

She stared at it, pulse racing. And then, slowly, she erased the words. Locked the screen. Slipped the phone back into her bag.

Across campus, West paused on a bench outside the gym, pulling out his own phone. Sophia's name sat in his recent calls, untouched. He typed:
I'm sorry. I miss you.

He didn't hit send either.

The messages sat unsent, like ghosts, the silence stretching between them.

And the ache—sharp, quiet, endless—remained.

Chapter Forty-Eight

Between the Lines

The blinking cursor mocked her.

Eliza sat at the dining table, laptop open, lyrics notebook beside her, textbooks scattered like collateral damage. One mug of cold tea, two open Google Docs, three half-finished verses—and still no song.

Her deadline for the ACL artist committee submission was in four days. Madison had been clear: *"Original work. Something that pushes you. Something that bleeds a little."*

And Eliza had been trying to bleed.

But the words weren't coming.

Outside the window, campus lights flickered like stars trapped behind glass. Inside, Finn paced the kitchen in gym shorts and a hoodie, quietly reheating leftover curry. His hair was damp from a late-night lift, his shoulders tight with exhaustion.

"You've been at that for hours," he said, carrying over a plate. "Eat something."

She glanced up. "I can't think about food. I can't think about *anything*. It's like every lyric I write sounds like someone else's song."

He sat beside her, nudging a fork into her hand. "Maybe stop trying to write what you think they want. Just… write us."

Eliza blinked. "What?"

He shrugged. "Write about *us*. The quiet stuff. The messy stuff. The truth. You said that's what your music's about, right?"

"I've already written our story. *Reclaim Me* was our story."

"That was a chapter," he said. "We're more than one song."

She looked at him—really looked. The smudge of ink on his wrist where he'd been taking notes, the small scar on his jawline from that game in October, the way he looked at her like she was still the only thing in the room.

"I don't want to disappoint anyone," she whispered.

He tilted his head. "You're allowed to be scared. Just don't let scared win."

Something in her chest cracked open.

She reached for her notebook—not to force anything, but to let it out. Slowly, words began to appear. Not about trauma. Not about reclamation.

But about staying.

About what it means to choose someone, over and over again, even when the world is loud and your faith is quiet.

The song started soft.

A verse about sitting on the floor with Thai takeout and unspoken apologies.

A chorus that repeated *"Still here. Still choosing."*

A bridge about how love doesn't need fireworks—just presence.

By midnight, she had two full pages of lyrics and a voice memo she didn't hate.

Finn dozed on the couch, notebook on his chest.

She watched him for a while, then whispered, "We're more than one song."

And went back to writing.

****

Eliza thought she would sleep forever after that night in Finn's arms. But morning still came, dragging with it the buzz of ordinary life: lectures, coffee runs, Sophia's relentless cheer, Van's easy jokes, West's restless silences.

Everything looked the same. But Eliza felt the shift—like her skin had been rewoven, thinner in some places, tougher in others.

Her notebook betrayed her in the quiet hours. Pages filled with scratched-out lyrics, margins littered with late-night fragments. She wrote until her eyes burned, but kept it hidden. Not yet. Not for the world to see.

But Sophia saw. Sophia always saw. She noticed the way Eliza's fingers twitched when music played, the half-hums in the kitchen, the secret song tucked in her guitar case like contraband.

"You're holding your breath," Sophia said one afternoon, perching on the arm of the couch while Eliza flipped through a battered notebook. "The only way to exhale is to let it out."

Eliza's laugh was small. "I'm not ready for people to look at me like I'm fragile. I barely got through my first open mic and that was only because I was so numb over what was happening between me and Finn to be scared."

"Then don't let them see you as fragile," Sophia said. "Let them look at you like you're fire."

That night, Sophia slid a sign-up sheet across the coffee table. The corner of her mouth tilted with mischief, but her eyes were serious.

"Open mic. Saturday. No one has to know. Just you, a stage, and whatever you're brave enough to share."

Eliza stared at it for a long time. Her chest tightened. Then, slowly, her pen scratched across the paper.

She didn't tell Finn. She didn't tell anyone.

But West saw.

He'd stopped by the campus coffeehouse later that week for an espresso, and his gaze snagged on the list taped crookedly to the bulletin board.

There it was: Eliza Monroe.

For a moment, he couldn't breathe. He stood with his coffee cooling in his hand, eyes fixed on the neat script like it might vanish if he blinked.

His first instinct was to text Sophia. To ask if she knew, if Eliza was ready. But his thumb hovered, then stilled. Sophia already knew. He could see it in the way she lingered near Eliza these days—protective but encouraging, a quiet anchor.

Later that afternoon, across the room, Sophia caught his gaze. Her expression softened for just a heartbeat then hardened as she looked away. She knew he'd seen. He felt the urge to hold her eyes, to say something, but he looked away first.

Because this wasn't about him. Whatever ache he carried, whatever ghosts haunted them, tonight wasn't his.
It was hers.

****

Saturday arrived with string lights and a packed coffeehouse. The little stage was barely wider than a dining table, but it gleamed under the soft amber bulbs.

Eliza sat backstage—if a curtain behind the espresso machine counted as backstage—her heart pounding against her ribs. Her hands trembled around the neck of her guitar.

"Next up," the emcee announced, glancing at the list. "Eliza Monroe."

The room quieted.

In the back corner, Finn's head snapped up. He'd been nursing a latte with Kai and West, and now his entire body went still. His chest constricted. He hadn't known.

She stepped onto the stage like stepping into fire, shoulders squared, chin lifted. She hadn't told Finn about the performance wanting to surprise him.

She adjusted the mic, exhaled shakily.

"I wrote this not long ago," she said softly. "It's called *Reclaim Me*. It's not just a song. It's a promise. To myself. And to the one person who never let me forget who I was—who I am."

Her eyes flicked to Finn. Held.

Then she sang.

It wasn't polished. It wasn't pretty. But it was raw—like every word had been torn from her ribs, beautiful in its' vulnerability. Her voice trembled in the verses, steadied in the chorus, soared in the final lines. When she hit the high notes, they cut through like a knife though warm butter.

The lyrics hit like truth. Pain, healing, defiance, reclamation—each syllable carved a space in the room. People leaned forward, hushed.

West felt the air leave his chest. It was like listening to someone rip open a vein and call it music. But what twisted the knife deeper was the way Sophia's eyes glistened beside him, her hands clasped tight in her lap.

When Eliza reached the final line—"*Reclaim me...*"—the silence cracked. The coffeehouse erupted. Cheers. Applause. Stomping feet.

But Eliza didn't move. She stared at her guitar, then at Finn across the room, his eyes shining.

It wasn't applause she'd come for. It was peace.

When she stepped off stage, Finn was there first. He wrapped her in trembling arms, kissed her hairline. "You just gave yourself to the world," he whispered.

She nodded, tears slipping down. For the first time, she believed she belonged. She knew that this was where she was meant to be.

West slipped out before the crowd thinned, jaw tight, chest burning. He didn't trust himself to stay.

Across the room, Sophia caught the door swinging shut. Her throat ached with two truths at once: pride for her friend, and an ache she couldn't quiet.

Chapter Forty-Nine

The Choice

By Monday morning, the video was everywhere.

Someone had filmed Eliza's set on their phone—shaky, grainy, but raw enough to go viral, at least on campus. It spread through group chats, music blogs, niche Austin Twitter threads.

Reclaim Me – An Original by Eliza Monroe.
You need to hear this.

One reviewer on a student-run blog called it *"The kind of song that hits you in the lungs, then the heart."*

Eliza stared at her phone like it was a live grenade.

"This was supposed to be private," she whispered to Finn that night.

"Sometimes the right words don't stay small," he said gently. "Sometimes they're supposed to get loud."

Her phone buzzed again. A new email.

From: Madison Kennedy
Subject: Reclaim Me

Eliza—

Darling friend! That song. That moment. The first thing I've seen in months that felt real. I know that you haven't had help pursuing your dream, but if you haven't already committed to working with someone, I'd love to talk. You have a story—and a voice—that matters. Coffee? Wine? Either way we need another girls night. Soon.

–M.

Eliza's pulse stuttered. For a moment, she almost forgot Madison wasn't just a friend she'd drifted into orbit with. Madison was a music rep. A PR powerhouse. A door.

Two days later, South Congress buzzed with tourists and neon. Madison was already seated at a café table, sunglasses perched on her head, lavender latte sweating in the heat.

"You showed," she said with a grin. "Means you're curious about what we can do together professionally."

Eliza smiled nervously. Sun glinting into her shades making her eyes water. "I'm… still figuring it out."

"Good. Let me help." Madison slid a folder across the table. "There's buzz around you now thanks to the viral video. I'm working on a side stage for ACL. Write something new. Maybe even perform with a backing set. If you have enough great material, I'll feature you so you can perform multiple originals. Committee meetings start next month—I want you on it."

ACL. Her name. A stage.

"I thought you repped real artists," she murmured.

"I rep real voices," Madison said. "And yours is one."

Eliza left with her heart in her throat, promo notes in her hand, a calendar alert titled **ACL Committee Kickoff – March.**

And as she walked down South Congress, her thoughts drifted—back to the first time she'd met Madison.

****

Flashback: City Limits

The city had pulsed around them.

She remembered standing just past the gates of Zilker Park, boots dusty, tank top sticking to her back, sweat beading at her temples, the distant sound of drums vibrating through the air like a second heartbeat. The Austin City Limits Music Festival was everything she'd hoped it would be—messy, loud, wild, alive.

She'd worn a vintage denim skirt and a tank top, her hair twisted into a loose braid, sunglasses perched on her head. Finn had run off to grab water and merch with a few of his teammates, and she didn't mind the space.

The music washed over her in waves. Big sounds. Bigger energy.

She'd wandered toward the smaller stage tucked behind a row of food trucks, where a folk trio had just started a stripped-down acoustic set. There were fewer people here, more space to breathe. She liked the intimacy of it—the raw lyrics, the soft edge to the singer's voice.

That's when a woman beside her muttered, "Finally. Someone singing about something other than cold beer, breakups, and trucks."

Eliza turned. The woman was in her early to mid-twenties, oversized sunglasses, a black leather mini, boots that screamed expensive. Her hair was straight, blunt-cut, shiny black like a raven's wing. She carried herself like someone used to being listened to.

Eliza laughed huskily. "Being a good Texas girl, I kind of like the truck songs."

"Sure," the woman said, grinning. "Until the third chorus and the girl hops in without asking if the AC works."

They shared a laugh, and the woman held out her hand.

"Madison Kennedy. PR for about half the bands backstage. You a fan or a musician?"

Eliza blinked. "Neither, technically. I'm a writer."

"Oh, a lyricist then. Or a '*I'm not a songwriter yet, but I write the hell out of people's pain*' kind of writer?"

"Something like that," Eliza admitted.

Madison sipped from her drink. "You've got the vibe. Stunningly beautiful. Smart eyes. Quiet type. Probably deadly on the page."

Eliza laughed. "That's weirdly flattering."

Madison tilted her head. "Weird but accurate. You published anywhere?"

"Once. A lit mag back in the spring. I mostly write short fiction, personal stuff. But I've been leaning into lyrics lately, just for fun."

Madison's eyes sharpened. "Good lyrics?"

"I think so."

"Email me," Madison said, fishing a card from her skirt. *Madison Kennedy – Artist Development & PR.*
"I know artists who'd kill for something that doesn't sound like it was built by a TikTok algorithm. If your words hit, I'll put them in front of the right ears. You have a gravity to you the draws people in."

Eliza took the card like it might burn her. "Seriously?"

Madison winked. "Don't act shocked. You've got that weird stillness around you. Like you've seen things most people write songs about. That's the stuff that sticks."

Before Eliza could respond, Madison turned, called back by someone from backstage. "Send me something real. Don't waste my time."

And just like that, she was gone.

Finn reappeared a few minutes later, shirt draped over his shoulder, two lemonades in hand.

"You look like you just saw a ghost," he said, offering her a cup.

"Not a ghost," she murmured, still dazed. "Maybe a door."

Back in the present, Eliza pressed her palm to the folder Madison had given her. The door was still there. And this time, it was wide open.

That night, she and Finn sat cross-legged on the floor with takeout cartons from their favorite Thai place scattered between them.

"I don't know if I'm ready," she confessed.

Finn cupped her jaw. "You don't have to be ready all at once. Just want it enough to keep walking."

"I do want it. But I'm terrified."

"Then it probably means it matters."

Her chest cracked open. She picked up her notebook. And the words began.

Not about trauma. Not about reclamation.
But about staying. Choosing. Loving.

By midnight, she had two full pages of lyrics. Finn slept on the couch, notebook slipping from his chest. She watched him, whispered, "We're more than one song."

And wrote until dawn.

Across the room, Sophia typed on her laptop, earbuds in, working late. West passed by on his way to the kitchen. He paused, watching Sophia's shoulders tense, her fingers hover, then type again. She was writing encouragement to Eliza, he could tell—he recognized the tilt of her head when she was pouring herself into someone else.

He wanted to step closer, to say something—anything—but his throat tightened. Instead, he filled a glass of water and slipped back down the hall.

Sophia felt him there. Didn't look up. Didn't need to. The air shifted in his wake, and the words she typed came slower, heavier.

Chapter Fifty

Still Here

The bar was tucked behind a vinyl shop on East 6th. A little indie hideout with live jazz, low lighting, and an old upright piano wedged into the corner. Eliza arrived early—because she always did—and ordered a lavender gin and tonic she wasn't sure she liked, just to feel like she belonged.

Madison swept in ten minutes later, silky black hair, all heels, red lipstick, and quiet authority. She kissed Eliza on the cheek like they'd been meeting for years.

"Monroe," she said, sliding into the booth. "You look like you're either about to perform or confess to murder."

"Honestly? I'm considering both."

Madison raised an eyebrow, signaling the bartender. "Whiskey sour. Extra lemon. And spill."

Eliza took a deep breath. "I've been writing. A lot. But I'm also… drowning. I missed two classes last week. I've got three lit papers coming up, and my professors' shadows still haunt the back of my syllabus."

"You're still recovering," Madison said gently. "But also—welcome to the grind. What's really going on?"

Eliza hesitated. "What if I'm not cut out for this?"

"This being…?"

"Music. Performing. Creating at this level. What if I'm just… a lit student who wrote one good song out of trauma?"

Madison didn't blink. She leaned in, voice low. "Okay. First? That's a garbage question. Let's start there."

Eliza blinked. "Excuse me?"

Madison smiled tightly. "You don't get to use the worst day of your life as the watermark for whether or not you deserve to take up space now. 'Reclaim Me' wasn't just raw—it was crafted. Your new song? Even more so. You're not just an artist because you survived something. You're an artist because you *make meaning* from it."

Eliza stared at her drink.

"You're scared," Madison continued. "So what? If fear was the deciding factor, no woman in the industry would ever make it past open mic night. The question isn't 'Are you scared?' It's, 'Are you willing to risk discomfort for the life you actually want?'"

Eliza swallowed hard. "I don't want to abandon everything else. My degree matters. My writing matters."

"Great. Then integrate it. Be the girl who writes *and* sings. Who studies literature and headlines a stage. This world doesn't need another safe brand. It needs *you*. The whole messy, brilliant, dual-major you."

Eliza let the silence settle.

Outside, rain streaked down the bar windows. Somewhere behind them, a saxophone moaned low and soft.

Madison reached into her bag and slid over a folded piece of paper.

"What's this?"

"A list of indie labels. Artists looking for collaborations. Producers who've been asking for something 'real.' Just names. No contracts. But I want you to *think bigger,* Eliza. The door's open. You just have to decide if you're walking through. There's an artist, Brooks Atwood, I represent that would create soulful harmonies with you. Gorgeous baritone, just yummy. Similar style. Also, I rep a band called the Saints & Strangers also out of Austin that Id' like you to sing and maybe do some songwriting collaborations with. Just some thoughts."

Eliza looked at the names. Then back at Madison.

"Why me?"

Madison gave a small, tired smile. "Because when you opened your mouth at that open mic, the whole room leaned in. You didn't just sing. You made people *feel*. That's rare."

Eliza folded the paper gently. "Okay," she said. "I'll try."

"No," Madison said, sipping her drink. "You'll *do*. Trying is for maybe. This—" she tapped the table—"this is yes."

For now it was the opportunity Madison presented that filled her mind pushing out the darkness.

****

Eliza found Finn on the rooftop of their apartment building, legs kicked out, hoodie pulled low. He was eating an entire bag of kettle chips, drinking beer, and watching the lights of downtown Austin flicker like fireflies in the distance.

He looked up as she approached.

"You okay?" he asked. "You've got that face."

"What face?"

"The 'I either landed a record deal or failed a midterm' face."

She sat down beside him, cross-legged, the list from Madison still folded in her pocket.

"I met with Madison."

He waited, chewing slowly.

"She wants me to think bigger. She thinks I could... actually *do* this. Write. Perform. Be something more than a girl who sings in coffeehouses when the semester lets her breathe."

Finn tilted his head. "And what do you think?"

Eliza hesitated. "I think I'm scared. But I also think I want it. And that scares me more."

He set the chips aside, turning toward her fully. "Eliza... you don't have to stay small just to be safe. Or to stay close to me."

She blinked. "What?"

"I've seen the way you light up when you write. When you sing. When you *belong to your own voice*. That's not something you can bottle up just because college is hard or we're still figuring us out."

He reached for her hand, squeezing it. "I didn't fall in love with someone who plays it safe. I fell in love with someone who turns pain into power. So yeah… go big. Go loud. Just don't leave me behind, okay?"

She laughed softly, blinking fast. "Never."

Later That Week – Campus Recording Studio

The space was small. Just one microphone, a bare stool, a black curtain backdrop, and a handheld camera propped on a tripod.

Sophia sat at the soundboard, her boots kicked up on the edge. "Alright, superstar," she said. "You've got fifteen minutes and a busted mic cable. Let's make some magic."

Eliza smiled nervously. She wore jeans, a gray V-neck, and no makeup. Her guitar sat in her lap like an anchor.

"I don't know if this is ACL-worthy," she muttered.

"Good," Sophia said. "Then it's probably real."

Eliza took a breath.

Then another.

Then let the first note fall from her lips like truth.

Still Here
Lyrics by Eliza Monroe

Verse 1
I don't shine loud, I don't blaze bright
But I stay when the room runs out of light
I'm not the girl they cheer for first
But I've walked through fire without burning worse

Pre-Chorus
And I've learned love isn't always clean
But it's in the quiet, the space between

Chorus
Still here, still choosing
Even when it's messy, even when we're losing
Still yours, still true
Even when the world forgets what we've been through
I don't need a perfect start
Just a place inside your heart
Still here
Still loving you

Verse 2
I've cracked and bent, but never broke
I've carried dreams wrapped in secondhand hope
I don't promise easy, don't promise gold
But I'll hold your name when the nights get cold

Pre-Chorus
We don't have to be some shining scene
Just steady hands and in-between

Chorus
Still here, still choosing

Even when it's messy, even when we're losing
Still yours, still true
Even when the world forgets what we've been through
I don't need a perfect start
Just a place inside your heart
Still here
Still loving you

Bridge
And when the lights fade down
When the noise all falls away
I'll be the breath you didn't know you were holding
I'll be the home you choose to stay

Final Chorus
Still here, still choosing
Even when it's hard, even when we're bruising
Still yours, still true
Even when the silence cuts us in two
I don't need a perfect start
Just your hand against my heart
Still here
Still loving you
Still here
Still loving you

By the time she hit the last chorus, she wasn't thinking about Madison. Or ACL. Or fear.

She was just… singing, feeling.

When she looked up, Sophia was crying. Quietly. She noticed that Rhetta was there too.

"You're gonna wreck them," Sophia said. "And I can't wait to watch."

Watching from the back of the room, Rhetta winked and held up her Shiner Bock. Madison had invited her to the performance. She caught Eliza in a hug after whispering, *"You're ready for a bigger stage, sugar. Don't you dare tell yourself otherwise. I'm proud of you."*

Eliza knew in that moment she was doing what she was created to do. Her soul sang.

Chapter Fifty-One

Where the Light Lives

Eliza had called it "a getaway."
Finn had called it "a reset."
West had called it "bullshit."

And Sophia—well, Sophia hadn't called it anything. She'd just folded her arms, stared down into her tea when Eliza pitched the idea, and muttered, *"You're meddling."*

But here they were anyway.

The gravel crackled under the tires as Finn's truck wound its way through the pines. Snow dusted the branches, glittering faintly in the weak afternoon light. The cabin appeared like something out of a painting—log siding, smoke curling faintly from the chimney, a porch swing that looked ready to creak at the first touch.

"Quaint," Sophia murmured from the backseat, her voice clipped.

"Creepy," West countered, not bothering to remove one earbud.

Eliza shot them both a look in the rearview mirror. "Neutral ground," she said firmly. "That's all it is."

Finn squeezed her knee where his hand rested. His voice carried the calm she didn't have. "We could all use a weekend out of the city."

West grunted something unintelligible. Sophia went back to pretending her laptop screen held her full attention, though Eliza had noticed she hadn't typed in fifteen minutes.

By the time Finn parked, tension was coiled so tightly in the cab that Eliza could practically *feel* it pressing at her ribs. She drew in a slow breath of pine air as she stepped out.

The cold slapped her cheeks immediately, but it was a bracing kind of cold—the kind that woke you up, that made your lungs sting in a good way. She thought, *Maybe that's what they need. A shock. A start.*

Inside, the cabin smelled faintly of cedar and woodsmoke. The floorboards creaked under their boots. There were mismatched mugs lined up above the sink, a stone fireplace blackened from years of use, wool blankets folded neatly across the couch.

West set his duffel down with a dull thud in the far bedroom without a word. Sophia drifted into the kitchen, tugging off her gloves slowly, eyes cataloguing everything as if she was gathering evidence.

Eliza lingered by the window. Snow drifted lazily down through the branches, fat flakes that caught the light like sparks. The sky had that soft, silver hue of early winter—the kind of cold that pressed against the glass but couldn't quite reach you if you were wrapped in the right arms.

Finn joined her, sliding his hands around her waist and pressing his cheek to her temple. "It's good here," he murmured.

"It's quiet," she said softly.

"You deserve quiet."

She leaned into him for just a moment before pulling away. Quiet wasn't the goal. Quiet was just the staging ground.

****

Dinner smelled like tomatoes, cumin, and something faintly smoky as chili bubbled on the stove. Finn hummed under his breath, wooden spoon scraping gently against the pot. West leaned against the counter, arms folded, his broad frame blocking half the kitchen light. Sophia perched on a barstool, scrolling absently through her phone until Eliza plucked it away.

"House rule," she said. "No phones unless it's music or emergencies."

Sophia arched a brow. "Dictatorship much?"

"Cabin democracy," Finn corrected cheerfully. "Majority vote. You lose."

By the time they all sat at the table—knees bumping under the small wood surface, bowls steaming—the edges had softened slightly. Sophia rolled her eyes at West's appetite when he polished off his first bowl in record time. But when she refilled his bowl without comment, West muttered, "Thanks," so low it almost disappeared.

Eliza saw Sophia's hand pause for a half-second before withdrawing. Saw the flicker of something cross her face. Hope, maybe. Or ache.

Later, Eliza insisted on a board game.

"Absolutely not," West said immediately.

"Absolutely yes," Eliza shot back. "Cabin tradition. Finn, back me up."

He grinned. "Nothing says team bonding like a classic game of Risk where it's everyone for themselves."

Sophia snorted but joined, arms folded tight at first. By round three she was accusing West of highway robbery with such dramatic flair that even he cracked a grin. His teeth flashed, quick and startling in the firelight.

Eliza caught Finn's eye and mouthed, *See?*

Finn's answering smile was softer. *Maybe.*

Morning came gray and quiet, frost feathering the windows.

Sophia padded out in thick socks, a blanket wrapped around her shoulders. Her glasses slid down her nose, hair tangled in loose copper waves. She froze when she saw West at the stove, coffee already steaming.

For a second they just stared.

Then Sophia cleared her throat. "You make enough for two?"

West's voice was gravel rough from sleep. "Yeah." He pushed a mug across the counter.

Her fingers brushed his when she took it. The touch was fleeting, accidental. But Sophia's heart stuttered anyway. She turned quickly, pretending to sip.

From the bedroom doorway, Eliza watched with a grin she tried to smother.

Later, while hauling logs in from the porch, Eliza pressed. "So?"

Sophia shot her a glare. "So what?"

"So... coffee."

Sophia huffed, stacking wood into her arms. "He poured coffee. That's not reconciliation."

"Eliza Monroe," Sophia muttered, "you're insufferable."

But there was no real bite behind it.

Inside, Finn found West leaning into the fridge. "You're brooding less," he remarked.

West raised a brow.

"Brooding makes people assume you hate them," Finn continued lightly. "If Sophia thinks you hate her, this weekend's a waste."

West shut the fridge slowly. "I don't hate her," he said finally. His voice was low, weighted.

Finn's expression softened. "Then don't make her guess."

The second night, Eliza decided to stop waiting.

After dinner—roast chicken and potatoes, the kind of meal that warmed even stubborn silences—she set her fork down and looked directly at Sophia. Then at West.

"Okay," she said firmly. "Honesty hour."

Sophia stiffened. "Please tell me this isn't truth or dare."

"No dares," Eliza promised. "Just truth. Because you two are driving the rest of us insane."

Silence slammed down. West's jaw ticked. Sophia's cheeks flushed.

"Eliza—" Finn started, warning in his tone.

But Sophia surprised them all. "She's right," she said quietly. Her voice trembled, but she lifted her chin. "We've been… avoiding."

West shifted in his chair. "Yeah. I'm good at that."

The fire popped, sending sparks up the chimney.

"You hurt me," Sophia whispered.

West's throat bobbed. "I know."

"And I don't trust easily."

"I don't expect you to."

She looked at him then, really looked. Saw the exhaustion in his eyes, the stubbornness in his set jaw, but also—God help her—the raw honesty underneath.

"Then why are you here?" she asked.

He swallowed. His hands curled into fists on the table. "Because you're it for me. Even if I don't know how to prove it yet."

Her breath caught.

Eliza reached for Finn's hand under the table, squeezing hard.

Sophia didn't answer. Not yet. But she didn't look away, either.

****

Later, long after the others had drifted to bed, Sophia stepped onto the porch. Snow fell silently in the yellow glow of the porch light, blanketing the world in quiet. She wrapped a wool blanket around herself, pulling it tight.

Her phone pinged with a text message from West. "forgive me. can we talk?"

She didn't text back. Didn't call back. Her heart hurt. She had never felt one tenth of what she felt for West for any other guy. She didn't want to move on without him. He was a big, tattooed risk but one she was finally realizing she needed to take. Regret would be a bitter pill if she didn't take the chance to be with him, really know him and let him know her. When he had said that she was it for him that night she was blown away and it made the ground shift beneath her.

The door creaked. West stepped out, holding two mugs. Steam curled up into the night.

"Second attempt," he said, handing one over. "Better cocoa this time. You didn't text me back. Thought I'd take a chance."

She accepted it, warming her hands. "Not bad, thanks," she admitted after a sip. "You know I love those little marshmallows."

He leaned against the railing, shoulders massive even in his hoodie, breath fogging in the cold. "You're quiet tonight."

"So are you."

"I'm trying not to mess this up," he confessed.

Sophia tilted her head, studying him. "Talking helps."

He stared into his mug for a long moment. "I've never had a future to think about. Not one that wasn't mapped by someone else. Football. Pain. Family. A name I didn't ask to carry."

As he spoke, memory came unbidden—bright and brutal. He could still feel the cracked cement under his fists that night in the fight club, his knuckles raw and splitting, the roar of the crowd like thunder inside his skull. The copper tang of blood had coated his tongue, sweat burning his eyes, but none of it dulled the sharper ache: Sophia's voice echoing in his head, the last words she'd thrown at him before everything broke. *You don't know how to love anyone without destroying yourself first.*

He had fought harder that night, trying to silence it. Trying to silence *her*. But when the match ended and the crowd dissolved, he'd been left with nothing but bruises and the truth: she was right. He didn't know what it meant to have something worth keeping.

He blinked hard, snowflakes catching on his lashes, and forced himself back to the present. "That's all I've ever known," he admitted hoarsely. "Hurting. Breaking. Carrying things I didn't choose. But you..." His eyes lifted to hers, steady and aching. "You make me want something different. I just don't know what that looks like yet. But I want to learn."

Sophia's chest ached, her breath caught somewhere between past and present. Without warning, her mind slid back to the fire escape—the night he'd climbed up, bruised and restless, his hoodie damp with rain. She'd been angry with him then, but when their eyes locked, the anger had cracked into something else. He'd kissed her like the world might collapse if he didn't, like he was holding onto the one solid thing he trusted not to vanish.

Even now, standing in the chilled balcony, she could feel the ghost of that kiss on her lips. The way it had scared her. The way it had lit something she couldn't put out.

Her throat tightened. She reached for his hand, guiding it to her chest. His palm rested over her heartbeat, steady and strong.

"Then let's learn," she whispered. "Together."

He didn't kiss her. Not yet. Instead, he pressed her hand to his chest in return, letting her feel the thud of his own heart. A vow without words.

She met his eyes, raising and turning over his hand, she kissed the inside of his wrist.

For the first time in months, silence between them felt like safety.

"I'm sorry," she added. "For what I said before. For not knowing what you were holding back."

"I deserved it," he said, ice blue eyes gleaming with feeling. "But I've want to fix things, Soph. And I want to fix *this. Us. Take the chance.*"

She stepped closer. Looked up at him.

"You're still an idiot," she said tears filling her eyes. "We were supposed to be done."

"But you're *my* idiot and I'm yours. Let's do this. Us."

Eliza didn't wait. She just leaned up and kissed him—fierce, certain.

And this time, he didn't shut down. She felt so good, right. He felt a strange peace come over him at her words, as her soft voluptuous curves melted perfectly into the hard planes of his body. The rightness of it filled him.

"Missed you baby," he said gently nuzzling her neck, breathing in deeply, taking her jasmine and passion flower scent into himself. "Wanna be with you. For real. Not just to scratch an itch."

He wrapped his arms around her like he finally believed she wouldn't vanish. Grinding her body into his hard needy one, showing her with his body how much he missed her, feeling her heat.

There and then they both decided to *stay*. Give it a real shot.

That night, passion reigned, everything didn't magically heal but their commitment to try, to exclusively move forward together, was foreign but right. As their bodies found a rhythm together, both drowned in the headiness of sharing. Body. Mind. Soul.

Things got *clearer*. Sophia had West. West had Sophia.

And for the first time in a long time, they didn't feel alone in the dark.

****

Inside, the fire burned low, glowing embers casting long shadows across the stone walls. Eliza curled into Finn's side, her head heavy on his shoulder, body still tingling after their intense lovemaking.

"I think it worked," she murmured.

Finn kissed her hair. "No," he corrected gently. "*They* worked. We just gave them a place to start."

Eliza smiled faintly, her chest full. Around them, the cracks were still raw, the wounds not yet fully healed. But this—this warmth, this weekend, this fragile beginning—was where the light lived.

Where healing began.
Where love, tentative and stubborn, proved it was still worth fighting for.

Chapter Fifty-Two

The Things We Dreamed

The cursor blinked like a dare.

Eliza sat cross-legged at her desk in their off-campus apartment, the afternoon sun slanting across the blinds. Outside, Guadalupe Street buzzed—bus brakes, horns, some kid blaring country out of a truck with a Longhorn decal.

Her laptop glowed with the finished manuscript. One hundred and fifty pages of her—essays and stories stitched together from scraps of late nights, café corners, memories that cut but healed in the telling. They weren't perfect, but they were alive.

Her thumb hovered over the "submit" button for the New Voices competition.

The weight of it pressed down. She whispered, "What if it changes everything?"

The door creaked. Finn leaned against the frame, hair damp from practice, jersey tugged loose over broad shoulders. He grinned that crooked grin that had been wrecking her since they were sixteen.

"You gonna hit send," he teased, "or do I gotta tackle you for the laptop?"

She laughed shakily. "I'm scared."

"Of what? You've survived worse than rejection."

Her throat bobbed. "Of becoming someone. Of things changing again."

He crossed the room, kneeling so his eyes met hers. He slipped a calloused hand over hers, steady. "You're already someone, Liza. This just lets the world in on it."

Her breath caught. He pressed a kiss to her temple.

"Do it," he whispered. "Hit send. Let 'em see what I already know."

So she did.

The page refreshed, and it was gone. She leaned back, heart pounding, while Finn smiled like he'd won something too.

****

Two days later, Austin was painted burnt orange. It was game day.

Fans filled the streets around Darrell K Royal–Texas Memorial Stadium, trucks flying Longhorn flags, pit smokers sending up clouds of brisket and sausage. Someone had Bevo painted across their chest. The Tower in the distance already glowed faint orange in anticipation.

Eliza wore game-day armor: red Lucchese boots, cut-off denim shorts, and Finn's white number twelve jersey tied at her waist. Burnt-orange beads clicked at her wrist when she clapped.

Inside the stadium, the Longhorn band stormed the field, trumpets gleaming, drums hammering "Texas Fight." Bevo himself shifted in his pen at the sideline, horns glinting beneath the lights. The crowd screamed.

Finn trotted out, helmet tucked under his arm, shoulders squared. He looked larger than life, but she knew the boy beneath—the one who left sticky notes on her laptop, who kissed her hand when she was nervous.

In the First Quarter the snap cracked the air. Finn's first pass flew clean, slicing across the sky into a receiver's hands. The student section exploded, boots pounding aluminum.

Sophia was screaming beside her, hair whipping in the wind, eyes focused on West holding the defensive line. Van clapped once, arms crossed, expression tight but present.

The opposing defense pushed back hard. By the end of the quarter, the score was tied, tension like barbed wire in Eliza's chest.

Sunlight dipped during the Second Quarter, shadows stretching across the turf. Finn's spiral arced perfectly, landing in the end zone. Touchdown.

The stadium shook. The band blared, horns sharp against the roar. Eliza jumped, clutching Sophia in a half-hug, tears stinging.

Halftime brought the full band pageantry—cowboy hats, white boots, the Longhorn formation drawn across the grass. Eliza pulled Finn's jersey tighter, whispering prayers into the chill.

In the Third Quarter, a sack nearly took him down, her stomach lurching as he hit turf. He rose slow, shaking it off.

Her nails dug into Sophia's arm. "He's fine," Sophia murmured, though her voice trembled.

Then—magic. Third down, twenty yards, Finn broke free, juking left then right before delivering a throw that seemed impossible. Completion. First down.

The stadium went feral. Eliza's cheeks were wet and she hadn't noticed until Sophia wiped one away with her sleeve.

In the Forth Quarter the game was tied. Only three minutes left. The lights burned white against a navy sky.

Finn called the play. The snap flew. Time collapsed—one pass, one catch, six points.

The roar was thunder. The Tower in the distance blazed full burnt orange, the lit-up "1" declaring victory across the city.

Eliza was already running. She found him in the chaos, helmet off, hair damp with sweat, grin wild. She leapt, he caught her, spinning until her boots kicked the air.

"You did it!" she cried.

"No," he rasped, forehead pressed to hers. "We did."

Victory carried them to O'Malley's, the old bar on Guadalupe lit with neon beer signs and a Longhorn mural. A live band crowded into the corner, fiddles and steel guitar ripping through a George Strait cover.

The place was wall-to-wall burnt orange. Students still chanting "Hook 'Em!" hoisted pitchers of Shiner Bock, foam spilling. Baskets of queso fries and fried pickles covered sticky tables.

Eliza slid into a booth, still in Finn's jersey and boots, her voice hoarse. Finn never let go of her hand, thumb rubbing lazy circles against her palm.

Dillon and Kai arrived balancing trays of wings and nachos. Brooks and Merrick had flown in—Brooks slapped Finn so hard the glasses rattled.

"To the man of the hour!" Brooks hollered, raising his Shiner.

"To the draft combine!" Merrick added, quieter but proud.

The table roared. Finn laughed, but his eyes always circled back to Eliza, grounding himself in her smile.

Across the bar, Eliza noticed Dillon leaning close to a dark-haired girl in a UT sweatshirt. She was laughing at something he said, twirling her hair. Dillon's grin was all ease, no shadow of his old crush. Eliza's chest loosened.

The band switched songs, someone yelling for "Amarillo by Morning." Half the bar joined in, off-key but loud.

Finn leaned close, breath warm against her ear. "Hey," he murmured, "you tell Sophia about ACL yet?"

Her brows lifted. "Not yet. Still waiting."

"You should hear from Madison soon, right?"

She nodded, nerves sparking. She'd sent her demo weeks ago, hoping for a slot at Austin City Limits—a dream almost too big to say out loud.

Finn kissed her cheek, lingering. "They'd be idiots not to take you."

Her heart swelled so fast it hurt.

Later, as Shiner pitchers emptied and the band shifted to "Friends in Low Places," Finn pulled her up from the booth. They danced clumsily between tables, his hand hot on her waist, her boots scuffing the wood. She laughed into his shoulder, the smell of beer and cedar smoke heavy in the air.

When he kissed her, quick and fierce, the whole world blurred until it was just the two of them.

****

A few days later, Eliza was at her desk when the email arrived. Subject line: *Congratulations—Your Story Accepted for Publication.*

Her hands shook so badly she nearly dropped her laptop.

"Finn," she whispered. "I think I just got published."

He tossed his ice pack aside and lifted her straight off the chair, spinning like he had after the game. "I told you!"

She laughed through tears, clutching him. Not survival tears—becoming tears.

Eliza had cried once when she got her first acceptance into the college—this felt bigger. Felt like all of her hard work at UT and to get scholarships had been worth it. More intimate. Like the world saw her now, not just as someone who survived, but as someone who had something to say. Like an extension of her songwriting just in a different format and audience.

With the Tower glowing outside their window and his arms locked around her, it felt like Austin itself was opening the future for them—stadiums and stages, stories and songs.

And they would chase it all together.

Chapter Fifty-Three

Letting It In

The neon still hummed in Sophia's ears when she stepped out of the crowded bar, West's hand brushing low at her back as if to steer her through the crush. The UT game had ended hours earlier, Finn carried on the shoulders of teammates, West, Dillon and Kai included, Eliza spinning through his arms in new red Lucchese boots Finn had surprised her with and denim shorts, the night thick with Shiner Bock, tequila, and victory songs.

Inside, the jukebox had blared Willie Nelson between bursts of rowdy band music; Bevo's name had been shouted from three different tables. Dillon had disappeared with a brunette named Raven, who laughed too loud, Brooks and Merrick had been arguing about brisket, and Kai was teaching strangers the Longhorns' fight song with a pitcher of Shiner held high.

Sophia, though, had felt the edges of the noise pressing in. When West leaned down, his breath warm against her hair, and said, *"You ready?"* she'd only nodded.

Now, under the sharp cold of an Austin winter night, she let the air steady her lungs. West's truck waited at the curb. His hand brushed hers once, twice, before finally catching hold.

His apartment smelled faintly of detergent and something citrus from the candle Sophia had brought weeks ago and teased him for never lighting. Tonight, though, it glowed on the counter.

West stood in the middle of the kitchen wearing a dark apron, sleeves shoved up, hair mussed like he'd been dragging his hands through it. A skillet hissed with garlic and oil, steam fogging the small square window above the sink.

Sophia blinked. "You're cooking?"

"Don't sound so shocked," he said, turning a piece of chicken with exaggerated focus.

"I just... didn't expect *this*." She slid onto the counter, ankles crossed, red nail polish catching the overhead light. "What exactly is *this*?"

He squinted at the pan. "Chicken. Rice. Some kind of sauce thing."

She bit back a smile. "Ah, yes. The classic 'some kind of sauce thing.'"

"I YouTubed the hell out of it," he muttered, flipping the chicken. "Please don't die after eating it."

The smell filled the room—garlic sharp, oil smoky, rice sticking just enough to the pot to hiss in protest. West moved with a kind of brute concentration, shoulders taut, every motion deliberate, like football plays replayed in his head.

Sophia watched him, and something inside her softened even further. He could've just ordered tacos. He could've avoided this entirely. But here he was, apron and all.

Dinner was messy. The rice clumped. The chicken leaned toward overdone. The sauce thing was more like garlic oil with ambition. But they ate it side by side on his worn couch, knees pressed together, forks scraping from the same mismatched bowls.

Sophia leaned back, warmth spreading through her chest despite the uneven meal. West set his bowl down, rubbed a hand over his jaw. His eyes flicked to her, then away, as though weighing a play that might lose the game.

"You scare me," he said suddenly, voice low.

Her brows lifted. "I scare you?"

He nodded, gaze fixed on the half-empty bowl. "Because I've never wanted someone the way I want you. And not just your body. I mean—your voice. Your stubborn playlists. The way you fight for people who don't even fight for themselves."

The honesty cracked through her carefully built walls. For a moment, she said nothing, only watched him, his jaw flexing, shoulders taut as if bracing for her silence.

Finally, she whispered, "I'm scared too. Because you could break me. But I don't think you will."

His throat worked. Slowly, he leaned forward until his forehead touched hers. Their breaths mingled, silence thick with everything unsaid.

"I won't," he murmured.

The kiss that followed wasn't frantic. It was careful, heart-stopping, intense. Yet fierce. A reminder of their new-found commitment. His hands traced the edges of her ribs as though asking permission with every touch. Her palms slid to his jaw, grounding him, answering without words.

When they finally undressed, laughter slipped between kisses—the clumsiness of socks, the tangle of denim, the knock of a knee against the nightstand. It was messy, awkward, breathtaking. His hands shook not from lust but from awe, reverence threaded through every touch. She pulled him close, steadying his tremors with her steadiness.

Their bodies found rhythm slowly, less conquest, more connection.

Afterward, tangled in sheets that smelled faintly of detergent and garlic, Sophia lay with her cheek against his chest. His heartbeat thudded steady beneath her ear, anchoring her.

"I'm falling for you," she whispered.

He didn't answer right away. His fingers drew idle lines along her spine, mapping words before he spoke them. Finally, voice rough but certain, he murmured:

"Then let me fall with you."

She closed her eyes. For the first time in years, she didn't brace for impact.

Morning cracked soft and gold across the blinds. Sophia woke to the smell of burnt toast and the sound of West cursing low. She slid from bed, pulling his UT jersey over her bare legs, the sleeves hanging past her hands.

The kitchen was a battlefield: toast charred in the sink, eggs half-stirred in a pan. West stood with a spatula, hair sticking up, muttering.

Sophia leaned against the doorway, arms folded. "Domestic god, huh?"

He glanced up, ears red. "I was trying to make breakfast."

"You set bread on fire."

"I *toasted* it aggressively."

She laughed, the sound surprising her with its ease. Crossing the kitchen, she bumped his hip with hers, reached for the spatula. "Scoot. Let me."

Together, they salvaged eggs, sliced avocado, made coffee that was more drinkable than not. They ate barefoot at his counter, her in his hoodie, him in sweats, their knees brushing.

It wasn't perfect. It was better.

Later, West drove them to meet Finn and Eliza for brunch at Kerbey Lane, Austin sun warming the December chill. Inside, the place buzzed with hungover students and families in Longhorns gear. The clatter of plates and the smell of maple syrup and salsa blurred into a hum of warmth.

Eliza's boots were propped on a chair rung, her hair in loose waves, Finn's arm slung lazily around her. They looked lit from within—like a couple who'd survived fire and was now walking toward light.

Plates arrived in a rush: stacks of gingerbread pancakes dripping with butter, migas with jalapeños sharp enough to sting the air, queso that pooled golden in the center of the table. Coffee kept coming in mismatched mugs, thick and slightly burnt.

Dillon swaggered in late, hair mussed, a phone number scrawled on his wrist. "What'd I miss?"

Sophia smirked. "Other than you finding religion with a brunette last night?"

He grinned unrepentant, dropping into a chair. "Her name's Raven. Environmental science major. She quoted Willie Nelson at me. I'm basically a goner. We were on and off for a couple of years."

Eliza raised her brows, mock-stern. "So you've finally stopped pining after me?"

Dillon pressed a hand to his chest, dramatic. "You wound me. I have matured."

Laughter rippled around the table.

West met Dillon's eyes, "You remember Gracie, my step-sister? My dad said she's the lead in a ballet with a prominent ballet company in Chicago now. Apparently, she is all grace these days. A big change from when we first met her. Anyway, Dad and Virginia want us to join them for a family dinner when she comes in town in two weeks to celebrate. You up for it?"

Surprised and intrigued, Dillon responded flashing back to when her met Gracie. "Got it. No problem I can run interference for you, I've done it in the past."

Brooks and Merrick, already mid-argument, leaned in from across the booth.

"She hot?" Merrick asked winking.

Not missing a beat, Brooks jumped in, "She single?"

West flicked a beer cap at Merrick. Brooks got a punch to the shoulder. "No more of that."

"Franklin's brisket still runs this city," Brooks insisted, wisely shifting gears, stabbing his fork for emphasis.

"Please," Merrick shot back. "That's a tourist trap. Micklethwait's blows it out of the water. The smoke ring alone—"

"Boys," Eliza cut in, eyes twinkling, "we're eating pancakes. Chill."

The table dissolved into laughter again, warmth pulling Sophia deeper into the moment.

She let herself watch Eliza then—really watch. The way Finn leaned down, whispering something that made her blush. The way her eyes shone when he teased her about ACL.

"Any day now," Finn said between bites, his grin unshakable. "ACL's gonna call. Madison said submissions were strong this year, but yours— yours are gonna cut through."

Eliza ducked her head, fighting a smile. "Don't jinx it."

Sophia's chest tightened, not with jealousy but with something quieter— an ache that was half admiration, half longing. She knew what it meant to put your whole heart into a thing and wait to see if the world would take it.

Beneath the table, West nudged her knee with his. She glanced at him, saw the softness in his eyes, the silent acknowledgment: *We're not there yet, but maybe we could be.*

She didn't look away.

That night, back at West's place, Sophia stood on his porch, cold air brushing her cheeks. Inside, the candle still burned faintly citrus.

She thought of garlic and burnt toast, of pancakes and laughter, of the way his voice had broken when he said, *"You scare me."*

And for the first time in a long time, she let the thought land fully:

She wasn't just falling. She was letting herself be caught in arms that felt like forever.

Chapter Fifty-Four

The Doors We Choose

The email landed in Eliza's inbox with all the subtlety of an earthquake.

She had been standing at the kitchen counter with a mug of tea cooling beside her laptop, her hair half pulled up, still in Finn's oversized *Designated Driver* t-shirt from the night before. Her manuscript tabs were open, a handful of scholarship deadlines blinking red on her planner app. She wasn't expecting anything more significant than a spam message or a reminder from UT's writing center.

But then—

Congratulations. You've been selected to perform at Austin City Limits.

The words didn't look real.

Her stomach plummeted and then soared all at once, like she'd missed a stair step in the dark. She pressed a hand over her mouth. ACL. The stage she'd sat in front of for years, guitar on her knee, daring to dream. The stage she'd seen legends on, the kind of stage she never thought would be hers.

"Finn," she called, her voice sharp with disbelief.

He came out of the bedroom in sweatpants, his hair damp from a shower, scrolling absently through his phone. "What's up?"

Eliza turned her laptop so he could see. Her hands were shaking. "I—I think I just got in."

He froze mid-step. "Wait—ACL? As in… Austin City freakin' Limits?"

Her throat bobbed as she nodded. "Live. Side stage performing my original songs."

Finn let out a whoop so loud the neighbors probably heard, his phone forgotten on the couch. In two strides he had her lifted off the ground, spinning her like he did after touchdowns. "Songbird," he laughed, pressing his forehead to hers. "I told you, I told you, they'd be stupid not to take you!"

Tears slipped hot down her cheeks, and she didn't even try to stop them. "I don't—Finn, this is real. This is actually happening."

He set her down gently but kept her close, his big hands cupping her face. "It's more than real. It's you. All those nights you stayed up writing instead of sleeping, every song you played until your fingers bled, every time you thought no one was listening. They were. They are. And now the whole damn world gets to hear them."

Her chest ached with how much she loved him in that moment. How he never looked at her like she was too small or too broken. Only like she was enough.

The mug of tea had gone cold by the time she remembered to breathe.

The next week blurred.

Finn's phone never seemed to stop buzzing—coach Billings, scouts, even agents. ESPN articles featuring his stats were circulating, and whispers of the draft were turning into real conversations. His advisor at UT pulled him into meetings about spring showcases, about timing, about strategy.

Meanwhile, Eliza had an email chain with Madison, the ACL stage coordinator, locked at the top of her inbox. Setlists, rehearsal times, promotional photos—things she used to dream about scribbling into the margins of her notebooks now stared back at her in black and white.

But between them, between the chaos, was a question neither had spoken aloud: *What happens to us when our dreams start pulling us in different directions?*

One night, they sat at the small kitchen table with their laptops open. His calendar crowded with training sessions and interviews, hers filling with deadlines and publishing house shifts.

Eliza closed her laptop slowly. "Do you think we can do this?"

Finn looked up, tired but still smiling, his knee brushing hers under the table. "Do what?"

"Both," she said softly. "Our dreams. Us. I don't want one to cancel the other out."

He reached across and covered her hand with his. His palm was warm, callused from years of gripping a football, grounding her in a way nothing else did.

"Eliza," he said, his voice low but certain, "we've done worse. We've been through hell. This?" He gestured between their calendars, their looming futures. "This is the good kind of hard."

Her eyes stung, but she managed a shaky laugh. "It just feels so big."

"Yeah," he admitted, squeezing her hand. "But everything I want—ACL, the draft, whatever it is—it's only worth it if I get to come home to you."

Her heart slammed against her ribs.

"Finn—"

He cut her off with a grin. "So. We don't overthink it tonight. We eat leftover pizza. We watch whatever terrible rom-com you've got queued up. And then, tomorrow, we wake up and chase the hell out of these dreams. Together."

She exhaled, the tightness in her chest loosening. He made it sound that simple.

Maybe it was.

She squeezed back. "Together."

****

It was Finn's idea to sneak into the stadium.

Late on a Friday night, the UT campus quiet except for the buzz of Sixth Street traffic blocks away, he tugged her hand with a mischievous grin. "Come on, Songbird. I've got something to show you."

Eliza laughed nervously, glancing around. "Finn, we're gonna get caught."

"Nah," he said, leading her through a side gate he'd long since learned to jimmy open. "Perks of knowing the security schedule. Besides, what's college without breaking a few rules?"

She rolled her eyes but followed anyway, the cool night air lifting her pale blonde hair, the light making it appear to Finn as though it were silver moonlight, as they stepped onto the wide stretch of field. The stadium was dark except for the spill of moonlight and the glow of Austin's skyline in the distance. Empty stands rose like shadows around them.

It felt sacred, like stepping into a cathedral built for noise and now hushed for prayer.

"Wow," she whispered awed.

The lights were off, the stands empty, the silence vast. As he led her onto the field, hand in hand, the turf springy beneath their sneakers. The UT logo spread beneath their feet, silvered by the moon.

"Why here?" she asked, awed voice hushed.

"Because this is where I feel it most," he said, turning to her under the dark sweep of sky. "The pull. The weight. The love. I wanted you in the middle of it."

Her cheeks flushed, but she smiled. "Romantic football field, huh?"

He grinned. "You'd be surprised."

He pulled her close, kissed her slow, steady. She melted into it, the quiet of the stadium wrapping around them.

"Finn," she whispered, hesitant. "Out here?"

"Nobody's here," he murmured against her mouth. "Just us. Just this."

Her breath caught. He felt her waver—the shy tug of restraint. So he slowed, hands gentle at her waist. "We don't have too. Ever. But Eliza—

God, I love you. I want to love you here, where everything started for me. Where everything changed."

Her eyes shone in the faint glow of the exit lights. For a long moment, she searched his face. Then, trembling but certain, she nodded.

They lay down first, hand in hand, the field stretching out around them like a dark ocean. The turf was cool beneath Eliza's back, tiny rubber pellets pressing against her bare skin where her blush pink blouse had ridden up. It smelled faintly of cut grass and something synthetic, the scent of every game Finn had ever played here and the ghosts of the too.

Above them, the night was wide and endless. The stadium lights were off, but the stars were ruthless in their clarity, scattered in silver arcs across the black sky.

Finn propped himself on one elbow, looking down at her, green eyes glowing. His rough thumb electrified her as he brushed her cheek. "God, you're beautiful here. In my place. Like the stars just decided to land on this field and become you."

Eliza flushed, a laugh caught in her throat. "You're ridiculous."

"Maybe." His voice dropped, tender and sure. "But you're my Songbird. And I want to hear you here, even if it's just the sound of your breath."

The name—his name for her—melted her.

Her chest tightened when he called her Songbird. In the beginning he'd called her that, half-joking, but now it felt like something sacred.

"It's so quiet," she murmured.

"Not quiet," he corrected gently. "Just listening."

When he kissed her, the echo of it carried in the empty stands, as if the whole stadium leaned in to listen. She felt her own breath bounce back to her in the silence, magnified, vulnerable.

"Finn…" she whispered when his hands traced her sides, when his mouth found the hollow beneath her jaw then moved lower.

He paused, lifted his head. "Too much?"

She shook her head quickly, nervous but certain. "No. Just—here?"

"Nobody's here," he promised, voice low, steady. "It's just us. Just the stars. And I swear to you, Songbird, you're safe."

His patience unraveled her. Every hesitation, every shy glance melted under the heat of his gaze. He moved with a kind of awe, as if touching her was both permission and miracle. The turf was rough and cool under her back, his body hot above her, and when he entered her, the entire world seemed to still—just the sound of their breaths, her moans, and the faint creak of the bleachers in the wind.

Eliza gasped, clutching at his shoulders. The sensation was sharp, overwhelming, but his whisper anchored her.

"Breathe with me. Look at me."

She did. His green eyes were so open, so full of her, that she found herself letting go. Letting him in. The connection between them almost overwhelming her.

They moved together slowly at first, laughter breaking through nerves when their rhythm stumbled, then dissolving into sighs as they found it. Finn's hard and silky cock filling her so full, she couldn't help but scream his name into the moonlit stadium, digging her nails into his back, wrapping her legs around his waist as gentleness and reverence gave way to an almost savage passion.

Finn took her as though reminding himself that she was his.

Possessing her.

Filling her.

At once shattering her and remaking her.

Seeing his possessive, loving, and passionate gaze as he growled, "Come for me Songbird," made her orgasm rip through her whole body as she shattered in his arms.

"Finn!" Eliza screamed as the pleasure took hold.

His orgasm took him as her body clenched down on his hard length milking every sensation. Just as Her voice slipped free in a shuddering moan of utter satisfaction, Finn stilled, breathes coming in labored gasps, forehead pressed to hers, arms shaking, sweat glistening on his heated hard chest. Both of them utterly spent from the shared passion.

"That sound," he whispered. "That's my favorite song. The noises you make when I'm inside you that only I get to hear."

Slowly becoming aware of their surroundings, Eliza smiled up at Finn, satisfaction and love evident in the movement, as she felt the turf pressed into her shoulders, the faint smell of grass and rubber filling her lungs, her hair tangling with the fibers. The vastness of the field seemed to cradle them, turning their intimacy into something infinite.

Eliza felt the release still, when she came, it had felt less like breaking and more like opening, like stepping into a light she hadn't known she carried.

After, they collapsed side by side at midfield, sweaty and tangled, their chests rising and falling in sync. Finn tugged his jersey over both of them, a clumsy blanket against the night air.

For a while, they just breathed. The silence was thick, but not empty—it was full of what they'd made together, shared together, lingering in the air.

Finn lifted a hand toward the stars. "See that one?" He pointed. "That's the North Star. Used to think of it during away games, when I felt lost. Always points you home."

Eliza followed his finger, her cheek still against his chest. "Home," she echoed softly.

"And that," he said, shifting his hand, "is Orion. The hunter. Coach Billings used to tell us about him before night practices—said he was watching if we slacked."

She laughed quietly. "Of course he did."

Finn's voice gentled. "And that one, right there—the brightest. That's for you, Songbird. That's yours."

Her throat closed. "Finn—"

The stars above them blazed on, eternal and unblinking, while below, on the quiet field where dreams were born, two futures intertwined—sealed not with spectacle, but with breath, skin, and vow.

"You realize we're crazy, right?" she said, laughing softly.

"Crazy in love," he teased, nudging her shoulder.

She rolled her eyes but couldn't stop smiling.

He sobered then, turning to face her fully. "Eliza—whatever comes, scouts or stages, cities or contracts—nothing's bigger than this—Than us."

"I mean it." He kissed her temple. "No matter where I end up—draft, teams, the whole circus—you'll be the brightest thing I ever find in the dark."

Tears pricked her eyes. She pressed a kiss against his hard chest tracing the songbird tattoo over his heart, tasting salt, whispering, "Then don't ever stop finding me."

His arms tightened around her, his voice a vow. "Never."

"North of Always."

Her chest ached with the force of it—the magnitude. She leaned in, kissed him once more, and felt the future press close—not frightening, but alive.

Afterwards, as they walked off the field, hands still locked, Eliza glanced back. The dark turf stretched behind them, marked with invisible imprints of where they had lain. She knew she would carry this night forever, tucked in her like a secret vow.

For the first time, she didn't just believe in dreams. She believed in a future worth building. Together.

****

The scouts came sooner than he expected.

Finn knew whispers were circling after the championship, but seeing men in pressed polos and logo caps standing along the practice sideline made it real. NFL team reps. Not watching the team. Watching *him*.

He threw harder, ran faster, every muscle coiled with focus. He could feel their eyes measuring him in yards and dollars.

After practice, Coach Billings clapped his shoulder. "You've got options, son. They're circling because you've earned it. Don't get caught in the noise—keep your head. I've got a couple of potential agents for you to meet. They're bulldogs, but fair. Think it's time."

Finn nodded, but his pulse was wild. He thought of Eliza, of ACL, of the way her eyes lit when she talked about music like it was oxygen. Dreams were real for both of them now. Big ones. Dangerous ones.

That weekend, they met Van for coffee.

He looked older, quieter. The fire that had once burned hot under his trouble now flickered with something steadier. "Got accepted into a Master's Lit and creative writing program at Rice University out in Houston," he told them. "Figured it's time I stop burning bridges and start building something real."

Finn clapped his hand across Van's shoulder. "I'm proud of you, man. For real."

Van's eyes softened. "Don't waste your shot, Finn. And Eliza—don't shrink when the world hands you a stage. You both got more in you than most."

As he walked away, Eliza squeezed Finn's hand. The weight of Van's words settled between them—not heavy, but grounding. Paths were starting to diverge and it felt bittersweet.

Chapter Fifty-Five

Enchanted

The sky stretched wide and clean, a Texas September morning painted in blues so bright it looked washed new. Finn's old blue F150 rumbled along the highway heading west out of Austin, its windows cranked down to let in the Hill Country air. The scent of cedar and mesquite drifted in, mixing with the faint leather of the seats and the dust kicked up by eighteen-wheelers roaring past.

Eliza sat in the passenger seat, legs curled under her, her red Lucchese boots perched on the dash. She wore denim shorts and a red off-the-shoulder blouse covered in tiny white flowers. Her hair whipped in the wind, sun catching the strands in almost white gold.

Finn glanced at her for maybe the hundredth time that hour. He'd always loved driving with her—she had a way of filling silence with ease, either humming along to the radio or twisting around to point out things he'd never notice. Today, though, her laughter made him feel both grounded and jittery at once.

In the glove box, tucked deep beneath old maps and registration papers, was a small black velvet box that felt heavier than any football he'd ever thrown. His chest tightened just thinking about it.

"Peach stand's up ahead," Eliza said, pointing. "Want to stop?"

"Only if you promise not to eat the whole bag before we get to town."

Her grin flashed mischievous. "No promises."

He pulled off the highway onto the gravel lot of a roadside stand. Baskets of Hill Country peaches glowed golden-pink under the morning sun, the scent sweet and heady. A little radio perched on the counter crackled out George Strait, and an old farmer in a wide hat greeted them with a slow nod.

Eliza sampled one, juice dripping down her wrist. Finn watched her lick it away with a laugh, and the thought hit him sharp: *That's the woman I want beside me for the rest of my life.*

They loaded a paper sack with peaches, still warm from the sun, and got back on the road.

By midday, Fredericksburg buzzed with weekend life—tourists spilling down Main Street, fiddles playing from a side porch, flags snapping in the breeze. German bakery scents drifted out of doorways: strudel, pretzels, cinnamon sugar. The sidewalks were crowded with couples carrying wine bottles from the local vineyards, kids licking ice cream cones.

Finn parked on a side street shaded by pecan trees. He and Eliza strolled past antique shops and boutique windows, her hand slipping easily into his. She stopped to admire a turquoise necklace in one window, her reflection soft in the glass.

"You want to try it on?" he asked.

She shook her head, eyes lingering on the piece. "Not today. I'm already wearing something pretty." She lifted their joined hands.

His throat tightened. He almost said *wait until you see what's in my pocket*, but kept his mouth shut. Timing mattered.

They grabbed sandwiches from a café, ate them on a park bench while an older man strummed guitar nearby. Eliza leaned her head on Finn's shoulder, humming along absentmindedly.

For a few hours, they let Fredericksburg's easy charm carry them. Shops. Peaches. Laughter echoing down cobblestone. Finn was quiet at times, his nerves pressing. Eliza didn't push—she had always known how to let his silences breathe.

By late afternoon, the heat softened into gold light. Finn suggested they drive out to Enchanted Rock.

The state park sprawled wide, pink granite dome rising against the sky like something half-ancient, half-sacred. It was their spot. The place where they first kissed. Memories filled his thoughts but as he held Eliza's hand at that moment, it felt new.

The trail crunched beneath their boots, cedar and cactus dotting the scrub. That day the sun slanted low, warm but not brutal. Grasshoppers buzzed. Birds flickered between shadows.

"You're suspiciously quiet," Eliza said, eyeing him thoughtfully.

"Just pacing myself."

She arched a brow cheekily. "Or hiding something?"

His heart kicked. He forced a grin transforming his face from handsome to devastating in an instant. "Guess you'll have to climb and see."

They reached the summit as twilight poured across the Hill Country. The view stretched forever—rolling oaks, scattered ranches, the last of the sun melting into lavender haze. A faint breeze cooled their skin.

Eliza exhaled. "God, it feels like the whole world is open up here."

"It is," he said softly.

They spread out a blanket Finn had packed, the granite warm beneath them. Eliza lay back, eyes tracing the sky as stars winked alive one by one. The dome darkened around them, the horizon bleeding indigo.

She pointed upward. "There—that's the North Star."

Finn followed her finger. His chest tightened. Perfect.

He sat up, palms damp. The words he'd rehearsed in his head suddenly scattered, replaced by nothing but the memory of her laugh in his truck, her voice on the fire escape years ago, her faith in him when he didn't deserve it.

"Eliza." His voice roughened. She turned toward him, smile curious.

He took her hand, pressed it to his chest where his heart beat hard. "Do you remember the stadium that night? Lying on the turf, looking up?"

She nodded, eyes soft.

"You said the stars made you feel small but safe. That no matter what changed, the North Star would still be there. And I realized something that I think I've known for a long time—you're that for me. My constant. My compass. Wherever I go, you're what brings me home."

Her breath hitched. The realization of what was happening began to crash over her consciousness like a wave on the beach.

He reached into his pocket, pulled out the small velvet box, and flipped it open. The antique amethyst glowed deep violet in the starlight mirroring her eyes, the diamonds surrounding it catching faint sparks.

"Eliza Monroe," he said, voice breaking, "will you marry me?"

For a heartbeat, silence. Just the whisper of wind across stone. Her hands flew to her mouth, eyes shining wet.

Then she nodded fiercely, tears streaking her cheeks. "Yes. God, yes."

He slipped the ring onto her finger—it was perfect. She laughed through her tears, tackling him back onto the blanket. Their kisses were breathless, messy, salted with tears.

"Songbird," he whispered against her hair, "you just made me the luckiest and happiest man alive."

"You thought you weren't enough, I thought I wasn't enough. But together we've always been more than enough. You're my North Star."

She laughed again, the sound breaking and beautiful. "I love you, Finn Callahan"

"I love you more."

Above them, the stars stretched endless. The North Star glowed steady.

They stopped at Rhetta's farmhouse on their way out of town the next morning, sun still low over the fields. Her porch smelled of coffee and roses.

Rhetta opened the door, apron dusted with flour, and froze when she saw Eliza's hand.

"Lord have mercy." She clasped both of Eliza's cheeks, eyes brimming. "That ring—"

Finn grinned. "She said yes."

Rhetta pulled them both into a hug that smelled of cinnamon and lavender. Tears streaked her cheeks as she pressed her hands over Eliza's.

"You take care of each other," she whispered. "That's all I've ever wanted for you, girl. To be loved the way you deserve."

Eliza nodded, throat tight.

They sat around Rhetta's kitchen table, sunlight spilling through lace curtains, eating homemade biscuits with peach jam. Rhetta told stories about Eliza—struggling to learn chords, notes, stubborn songs she hummed before bed. Finn listened, squeezing Eliza's hand under the table.

When they finally left, Rhetta waved from the porch, her blessing trailing after them like a benediction.

As they drove back toward Austin, Eliza rested her head on Finn's shoulder, the amethyst ring winking every time the sun caught it.

For the first time in both their lives, the future didn't feel like something to fear.

It felt like something waiting, wide and bright.

Like a horizon they'd climb together. Like home.

Chapter Fifty-Six

Gearing Up

The week after Fredericksburg, everything seemed lit from within.

Eliza caught herself staring at her hand in random moments—on the steering wheel, while pouring coffee, while scribbling lyrics on the corner of a notebook. The amethyst glimmered with every flick of light, deep violet circled in tiny diamonds. People stopped her constantly: strangers, classmates, the woman at the H-E-B checkout who reached across the conveyor to take a closer look.

But more than the ring, it was the way Finn looked at her now. Like he had climbed the dome of the world and seen a horizon only the two of them could share. He was steadier, more open, more certain in a way that seeped into her own bones. They had each other and that was more than enough. It was everything.

She hadn't told Madison yet. She wanted to see her face when she did, to hold that moment between them like a secret. But ACL loomed, so big she could barely fit it in her chest.

ACL Prep

Madison paced Eliza's apartment living room, phone pressed between her ear and shoulder, red lips pursed, laptop open with color-coded tabs. She was wearing ripped black jeans and a sequined blazer at ten in the morning. Eliza swore the woman never slept.

"Two fifteen, North Tent, Saturday," Madison rattled off, snapping her fingers. "Private circle, industry only. But word is the *Chronicle* might send a scout. That means reviews. Reviews mean features. Features mean touring possibilities and better collaboration partners. You ready?"

Eliza's mouth went dry. She tugged at the hem of her chambray shirt, running her hands through her long tresses in agitation and excitement. "As ready as I'll ever be."

"Wrong answer." Madison dropped the phone onto the couch, eyes narrowing, full of sparks. "You're not just ready. You're about to blow them the hell away. Repeat after me: I'm not just ready—"

Eliza laughed nervously. "Madison—"

"Say it."

Eliza rolled her eyes but played along. "I'm not just ready…"

"I'm going to set fire to that tent."

Eliza snorted. "Madison."

"Say it."

She sighed, cheeks heating. "I'm going to set fire to that tent. Burn it down."

Madison clapped once, satisfied. "That's my girl."

Across the apartment, Finn leaned against the kitchen counter, half-smile curving his mouth as he watched the exchange. He was in a dark green henley, broad shoulders filling the doorway like he'd been built to anchor a room. Eliza caught his hot gaze and flushed, her hand brushing the ring. He winked. She blew him a kiss.

****

Early afternoon, Finn had a meeting with Coach Billings. Two NFL teams had called again—the Cowboys and the Falcons. His stomach churned as he tugged on a collared shirt, trying to flatten the wrinkle in the fabric. This felt like a dream. One he wasn't sure that he prepared for.

The next day was the big meeting. Finn hated suits. The collar itched. The tie was too tight. He could break a blitz but God help him in a button-up. Still, he sat tall, broad shoulders back, across from Coach Billings, the two scouts, along with the agent he'd hired at Coach's recommendation, and a team administrator with an iPad.

They asked about performance. Pressure. Academics. His shoulder health.

He answered calmly, confidently. But in the back of his mind, he was thinking about Eliza. About her sitting cross-legged on their bed, headphones in, chasing a melody.

"And if you're drafted?" one scout asked, pen poised, "are you ready to relocate? Hit the ground running?"

Finn paused. Thought about Eliza's music. The life they'd started building together. The way she looked at him when he wasn't wearing armor.

"I'm ready for what's next," he said, knowing that they'd find a way to make it work. "As long as I'm doing it with Eliza."

After his Earth shaking meeting, Finn parked his truck on the side of the street near a taco stand in East Austin that hadn't changed since high school. He spotted Merrick before he even got out—same floppy brown hair, same easy grin, still wearing those worn-in boots he swore were lucky. In town for ACL.

"Beer. I need a beer. Pronto." Finn calls out as he meets up with Merrick.

They slapped shoulders and laughed the way old teammates do, easing into the rhythm like no time had passed.

"Look at you," Merrick said, shaking his head. "Big time. UT starting Quarterback. I saw your name on ESPN last week. There's talk of you going Pro."

Finn shrugged, looking proud but uncomfortable. "Still just playing ball."

Merrick gave him a knowing look. "And still pretending like you don't know how good you are."

"Yeah, thanks for that," Finn replied shoulder checking Merrick. "West is in discussions with some pro teams. He had a helluva season as Defensive Lineman."

Merrick nodded his agreement as they sat at a metal picnic table under string lights, the smell of grilled onions and BBQ in the air. They talked about Fredericksburg, about old Friday night wins and Coach Howard's locker room rants, about how much smaller things feel once you leave.

"Seriously, you plan on going pro like West?" Merrick asked, halfway through his grilled shrimp and avocado taco.

Finn hesitated. "Yeah. A lot lately. Like I mentioned it's been under discussions. I just had a meeting with Coach Billings and there is interest from a couple of pro teams."

Merrick taking a pull from his Dos Equis beer looked at Finn impressed. "And?"

"And I'm scared if I chase it, I'll lose the other stuff. The stuff that actually *matters*."

Merrick was quiet for a second. "You mean Eliza."

Finn looked down. "Yeah. I finally got her back. Much as I love football; Eliza is everything to me."

"Then bring her with you," Merrick said simply. "That girl's been your North Star since we were sixteen. You think she's not strong enough to shine wherever you go?"

Finn's throat tightened. His Songbird was the most resilient, strongest woman he knew.

Maybe Merrick was right.

Maybe he didn't have to choose. Maybe they could create their path and forward together.

"You look good," Eliza said softly from the bed, knees drawn up, guitar balanced across her lap. She strummed idly, the tune not quite formed.

"You're biased."

"Damn right I am."

He came to sit beside her, stealing a kiss that tasted faintly of peach tea. Her hand lingered on his jaw, thumb brushing his stubble.

"You'll crush it," she whispered.

He nodded, though the weight in his chest was real. He'd faced down defensive lines twice his size without flinching, but the thought of leaving Austin—of being away from her, even for a season—scared him more than any sack.

Sophia & West

That night, they gathered at a taco truck off East Sixth—Sophia, West, Dillon, Kai, Brooks, Merrick. Picnic tables glowed under string lights, the smell of grilled onions and cilantro filling the air.

Sophia wore a sundress, her curls loose, her laugh softer than it used to be. She's traded her black moto boots for blinged out blue Corral cowboy boots. West hovered near her, pretending to study the chalkboard menu, but his eyes kept sliding toward her mouth, his on her thigh.

Dillon showed up late with a girl on his arm—tall, dark hair, bright lipstick. He introduced her as Mariah, and Eliza felt a twist of relief. He'd finally moved on from his ex Raven. She was awful.

They ordered tacos al pastor and queso, pitchers of Shiner Bock sweating in the heat. Brooks cracked jokes about Finn's "big-time quarterback swagger," and Merrick nearly spit out his beer laughing.

At one point, Sophia raised her glass. "To Eliza. To ACL. To finally letting the world hear what we've known all along."

Everyone clinked bottles, the sound sharp and sweet in the warm Austin night.

****

The ACL grounds in Zilker Park were already humming when she arrived with her guitar case housing her precious vintage acoustic Gibson Songwriter slung over her shoulder, rhinestone shoulder strap glinting for rehearsals. Volunteers rolled out cables like arteries, techs tested sound rigs with sharp pops of feedback, and the smell of trampled grass and fried food was already starting to hang in the October air.

Finn walked beside her, baseball cap pulled low, his hand brushing hers like he couldn't stop reminding himself she was real. Every once in a while, he glanced at the big North Tent stage where her name was printed—tiny, almost hidden, but printed all the same—on the day's lineup board.

"Songbird," he murmured, leaning down so only she could hear, "look at that. That's you."

Her throat tightened. "It's… small print."

"Doesn't matter. That's the print people are gonna remember after today."

She tried to laugh, but her stomach was already churning.

Madison waved from the soundboard, headset slung around her neck, clipboard in hand. She looked every bit the music exec she was becoming, sharp in ripped black jeans and spiked boots, eyes lit with a mix of calculation and pride.

Eliza stood on the empty practice stage, guitar strap biting into her shoulder. Madison paced like a coach prepping for the big game, arms crossed.

"Again," Madison called. "Lean into the last note. Make them ache for it."

Eliza adjusted the mic, took a breath. She thought of Finn in the stands, watching her under the stars. She thought of Rhetta's porch, of Sophia's belief. She let it all bleed into her voice until the note rang raw, until her chest vibrated with it.

"My soul felt that. You ready to do this?" Madison asked, clasping Eliza's slim shoulders.

"No," Eliza whispered.

"Perfect. The good ones are never ready."

They went through mic check. The sound in the empty tent was raw, too big, every note bouncing back like it was questioning her. Finn sat cross-legged in the front row of folding chairs, watching her like she was already the headliner he knew she could be. That gaze alone steadied her.

When she finished, Madison's grin spread wide. "That's it. That's the fire."

The city buzzed different on festival morning ACL weekend. Downtown streets flooded with people in boots and cutoff shorts, bandanas and flower crowns. Food trucks lined Zilker Park. The air smelled of barbecue smoke, fried funnel cakes, spilled beer.

Finn held Eliza's hand as they wove through the crowd, her boots crunching over trampled grass. Her stomach fluttered like a swarm of cicadas.

Madison appeared in a whirl of sequins and schedules. "North Tent. Ten minutes. Don't puke, don't cry, don't trip. Got it?"

Eliza laughed weakly. "Easy."

Finn kissed her temple. "Songbird, you've got this."

By Saturday afternoon, the grounds were a living organism. Tens of thousands of bodies pressed into the park, laughter and shouts mixing with the steady thump of bass from stages all around. The Texas sun slid lower, throwing everything into gold.

The tent pulsed with muted bass from the main stage nearby. Eliza peeked through the curtain: rows of folding chairs filled with agents, reviewers, musicians she'd admired from afar.

Her throat tightened. Her palms slicked.

Eliza's set time crept closer.

She sat backstage on a folding chair, guitar across her lap, staring at her setlist:

1.   *"Splinters and Light"*

2.   *"Ashes Don't Lie"*

3.   *"Reclaim Me"*

4.   *"Still Here"*

5.   *"Shatter "* (Encore song - new acoustic)

Her hands shook as she traced the words she'd written. *Shatter* was still raw, barely rehearsed. Madison had been hesitant to let her try it in a festival setting. But Finn had been adamant—this was the song.

Finn ducked in through the curtain, a bottle of water in hand. "Hey," he said gently. "Breathe. In through the nose, out through the mouth. Just like before games."

"You're ridiculous," she whispered, eyes lit with amusement, trying not to smile.

"Ridiculous enough to marry you," he shot back, low and certain.

Her chest ached with love. "Songbird's gonna be okay," he added, pressing the bottle into her hand. "This is your moment to soar. Let all that beauty, pain and brokenness out into the world. Let people know that they're not the only ones who feel those things."

She nodded, overwhelmed, unable to speak.

Madison squeezed her shoulders. "Breathe. It's just you and the song. Nothing else."

Finn caught her gaze from the side, steady as ever. He mouthed: *North Star.*

She swallowed hard, nodded.

Chapter Fifty-Seven

Spotlight

nstage—ACL

When her name was announced, Eliza stepped out. Light hit her first—hot stage lamps, brighter than the sun. Then came the sound. A wave of applause, a few whistles, the restless shifting of a crowd not sure what to expect. The tent wasn't packed, but it was full enough. The air smelled of dust and sweat, the trampled grass mixing with the faint sweetness of funnel cake drifting in from a nearby stand. From the next stage over, a bassline bled through like a competing heartbeat.

She stepped to the stool, adjusted the mic, and strummed the opening chords of **"Splinters and Light."**

Her voice shook at first, but steadied by the chorus. The song's imagery— fractured glass, scars that caught sunlight—poured from her like a confession. By the time she hit the bridge, she wasn't just singing; she was *releasing*. The crowd leaned closer. Conversations dimmed.

Applause rose like a tide when she ended.

She let it wash over her.

The second song, **"Ashes Don't Lie,"** was sharper—rhythmic strums, her voice low and fierce. Lyrics about rising from betrayal, about how fire reveals truth. By the second verse, the front rows were nodding along, some mouthing words they didn't even know yet.

"Reclaim Me" followed, a softer ballad. This one she played with her eyes closed, fingers trembling against the strings. A girl in the third row started crying. Madison, off to the side, folded her arms, eyes bright.

By the fourth track, **"Still Here,"** Eliza was fully inside it. Her voice rang strong over the bleed of bass from the other stage, a defiant anthem that had people lifting their phones to record, swaying in unison. When she belted the final line, *I'm still here,* the whole tent erupted in applause that rattled the folding chairs.

She stood, guitar in hand, and smiled through the mic.

"Thank you," she said, breathless. "Thank you for letting me share some time with you. These lyrics, these songs come from my heart, reminders that in love there is truth. And that love has taught me you can only find your strength once you're brave enough to break. True beauty is found in the broken places and how you put the pieces together. That pain makes room for love."

Locking eyes with Finn, "I love you Finn."

She dipped her head, waved, and started toward the wings.

But then it started.

A rumble at first. Stomping. Shouts. Whistles.

And then the glow of phones, hundreds of tiny lights lifted like stars inside the tent. The sound of feet stomping loud. The chant began to build:

"One more song! One more song!"

Her chest heaved. Tears threatened. She turned to Madison. Madison just nodded. *Do it*.

So Eliza walked back out, Gibson in hand, throat tight with gratitude.

The moment Eliza returned to the stage and stepped into the lights, the world shrank and swelled at once. The spotlight made her pale hair and delicate face seem to glow as though she were lit from within like some sort of angel or apparition.

The tent ceiling was low, canvas stretched taut, but the spotlights made it feel endless—white beams cutting through dust and heat like slices of heaven. Sweat already rolled down her spine, soaking the back of her sleeveless western slim cut dark denim rhinestone button down, with turquoise bolero, she'd thrown on over a thigh length denim skirt and her favorite red Lucesse boots. The smell was ACL in its rawest form: beer gone warm in plastic cups, sunscreen and cigarette smoke, the metallic tang of trampled fence wire somewhere near the crowd line.

Across the tent, Madison stood at the soundboard, her posture sharp as a tuning fork. She didn't sway, didn't blink—her entire body listening.

Eliza adjusted her beige Stetson, the rhinestone guitar strap, felt the familiar scrape of pick against callus, and stepped to the mic. Back into the light.

The crowd pressed in closer, a shuffle of boots and sandals, the crunch of crushed cans. Someone whistled. Another shouted her name.

She strummed the opening chord—low, minor, aching. She sat back on the stool, tucked pale, wavy blonde hair behind her ear.

"This is new," she told them. Her voice wavered. "It's called **Shatter.**"

The crowd hushed.

She strummed the opening chords, simple and raw. Her voice carried clear:

The words came quiet, almost hesitant, like she was whispering to herself. Lines about standing at the edge of herself, brittle and afraid to break. Images of glass so thin you could see through it but not touch, of nights when silence rang louder than any storm.

In love there is truth, in truth there is pain,
I broke to the pieces I couldn't contain.
But the cracks let the light seep into my skin,
Only when shattered could love begin.

Her voice cracked at the edges, husky, vulnerable. A girl holding herself together with guitar strings.

The audience leaned in. A man in a black Stetson bowed his head. A girl on someone's shoulders mouthed along, though she couldn't possibly know the words yet.

Her voice grew stronger with each verse, trembling less, filling the tent:

You can't be strong 'til you're brave enough to break,
Can't feel the joy 'til you've carried the ache.
Pain carves the space where the love can stay,
Only then, only then, can the light find its way.

The phones swayed like constellations. More people had come into the tent after her first couple of songs and now it was full to capacity.

Madison's eyes glistened. Finn, pressed against the curtain edge, having gone backstage before the Encore, looked at her like he was witnessing a miracle.

By the second verse, the guitar grew sharper, the strum harder. Eliza's boot tapped unconsciously against the plywood, syncing with the faint percussion layered in by the tech.

The lyrics sliced deeper now. Mirrors and fractures. Hands reaching for pieces of yourself you thought were gone. Her eyes stung, but she didn't look away from the crowd—she gave it to them raw, her voice quivering, defiant.

Somewhere near the front, a woman covered her mouth with her hand. Two college guys exchanged a glance like they'd been caught off guard.

During the bridge of the song, Eliza's voice dropped to a near-whisper. The guitar line thinned into something fragile, heartbeat-soft.

She sang of the aftermath—the long nights when you lie awake in the ruins, when all you can hear is your own breath. Of how ache itself carves space. Of how only by breaking do you find the room for tenderness to grow, for joy to live.

Silence swept the tent. People stopped shifting, stopped drinking, stopped breathing. For a heartbeat, the only sound was the faint bleed of bass from a stage half a mile away, pulsing like a distant storm.

And then—she lifted her chin, strummed harder, and let her voice go.

It soared, cracked once, raw and holy, but she didn't pull it back. The tent walls seemed to swell with it.

She sang of love not as safety, but as courage. Of choosing to open, to shatter, to let the light pour into the broken places. Of being remade by the very things that once undid you.

People cried out, clapped along, stomped boots against the plywood so hard the stage rattled. Dust rose in the beams of the spotlights, turning them into golden shafts.

Then her voice rose on the chorus. She sang about the truth love had revealed: that strength didn't come from never breaking, but from daring to splinter. That pain wasn't the opposite of joy but its doorway.

Her tone filled the tent, echoing against canvas, riding the air until it bled out into the night. The applause after the first chorus wasn't loud—just murmurs, shouts—but it carried the electricity of people realizing they were watching something real.

Then the final chorus rang out:

Shatter me, scatter me,
Pieces that bleed,
Are the pieces that need—
To be seen, to be free.
Don't hide the fall,
Let the cracks recall—
Only then, only then,
Can the light begin.

The final chord rang, trembling in her chest, vibrating the wood.

And then—silence.

For a suspended second, no one moved. The whole crowd stood frozen in the heat and sweat and dust, as if afraid any noise would break what she had built.

Then the roar came.

Thunderous. Hands slapping, boots stomping, whistles slicing the air. Shouts of her name. The audience cheered like she'd been theirs forever.

A wave of noise that hit her body like a physical force, warm and wild and alive.

Madison was clapping now, slow and deliberate, a huge smile tugging at her mouth.

Eliza staggered back from the mic, chest heaving, vision swimming in sweat and light. Completely spent.

The sound that continued was physical, crashing over her in waves. Eliza bent forward, overcome, and whispered into the mic: "Thank you. Thank you for listening."

Blowing a kiss to the audience along with a small wave. She headed out. When she finally stepped offstage, Madison caught her in a fierce hug saying, "This is just the start Eliza."

Her gaze found Finn in the wings.

He wasn't moving at first. Not clapping. Just watching her like she'd set the sky on fire. Then a huge smile lit his handsome, strong face, green eyes glittering, full of love and awe.

She was suddenly in Finn's arms a second later, being swept off her feet in a bridal carry and swung around, as Finn whispered in her ear so only she could hear:

"You shattered them, Songbird. And you lit them up. So proud of you."

And for that heartbeat, she wasn't in a festival tent, or on a stage, or even in Austin. She was in the truth of her own voice. Shattered and remade.

On the balcony back home hours later, long after the dust and roar of ACL had faded into the Austin night, Eliza and Finn sat on their apartment balcony.

The city hummed below—muffled music still bleeding faintly from Zilker Park, car horns echoing off downtown buildings, cicadas buzzing in the patches of dark between street lamps. Eliza curled into Finn's side, adrenaline spent, a sense of happy, satisfied exhaustion filling her. Wearing this years' ACL hoodie designed by her artist friend Amber Walker, who was on the same ACL planning committee with her and Madison this year— designed specifically for this years' festivities. Madison had one made specially for her that included a list of names, including hers, of the artists that had performed on the small stage with her. Mads was so thoughtful.

Her hair was still damp from a rushed shower, her voice hoarse from singing and shouting.

The amethyst ring glimmered faintly in the low light when she turned her hand. It still felt surreal, a jewel heavy with promise.

Finn, pulling her close: "That's our truth, Songbird. We're enough. Always."

And here, with Finn's arms wrapped around her, the night sky stretched wide, and the North Star holding steady—Eliza believed it.

Finn tipped his Shiner bottle toward the sky. "There," he murmured, pointing with his free hand. "North Star. Same one we saw at the stadium. Same one from Enchanted Rock."

Eliza followed his gaze. The sky was hazier here, city-lit, but the star still held steady, sharp as if it were meant only for them.

"Do you ever think about it?" she asked softly.

"What?"

"That it's... always there. Even when we can't see it."

Finn rested his chin lightly on the crown of her head. "Yeah. That's us, Songbird. Doesn't matter where we are, what changes, who's watching—we'll always find our way back. Just like that star."

Her throat tightened. She pressed closer, listening to the steady thrum of his heart.

For a while, they didn't speak. Just breathed in sync, the night stretching quiet and full around them. Below, a car radio drifted faintly up—some country song about forever. Above, the North Star burned like an ancient vow.

Eliza tilted her head back, whispering, "Tonight didn't even feel real."

Finn smiled against her hair, inhaling its' musky lavender-vanilla scent. "It was real. You shattered them," he said gripping her body tightly to him, fitting them together, two broken pieces who together become whole. "And tomorrow, the world's gonna know it. Songbird, remember who knew it first and loves you most. You're always mine. North of Always."

She closed her eyes burrowing her face into his warm, hard chest. "Remember my love that you're always and ever mine. Till the stars fall from the sky and beyond."

The fear that had always shadowed her dreams felt lighter now, like it had cracked open, making space for something bigger. Like everything was possible.

She thought of the lyrics she'd sung into that mic: *Only then, only then can the light begin.*

As they came together passionately heralding that The light had begun.

Epilogue

North Again

Eliza & Finn

Finn – Letting Go, Leaning In

Seven years.

That's how long it had been since Enchanted Rock—since the amethyst and diamond ring, since promising Eliza forever under a sky the color of fire. Seven years of moves, trades, cold northern cities, heat-warped Texas summers. Seven years of road games, hotel rooms, holding on tight.

Football had given me everything I thought I wanted. And yet, by the end, the bruises lingered longer. The injuries more significant. The flights got heavier. And every time I saw Eliza alone in a crowd, or caught her singing through a grainy livestream because I was three states away—I knew.

It was time to stop chasing stadium noise and start putting down roots.

So when the University of Texas called, offering me a spot as assistant coach and commentator, I didn't hesitate. The league had been a chapter. Texas would be the rest of the book.

Coaching meant mornings on the practice field instead of endless airports. It meant breaking down film with kids who were hungry, who reminded me of myself at nineteen—wide-eyed, carrying too much weight, needing someone to say, *you're more than your stats*.

It meant I could come home at night to the only person who had ever mattered more than the game.

Eliza had grown too.

When we met, she scribbled lyrics in margins, hiding them like secrets. Now, those words traveled farther than either of us imagined.

Her band, *Saints and Strangers*, had grown from Austin dives to ACL's main stage. Madison still managed with her sharp-eyed devotion, keeping the chaos in line. They toured summers—Denver, Nashville, even London once—but they always came back here.

She'd been a guest on *The Tonight Show*, boots tapping against polished studio floors, Fallon laughing at her sharp wit. She'd been profiled in *Rolling Stone*, her voice described as "dust and wildfire." She'd written songs for country stars who sent her thank-you flowers she stuck in beer mugs on our table.

And still, she came home to the balcony, in the house we bought putting down roots, hair messy, guitar in her lap, singing for me first. Always for me first.

Sometimes, when the noise of our days dulled, I'd replay the wedding like film.

Golden hour at Enchanted Rock, the heat fading, sky painted with streaks of fire. Her dress fitted and satin at the top, tulle spilling into lace songbirds embroidered on the hem. White Lucchese boots peeking out because she wouldn't be Eliza without them.

I'd worn a western-cut suit that felt like it belonged on me and my Stetson of course.

We said vows with voices thick and hands steady, and then we each released a bird into the sky. They rose together, tiny silhouettes against the endless blue of the Texas sky.

The next weekend, the reception at The Line Hotel in Austin turned into a blur of stomping boots, tequila toasts, Madison crying quietly during Eliza's song. I danced until my shirt stuck to my back, kissed my wife under string lights, and knew—I'd never want for anything else.

Now, mornings started with grass.

Whistles blew sharp across the UT practice field, cleats pounded turf, and I stood at the fifty-yard line, hollering corrections that sounded harsher than they were.

These kids reminded me of myself at nineteen. Hungry. Desperate. Carrying the belief that if they weren't perfect, they weren't enough.

One of my linemen, Reyes, jogged over, helmet in hand, chest heaving. "Coach, I don't think I can keep up with these drills."

I clapped him on the shoulder. "Listen, you don't have to be perfect. You just have to show up. Every damn rep. That's how you win."

He nodded, shoulders loosening like no one had told him that before.

When practice ended, I headed to the commentary booth for a segment. Talking football to a camera wasn't like playing it—but I'd learned how to break plays down, how to show fans the grit that went unseen. And when I looked down from that booth and spotted Eliza sometimes in the stands, scribbling in her notebook, I thought: yeah. This is the right field.

Eliza called me from Denver one night. The line crackled with noise—laughter, tuning instruments, the thrum of a crowd just beyond the curtain.

"Wish you could see this place," she said breathless. "It's packed. Madison says they're here for us."

"They are," I told her. "Go burn it down."

Later, I watched a fan-posted video. She stood center stage, hair wild, spotlight catching her boots. She sang *Reclaim Me,* a song she once wrote on our kitchen floor in tears. Now the crowd shouted it back at her word for word.

Her voice was sharper now. Fuller. She carried herself like someone who knew her worth, but never forgot what it cost to learn it.

I closed the video and whispered into the empty room, "Proud of you, Songbird."

Saturdays, we volunteered at the community center.

Eliza led songwriting workshops, a circle of kids with guitars too big for their laps, notebooks covered in doodles. She crouched low, listening, nodding like every lyric mattered.

I played ball with the younger ones out back, teaching spirals, letting them tackle me until I groaned dramatically.

One boy, maybe twelve, lingered at the edge. He had that look—I knew it. The look of someone who'd been moved around too much, who was bracing for goodbye.

"You play?" I asked, tossing him the ball.

He shrugged. "Not good enough."

I caught his eye. "Hey, I used to think that too. Truth is—you don't have to be perfect. You just have to keep showing up."

Later, Eliza strummed a guitar, leading the kids in a chorus she made up on the spot. I watched their voices lift together, small and cracking, but alive.

We left that night hand in hand, quiet.

"That boy," she whispered, eyes wet. "I saw myself in him."

I squeezed her hand. "Yeah. Me too."

That's why we kept showing up. That's why we gave.

Because love had found us when we thought it never would. The least we could do was pass it on.

The night I told her I was done with the league, I thought I was the one bringing the surprise.

But she had one too.

"I'm two months pregnant," she whispered, tears cutting trails down her face. I wanted to wait to know for sure that it'd stick.

My knees nearly buckled. We'd been trying but not trying for a couple years. We had a couple of pregnancies that miscarried which left us both broken. Committed, we didn't give up on our dream of having our own family. All the stadium roars in the world couldn't touch that moment—the world shrinking to her heartbeat and the promise of another one on the way.

We sat out on the balcony that night, city humming below, her hand on her belly, my arm around her.

"Our biggest adventure yet," I murmured.

She laughed. "Bigger than ACL? Bigger that a Bowl Game in the NFL?"

"Way bigger."

A week later, she played me the new song.

Cross-legged on the rug, guitar in her lap, hair falling in her face. The lyrics told our story—not polished, but raw.

We were splinters, we were light,
We were wrong turns in the night.
But the cracks became the place
Where the stars could start to rise.
Now the smallest surprise
Is the greatest truth we've known—
Love makes a house a home.

Her voice cracked at the end.

I pulled her close, whispering, "That's the most beautiful thing I've ever heard."

And it was. Because it was us. Because it was forever.

Seven years later, forever didn't look like perfection. It looked like cracked sidewalks and roots in Texas soil. It looked like her voice filling stadiums and classrooms, like kids clutching guitars too big for them. It looked like quiet mornings on the balcony, my hand over hers, waiting for the kick of new life.

Forever was the North Star—sometimes hidden, sometimes faint, but always there when you remembered where to look.

And standing here with Eliza's hand in mine, Austin spread below us, the world waiting for our next chapter—

I knew.

We were home.

Small Surprises

– by Eliza Monroe

Verse 1
We were splinters, we were light,
Wrong turns in the quiet night.
Every break, every scar we hide,
Led us closer to the other side.

Pre-Chorus
And the cracks became the place
Where the stars could start to rise,
Where the dark gave way to grace,
Where the truth lit up our lives.

Chorus
It's the small surprises that carry us through,
The gentle reminders that love makes us new.
From the ashes we grew, from the storms we survived,
It's the smallest surprises that keep us alive.

Verse 2
You were fire, I was stone,
We learned how to build a home.
Every silence, every fight,
Taught us how to hold on tight.

Pre-Chorus
And the cracks became the door
Where forgiveness found its way,
Where we weren't afraid no more,
Where the night turned into day.

Chorus
It's the small surprises that carry us through,
The gentle reminders that love makes us new.
From the ashes we grew, from the storms we survived,
It's the smallest surprises that keep us alive.

Bridge
Now there's a heartbeat we can't see,
A song that's waiting patiently.
Every stumble, every fall—
Love was the greatest gift of all.

Final Chorus
It's the small surprises that carry us through,
The baby steps rising, the proof of what's true.
From the ashes we grew, from the storms we survived,
It's the smallest surprises that keep us alive.

Outro
We were splinters, we were light…
Now we're stronger, side by side.
Love makes a house a home,
And surprises make it shine.

Epilogue (Bonus)

Quiet Light

Sophia & West

The storm had passed, but Austin still smelled like rain. Damp cedar, hot asphalt, and that faint metallic tang that came after lightning had scraped the sky. Street lamps caught puddles in golden rings, the sidewalks shining like polished glass.

West stood on Sophia's stoop with a paper bag tucked under his arm. The Thai place down the block had run late—every order piled high, the air inside thick with cilantro and spice—but he'd waited. Tonight felt worth the waiting.

When she opened the door, barefoot, hair loose around her shoulders, wearing one of his old UT football jerseys over cutoffs, West felt something loosen in his chest.

"You're late," she said, though her smile betrayed her.

"They only had one order of dumplings left," he answered. "I fought for them."

"You probably glared until they gave up."

"Charm," he corrected, brushing past her into the kitchen. "Pure charm."

She laughed—low, warm, quick to vanish but real.

They ended up on her balcony, cartons open, chopsticks clumsy in his hands. The storm had left the air softer, cooler. Below them, the city hummed—horns, laughter, a band spilling out from a bar three streets away.

Sophia ate noodles straight from the carton, hair falling into her face. West chewed on a dumpling, watching her from the corner of his eye.

"You ever think about how far we've come?" he asked.

She shot him a wry glance. "Since when? Since last week when you burned pasta and nearly set off my smoke alarm?"

"Since the fire escape. Since the retreat."

Her expression softened. Rain on rusted metal, his voice rough and reckless. The first night she realized he wasn't invincible, and maybe neither was she.

"I thought you were going to ruin me," she said quietly.

"I thought you were going to run."

"And yet here we are."

"And here we stay," he murmured.

The silence that followed wasn't empty. It pulsed between them, charged with something steady, like the afterglow of lightning.

Later, she curled onto the couch with a blanket over her legs, hair damp from a shower. West leaned against the opposite armrest, sketchbook balanced on his knee. His pencil moved fast: lines, smudges, shadows.

Sophia tilted her head. "Are you drawing me again?"

"Maybe."

"I'm not a muse, West."

"You're wrong," he said simply. "You're exactly that."

Her breath caught. "That's terrifying."

"Why?"

"Because muses disappear. They burn bright and vanish. They're never real."

He set the pencil down, leaned closer. "You're real to me."

Her throat tightened. She looked away, to the window where city lights flickered like stars blurred by clouds. "Do you ever get tired of fighting?"

"Fighting what?"

"Everything. Ourselves. The world. Everyone's idea of who we're supposed to be."

He thought of the fight club nights, the taste of blood, the rush of fists connecting, the emptiness afterward.

"Yeah," he admitted. "But I'm not fighting alone anymore."

Her eyes shimmered, lashes damp. "Neither am I."

It had been a struggle keeping their relationship on track after he got picked up in the draft by the Houston Texans.

Six months later they got a place in the Heights area of Houston and moved in together.

A few weeks after, she printed out her story. She'd written it in fits and starts, late nights with tea going cold beside her, mornings when West was still asleep and she could type with the quiet hum of his breath in the background.

When she finally handed the pages to him, her hands shook.

"You don't have to like it," she warned. "You don't even have to finish it. Just... tell me if it feels like me."

He read every word. Slowly. Carefully. His jaw tightened in places, his throat worked in others. When he finished, he didn't say anything at first. Just set the pages down like they were breakable.

Then: "Soph... this isn't just good. This is you letting people in. And it's beautiful."

Her heart stuttered. For once, she didn't deflect. She just let the words sit, warm and heavy in her chest.

A week later, she submitted it to a small literary journal out of Houston. No fanfare. Just an email and a deep breath. And West, sitting beside her, their knees touching, whispering, "Proud of you."

For him, the shift came one night when his phone buzzed: another text, another invitation to fight.

He stared at the screen for a long time. The rush it promised was familiar —blood, adrenaline, the illusion of control. But he pictured Sophia's face if he came home bruised again. He pictured the way she'd said we stay.

And he deleted the message. Blocked the number.

He didn't tell her right away. But weeks later, when he finally said, "I think I'm done with that life," she didn't ask questions. She just reached for his hand, laced her fingers through his, and said, "Good."

In their converted garage which was transformed into West's gym, workout equipment, and a weight rack shared space with a large punching and kickboxing bag suspended.

One evening in November, they drove out past the city, windows down, air crisp with cedar smoke from backyard fires. West pulled off onto a dirt road, the kind he used to drive down when he needed to hit something. This time, he spread a blanket in the bed of his truck.

They lay back, shoulder to shoulder, watching the stars.

Sophia pointed upward. "There. Orion's Belt ."

He smiled faintly. "Funny how it keeps finding us."

Her voice was soft. "Even when the sky's crowded, it's still there."

"Just gotta remember where to look," he said.

She turned toward him, her face haloed in starlight, copper hair gleaming. For once, there was no guard in her eyes, no wall. Just truth.

"You make me brave, West," she whispered.

He reached for her, tucking a strand of hair behind her ear. "You make me stay."

And under the wide Texas night, with the stars burning ancient and sure, neither of them ran.

They didn't need a stage. They didn't need applause. Their love wasn't a spotlight—it was a lamp in the dark, steady and quiet, enough to light the path forward.

Not shattered. Not perfect.

Just two people learning, day by day, how to stay.

And maybe that was forever.

West thought so, proposing to Sophia by the waterfall in Houston. She said yes.

The lights at the Continental Club in Austin dimmed low, the stage washed in a soft amber that made Eliza's guitar gleam like something alive. The *Saints and Strangers* had just ripped through a rowdy, fiddle-heavy number that had the dance floor packed shoulder to shoulder, boots stomping in rhythm. Sweat and Shiner Bock filled the air.

Then she stepped forward, adjusting the mic, eyes soft as they scanned the crowd.

"This one's... new," she said, her voice just loud enough to carry, but still intimate, like she was confessing something to a room full of friends. "It's about the way life sneaks up on you, about the things you don't plan for but end up meaning the most."

The chatter dipped. Someone near the bar shushed his buddy.

Eliza strummed the opening chords—gentle, fingerpicked, the kind of melody that made you lean in. Madison, perched at the soundboard, had the levels dialed in perfectly: just her voice, her guitar, and a hush that settled like reverence over the club.

Verse 1

We were splinters, we were light,
Wrong turns in the quiet night…

Her voice was low, almost a whisper, but clear. The kind that felt like it was coming from the inside of you instead of the stage. Couples on the floor swayed unconsciously. A waitress froze with a tray of Lone Stars in hand, just listening.

Pre-Chorus

And the cracks became the place
Where the stars could start to rise…

The steel guitar slid in, subtle but aching, and Brooks on percussion brushed the snare with the softest whisper, like a heartbeat.

Chorus

It's the small surprises that carry us through,
The gentle reminders that love makes us new…

Her voice soared now — still raw, but big enough to fill the room, to press into every corner. Phones lifted, recording. A woman near the stage had tears streaking her cheeks.

Verse 2

You were fire, I was stone,
We learned how to build a home…

Eliza's boot tapped against the worn wooden stage, syncing with Dillon's bass line. The song was growing—like a memory gathering momentum.

Bridge

Now there's a heartbeat we can't see,
A song that's waiting patiently…

Here, she closed her eyes, hand pressing against her chest as if she could already feel the small life inside her, even though the crowd didn't know. Finn, leaning against the back wall, swallowed hard, his eyes locked on her like there wasn't anyone else in the room.

Final Chorus

It's the small surprises that carry us through,
The baby steps rising, the proof of what's true…

Now, the whole crowd was swaying with her. The chorus landing like a promise, warm and unshakable. Boots stomped gently in time.

Outro

We were splinters, we were light…
Now we're stronger, side by side…

Her voice dropped to a hush again, the band falling away until it was just her and the guitar.

The last chord rang, trembling in the amber glow.

Silence.

Then the room erupted. Stomps. Whistles. Shouts of her name. People rose from their chairs like they'd just seen something holy.

Madison, stone-faced as ever, allowed the faintest smile.

And Finn—he just pressed his hand to his chest, like he was holding the whole world in place.

****

If you enjoyed Eliza's songs, sign up for my NEWSLETTER and get a FREE North of Always Lyric Songbook that includes the songs from the book.

****

Enchanted Rock Romance continues with a story that'll make you swoon on the roller coaster ride experiencing Amber and Merrick's love story in **South of Hope**. Here is a **SNEAK PEAK at Book 2** in the Series.

Enchanted Rock Book 2

South Of Hope

Sneak Peek

A guarded artist. A restless bull rider.

A summer that changes everything.

Amber Walker lives a quiet life of canvas and color—until Merrick Holt rolls into town. Their chemistry is immediate, but with a rodeo schedule and rising art world attention, they'll have to learn that staying in love takes more than falling.

For readers that love:

Second chance

Opposites attract

Surprise pregnancy

Prologue

The Shocking Encounter

His sapphire eyes glared at her, cutting through the spring sunshine that danced over the sleepy sidewalks of Fredericksburg, Texas. The quaint charm of the historic Hill Country town—stone storefronts, wine bars, and German bakeries—felt like a cruel contrast to the emotional storm unraveling in the middle of the town square.

Then Merrick's gaze dropped—slow, deliberate—to her slightly swelling belly and the curve of her extremely fuller-looking breasts, emphasized by her tightly fitted shirt. His eyes were hard, lips twisted into a smirk that didn't hide his disgust. Eyes that used to reflect only love.

"Whose is it?" Merrick asked, voice low but sharp as broken glass. It was a question asked by someone who didn't want the answer. Amber winced as if he'd slapped her.

She felt the weight of his scorn like a stone pressing on her chest. Her sun-streaked blonde hair fell over her tanned face as she bowed her head, hoping to hide from the prying eyes seated along the cafe patio behind them.

"Just leave me alone," she said, voice trembling. "Haven't you done enough?"

"That's rich coming from you," he snapped back. "Is Daniel proud of getting you knocked up?"

His voice echoed off the stone buildings like a gunshot. Her knees went weak, her whole body vibrating with embarrassment and fury. Around them, the small-town chatter halted. Glasses clinked, forks paused mid-air.

She turned quickly, nearly stumbling over the curb beside the market's old stone fountain. Her boots caught on the uneven cobblestone. She had to get away—right now. From him. From the questions. From the past. From the pain of his rejection. The derision in his eyes cutting.

Amber cupped her belly, eyes stinging. She whispered, "I still love you." Whether the words were meant for the child growing inside her or for the man she once thought she would marry, she didn't know.

In the distance, the outline of Enchanted Rock loomed on the horizon like a silent witness, its ancient pink granite bathed in late afternoon light. How many times had she and Merrick climbed that rock together, believing the world was theirs?

That felt like another lifetime.

Before

Amber was psyched. Twenty-one. She was finally legal. While her college friends had teased her for not drinking before, she loved the idea of saving moments—marking time with meaning. And turning 21 in Fredericksburg during peach blossom season? It was perfect.

Lina, Christine, and Heather—her closest girlfriends since their freshman year at the University of Texas—had planned it all: bar-hopping down Fredericksburg's historic Main Street, tasting wine at the Hill Country's famed cellars, and ending the night watching stars from the summit of Enchanted Rock. Wild and magical. Just like they imagined their twenties would be.

Back at the Airbnb, the apartment was a riot of color and music. Amber's vintage record player spun Abba and early Taylor Swift as the girls rummaged through suitcases, swapping outfits and stories. Amber was about to wear her usual—modest, fitted jeans and a flowy blouse—when Christine raised an eyebrow.

"Don't wear that!" she said, rifling through the pile and pulling out a low-cut black tank top. "You've got curves, girl. Celebrate them. The guys are going to lose it when they see you."

Amber hesitated.

At 13, she had nearly been raped by a boy she knew—an older lifeguard at the town pool near her childhood home outside Fredericksburg. He was popular, a rising football star, and untouchable. She'd never told anyone. Not after seeing what happened to Sarah, the girl who *had* come forward the year before. Sarah was shunned—labeled a liar, a slut, a threat.

Amber would never put herself in that position. The scars were quiet but deep, shaping how she dressed, how she flirted—or didn't—and how she viewed intimacy.

Still, tonight was different. Tonight was hers.

Lina leaned into the mirror, expertly applying gloss. "We'll start at Streamline, then work our way down the strip. Maybe we'll meet some men who don't still live with their mothers or throw beer cans off tailgates."

"Not Brett," Heather added with a groan. "Please, no Brett."

Brett—Lina's older brother—had once played football with *him*, the lifeguard. The same arrogant pack of small-town gods who never got held accountable. Even here, in Fredericksburg—surrounded by wineries and wildflowers—the past felt close. Too close.

Amber tucked her hair behind her ear, steeling herself. The truth was, she didn't want Brett there either. Not because of a grudge. Because the sight of him was a reminder of what she never said out loud.

Meanwhile, just a few blocks away…

Merrick sat at the ranch office, the dusty blinds letting in slats of golden light. His father had died three months ago—an old rodeo man, proud and stubborn, and now Merrick had inherited the wreckage. Cattle, debt, an aging farmhouse on the edge of town, and books that didn't add up.

He'd buried himself in the numbers, in the dirt, in the long days of trying to keep the family name from being sold off in foreclosure.

Matthew, his best friend since high school, popped his head in. "Come on. One night out won't kill you. Let's hit the bars. You can pretend you're not a broke-ass rancher for a few hours."

Merrick sighed, rubbed the bridge of his nose. He wasn't one for crowds or small talk—but something about tonight felt like it might be different.

"Alright," he muttered. "Let's go."

Outside, the Texas sky was shifting from blue to velvet. A soft wind carried the scent of peaches and limestone. Somewhere down Main Street, Amber was laughing over her first glass of wine. Somewhere, fate was stirring.

And not far off, Enchanted Rock stood quiet and waiting.

South of Hope — Available on Amazon in 2026

Thank you for reading!

If you enjoyed my book please leave a 30 second review on Amazon or Goodreads.

<u>Enchanted Rock Romances</u>

While each of the four books in the series can be read on their own, they are interconnected — so for reader clarity, to enjoy the full Enchanted Rock Romance experience, here is my recommended order:

North of Always (Eliza & Finn)

South of Hope (Amber & Merrick)

East of Desire (Madison & Brooks)

West of Forever (Gracie & Dillon)

Acknowledgements

Dedications

Romance novels have been my heartbeat since I was a teenager—my escape, my comfort, my thrill. Those pages full of swoon-worthy book boyfriends and strong, beautifully flawed heroines taught me about love, resilience, and the messy wonder of being human. They were my constant companions through every season of life, and I'll forever be grateful to all the incredible authors who've filled the world with their stories. You've made the hard days bearable and the good days even better.

To my readers—thank you for opening your hearts to the *Enchanted Rock Romances*. These stories are my gifts to you, wrapped in all the emotion, hope, and love I could pour into them. I hope they lift you, move you, and remind you that connection—real, honest, imperfect connection—is everything.

To Vesa, my forever Lovey—your love, patience, and unwavering belief in me made this dream possible. You've been my anchor and my inspiration, the quiet strength behind every word.

My loving mother, Rose-Mary, who started and supported my life's adventures and used to chide me as a teen when I read under the blanket at night because I couldn't put a book down until I'd finished. See…I was right…who needs sleep when there's a story waiting?

To Mel, my sweetness—you remind me every day to stay curious, to reach farther, and to keep saying yes to life.

To my editors, Laura Calaway and L.F. Howard—thank you for seeing what this story could be, for your sharp insight, kind encouragement, and for helping me bring Eliza and Finn's world to life.

And to God, for His infinite grace—and for the storm that changed everything.

Five years ago, breast cancer tore away my fear and handed me courage. It forced me to live deeply, to write boldly, and to choose joy without apology. This book, *North of Always*, is my bell-ringing moment—my celebration of survival, love, and second chances.

Writing is my freedom now. My way of saying: I'm still here. And I'm just getting started.

About the Author

Jules Woods is the author of the *Enchanted Rock Romance Series—North of Always, South of Hope, East of Desire,* and *West of Forever*—a collection of emotionally rich contemporary romances set in the heart of the Texas Hill Country.

A Texas native, Jules writes love stories that explore resilience, passion, and the quiet power of second chances. Her novels are known for their lyrical writing, heartfelt chemistry, and characters who feel as real as the places they call home. Readers describe her stories as *"full of longing, lyrical writing, and unforgettable chemistry"* and *"a gut-punching love story with the softness of poetry and the fire of first love."*

When she's not writing, Jules is an artist, photographer, and traveler who finds inspiration in landscapes, connection, creative expression, and a glass of wine. A devoted, mother, cat lover and believer in true love, she married her own real-life hero and pours that same warmth and authenticity into every book she writes.

Sign up for my newsletter to discover exclusive bonus material, special offers, and be the first to know by joining my mailing list.

CONNECT WITH JULES

JULES WOODS:

www.juleswoods.com

AMAZON:

https://www.amazon.com/stores/Jules-Woods/author

INSTAGRAM:

https://www.instagram.com/JulesWoodsAuthor

FACEBOOK:

https://www.facebook.com/JulesWoodsAuthor

BOOKBUB:

https://www.bookbub.com/authors/jules-woods

WEBSITE   **AMAZON**

Special offer! If you Enjoyed Eliza's songs, sign up for her NEWSLETTER (www.juleswoods.com/contact) and get a free **North of Always Lyric Songbook** that includes songs from the book.

Book Club

Questions

Character & Relationship Dynamics

1. **Eliza and Finn's bond began in trauma.** How does that shared past shape their love as adults — both the beauty and the toxicity of it?

2. Do you think Finn truly understands the depth of Eliza's trust issues, or does he underestimate them?

3. **Eliza's songwriting** becomes a form of healing and self-expression. What do her lyrics reveal that her words can't?

4. Finn's rising fame puts him under a spotlight he never asked for. How does public pressure test private love?

5. **Ava's manipulation** plays a pivotal role in the story. Do you see her as a pure villain, or is she a symptom of the world Finn and Eliza are navigating?

Themes of Trust, Trauma & Healing

6. The novel deals with the idea that **healing isn't linear.** How do both characters show progress — and relapse — in their emotional growth?

7. Eliza's instinct is to run when she's hurt. Finn's is to fight. How do those survival strategies collide and evolve?

8.   What role does **forgiveness** play in their story — and do you think Eliza forgives Finn, or simply chooses him again?

9.   Both characters have to rebuild a sense of safety, not just with each other but within themselves. Who do you think grows more by the end?

Setting, Style & Symbolism

10.   Austin, Texas, is more than a backdrop — it's a character. How does the city's creative energy and chaos mirror Eliza and Finn's journey?

11.   The title *North of Always* suggests direction and constancy. What do you think "North" represents for Eliza and Finn?

12.   Music and football — Eliza's art and Finn's sport — are both about rhythm, drive, and vulnerability. How do those parallels play into their story?

Romance, Tension & Tropes

13.   This novel plays with several beloved romance tropes (best friends to lovers, second chances, found family). Which one resonated most and why?

14.   There's a fine line between **loyalty and codependence** in their relationship. Where do you think the story lands on that spectrum?

15.   The ending is hopeful but not perfect. Did it satisfy you? What do you imagine for Eliza and Finn's future beyond the final page?